FIFTY YEARS AFTER

David S. Britton

> The judgement of this court is that you be taken from hence to the place from whence you came,
> and from thence to a place of execution,
> where you shall be hanged by the neck until you be dead;
> and may God have mercy upon your soul.
> *The traditional words of the sentence of death in a British Court*

> *What did he know, and when did he know it?*
> US Senate Watergate Committee

> Two households, both alike in dignity
> From ancient grudge break to new mutiny
> *From the Prologue to "Romeo and Juliet"*
> Life – is a tale told by an idiot, full of sound and fury,
> signifying nothing.
> *Macbeth Act 5 Scene 5*

CONTENTS

Part One: The Search for the truth (1959 -2010).. 1
1: Christmas Eve 3
2. Murder casts its long shadow 12
3. The Diary 22
4. An Old Romance 32
5. The Trial of Mark Smith 41
6. Fifty Years Later 60
7. Philip Stewart, M.P. 75
8. The Hacker 81
9. The Trial Revisited 85
10. The Stewart and Buchan files. 90
11. Stewart versus Greenway 102
12. Lord Albert Corrigan 115
13. Wilfred Martens 130
14. Luke Smith 135
15. Greenway versus Stewart 140
16. Jennifer Brown 149

Part Two: Preparing the Case (February to April 2010) 159
17. Cambridge 161
18. Return to Buckinghamshire 172
19. Decisions 188
20. Case Conference 206
21. Kidnap 220
22. The new Police Team 244
23. The Deadly File 275

Part Three: The Philip Stewart trial (May to September 2010) 283
24. Appeal 285
25. Preparing for Trial 296
26. The Opening Phase 340

27. The Trial opens 347
28. Voices from the Past 378
29. Philip Stewart 408
30. The final day 437

Part Four: Death comes as the end (2010 to 2012) 447

31. The end of the Stewart Gang. 449
32. The Final Curtain 458

Fifty Years After

Part One

The Search for the truth (1959 -2010)

**Two households, alike in dignity,
From ancient grudge, break into new mutiny**
(Romeo and Juliet Prologue)

Fifty Years After

1: Christmas Eve

December 24 1959
Marcus Greenway paused in his headlong rush to look at his watch. It was half past three. He sighed, brushed the snow out of his eyes, and resumed his search for the perfect Christmas present for his future girlfriend. Evelyn James would be his first girlfriend, and, at eighteen, Marcus was besotted with the slim, blond haired, sixteen year old. Marcus desperately wanted to impress her. So far he had been too shy to approach her, but Marcus thought that an inspired Christmas present might do the trick and see off his rivals, especially Philip Stewart, his classmate. Marcus realised he did not know Evelyn well enough to choose what she would really like. He had saved thirty pounds and it was burning a hole in his pocket – but, despite spending over three hours on the search, he had yet to find that perfect gift.

Sighing with resignation, Marcus entered his fifteenth shop of the day, a reputable, but relatively cheap, jewellers. He moved around the shop, staring at the items under the glass cases, becoming more and more depressed as he saw that the items he liked were too expensive for him and he did not like those he could afford. He walked around the shop as his spirits continued to fall and was about to leave yet another shop when his eye caught something almost out of his sight – a fake diamond necklace priced at twenty-eight pounds. Something told him that Evelyn would love it and it was just within his price range. With what he had left over he could even buy her a special "girlfriend" Christmas card. He smiled, approached a shop assistant diffidently, and asked for the necklace. The young woman smiled back, fetched it for him, took his six five pound notes, gave him two one pound notes back, and asked him if he wanted it wrapped.

"Yes please," Marcus answered. "I'm no good at wrapping presents, and this one's special."

"Is it for your Mother or your girlfriend?" she asked.

"My girlfriend," Marcus answered, blushing to his roots.

The girl grinned as she wrapped the gift and handed it over.

Marcus pocketed the little package, smiled with relief, and left, thanking the assistant and wishing her a happy Christmas.

He left the shop and retraced his steps to the cards shop he had visited earlier. Here the search was a lot easier. He found the cards he spotted on his first visit and selected one, which was especially romantic. He bought the card and left the shop, running into his rival as he closed the door.

"Merry Christmas, Marcus," Philip greeted him.

"Merry Christmas, Philip," Marcus grunted in reply.

"I've just seen Evelyn James," Philip told him after a silence that embarrassed both of them.

"So what?" Marcus answered, affecting to be unconcerned.

"I've got to find her a good present. She won't be impressed by rubbish."

"You can't buy her love. She's a classy girl," Marcus responded. "I wouldn't even try," he added.

"Liar!" Philip answered with a grin. "I've watched you when you're on duty, stripping her with your eyes. You can't wait to get into her knickers; if she lets you, of course."

"Speak for yourself, Philip. Evelyn knows that I would treat her with respect."

Philip laughed.

"She wants action, not respect. She's like all girls. They're all the same."

"Says you! Evelyn's different. She wants love and respect – not sex."

Fifty Years After

"Marcus, you may deceive yourself, but you can't deceive me or her. You want to fuck her as much as I do! She knows that – but she also knows I'm more honest about what I want. She'll go with me, you wait and see."

Philip paused before turning away and throwing a final comment at Marcus as he did so.

"Meanwhile, I'm going to buy her love. We'll see then whether she prefers respect or expensive presents."

Marcus did not reply, contenting himself with shaking his head sadly, and turning away in silence. He still had to buy gifts for his parents and his younger brothers.

Marcus walked away in the opposite direction to that taken by Philip. He felt despondent; even though he was convinced that his gift would impress Evelyn. Philip was, he knew, right in what he had said about Marcus, and, he feared, was right about Evelyn as well. He knew that the stakes were levelled against him. He, the son of a local barrister, could not compete in the cash stakes with Philip, the son of a wealthy man, a man who had built up a successful construction business. Marcus did not believe his own brave words and alleged belief that Evelyn was a high-principled girl who shared what he tried to convince himself were his own ideals.

"I've bought her present and her card. I'll write a message and drop them in her door as I go home," he thought, as he entered another shop, bent on the less exacting task of buying gifts for his family.

Philip walked away, bent on his own shopping expedition. He dismissed his meeting with Marcus in one word, "Wanker!" expressed vehemently under his breath, as he entered an expensive perfumery. Here he wondered among the shelves, studying the names and prices on the bottles, before buying the most expensive.

"That should convince the greedy bitch," he thought. "After I've had her, that pious fool, Marcus, can do what

Fifty Years After

he likes with her. I'll have won the battle, that's all that counts."

With that thought, he took the expensive looking box to the counter, paid the required price, and asked the shop assistant to wrap it for him. She did so, and he walked away without another word.

"You rude bastard," the girl thought, as she turned to her next customer.

Sixteen year old Mark Smith was also shopping in the High Street that day. He had travelled with his parents from Jamaica on the "Empire Windrush." His father worked as a conductor for London Transport, while his mother had joined the National Health Service as a nurse. Mark had left school at fifteen and after struggling to get a job took up an apprenticeship in a local printing firm. He, too, was buying Christmas presents for his family. Unlike Philip and Marcus, however, he had bigger problems than vying for the affections of a sixteen year old white girl. Indeed, the very thought that he might be interested in such a person would have horrified both him and his parents. It would not work any way in a town where every vacant house or flat being offered for rent had a sign saying "No pets, no children, no blacks." Even in the shops, he noticed, the white shop assistants seemed reluctant to serve him. If a white person joined the queue behind him, he or she always got served before him. As he made his way along the High Street, Mark passed both Marcus and Philip in turn, not knowing or noticing them. They, however, noticed him, and both stood their ground as he approached, forcing him to step onto the road to pass them. Philip and Marcus agreed on very little, but they did agree that people like Mark should not be in Britain.

His mission finally, accomplished, Marcus set off for home, taking a roundabout route, and hoping to run into Evelyn on the way. His heart beat faster as he entered the road where she lived and approached her house.

Fifty Years After

"Please God, make her like my present," he prayed.

Shyly he approached the front door and rang the bell. His heart beat even faster as he heard footsteps inside and saw a shadow approach the door. He half hoped it was Evelyn and half hoped it was not. The door opened at last, and Evelyn's mother stood there, wearing an apron over her flowery dress and obviously had just come from the kitchen from where he could smell the smell of cooking.

"Hello Mrs James," Marcus began in response to the big woman's smiled greeting. "Merry Christmas. I've brought a present and a card for Evelyn."

Shyly he offered the gaily-wrapped package and the boxed card to her, but she smiled and refused to take them from him. Instead she turned away and called up the stairs.

"There's a boy here with a present for you Evelyn. You'd better come down and see him."

Marcus's heart quickened as he heard Evelyn's voice floating down the stairs.

"Who is it Mum? If it's Philip Stewart tell him to fuck off. He's only after one thing."

Mrs James looked embarrassed at her daughter's language.

"I'm sorry you heard that, dear," she said to Marcus. "Is your name Philip?"

"No, Mrs James. I'm Marcus. I go to the same school as Evelyn."

Mrs James called this information up the stairs and, a few moments later, Evelyn walked warily down the stairs to replace her mother at the door.

"You'd better come in," she said hesitantly, indicating the door that led from the small hallway into the Sitting Room.

Marcus followed Evelyn into the room. He noticed that it was neatly, but sparingly furnished. The floor carpet was brightly coloured, mainly red and blue, with a flowered pattern, which Mrs James obviously favoured. He noticed that everything in the room suggested that they were struggling to make ends meet. Despite this the room contained a coffee table and a three-piece suite as well as a television set, which, at this time of the day, was switched off. Instead, a radio blared light music from somewhere inside the house. He sat down on the sofa, and Evelyn sat on one of the chairs, facing him. Her face showed how puzzled she was at this unexpected visit.

Marcus suddenly began to doubt. Had he made a fool of himself offering a present to a girl who did not care about him?

"I've seen you at school," Evelyn began. "You're one of the Prefects aren't you?"

"Yes," Marcus replied. "I'm called Marcus Greenway, and I've fancied you for a long time."

"You've never told me," she replied simply. "You're about the only boy in the Sixth Form who hasn't!" she added.

"That's because I thought you would say 'no'," Marcus replied. "I thought that you were keen on Philip Stewart."

"That creep!" she said dismissively. "I wouldn't go out with him if he was the only man left in the world. He wants to get his hands inside my knickers and thinks he can buy me. It's almost like he thinks I'm some sort of prostitute who can be bought. Well, he's wrong. I'm not a prostitute and I can't be bought."

Marcus did not know how to respond to this. Nervously he produced his gift and card.

"I bought you this," he said. "I hope you like it – but I'm not trying to buy you."

Evelyn took the gift and looked first at the wrapping and then at the face of her suitor.

"Can I open it?" she asked.

"You should really wait until Christmas Day," he replied. "But if you want to, then do so." Evelyn nodded and slowly and patiently opened the parcel, trying to save the wrapping paper. Finally, she pulled the paper away and revealed an oblong cardboard jewellery box. She opened it

Fifty Years After

eagerly and her eyes widened as she looked at the necklace inside.

"Is this really for me?" she asked. "It must have cost you a fortune."

"It's what you deserve," Marcus replied, saying the first thing that came into his mind.

Evelyn stood up and walked over to him. She sat down next to him, grasped his hands and leant over and kissed him. He kissed her back and they remained locked together mouth to mouth for what seemed an age before Marcus pulled his face back and asked quietly.

"Would you come to the pictures with me on Boxing Day. There's a good film on. Gregory Peck is in it."

"Promise me that you're not like the other boys," was her answer. "If we see the film, you can kiss me but I don't want your hand up my skirt. If you do that I'll walk away and leave you."

"I promise," Marcus answered.

"Then I'll come," she said, putting her arms around him and kissing him again, just as the doorbell rang and they heard her mother answer the door.

"Is Evelyn in Mrs James?" Philip asked.

"She's not, Philip," Mrs James lied. "She went out shopping two or three hours ago and is going to meet her Dad, to help him bring back our Christmas shopping."

"Well, please give her this present for me," Philip said, his disappointment sounding in his voice.

The door closed and the Sitting Room door opened, revealing Evelyn's mother to the two teenagers locked in each other's arms.

"I see you've made friends already," Mrs James commented drily. "If you're interested, Evelyn," she added, "Philip's left this for you."

She handed the parcel to Evelyn who looked at it disinterestedly.

"It looks like perfume," Evelyn said. "He always buys the most expensive perfume. He doesn't seem to realize it's not the price but the brand that I look for – and he never gets it. You take it Mum. You can either use it or give it to someone who likes it."

Mrs James took the parcel back.

"Thank you dear," she said, looking at the box stripped of its wrapping paper. "I see you couldn't wait," she added.

Evelyn grinned at her

"Look what Marcus bought me, Mum."

She showed her mother the necklace.

"It's lovely. I'm going to wear it on Christmas Day and keep Marcus' card until then."

Mrs James admired the necklace, handling it before returning it to her daughter.

"You chose well Marcus. Evelyn has always loved pretty jewellery and this is very pretty."

"Thank you, Mrs James."

Marcus paused and looked at Evelyn, asking her without words. She nodded.

"Would you allow me to take Evelyn to the cinema on Boxing Day?" he asked.

"Will you treat her like a lady?" she asked.

"Of course," he replied.

"Well, if she wants to come with you, I won't stop her."

She turned away from them.

"I've got to go back to the kitchen, Evelyn. Go and make Marcus some tea. It's cold outside and he needs warming up before he goes back out."

Evelyn followed her mother out of the Sitting Room and Marcus was left on his own.

"Result!" he said to himself, as he waited for Evelyn to return.

Mark, meanwhile, had completed his shopping and was on his way home. He lived in Evelyn's neighbourhood, although neither teenager was aware of the other. Loaded down with shopping bags, he struggled through the snow, which was growing steadily stronger, buffeted by a driving wind that froze his body, despite his many layers of clothing under his

Fifty Years After

duffle coat. His hood was up and his scarf was across his mouth; but none of this helped him combat the cold. The only result was that his downcast eyes did not see an angry Philip striding towards him, muttering under his breath about ungrateful girls. Philip did not see Mark either, and, as a result, the two boys crashed into one another, causing Mark to drop his bags, fortunately without breaking anything, and exacerbating Philip's anger.

"Get out of my way, Nigger," Philip snarled.

"Why?" Mark answered. "I've as much right to walk on this pavement as you have – and you may have broken my mother's Christmas present."

"Tough!" Philip answered. "The only present I would give you would be your ticket back to Bongobongoland."

Mark seethed at this latest example of racism directed against him. All his instincts told him to hit the smirking white racist in front of him – but he knew that the Police would blame him for the fight that would follow, so he turned away.

"Go on then, you coward. You come here, take our jobs and houses and rape our girls and you haven't got the guts to stand up for yourself," Philip taunted.

That was simply too much. A red mist suddenly descended on Mark. He swung around and smashed his fist into the face of the white racist teenager who had taunted him. Philip staggered back as his nose suddenly spurted blood, and Mark picked up his bags and calmly walked away, breathing deeply. Philip wanted to chase after the black teenager's retreating back but knew he wasn't strong enough or brave enough to tackle him alone.

The three boys returned to their homes at about the same time, but with different emotions. Marcus was on cloud nine. Philip was hurt and angry. Mark felt humiliated and ashamed of himself for reacting in the way he did. And. in these separate ways, the three teenagers waited for Christmas 1959 to begin next day.

Fifty Years After

2. Murder casts its long shadow

Christmas Eve 2009
Jonathan Greenway arrived at the entrance to his grandparents' grace and favour government country estate in Buckinghamshire. The twenty year old Information Technology student drove down from his university lodgings in Cambridge and was waved to a halt by two police officers standing on guard at the gate to the estate. Jonathan rolled down his window and addressed the officers.

"What can I do for you, Officer?" he asked

"You can identify yourself for us. Who are you and what are you doing here?" the younger officer asked.

Jonathan smiled.

"My name is Jonathan Greenway. I'm a student from Cambridge University and I'm the grandson of Sir Marcus and Lady Evelyn Greenway. The reason why I'm here is because they have invited me to spend Christmas with them."

"Can I see your driving licence, sir?" the older officer asked.

Jonathan reached into his inside pocket, pulled out his wallet and withdrew a photo card, which he handed to the officers, who studied it, before returning it to him with a smile.

"That's all right, sir. You can pass through. I hope we haven't offended you, but we can't be too careful in these days what with the Jihadists and the Irish Republican terrorists and all."

"Not to mention Sir Marcus's political enemies who've been trying to destroy him," the younger man added.

Jonathan took back his driving licence and returned it to his wallet with a smile, before pocketing the wallet and driving carefully through the now opened gates into the estate as the older officer picked up a phone and

Fifty Years After

telephoned through to the house to report the visitor's arrival.

Jonathan drove the mile or so from the gate to the house. He stopped in the driveway in front of the house where he was met by the butler, who took his bags and car keys. He passed Jonathan's keys to Sir Marcus's driver, who drove the car around to the side of the building, where he parked it in one of the garages. Meanwhile, a housemaid took Jonathan's bags to his room, where she unpacked them and placed his clothing and other belongings in appropriate places, and the Butler showed Jonathan into one of the Reception Rooms, asked him to sit down, showed him where the drinks cabinet was and went to fetch Lady Greenway. Jonathan selected a medium sherry and poured himself a double. He sat down and waited, while the routine of the great house went on quietly around him for the best part of half an hour. Jonathan looked around the room. He noticed that it was elegant rather than comfortable, characterless and plainly government inspired. He guessed that civil servants rather than his grandparents had chosen the furniture.

As he waited, Jonathan thought about the details of Sir Marcus's remarkable career. Trained as a solicitor, he married his childhood sweetheart at the age of nineteen, before being called to the bar, following in his father's footsteps. He recalled that father and son had been involved in a very controversial murder case involving a young black male who was hanged for murdering a young white woman. He remembered that there had been a lot of debate about that case, and resolved that he would Google the case and find out more. After it, his great grandfather had become a judge and his grandfather had gone into politics, joining his local Conservative Association and becoming a political assistant to one of the MPs. When the MP died, he was selected to defend the seat, and won it. From there, his rise to power was swift, and, by the age of

Fifty Years After

thirty-eight he was a Cabinet Minister. Eventually, having been a successful Chancellor, he was elected Party Leader and became Prime Minister, winning power in his own right at the 2008 General Election. Since then he had been struggling with a major financial crisis and had begun to face awkward questions about his own past and those of many of his associates in the press, in social media and on both television and radio. Jonathan did not know the rights and wrongs of it, but he had experienced some of the fallout as the Press, anxious to get more information on the Greenways, hounded his family.

The door opened and Lady Greenway entered. She was very different from the rather shy and awkward Evelyn James who received the Christmas present from young Marcus Greenway fifty years earlier. Lady Evelyn Greenway was composed, elegant and rather austere. She carried herself with confidence and dressed in the simple way that only the wealthy and powerful can carry off. She crossed the room swiftly and embraced Jonathan.

"Jonathan, how lovely to see you. Your parents and brothers are coming down later today. Sir Marcus will be down tonight."

"Grandma, it's lovely to meet you too. It's been a long time."

"Too long."

"And I've never been here before."

"Then I'll show you around later. How are you doing at University?"

"I'm reading IT. It's my second year. It's an interesting course – but I do need a much more powerful and modern computer. Mine is old, weak and slow."

Evelyn smiled.

"So I heard," she commented. "We'll have to see what we can do about it."

Jonathan nodded and smiled at Evelyn. He had always loved his Grandma, who had earned his love by usually supporting him in his battles with his parents. She tolerated his teenage mood swings where his mother and father tried to fight them.

Evelyn stood up.

"Come on, Jonathan, if you're going to see the garden, we'd better get going, before it gets dark."

Jonathan nodded, swallowed the last of his sherry, and stood up. He followed his grandmother out of the room, closing the door behind them.

Following their tour of the house and gardens, Evelyn took Jonathan to his room and left him to freshen up for the evening. Following a brief shower, he half dressed in the formal style required by the household for the main evening meal and turned to his laptop. Jonathan's interest had been aroused by his musings over his grandfather's career, and particularly the incident of the trial. It took some time, but, eventually, he managed to track down a record of the trial in Google. Plainly, he thought, his Grandfather's emergence at the top of the political tree had caused others to research the story. He was surprised to see that the case had caused a huge amount of controversy at the time and that a number of books had been written about it, both by lawyers and by historians. He found two articles especially interesting. The first was a front page from the North London Daily Herald of June 23rd 1961, announcing the verdict. Jonathan downloaded it and read it.

The title of the article was "Teenage girl's slayer condemned to death". The article read:

"An eighteen year old Black man, Mark Smith, who came to Britain from Jamaica a few years ago in the "Empire Windrush" was condemned to hang today in the Old Bailey for the murder of the white teenager, Janet Brown. Judge Thomas Williams commented that the evidence of Philip Stewart, the boyfriend of the dead girl, who had witnessed the fatal gunshot, was decisive. He expressed

Fifty Years After

shock and horror at the nature of the crime, commenting that he thought that it showed that the Government's policy on allowing wholesale immigration from the West Indies was misplaced. Donning the black cap, he said that he hoped the black community would take note that white girls are not available to be slaughtered by black boys angry that they had jilted them. Smith had pleaded not guilty, but his barrister had not called him to give evidence."

On July 15th 1961, the same newspaper carried a second story about the case. A brief paragraph on the front page, under the title, "Killer hanged", read:

"The murderer of Janet Brown, 18 year old Jamaican, Mark Smith, was hanged at 8 am this morning in Wormwood Scrubs Jail. Other prisoners expressed their protest by banging on their locked cell doors at the time of the execution and a large crowd of protestors gathered outside. Later, a notice of the execution and burial of Smith inside the prison yard was pinned on the main door of the prison. The Herald understands that Smith's family were allowed to spend time with him yesterday following the Home Secretary's rejection of his appeal for clemency yesterday morning. The prisoner had the traditional last breakfast of his choice at 7 am."

Jonathan read these two articles again, slowly, and then looked at other, more recent, contributions on the trial. He noticed that there seemed to be considerable unease about the case and the verdict. There had been so much unease that there had actually been an attempt to get the verdict dismissed as unsafe and an official pardon for Mark Smith, although it had come to nothing. However, he also learnt that the case still caused anger and resentment in the Afro-Caribbean community. Jonathan noted the reference to the role of Philip Stewart in the trial and resolved to ask Sir Marcus if he could tell him more about it.

Fifty Years After

His meditations and researches were brought to an abrupt end by the sounding of the dinner gong below in the hall. Hastily donning his dinner jacket and tie, Jonathan switched off his laptop, and made for the Dining Room.

Jonathan was almost the last into dinner. His parents and brothers and his grandmother were already seated and their host was the only other person missing. He had arrived from Downing Street and was expected any moment. Jonathan noted that his brothers seemed very happy to see him, but that his father seemed displeased. Jonathan thought it was because he was late, but he reflected, his father seldom seemed pleased with what he did. His mother, however, smiled encouragingly at him, and Lady Evelyn greeted him and told him to sit beside her.

"Now I've seen my eldest grandson again after so long, I'm not going to let him get away from me," she said to the room in general, but glancing meaningfully at her son, who grunted his assent.

Shortly afterwards, Sir Marcus entered the room, and took his seat at the head of the table. He greeted everyone before looking at the Butler and clapping his hands for the meal to be served. Jonathan sat quietly between his grandmother and his mother, listening to the conversation between the four older members of the party.

"How's it going?" Jonathan's father, Martin Greenway, asked his father.

"Badly," Sir Marcus replied. "I hoped after the Election to have a few years of quiet endeavour in which to carry out my promises, but I've not had a moment's quiet since June 24th, 2008."

"I know there have been some problems," Martin responded, "but surely it's not as bad as all that?"

"You don't know the half of it, Martin. The banks are on the verge of collapse. We have so-called asylum seekers besieging the depot in Calais. The papers are full of stories about MPs on the fiddle. The Russians are

Fifty Years After

playing dangerous games in Eastern Europe and the Middle East. A gung-ho American President is threatening all-out war with the Muslims and I have the usual idiots in my Party trying to make a fuss about our membership of the EU."

"It could be worse, Marcus," Evelyn commented. "At least no one is trying to drag you into Malcolm Kent's war plans!"

"Malcolm Kent is!" Sir Marcus answered bitterly. "And our generals seem to agree with him."

"President Kent has always been that way," Jennifer Greenway (Jonathan's mother) commented. "Surely it doesn't concern us?"

"I don't want to preside over a second 7/7 or 9/11," Sir Marcus answered.

That comment sobered them as they all remembered the Jihadist bombs in New York and London and the hundreds of deaths they caused. Silence fell on the gathering as the main course was followed by the sweet. Into this silence, to the surprise of everyone, Jonathan asked the question that had been tormenting him all evening.

"Who was Philip Stewart, Grandpa?"

Martin Greenway looked angrily at his son and Sir Marcus looked surprised. Neither answered. Instead it was Lady Evelyn who answered Jonathan's question.

"Philip Stewart was the little creep who thought he could buy my body for a bottle of perfume," she answered simply.

Sir Marcus made a mock objection.

"That's unfair, Darling. We mustn't call Lord Stewart of Little Wittering a creep. It's unfair to those who are creeps!"

Evelyn laughed.

"Unfair, perhaps, but still true. Before you came to see me in Mum's house he'd been creeping around me for weeks."

She turned and spoke to her grandson.

Fifty Years After

"You must know the sort of boy he was – I'm sure you've met the type."

"What type, Grandma?"

"The type that likes to collect girls as a sort of prize. They trick or force the girls into having sex with them and then boast to everyone else about it."

Jonathan grinned.

"Oh yes, Grandma, I know the type. Several of the male students in my college are exactly like that."

Evelyn smiled at him.

"I thought you would, Jonathan. Well, Philip Stewart was like that. He wanted to hang me on his prize belt. I refused him and became your Granddad's girlfriend, but that didn't save me. He told everyone that he'd slept with me and that I was easy-pickings. His exact words, someone told me, were 'She was gagging for it.' When your Granddad heard what he was saying, he found him one night and gave him a good thrashing. I'd never seen Marcus so angry. Certainly I've never seen him so angry since. He's usually very mild and calm. He wasn't then!"

Sir Marcus interrupted the conversation, emphasising his points by waving his spoon at Jonathan as he spoke.

"Philip Stewart was and is a louse. He told me that every girl wants a man to get into her bed. Actually his words were 'to get into her knickers'. He told me that that was all your Grandma wanted and he was going to take her. I actually believed him for a moment, but decided I would take my Christmas present to her anyway. That's when I learnt just how wrong he was. Anyway, when he later spoke about Evelyn in the way he did, I saw red, and fought him. He hurt me, but I hurt him a lot more, and he certainly stopped abusing Evelyn. I was wrong though, because violence isn't the answer. Never forget that young Jonathan."

He paused, put his spoon down, and continued.

"Anyway, why do you ask?"

"I was thinking about you when I was waiting for Grandma after I arrived, and I remembered that murder trial you and Great Grandpa were involved in. When I got back from my walk with Grandma I looked it up on Google and discovered that Philip Stewart was the chief witness. So I wondered who he was."

Sir Marcus looked startled for a moment and the rest of the table was silent. Martin glared angrily at his son, who ignored him, concentrating on his Grandfather, who eventually began to speak again.

"I remember the trial of Mark Smith very well. It still haunts me in fact. Philip was doing what Philip always did, knocking up a girl. In this case the girl was already in a relationship, like Evelyn was with me. In her case it was with Mark Smith. It was very dangerous, in those days, for a white girl to be seen with a black man, but the two were in love. Philip tried to break it up. I understand that he caught them both naked and having sex and pulled the boy off the girl. Apparently there had been some sort of run in between the two before and Philip recognised Mark. At any rate he beat the boy up well and truly. Philip claims that he then went over to assist the girl to get up and get dressed, believing she was a rape victim, when Mark suddenly went to his clothes, took a gun from his pocket, pointed it at Philip and fired two shots. Both shots missed Philip and hit the girl, killing her instantly."

Sir Marcus paused once more, picking up his wine glass by the stem and fiddling with it. Finally, he resumed, but with less conviction.

"That was the story. Mark's barrister tried to shake it but didn't really succeed and Mark wasn't asked to give evidence in his own defence. There was little forensic evidence and the only witness was Philip. Philip was and still is a womaniser and a liar. I've always been troubled by the verdict. My father was the Prosecutor and certainly he had no doubts. Neither did the Home Secretary who rejected Mark's appeal, when I spoke to him about the case years later."

"Did you speak to Philip about it, Granddad?"

Sir Marcus hesitated before answering.

Fifty Years After

"No, Jonathan. I've never spoken to him about it."

"I read that there are some books written about the case. Do you have any that I can read?" Jonathan asked.

"Oh for Heaven's sake, boy. Leave it alone!" Martin ordered.

"No, Son," Sir Marcus responded. "The boy's entitled to know the truth."

He turned back to Jonathan.

"Once we've got through Christmas Day, young Jonathan, come and join me in my study. I will lend you the book you want. In fact, I'll do better than that – I'll give it to you as a present. I'll also allow you to read through the diaries I wrote at that time. Only your Grandma has ever read them apart from me."

"I blushed when I read them," Evelyn commented, "but you youngsters aren't half as squeamish as we were so I doubt that you will find them as shocking as I did."

Jonathan laughed, relieved that he had got away with what he recognised was a social faux pas.

"I'll tell you, Grandma, when I've seen what Granddad wrote that he did not intend other people to see."

She laughed as well, and the conversation moved on to other issues, until the party broke up. Sir Marcus took Martin and Jonathan to the Drawing Room to drink brandy while Lady Evelyn took Jennifer and the two younger boys to the Sitting Room, where coffee was served.

3. The Diary

December 26 2009
Christmas Day passed in a whirl for Jonathan. The Christmas routine absorbed everyone in its relentless onward movement. All that really registered for Jonathan was his gift from his grandparents – a top of the range laptop to help him with his studies, as Lady Evelyn had hinted to him the day before. Otherwise the helter-skelter of big meals, family games and drowsy post-prandial debate passed him by, as did the cheerful camaraderie of his mother, the continued disapproval of his father and the juvenile (as he thought) antics of his younger brothers. He even failed to notice the slight frostiness he had caused between his grandparents. Jonathan's mind was on Boxing Day.

Eventually the pleasure-filled day passed and Jonathan was able to retire to the seclusion of his bedroom, where he was, at last, able to set up his new laptop. He did this with great pleasure, as he saw how much more powerful it was than his old one. Using his new computer, he accessed the Google files on the various characters in the Mark Smith Murder Trial. He found very little about Janet Brown, except that she was eighteen when she was killed and seemed to be a working class girl. She worked as a shop assistant in Rosemary's, a local clothes shop specialising in women's clothing. Mark Smith, he learned, had not finished his apprenticeship as a printer and was working in a local printing company. Other than that, the story he had read in the Herald article was repeated. Jonathan was puzzled. The story, as told in the newspaper and repeated in the articles on Google, suggested that the charge of Capital Murder was wrong. He felt that Manslaughter would have been more appropriate. He wondered if the charge and the verdict were due to racism

Fifty Years After

and the fact that a black boy and white girl were making love.

He turned to the career of Philip Stewart, and here he was luckier. Philip had never married but was known as a good family man. Philip entered politics with the Labour Party and the Trade Union Movement. A wealthy man, he was on the right wing of the Labour Party. He served in the last Labour Government as Secretary of State for Trade and Industry with some success, and went to the Lords after the defeat of that Government in the 2002 General Election and the loss of his Parliamentary seat in Marchfield West. While he and Sir Marcus were both in the House of Commons, the two men had often been at each other's throats. Since Sir Marcus had become Prime Minister, Philip had been a persistent and nagging critic from his seat in the Lords.

Jonathan found all this to be interesting, but unhelpful in his search for Philip's role in the murder trial. Something seemed wrong about his story. If Mark wanted to rape Janet, Jonathan mused, he would scarcely have found a place public enough for Philip to have discovered them. If Janet and Mark were lovers and looking for a place where a black boy and a white girl could have fun together without provoking public hostility, they would also have been very careful to select somewhere secluded. So how could Philip Stewart have found them?

Jonathan searched through all the references in the Google pages but found nothing about Philip's role in the Martin Smith trial except references to his having been the prime witness for the Prosecution. He was no luckier looking up Sir Marcus and, when he looked for Sir Walter Greenway, he found very little. The article in Wikipedia simply gave a chronological list of important events known in the barrister's life and a two sentences entry on the Mark Smith trial which said that Sir Walter had led the

Fifty Years After

prosecution of Mark Smith and was a witness at his execution.

Jonathan finally gave up his search with a sigh. He realised that he would have to rely on what Sir Marcus chose to reveal to him next day. He wrote down a number of questions he felt he needed answers to.
1. What was known about the two lovers?
2. Why was Philip Stewart present at their tryst?
3. What, if anything, was Sir Marcus covering up?
4. Why was Mark Smith executed?

He felt that, if he could get answers to any of these questions, he would be closer to learning the truth about a case that seemed all wrong to him.

Next morning, following a late breakfast, Sir Marcus took Jonathan to his study, and invited him to sit in one of the deep leather chairs which were provided for visitors to the room which, apart from Sir Marcus's desk and drinks cabinet, was more like a library than a study, since the walls were lined with shelves which were full of books. Jonathan looked around as Sir Marcus walked across to his drinks cabinet, took two stemmed glasses with large bowls, which Jonathan recognised as brandy glasses, and poured two generous shots of brandy into them. He saw that there were two gaps in the serried ranks of books and guessed that the two books on his grandfather's desk accounted for the gaps. Sir Marcus returned to where Jonathan was sitting and handed him one of the glasses, before sitting down in another of the leather chairs and drawing it up to face his grandson.

"I always believe that a glass of brandy assists a good chat, young man," he said, placing his glass on the small coffee table that separated grandfather and grandson. "Now, what did you want to talk to me about?"

"Lots of things, Grandfather, but could we start with that trial?"

Fifty Years After

Jonathan thought he saw a shadow cross Sir Marcus's previously smiling face. However, if it was, it was swiftly replaced.

"Why are you so interested in that case?"

"I wasn't until yesterday. In fact, I didn't even know about it until I read a newspaper story about a possible appeal to you from the Smith family to open a public enquiry into the case."

Sir Marcus nodded.

"Yes, I've heard about their campaign. 'The Express' seems to have thrown their weight behind it. I'm minded to ignore it."

Jonathan was surprised and said so.

"Surely, Grandfather, the easiest way to put the case to bed is to hold a public enquiry?"

Sir Marcus laughed.

"The only reason a politician ever launches a public enquiry is when he wants to kick something into what we call the long grass. You set up an enquiry, give it a long and complicated brief, which it can never actually fulfil, and solemnly instruct the Chairman to leave no stone unturned and take as much time as he needs to reach the truth. Then you hope that he will take you at your word and that, by the time he produces his report you're long gone. If you're still there you simply make a public statement in the House announcing that you accept the findings, thank the chairman and forget all about it."

"That seems somewhat cynical Granddad."

"You're still very young, Jonathan. You will learn, as you grow older, that all politicians are cynical. The nature of politics makes us so. I'm always polite to Philip Stewart and he is to me – but I would dearly like to stick a dagger in his back and I know he would like to do the same to me! But, we are publically opponents but also colleagues, with whom sadly we disagree, and we treat each other with respect. You can call it cynical if you like – but that's the way the game is played."

Jonathan sipped some of his brandy. Sir Marcus followed him with his blue eyes.

"It's a good brandy. President Le Saux gave me a case when I visited Paris last year."

"Yes, it's nice, Granddad," Jonathan agreed, putting his glass down again.

"I understand that you worked with Sir Walter on the case, Granddad. What exactly did you do?"

Sir Marcus smiled.

"Not a lot, Jonathan. I was his clerk. I read the papers and assembled them in order for him. A solicitor did all the interviewing and other donkey work."

"There's lots of things that don't make sense to me in that trial, and I wondered if you can explain them."

"I can try. What's troubling you?"

"I know what Philip Stewart said happened, but not what Mark Smith said. What was his story?"

Sir Marcus paused before answering, sipping his brandy and plainly gathering his thoughts. Finally, he put his glass down and began to speak.

"This was never stated in court, but it's what Mark told the police who questioned him. He and Janet had been going out together secretly for some time. They kept their relationship secret because neither his parents nor Janet's approved. That sort of thing wasn't done in those days. Blacks and Whites did not go together, certainly not men and women in a sexual relationship. However, that's what Mark claimed these two were having. As we told you two days ago, Philip Stewart was and is what is called a male predator."

"Was he prepared to rape a woman if she resisted his advances?"

"Oh yes, certainly. We all knew of several cases where the girl complained about being forced into sex."

"How did he get away with it?"

"In those days the courts didn't take rape all that seriously, especially among teenagers. In any case, his family had money and the girl could always be bought off."

"What if she became pregnant?"

"There were always doctors willing to do an abortion if paid enough."

"I thought it was against the law!"

"It was," Sir Marcus agreed, "but that didn't stop it. It's one reason why abortion eventually was legalised."

Jonathan took this in, sipped some more brandy and continued.

"How did Philip become involved?"

"He saw Janet Brown, who was, incidentally, a very pretty girl, and wanted her to add to his collection. He began to stalk her and that's how he caught her with Mark. Mark said that he and Janet had found a quiet and secluded spot, and began to have fun together. One thing led to another, and, eventually, both were naked and were having sex when Philip suddenly appeared. He looked outraged at what the two were doing and ordered them to separate. Mark said he obeyed, only for Philip to kick him hard between the legs."

"Ouch!" said Jonathan involuntarily.

"Exactly," Sir Marcus concurred. "Mark said he was doubled up as a result when Philip gave him an uppercut to the chin that almost knocked his head off. When he recovered consciousness he found the gun in his hand and Janet lying dead with two bullet wounds to her body. He was still naked, as was she, and Philip Stewart was standing nearby with a police constable, who arrested Mark, ordered him to dress, cuffed him, and put him in a police car to be taken to the nearest police station."

Sir Marcus paused, poured himself some brandy, and then concluded.

"That was Mark's story, but it was never told in court."

"Why not?"

"I think his barrister knew that the all-white jury would never believe it. The only alternative was that Philip had shot Janet and that Mark and Janet were having consensual sex together. Such a thing in 1961 was almost unheard of. It was much easier for the Jury to believe Philip's story that Mark tried to rape Janet and brave Philip tried to save her, causing Mark to try to kill him, but killing Janet instead."

Jonathan looked pensive.

"What did you think Granddad? You said you knew all about Philip. Did you know anything about Mark?"

"Nothing."

"Didn't Sir Walter try to find out anything about him, to throw light on the conflicting stories?"

"It wasn't his job, Jonathan. It was the job of the police and the officer in charge, D.I. Alasdair Buchan didn't bother."

"Why not? Surely that was the least he should do?"

"Jonathan – we're talking about 1961. In 1961 if a black boy was caught with a gun in his hand and a dead white girl at his feet, and both are naked – then he had tried to rape her, she resisted, and he killed her. There was no chance that anyone would believe Mark's story - so why bother to get him to tell it? Instead the barrister tried to get him off on a technicality."

"What was the technicality?"

"That the charge was wrong."

Jonathan smiled sadly.

"That was another thing that worried me, Granddad. It was the wrong charge. If Philip Stewart's evidence was true: then Mark was guilty of manslaughter not murder."

"That's what the lawyer tried to argue – but the Jury didn't accept it."

"The Jury might have thought that, Granddad, but surely your father didn't? He knew the law, so why didn't he get the charge altered?"

"My father was of the same mind as the Jury. He said to me that if other black boys copied Mark; then no white girls would be safe. The Judge felt the same."

Grandfather and grandson sat together, facing one another, in silence, as Jonathan absorbed what Sir Marcus had just told him. Finally, after five minutes, Sir Marcus stood up and went to his desk. He came back with the two books. One he placed on the floor. The other he handed to Jonathan.

"This is the best account of the Smith Trial. It was written a couple of years later when the debate about Capital Punishment was reaching its conclusion. It reflects the atmosphere of the time and includes a full transcript of the trial. Take it home with you as an extra Christmas present from me."

"Thank you, Granddad."

Jonathan paused, feeling awkward.

"What is it that's still worrying you, Jonathan?"

"What did you think about Mark and Philip's stories?"

Sir Marcus silently poured out another shot of brandy for them both and took a long sip from his own glass as he thought of his answer. Finally, just as Jonathan began to conclude that he wasn't going to answer, he spoke somewhat hesitantly.

"I don't know, Jonathan. I never spoke to Mark or his family, or the members of Janet's family."

"And Philip?"

There was a significantly longer pause before Sir Marcus answered.

"I hated Philip Stewart for what he said about Evelyn, which you will read about in my diary. I have never spoken directly with him since the day I found out. I heard what he said in court."

Marcus paused to sip his brandy. He looked fixedly at Jonathan, almost challenging him to believe him. Jonathan did not respond. Eventually Marcus continued.

"I know enough to know that what Mark said about his relationship with Janet could be true – but I don't think that Philip murdered her – which is the only other alternative to the story that the court obviously believed."

Jonathan sat quietly, sipping his brandy. He was grateful that he had the glass to cover his doubt and confusion. He had always loved and respected Sir Marcus. He thought of him as an honest man, and, as far it was possible to be one, an honest politician. However, he was convinced that Sir Marcus had just lied to him. He could not understand why or how the lie had been said. He didn't even know for sure what the lie was – but he was certain there was a lie there and he was saddened by it. Sir Marcus studied his grandson. He was aware that something was obviously wrong. The previously warm atmosphere between them had chilled suddenly, but he did not know why or how it had happened.

"What's wrong, Jonathan? What's worrying you so suddenly?" Sir Marcus asked.

Jonathan shook his head, as if to clear it.

"Oh, it's nothing, Granddad. I'm still a little confused, but I'm sure the book will tell me all I need to know. Thank you for giving it to me."

Sir Marcus smiled in relief. He was glad to have got this potentially awkward interview over.

"You won't have time to read it here, though, Jonathan."

Sir Marcus handed him the other book.

"This is my diary. I promised you that I would let you read it. It will tell you most of what you want to know about me and Evelyn and my life until I became PM. It doesn't contain anything controversial and only goes from 50 years ago when I first met your Grandma until I became Prime Minister."

"Don't you keep a diary now, Granddad?"

Sir Marcus smiled.

"Oh yes – but now it's on my laptop, double protected by passwords, together with controversial stories from earlier. Experience has told me that it only takes a lucky burglar and the national press has all your secrets?"

Jonathan smiled at him.

"Does this file contain what you really think about my Dad?"

Sir Marcus laughed.

"Listen grandson, I used the word 'controversial' to describe what I put on my file – not 'incendiary'!"

Both grandfather and grandson laughed as Jonathan took the two books and left the study.

4. An Old Romance

December 26 2009
Jonathan settled into his room, opened the big black covered hardbound notebook, and began to read. The first entry was dated December 24th 1959 and told the story outlined in the first chapter, except with the addition of a lot of exclamation marks. Jonathan read it with a smile, showing empathy with the young Marcus, remembering how he felt about his first girlfriend. He recalled the "Will she? Won't she?" "She loves me; she loves me not," moments with a smile. He passed on to the second entry – December 25th and saw that Marcus had stuck in a Christmas card. He opened it. There was nothing special about it – it was the sort of cheap card you could buy in any supermarket. What was special was the message:

"To my first boyfriend, the one I've always wanted. Merry Christmas from Evelyn – your new girlfriend."

Jonathan counted at least twenty kisses on the rest of the card. Underneath it was pasted a small black and white photo. It was the sort taken by a box camera with a fixed lens, he thought, and slightly out of focus and shaky – but it clearly showed a pretty teenaged girl with light (probably blond) shoulder length hair smiling out at him. Underneath it, Marcus had written, *"My girlfriend – Evelyn."*

Jonathan nodded gently as he studied the photo, and then turned as he felt a light hand on his shoulder. He turned around to look into the smiling eyes of his Grandmother.

"I thought you'd be here, reading the diary," she began. "I came here to tell you my side of the story."

She looked at the card and the photo.

"I gave your Granddad that photo when he came round to see me on Christmas Eve. What he doesn't know was

Fifty Years After

that I had dreamed about his being my boyfriend for months – ever since he kept me in detention for being cheeky to him. I wanted him to keep me in so I could say I'd spent the evening with him!"

Jonathan laughed.

"I see that girls haven't changed much in fifty years, Grandma," he said.

Evelyn laughed as well.

"We haven't changed much in 2000 years, yet alone 50, young Jonathan! When we want a man, we have our ways of getting him! Marcus didn't just get the idea that he fancied me. I got a friend to tell him that I fancied him. It worked – as you see."

Jonathan smiled at Evelyn as he studied her youthful figure in the photo.

"You haven't changed too much over the years, Grandma," he said.

"Don't be silly, Jonathan," she replied. "You sound like your grandfather. Of course I've changed! My hair's grey instead of blond, for a start."

"And you're mature and elegant rather than young, vivacious and naïf," Jonathan added.

"What you mean is that I've grown old and lost my youthful figure," Evelyn said sadly. "You're like Marcus, skirting around sad facts with bold phrases."

Jonathan laughed.

"You're right, Grandma – but I can see the light of mischief in your eyes. The teenaged girl hasn't entirely disappeared."

Evelyn looked at Jonathan with new respect.

"Your father doesn't do you justice, Jonathan. That was an amazingly accurate observation for one so young to make."

She paused, smiled, and then continued.

"Now let's read what my husband wrote about our first date."

Fifty Years After

Jonathan turned back to the book and began to read Marcus's careful and upright hand writing aloud.

Christmas Day (December 25th) 1959
I have always loved Christmas. We got up early and had a special breakfast together. It's the only time we eat with Dad, who's usually too busy to spare time to join us. Then we gathered around the Christmas tree and opened our presents. We all bought each other the usual mixture of toys, clothes and books, etc. The usually quiet and tidy room became a riot of shouting and tearing, as presents were given, opened and thanks offered. The floor became covered with torn strips of brightly coloured paper and ribbon, casually thrown away – to be picked up later. Dad watched us with a smile on his face. That was the closest he ever came to being happy. Dad was usually a stern man. I suppose that's why he's a Prosecutor at the Old Bailey. Anyway, we filled in the morning while Mum prepared lunch (Turkey, etc.) and we three boys were washing up as we normally do on Christmas Day, when the doorbell rang. Mum answered it and we heard voices from the Hall before she came into the kitchen and said to me "There's a girl at the door for you." My two brothers began to chant, "Mark's got a girlfriend! Mark's got a girlfriend!" They always call me Mark instead of Marcus. I told them to shut up and went to the door.

I was surprised to see Evelyn there, even though I had written my address in my card, hoping she might come to see me. I tried to be formal, like I was told you were supposed to be when someone from the opposite sex comes to see you.

"Hello, Evelyn," I said, "what a lovely surprise!"

"I've brought you a Christmas card," she said shyly. "I didn't have time to buy you a present – so I've brought you myself."

"I didn't say that to him," Evelyn commented. "I said, 'I've come to see you instead of bringing you a present. So

I suppose I am your present.' It worked anyway," she continued smiling, "because he invited me in to see his family."

She commented that Sir Walter seemed unhappy that she was there but that the rest of the family seemed to accept her. A point that Marcus had smoothed over in his diary. However, he had used her visit to get out of the washing up and the two had gone out for a walk together and, eventually, ended up in one another's arms after making love in a greenhouse in the nearby park. Marcus knew where the key was kept because he knew the park keeper. As he read through the diary with Evelyn she frequently interrupted to explain how Marcus's words had rewritten what had actually happened to suggest that she had led him on, whereas the truth was that they were both equally responsible for the way the tryst developed.

The description of their love making was quite graphic and Evelyn smiled as she recalled what happened and corrected the account. Jonathan read the diary and listened to his grandmother open mouthed as what both were saying was totally at odds with what he expected of young people in the 1960s or the much older couple that he knew now. Evelyn summed up her feeling in these words:
"I knew my Mum would kill me if she knew what I had done and my Dad would throw me out of the house if I got pregnant – but I didn't care. Marcus was the man of my dreams and I'd got him."
Jonathan, deeply moved, put his arm around his Grandmother.
"You loved him a lot didn't you?"
She nodded.
"Do you still love him?"
"Yes – and I won't allow anyone to hurt him. He's very vulnerable, as I'm sure you know."

Fifty Years After

Jonathan nodded and returned to the diary, only to look up in surprise.

"His account of your walk ends there and he doesn't write about your date on Boxing Day."

Evelyn smiled.

"I'm not surprised. It's probably in his secret diary, which I've never found, incidentally. I imagine he was too embarrassed to write about it in this, semi-public, diary."

Jonathan was intrigued.

"Why? What happened?"

Evelyn laughed, remembering Marcus's shocked reaction at what she did.

"That's for me to know and you to wonder about, Jonathan," she said teasingly.

She grinned again.

"I'm going to embarrass him all over again by asking him."

Jonathan looked lovingly at his Grandmother, who was plainly, in her mind, a teenaged girl, newly in love, all over again.

"You're right, Gran," he said, "You were a minx and secretly, you still are."

Evelyn smiled at him.

"Why thank you, young sir," she replied gravely. "I'm glad you recognise it."

They returned to the Diary. There were a few brief comments about school and schoolwork and the improvements being made in the house as well as references to a number of more conventional visits and outings that Evelyn and Marcus made together. The next substantial entry was for about three weeks later.

<u>January 18th 1960</u>
Philip Stewart is a bugger. He's never accepted that he tried and failed to get my Evelyn. She's told me what the other girls say about him and that's confirmed all my negative feelings about him. There's an old fashioned

word that describes him. He's a cad! I heard him saying the most outrageous things about my girlfriend today when she was present to hear him. I walked into the Prefects' Room to find Evelyn standing there. This surprised me because she's not allowed in there because she's too young to be a Prefect. However, I learnt later that she'd come to confront Philip because he'd told everyone that he'd got inside her knickers as he put it. He told everyone that she came to him, begging to be 'done' by him and he was happy to oblige. He said that she took her skirt and knickers off for him to make it easier. Finally, he said that she said that he was better at it than I am. That was the point when I entered. I asked one of the other prefects what was going on when Evelyn suddenly slapped Philip hard across the face.

"Don't ever say anything like that about me or about Marcus again. He's three times the man you are!"

Philip was about to hit her back when he saw me and stopped.

"Don't you dare touch her!" I said to him.

He sneered back at me. "If I did, what do you plan to do about it, you Wanker?"

I walked over to him and put my arm around Evelyn to shield her. Then I spoke quietly to him.

"If you want to know what I will do, meet me after school and I will show you."

Then I took her away. Philip must have thought I was grandstanding because he turned up after school, just as Evelyn and I were leaving. He had some of his mates with him and I had three of my friends, as well as Evelyn with me.

"So you've come," I said, as I walked over to him. "I didn't think you had the guts!"

He sneered at me.

"Who do you think you are?" he asked, "Floyd Patterson?"

I didn't answer. I just squared up to him and waited. He rushed at me, arms waving. I hit him four times, twice in the stomach and twice on the chin. Then I turned away and left his friends to pick up his prone body. He obviously didn't know I belong to a boxing club. He didn't meet Floyd Patterson. Instead he met Marcus Greenway. However, I don't think that Patterson could have done a better job on him!

Jonathan looked at Evelyn who looked proud at the memory.

"You didn't know that your grandfather could fight, did you?"

"No, Grandma."

"Few people did. Even I didn't know until then. However, no one dared challenge him once the story got around the school and Philip kept well out of our way."

Evelyn went on to describe how people at school still avoided upsetting them even when they discovered that she was pregnant and Marcus was the father. However, their families were upset with them both and forced them to leave school and to get married. They both noted that Marcus did not appear to have written about this.

"I suppose the baby was my Dad," Jonathan commented. "Is that why you didn't have another child?"

Evelyn laughed.

"You might think that! Martin was always bad tempered – even in my womb. He gave me hell when he came out and damaged me so much inside by his kicking that I could not have another child. We tried – but the doctors warned us that I couldn't have a second child and they were right."

"So that's why Grandpa hates my father!"

"You are very perceptive, Jonathan, and probably right. Marcus was and is fiercely protective of me, and hates anyone who tries to harm me. I think he feels that Martin's one of them. It's not fair, of course, since it was hardly Martin's fault. But, then, life isn't always fair."

"How long did Sir Walter remain angry with Grandpa?"

"For quite a long time. It was actually the Smith Trial that brought them back together."

Can I ask you two more questions, Grandma?"

"Yes – ask as many as you like."

"The first is what did Granddad say when you first told him you were pregnant?"

"He went white and then very cool. 'We'll have to get married quickly,' he said, 'and tell our parents why. They won't like it – and I'm sure my Dad will beat me. But I think that's all he'll do.' I told him that my Dad would certainly beat me. We were both right. But – your Granddad never tried to evade his responsibilities and he never suggested that I have an abortion."

"The other question is about the murder trial."

"Why are you so interested in that?" Evelyn asked.

"Granddad asked me the same question, Gran. My answer is that I find the case puzzling. He told me a lot about it, but I am still puzzled."

"I'm not surprised, Jonathan. I'm still puzzled about it and I lived through it. What do you want to know?"

"What did Granddad really know about it and what does he really think about it?"

"Those are the questions that worry me too, Jonathan, if I'm honest. There is something that doesn't quite make sense. Marcus's attitude to the case changed at a specific point. Before that he was quite excited to be helping his father prosecute an important case. Then he became apprehensive, may be, and even worried about it."

"What caused the change?"

"It's easier to say when it happened rather than why. I don't know the why – but I do know the when. It was after he talked with Philip Stewart."

Jonathan was shocked at this. He had twice heard Sir Marcus deny ever discussing the case with Philip Stewart.

"Did he say what Philip Stewart told him?"

Fifty Years After

"No, and he went further. He ordered me never to talk about Philip Stewart again. That's why your father was angry when you mentioned Philip's name. He knew what Marcus had ordered. I'm somewhat surprised that Marcus spoke to you about it. He hasn't spoken to anyone about that case since the boy was hanged."

"How did he behave on the day of the execution?"

"That's another odd thing. Your Granddad is not a religious man, but he went to Church that week, made his confession to one of the priests and attended Mass on the actual day of the execution. He was, as close as he could get it, actually receiving the host as the trapdoor was pulled on that unfortunate boy."

Jonathan sat silently, head in hand, staring at the open pages of the Diary that purported to say everything about Sir Marcus Greenway's life but which actually said very little. His grandmother looked at him with silent compassion. She saw a great deal of her husband in her grandson, and loved him as much as she loved Marcus.

"Is there anything else, son," she asked gently.

"No, Gran," Jonathan answered. "However, if I find anything about you in the rest of this diary can I ask you about it?"

"Of course you can," she said, "but I don't think there's anything more of importance in the diary which relates to me. Most of it is boring political stuff. You might find it interesting. I find it tedious."

With that, she stood up, squeezed Jonathan's shoulder affectionately, and walked from the room, leaving Jonathan to continue reading.

5. The Trial of Mark Smith

June 22 and 23 1961
Number One Court at the Old Bailey was packed. The Smith case had roused tremendous interest and great passion in the popular press and the visitors' gallery was packed. All eight members of the Smith and Brown families were there and everybody craned forward to get their first sight of the slight figure of the young black defendant as he entered the dock. Mark Smith was plainly nervous as he saw the crowded courtroom and he turned around to see if his family were there. Seeing the familiar figures of his father (Abraham), his mother (Winfred), and his younger brothers (Luke and Matthew), he felt less isolated and smiled nervously at them. The boys waved and his parents smiled back encouragingly. Further away he saw the figures of Janice and Thomas Brown (Janet's parents) and her siblings (Jennifer and Tom). They stared at him expressionlessly. He turned away as the Court Usher called them all to stand as the Judge entered.

Thomas Williamson was sixty years old. He had been a judge for over fifteen years and was now the Recorder of London. For him, the slim eighteen year old was just another in a long line of accused persons awaiting justice. He would have been sorry for the young man had he not been black. Thomas had very strong feelings about what he saw as the invasion of West Indians, taking British jobs and houses and swelling the numbers of the unemployed and homeless white residents of the capital, many of whom turned to crime and appeared in his court day after day. Still, he thought, "I must ensure he gets justice." He sat and everyone in the Court sat as well. Only the Clerk of the Court remained standing.

"Would the Defendant please rise," Thomas said.

Mark stood up nervously, fingering the tie he had put on that morning for the first time since his arrest two months previously. It was the tie that Janet had bought him for last Christmas.

"Mark Smith you are charged with the capital murder of Janet Brown on April 26th 1961. Do you plead guilty or not guilty?" the Clerk intoned.

Mark was silent as the twelve members of the all-white and all-male jury stared at him.

"Did you hear the question Mr Smith?" Thomas asked.

"Yes, My Lord," Mark answered.

"Well then, what's your answer? Are you guilty or not guilty?"

"Not guilty, My Lord."

"Thank you Mr. Smith. You may sit down."

A sigh of relief went through the courtroom as the tension caused by Mark's delay in answering the charge subsided.

Sir Walter Greenway stood up and introduced himself to the Judge.

"I'm Sir Walter Greenway, My Lord. I'm prosecuting this case. My colleague, Albert Corrigan is conducting the defence."

Albert stood up and bowed to the Judge, who addressed him.

"I don't think I've ever heard you in my court Mr. Corrigan. You seem very young. Is this your first case?"

Albert looked as nervous as Mark.

"Yes, My Lord. I was only called to the Bar a month ago."

"I see," Judge Williamson said in what he thought was his kind tone. "If you find yourself in difficulties in the legal aspects of this case, just ask me and I'll guide you through."

"Thank you, My Lord," Albert replied and sat down relieved.

Thomas turned to Sir Walter.

"Now, Sir Walter, would you begin your case."

Fifty Years After

"Certainly My Lord," Sir Walter turned to face the Jury. "This is essentially a simple, but sad, case, members of the Jury. On April 26th last, a young woman, Janet Brown, was returning home across a Park in Marchfield. She was taking a short cut often used for that purpose. In that Park she had the misfortune to run into the Defendant who seized her by force, pushed her into the trees and stripped her naked. He forced her to the ground among the bushes and raped her. Fortunately, at that moment, another young man, Philip Stewart, happened to be also crossing the Park. He heard Janet's cries and hauled the defendant off, kicking him in the groin and knocking him out with two punches to the chin. He then chivalrously went to assist the young victim to her feet. At that moment the Defendant recovered consciousness, went to the pile of clothes he had discarded and took a revolver from his jacket pocket. He fired his gun twice, apparently at Mr Stewart, but, in his anger, he missed his target and hit Janet instead, killing her instantly. Mr Stewart bravely knocked the gun from the Defendant's hand and, having once again rendered the Defendant incapable of any action, called a policeman, who affected the arrest. You will hear from the Police Officer involved, from the Detective Inspector who interrogated the Defendant, the forensic scientist who examined the body of the deceased and the young man who bravely tried to save the young girl who had been thus foully raped."

The first witness was Police Constable Anthony Adams. He described how he had become involved.

"I was on my beat which runs alongside the Park in Marchfield when a young white male whom I later knew as Philip Stewart ran out of the gate and called me over. 'There's been a shooting,' he said, 'and a girl is dead.' I ran with him to the scene of the crime and found the Defendant kneeling beside the body of a white female of about eighteen years of age, who I later discovered was called Janet Brown and who had been shot twice in the

Fifty Years After

region of the heart. Both she and he were naked and there was a revolver which appeared to have been fired on the ground beside the defendant."

"What did you do?" asked Sir Walter.

"I ordered the defendant, who I learnt was called Mark Smith and that he was 18, to put his clothes on. He did so, and then I asked what had happened. He said that he and the girl were having consensual sex together when Mr Stewart arrived. He and Mr Stewart had been involved in an incident two years ago; apparently, when he claims Mr Stewart racially abused him and he hit him before walking away. He said that Mr Stewart dragged him off his girlfriend and kicked and punched him, knocking him out. When he recovered, he said he found a revolver in his hand. He claimed not to have seen this weapon before. Then he saw Janet lying on the ground, among the trees, unmoving. He went to see how she was, only to discover that she had been shot and was dead. That's when I found him. I arrested him and took him back to the Station, where I handed him over to D I Buchan."

"Did he try to resist arrest?"

"No, My Lord. He seemed quite passive – as though his violence had been sated."

Albert stood up.

"Objection, My Lord. The witness is stating his opinion, not fact."

Thomas upheld the objection and told the jury to ignore the comment, and Sir Walter sat down. Albert only had one question.

"Did the defendant appear to know what had happened?"

PC Adams thought for a moment before speaking.

"I thought he appeared confused, almost stunned. It was as though he didn't know what he had done."

"Thank you, Constable Adams. That's all I want to ask."

Fifty Years After

Detective Inspector Buchan followed the Constable and basically repeated the story the Constable had already outlined.

"Smith appeared unaware of what exactly had happened. He claimed to have been having a long term relationship with Janet Brown and that they had met by arrangement for sex in the Park. Apparently both of them felt that their parents disapproved of the relationship and so the Park was the only place they could meet. Mr Stewart disturbed them while they were fully engaged and dragged Smith off by main force and knocked him unconscious. Smith denied recovering and shooting his alleged girlfriend by accident as he was trying to kill or at least wound Mr Stewart. He claimed that he woke up and found the gun, which he said was not his, in his right hand. I tried to shake his story, but he would not budge from it. As a result, I wrote out his statement, got him to sign it, and charged him with the murder of Janet Brown."

Sir Walter asked no further questions, and Albert took over.

"Inspector Buchan did you say that Mr Smith woke up and found the gun was in his right hand?"

"Yes, My Lord."

"His **right** hand?"

"Yes, My Lord."

"With what hand did he sign his statement?"

"His left hand, My Lord."

".... His **left** hand?"

"Yes, My Lord."

Thomas leaned forward.

"What point are you trying to make Mr Corrigan?"

"Mark Smith was **left** handed, My Lord. He would not have fired a gun, his or anyone else's, with his **right** hand."

"Do you agree with that comment Inspector Buchan?" the Judge continued.

"It would be unusual, My Lord, I agree – but in moments of stress people do odd things. Smith may have grabbed the gun with his right hand and fired it without shifting hand. It might explain why he hit Janet Brown instead of Philip Stewart."

The Judge appeared satisfied and Albert let the Inspector go.

James Arthur's evidence completed the first morning of the trial. He was introduced as a leading forensic scientist who had examined Janet's body and samples of powder taken from Mark's right hand.

"What did you find Mr. Arthur?" Sir Walter asked.

"The deceased was a young white woman of just over 18 years of age. She had been killed by two shots. One entered her heart and the other entered her chest, close to her heart. The shot to her heart killed her instantly. Both shots were fired from the gun that was taken from the defendant and which bore his fingerprints. I examined the white powder taken from the Defendant's hand and it was gunpowder."

"What does that mean to you, Mr Arthur?"

"The Defendant, Mark Smith, fired the two shots, one of which wounded Janet Brown and the other killed her. So, I believe that Mark Smith shot and killed Janet Brown."

Sir Walter sat down and Albert took over.

"Is it possible that two people fired shots at Janet Brown?"

James Arthur looked surprised at the question.

"It's possible," he eventually said reluctantly, "but there's no evidence of it."

"Let's suppose that the killer of Janet Brown disabled Mark Smith and then fired the shot that killed his girlfriend. That's the one through the heart. Then, to frame Mark for the murder, he placed the gun in Mark's right hand, not knowing that he was left handed, and fired it a second time at the girl's body, placing his fingers over the unconscious Mark's. Is that not possible?"

Fifty Years After

"It's possible," James conceded, "but that's the stuff of detective fiction, not detective fact. All the evidence I have suggests that Smith fired both shots. His fingerprints are on the weapon, there was powder on his hands and no evidence of any other person involved."

"If that person wore gloves and later destroyed them, there would be no evidence of a third person would there?"

"That's true, My Lord. But that's a lot of ifs. I deal in the facts that I see, not possible alternative theories."

Albert Corrigan admitted defeat and sat down. The Jury looked unimpressed as they left the Jury Box, preceded by the Judge, who had reminded them not to discuss the evidence, and the court emptied as everyone went for lunch.

The evidence of Philip Stewart dominated the afternoon. Sir Walter called him to the witness box as soon as the session began. He took the oath and introduced himself as Philip Stewart, twenty years old and a Director of Stewart Enterprises – his father's firm and a big employer in North London. Sir Walter then asked him to describe what happened on April 26th.

"It was a pleasant evening, My Lord, and I had just had a large dinner."

He looked at the Jurors as he continued.

"We Company Directors often have large dinners, that's why so many of us develop large bellies."

He rubbed his stomach ostentatiously, causing many of the Jurors to laugh as he obviously intended. He turned back to face Sir Walter.

"Anyway, I decided to walk off the effects of the over eating and turned into the local Park. As I was walking in the Park I saw a couple of people ahead of me – a white girl and a black man. He seemed to be manhandling her and I quickened my step as I saw the two of them leave the path and go in among the trees and bushes at the side. When I reached the place where I had last seen them, there

Fifty Years After

was no sign of them, but I did hear the girl cry out the word 'No', followed by 'Leave me alone.' I rushed into the trees in the direction of the cry and found the two of them, both stark naked with him lying on top of her with his cock plainly inside her. He was moving up and down on top of her and she was struggling to push him off – but he held her down with his arms."

He looked at the Judge.

"He may look thin, meek and mild, but he's a strong bastard, especially when he is crossed and showing his temper – like all Niggers."

The Judge rebuked him.

"We don't use swear words like Bastard or crude words like cock in my court, Mr Stewart, whatever you use in your boardroom. The Minute taker will replace the first offensive word with the word penis and delete the second entirely."

"I'm sorry, My Lord. I forgot myself."

The Judge nodded.

"That's all right Mr Stewart. I understand. Just don't offend again. Continue with your evidence."

"Thank you, My Lord. I rushed in, grabbed him by the shoulders and pulled him off the girl. I was right his co--- penis was large and hard and her genitalia had obviously been forced. I pulled him around to face me and kicked him in the genitals to disable him temporarily and then punched him hard on the chin twice, as his body buckled under the shock of the kick. He fell back and lay still. I went over to the girl to help her to her feet, brush her down and get her dressed when I heard a sound behind me. I looked around and the man I now know as Smith had got to his feet and had a gun in his hand. He shouted 'I'll get you, you cunt!' I'm sorry, My Lord, but that's the word he used. Then he fired twice, missing me and hitting the girl, who fell down at once. I turned and knocked the gun out of his hand before he could fire a third time and then hit him very hard on the chin again. This time he was out for the count. I took my tie off and tied his hands behind his back so he couldn't escape, checked that the girl was dead, and went to get the police."

"Had you had any dealings with Mr. Smith before?"

"No, My Lord."

"He said that you had racially abused him and he hit you. Is that true?"

"No, My Lord."

"So you had never seen the Defendant before that day?"

"No. My Lord."

Sir Walter sat down.

"Mr Stewart, you appear to be a very public spirited gentleman. Is that not so?" Albert asked.

Philip preened himself.

"I try to do my bit," he replied.

"Very commendable I'm sure," Albert responded drily. "Would you have been so concerned had Mr Smith been a white man?"

"Of course, no man should force a woman to have sex against her will."

"What if Janet Brown had been a black girl?"

Philip laughed.

"That's a case of dog bites dog rather than dog bites man. Those Niggers copulate in the bushes all the time. I've seen them. They don't have homes in Bongobongoland, I suppose and so they breed in the open without shame. Many of them don't wear any clothes anyway – so why should they care?"

"I believe that Mark Smith lived in Marshfield – not Bongobongoland," Albert observed drily.

"That's where his family were shacked up. They're all the same. They take our homes and our jobs and now they're after our women. It's wrong. Someone should stop it."

A man in the gallery clapped and the Judge ordered him to be taken out.

"This is a law court," he said, "not a public theatre. Mr Stewart, you should remember that as well, and stick to the evidence."

"Yes, My Lord. I'm sorry, My Lord."

Albert Corrigan paused, returned to his seat and picked up a piece of paper, which he affected to read, looked at the Jury and returned to face Philip.

"I get the impression, Mr Stewart, that you hate black people. Is that true?"

"I don't hate Black people so long as they keep in their place."

"And where's that?"

"Bongobongoland."

"Mr Smith was never in Bongobongoland, wherever that is and if it actually exists, which I doubt. His family came from Jamaica on the 'Empire Windrush' at the invitation of the Government."

"I don't care who invited them. They should've stayed in Jamaica, if that's where they came from."

"They came here because there was no one to drive the buses."

"So they say! I think they came here to steal our houses, jobs and women."

Albert felt that he had got as much as he could from that issue and changed the subject.

"You say that you punched Mr Smith at least three times and knocked him out twice."

"That's right."

"Didn't you hurt your hand?"

"No."

"You hit him on the chin, Mr Stewart. That's hard bone. Your hand was unprotected. You must have hurt your hand as much as you hurt his chin."

"No. My gloves protected me."

"Why were you wearing gloves?"

"It was cold."

"Did you keep them on during the whole of this incident?"

"Yes."

"What did you do with them afterwards?"

"I threw them into the rubbish bin when I got home."

"Why?"

"They got torn in the struggle."

"What struggle? You said you kicked him and then hit him. He doesn't appear to have fought back at all."

"I probably tore them when I hit him," Philip answered sullenly.

Albert changed tack again.

"After you knocked out Mark for the first time you moved over to assist Janet. Where was she?"

"She was lying on her back on the ground, with her legs spread out, under a tree shielded by some bushes."

"Did she try to get to her feet?"

"Yes."

"And you moved over to help her?"

"Yes."

"What did you do?"

"I reached down and pulled her to her feet and told her to put her clothes on."

"And that's when you heard footsteps behind you?"

"Yes."

"How did you hear him, since he was naked?"

"I heard a twig snap."

"What did you do?"

"I turned around and saw Smith who was standing, pointing a gun at me."

"In what hand was he holding the gun?"

"The right hand."

"Was he shaking or showing signs of emotion?"

"No."

"And yet he told you he was going to kill you?"

"Yes."

"Why?"

"I don't know."

"What did you do when he made this threat?"

"Just stood there."

"Where was Janet Brown?"

"To the left of me, trying to pick up her clothes."

"You did not move to protect the girl you thought was being raped earlier?"

"No."

"Why not?"

"I didn't think and there wasn't time."

"How long do you think there was between your rescue and the return of the Defendant with the gun?"

"Two or three minutes."

"So you didn't do a very good job then did you?"

"What do you mean?"

"I ask the questions, Mr Stewart – but I will answer this one since you seem not to understand me."

Albert paused for effect before continuing.

"You claim that you knocked Mark Smith out, then went to help Janet Brown to her feet, telling her to get dressed. Incidentally, when she picked up her clothes, did she face you and the defendant or have her back to you?"

"She was facing us."

"Was she standing or leaning over?"

"She was standing."

"So she was naked, holding her clothes, and simply standing facing two apparently strange men?"

"That's right."

"How many girls do you know who stand in the nude facing two men unless as a result of force?"

"I don't know enough girls as well as that to know."

Albert laughed.

"I don't have any personal experience of that kind, but I know enough of women's natural demeanour to know that what you describe is highly unlikely, especially if one of you had just raped her. I think you're lying Mr. Stewart."

"No, My Lord. I'm telling the truth."

Fifty Years After

There was a long pause before Albert threw his last question at Philip.

"I put it to you Mr Stewart that you were not in that Park by accident. You were following Mark and Janet because you wanted Janet for yourself and were jealous of Mark who you recognised as the man who hit you two years previously. You are a racist who hates black people and that simply made things worse for you. You wanted revenge by taking his girl from him. So you interrupted them in their lovemaking and attacked Mark, incapacitating him. I think that Janet told you to leave them alone and clear off. You got angry because of this and shot her dead. Then, frightened at what you'd done, you decided to frame Mark and get the state to kill him for you. So you placed his unconscious hand on your gun and fired a second bullet into Janet's already dead body, before going to fetch the Police. You didn't tie up Mr Smith because you didn't have to do so – he was still unconscious. That's why the Constable didn't mention the fact that Mark's hands were tied. Is that not the truth?"

"No," Philip shouted, "It's a lie."

"There's no need to panic, Mr Stewart," Albert concluded, "We're only trying to get to the truth here and prevent a second innocent person being killed."

He sat down and Sir Walter stood up to ask a final question.

"Did you shoot and kill Janet Brown, Mr Stewart?"

"No. My Lord, I didn't."

"Did you see Mark Smith fire two shots at Janet Brown; two shots that killed her?"

"Yes, My Lord, I did."

"Thank you Mr Stewart."

That ended the first day of the trial.

The second and final day opened with a sensation. Albert Corrigan stood to address the Court and announced that he would not be asking the Defendant to go into the Witness Box.

"It is not necessary," he said. "Mark's story has been told twice and there are no supporting witnesses. It's a case of his story against Philip Stewart's story. Either Janet and Mark were lovers, and there are no witnesses to that, or they weren't and Mr Stewart is the only witness to that."

At that point Marcus Greenway, sitting beside his father and shuffling papers for him, noticed that Janet's sister, Jenifer left the court in apparent distress. He followed her and returned about ten minutes later to have a whispered conversation with his father, which ended with Sir Walter shaking his head, and Marcus returning to his papers.

Albert continued his presentation.

"Mark Smith, in his statement, confirmed by both P C Adams and D I Buchan, states that he and Janet were lovers. Their romance was frowned on by both sets of parents, because mixed marriages are, to say the least, problematic, in Britain at the moment – even in London, which is probably more tolerant than the rest of the country. As a result, they were forced to have their trysts outside in the Park rather than in one or the other's house when the adults were out as most teenagers do. He claimed that Philip Stewart hated him because he was black and had deliberately abused him because of his race when they met in the street on Christmas Eve 1959. Mark said he punched Mr Stewart on the chin and left him. He also said that Janet had complained that Mr Stewart had taken to following her about and had also propositioned her once. Mark said Janet rejected Philip Stewart."

Albert paused for effect and looked meaningfully at the Jury before continuing.

Fifty Years After

"The two apparently met by arrangement in the Park that afternoon. They intended to have sex together and they did what any couple in that situation would do, found a secluded place, stripped off and began to make love. Both were unaware that Philip Stewart had followed them until he interrupted their lovemaking, dragged Mark off, abused and assaulted him, and knocked him unconscious. So far, allowing for different emphases and starting points, the stories of the two principles concur. But now there is a difference. Mark says that he did not recover consciousness for some time, and when he did he found a gun in his hand and his girlfriend shot dead. Philip Stewart says that Mark recovered quickly, took a gun, fired it twice at Philip but hitting Janet by accident and killing her. He then claims that he subdued Mark for a second time before fetching a policeman to arrest him."

Albert walked over to the jury box, and faced them directly.

"Members of the Jury, you know that one innocent young person has already died in this sad case – that's why we're all here, to find out and decide what happened. I fear that you are being invited to send a second innocent young person to his death. You have two conflicting stories and you have to decide between them. Mark has never wavered in his account, despite, presumably being put under immense pressure by D I Buchan to confess to a crime he claims he did not commit to save us all time and possibly get a lighter sentence. On the other hand, Philip Stewart's story is full of holes. An apparently homicidal rapist is twice knocked out. That same man is tied up one minute but not the next. A left-handed man apparently decided to shoot another man with his right hand. Mr Stewart is conveniently wearing gloves, which he also conveniently throws away afterwards. You might think all these things to be odd. I certainly do. You might conclude that Philip Stewart was lying to you, as I do, and wonder, like me, why he did so. You might also conclude that Philip Stewart hates black people and especially hated this young black man, and you might ask yourself why."

He turned away and returned to the centre of the Court, between the Judge and the Defendant, to reach his conclusion.

"I believe that there is enough doubt in this case to cause you to dismiss it outright and find Mark Smith not guilty. But, if you do believe Philip Stewart's story, then you must still find Mark Smith not guilty of murder. The death of Janet Brown was, according to the Prosecution's only witness to the actual event, a tragic accident. Philip was the target, not Janet. In that case the charge should have been manslaughter."

Albert sat down and Sir Walter took his place.

"I feel we should congratulate Mr Corrigan Members of the Jury. He has argued a hopeless case with passion and considerable erudition. He will, I am sure, with more experience, make one of the great advocates. However, here he is wrong. This is an open and shut case. Mr Smith (witnessed by Philip Stewart, and confirmed by James Arthur, the Forensic Scientist who examined the gun, the body of Janet and the powder taken from Mr Smith's right hand) killed Janet Brown. They agree that Janet was shot twice, once in the heart and once close to her heart, while she stood or sat, naked, facing her assailant. They agree that the man who fired the gun and killed Janet Brown was Mark Smith. We don't know why he did it, except that it seems she was not his intended target. Mr Stewart was. That makes no difference in law – he shot and killed Janet Brown, and for that reason you must find him guilty of Capital Murder."

Fifty Years After

Sir Walter sat down and Thomas turned to address the Jury.

"Members of the Jury, you must shortly go out and decide your verdict in this case. You must go by the evidence presented and not be influenced by the fact that Mr Smith did not give evidence. There is no obligation on him to do so. Nor must you wonder about motive or discussions about Mr Stewart's alleged racism. The only question for you is did Mark Smith shoot and kill Janet Brown? Don't concern yourself over the issue of manslaughter. It does not arise here – because the killer used a gun and that constitutes a capital crime. Nor should you be concerned with Mark Smith's youth. He is old enough to know right from wrong, old enough to have sex with a girl, and old enough to go to work. Therefore, he is old enough to take the full consequences of his actions. You must go out now, elect a foreman and reach a verdict that satisfies you all. If you have any reasonable doubt that Mark Smith shot and killed Janet Brown, you must find him not guilty. If, however, you find no reasonable grounds for doubt, you must find him guilty."

The Jury were out for just half an hour before returning to the Court. The Judge ordered Mark to stand and the Clerk of the Court called on the Jury Foreman to stand.

"Have you reached a verdict on which you are all agreed?" he asked.

Matthew Albright, the Jury Foreman, replied, "Yes, My Lord."

"Do you find the Defendant, Mark Smith, Guilty or Not Guilty of the murder of Janet Brown?"

"Guilty, My Lord."

"And is that the verdict of you all?"

"Yes, My Lord."

The Foreman sat down.

Thomas spoke to Albert.

Fifty Years After

"Do you have anything to say in mitigation before I pass sentence Mr. Corrigan?"

"Only that my client was of previous good character, has a responsible job, and, at best killed Janet Brown as a result of a tragic accident for which he has already paid heavily."

Albert sat down as Thomas began to speak to the still standing Mark, who was showing signs of shock at this verdict and its inevitable consequence.

"Mark Smith you have been found guilty of the capital murder of Janet Brown, possibly, although not certainly, following her rape. We cannot permit visitors to this country to take local girls, abuse them and kill them. There has to be an example made, and, sadly for you, you are that example. Whether you intended to or not, you took an innocent girl's life by shooting her. The law is quite clear what the sentence for that is, and, even though you are very young, you are old enough to know better and take the full consequence of your actions."

The judge paused to put on the black cap.

"Mark Smith, the sentence of this court is that you shall be taken from hence to the place from whence you came and from thence to a place of execution where you shall be hanged from the neck until you be dead. And my God have mercy on your soul."

The judge looked at Mark's shocked and devastated eyes from which tears were beginning to flow. He turned away and spoke to the two prison officers acting as his escorts and guards.

"Take him down."

The now openly weeping Mark was taken away and the judge, after thanking the jury, rose and left the Courtroom, followed by the rest of the public. The trial had lasted just six hours.

Three weeks later, as described in the North London Herald, following the rejection of Mark's appeal by the Appeal Court and of his appeal for clemency by the Home Secretary, Mark was hanged on July 14th 1961.

6. Fifty Years Later

January 1st 2010.
Sir Marcus Greenway was in an ebullient mood on New Year's Day. The family had celebrated long into the night the previous evening and he had prepared a New Year's Day surprise for his grandson. Martin announced at breakfast that he was taking the rest of the family out to join the local hunt. He invited Sir Marcus and Jonathan to come with them. Sir Marcus said he was busy and Jonathan said he did not approve of any form of fox hunting. He resisted all blandishments. Eventually his father gave up, calling Jonathan a wimp as he stalked out of the dining room.

Lady Evelyn grinned at Jonathan.
"He doesn't like you much," she said. "You must try harder to accommodate him. He's your father remember, and you're his eldest son."
"It runs in the family, Darling," Sir Marcus replied. "I didn't get on with my father; Jonathan's father doesn't get on with me; and Jonathan doesn't get on with Martin."
"But you made it up with Walter, remember; so Jonathan can do the same with Martin, even if I have to knock their heads together to achieve it," Evelyn said determinedly.
Marcus looked at Jonathan's determined face and smiled wryly at his wife.
"Good luck with that, Darling. I think you'll need a sledgehammer!"

Evelyn did not reply and Marcus changed the subject.
"How are you getting on with your reading, young man?"
"I've worked through your diary, Grandpa, and read the transcript of the Smith Trial, although not the book itself yet."

Evelyn interrupted.

"You're a wicked man, Marcus. You cut out all the best bits from your diary and I had to fill Jonathan in."

Marcus laughed.

"I bet you did! And - I bet you enjoyed doing it! You're still a teenager at heart, Darling."

Evelyn smiled the cheeky smile she had used when Marcus first knew her, and he guessed he was in trouble. As soon as she began to speak, he knew he was right.

"You did not include our first planned date – the Boxing Day trip to the alleged cinema that was in fact the park greenhouse."

Marcus blushed like a teenager as he remembered that day.

"I never asked you – how did you manage to take my knickers off and put them back on with your brothers around?"

"I never took them off, except when I went for my bath – so they never saw them."

"That was a cheat! My sister saw me wearing your pants and got me to tell her everything we did."

"Everything?"

"Everything."

"No wonder she grinned at me when I called to collect you! I wondered why at the time."

"You can tell Jonathan the whole story now can't you? Then he can be your official biographer. You need people to learn your story."

Marcus groaned inwardly. He should have expected this he realised when he let Jonathan read his diary. He decided to make the best of a bad job.

"I will give you a USB key this afternoon. You must promise not to let anyone see the files on it except your Grandma. She'll kill you if you don't let her see what's on there."

"Too right, Darling," Evelyn commented with a smile. "I assume you're going to give him access to your private diary."

"That's right – but you must promise something else, Jonathan."

"What's that, Grandpa?"

"You won't publish anything without showing your Grandma and me first."

"I promise."

Marcus smiled. Evelyn gave Jonathan a hug.

"I'm glad you persuaded Martin to include him in our invitation, Marcus. Our grandson is much more like the son I wanted than the son we actually got!"

"Hush, Darling. What happened to you because of Martin wasn't Martin's fault and we've both been too hard on him. I'm going to try to repair the breach between us. I intend to invite him to come with me when I next go to Sandringham."

"He'll like that," Evelyn commented. "It may do the trick. Remember to talk to him about Jonathan and the need to be kinder to his son."

Marcus nodded. He turned back to talk to Jonathan.

"Did you find the trial transcript interesting?"

"I found it confusing, Grandpa."

"Why?"

"The verdict seemed perverse and the sentence unjust."

"The sentence was what the law prescribed in 1961."

"But surely not for an 18 year old boy? The age of majority was 21 then!"

"Yes, that did surprise me," Sir Marcus commented, "but, remember, the Judge alluded to his age as not being a factor to consider."

"The Home Secretary should have done so, though," Jonathan pointed out.

Evelyn interrupted.

"What you don't know, Jonathan was how racist the country was at that time. The popular press was baying for

Mark Smith's blood. The Home Secretary would have committed political suicide by reprieving him."

"There was another thing which I did not understand, Grandpa, and it concerned you."

"What was that, Jonathan?"

"On the second morning, when the defence lawyer said he was not calling any witnesses, Janet Brown's sister left the court suddenly and you followed her. You returned shortly afterwards and had a whispered conversation with your father who appeared to shake his head at you. What happened?"

Sir Marcus poured himself a second cup of (nearly cold) coffee and drank it at a gulp to gain time to think. Then he moved his chair around to face Jonathan and Evelyn and began to talk.

"As I told you, Mark's defence against the charge of rape was that he and Janet were boyfriend and girlfriend and had been going out for some time. Because of the racism of that era, he and she felt unable to make love with each other at either's home, but both had got to the point when they felt they wanted to do that. They were much slower than you and me, Evelyn!"

Evelyn grinned at the memory of their first date.

"He also said that Philip had been following Janet about and trying to seduce her. We would call it stalking now – and it's an offence. It wasn't then. Albert Corrigan said there were no witnesses to back Mark's version of events, and that's when Jennifer Brown got up suddenly and left the Court. I suspected that she disagreed and went out to ask her."

"What did she say, Grandpa?"

"As far as I recall she said that Mark and Janet had been boyfriend and girlfriend and that Philip Stewart had tried to molest Janet."

"Did she say when this happened?"

"I asked her and she said it was the day before she was killed."

Fifty Years After

"And that was the end of the conversation?"

"Not quite, Jonathan. She told me that she did not believe that Mark had a gun or that, if he had, he would have shot Janet, even by mistake. She believed that Philip had shot Janet deliberately because of what she had done and said the day before and he had framed Mark to punish him."

"Is this what you told your father when you went back into Court, Grandpa?"

"Yes."

"What did Sir Walter say?"

"I remember his words well, Jonathan. He said, 'That's all very interesting, my boy. But it's his Defence Barrister who should introduce the evidence. It's not our responsibility to do his job for him. He obviously doesn't give much credence to Jennifer Brown as a witness, otherwise he'd have called her.'"

Sir Marcus looked at his watch and stood up.

"I'm sorry but I've got to go now. I wasn't lying to Martin when I said I have work to do this morning. I have the Master of the Rolls and the Attorney General coming to see me to discuss this blasted mess that the MPs, including some of my ministers, damn them, have got into over their expenses."

He paused and then smiled at Jonathan.

"On reflection, young Jonathan, I'll introduce you to the Master of the Rolls. In view of your interest in the Smith Case. I think you would like to meet him. You will have a lot to talk about."

This intrigued Jonathan.

"Who is the Master of the Rolls and why should I want to talk to him, Grandpa?"

"He is one of the most senior of our judges and a member of the House of Lords. His name is Lord Corrigan, but you know him better as Albert Corrigan. I will call you down to meet him when we've finished our business."

Jonathan thanked Sir Marcus, who nodded his appreciation, and left the room to go to his study, followed by Lady Evelyn who was leaving to attend a function in the nearby village. Jonathan returned to his room and began to read the text of the book on the Trial, rather than the Appendix, which had contained the transcript, which he and Evelyn had read together. He heard the doorbell ring and guessed that signalled the arrival of his Grandfather's guests. Later he went down to the dining room where the butler served him a light lunch, which he ate alone, before returning to his room to resume his reading. Later still he heard the sound of a car being driven off. Shortly afterwards he heard the discrete tap on his door, which he had been so eagerly awaiting.

"Sir Marcus said you should come down to the study now, Sir," the Butler said.

"Thank you, Jenkins," Jonathan called out, as he rose, straightened his tie and adjusted his jacket before opening the door and leaving the room.

When he entered the study, Jonathan found his Grandfather sitting and sipping his favourite brandy with a man of about the same age, but taller and greyer, and, Jonathan thought, more distinguished looking, who was also holding a brandy glass, He noticed a third, empty, glass was on the circular mahogany table and a third leather armchair had been drawn up to it.

The two men looked up as he entered. Sir Marcus smiled at him and waved him to the empty chair, and, as he sat down, filled Jonathan's glass for him. Sir Marcus turned towards Lord Corrigan.

"Albert, this is my grandson, Jonathan. He's got an incorrigible curiosity, and, like all the Greenways, if you set him on the scent, he's like a foxhound. He'll continue to worry away at the problem until he's shaken the truth out of it."

Fifty Years After

Albert Corrigan laughed.

"Then Jonathan is just like you, Marcus. I'm sorry for the country if another Greenway is haunting the land!"

He turned to Jonathan.

"I'm pleased to meet you, Jonathan. I'm Albert Corrigan. People call me lots of names. Some I like and some I don't. Technically, I'm Lord Corrigan. But you can call me Albert."

Albert paused after this long introduction before resuming, just as Jonathan was about to answer him.

"What fox has your Grandfather set you on?"

"The Mark Smith Trial, Sir. I've been researching it and have just read the transcript."

"I'm Albert, not 'Sir'."

"I'm sorry, Albert – but I was always told to address my elders and betters as 'Sir'. I will try to remember."

"Good," Albert commented. "Why are you interested in this trial?"

"It was when I came down here that I remembered there had been a big trial Granddad was involved in when he was young and so I looked it up and the more I read about it, the stranger it seemed."

"I remember it as though it was yesterday," Albert Corrigan said. "It was my first big case and I lost it. My client was hanged and I always felt that I had let him down."

"You didn't let him down, Albert," Marcus commented. "You missed a trick or two because of your inexperience, but I don't think it made any difference."

"Probably not, Marcus," Albert agreed, "but I wish I had done more to try to save the lad. He was innocent of any crime you know!"

"I know you think that, Albert. Many people agree with you, but sometimes the law fails people and it may have failed Mark Smith."

"I know it, not think it," Albert corrected, "and I know you know it, too."

Fifty Years After

"You may think that, Albert; but I could not possibly comment," Marcus replied.

"I disagree with Grandpa," Jonathan said suddenly, interrupting the conversation between the two elderly men. "I believe you did let Mark down, Albert."

Albert Corrigan turned to face Jonathan in surprise. For a moment, lost in their reminiscences of the trial, the two men had forgotten Jonathan was there.

"Why do you say that, young man?" Albert said sharply

For a moment Jonathan heard the Master of the Rolls speaking, rather than the kindly old man.

"Why didn't you call Jennifer Brown and Mark Smith to give evidence? They would have pointed the finger clearly at Philip Stewart as the killer. You had already shown that there was great doubt about Philip Stewart's evidence. Jennifer would have completed that picture."

"Sir Walter would have destroyed her, Jonathan. Jennifer was only 14. He was one of the fiercest cross-examiners on the circuit. She would have been presented as what the press in those days termed 'a Nigger lover' – pardon my use of the N word - and she would possibly have been rejected by her parents because she had embarrassed them."

"But, surely, that should not have been a consideration? If her evidence caused Mark to be acquitted and the real murderer to be hanged, surely that is all that mattered?"

"You're very young, Jonathan, and you've grown up in a very different world, thank goodness, to the one your grandfather and I grew up in. Do you know any white-black romances?"

"Of course," Jonathan replied promptly. "I've got a black girlfriend, and many of my Uni friends are the same. What of it?"

"It's taken us a long time to reach that point, Jonathan," Albert answered seriously. "Even today there would be people, mainly of my generation it's true, who believe that a black man going out with a white girl or vice versa is scandalous. Virtually everyone thought that in 1961, including both Mark's and Janet's parents."

"But surely, Albert, the Jury would have accepted the truth, even if Mark was subsequently ostracised?"

"Have you told him about Jack Stewart, Marcus?"

"No, Albert. You tell him."

"Who was Jack Stewart?" Jonathan asked, taking a sip from his refilled brandy glass.

"I assume you've heard of the Kray brothers," Albert responded.

"Yes. Everyone's heard of the Krays. There's a film out about them. They were East End gangsters in the 60s and 70s.'

"Right," Albert answered. "Well Jack Stewart was similar, but less well known, except among the police, who he was careful to keep bribed to look the other way. On the surface he was a successful businessman, but underneath he was a vicious criminal who operated mainly in North London at the same time as the Krays. They knew about each other and avoided treading on each other's toes."

"Was Philip Stewart part of the Gang?" Jonathan asked.

"That's a good question, Jonathan. The answer is that we don't know, but, if he was, it explains where the gun came from. He was devoted to his father and it would be logical that he was fully involved in his father's activities, both legal and illegal."

"How does Philip's father's activities come into the trial?" Jonathan asked. "There wasn't any reference to him in the records or in the book I'm reading. I've gone through the index at the back and the only Stewart mentioned is Philip."

"I didn't know it at the time, Jonathan, but three of the Jurors, including the foreman were connected with Jack Stewart, either with his legitimate businesses or his criminal businesses. They either cajoled or bribed the other

Fifty Years After

nine. Why else do you think they only took twenty minutes to reach their verdict? Remember, too, all of them were white men, so most needed little convincing. The murder charge against Mark was toxic in the atmosphere of the time."

"But…" Jonathan said.

Albert cut him off.

"Sir Walter was briefed that there was no doubt about the guilt of Mark Smith. Inspector Buchan felt the same way, and Judge Williamson was a former follower of Sir Oswald Moseley. I didn't call Mark to give evidence because I knew that Sir Walter would tear him to pieces and I wanted to leave him some dignity even if that dignity was in death. At least hanging is quick and relatively painless they tell me, if it's done properly."

"Did you think that the Jury had been bribed?" Jonathan asked.

"No," Albert replied. "However, I knew they were hostile to me and to Mark. You can tell, as your Grandfather will tell you. He got some trial experience before he became a politician."

Sir Marcus nodded and sipped his brandy meditatively.

"The truth is, Jonathan, that Mark was like the fox tracked to his den by the fox hounds and surrounded by them - trapped and surrounded by his enemies. That trial could only end one way – with his conviction and execution. He was murdered just as surely as his girlfriend was: the murderer was Philip Stewart, backed by his father."

The three men sat silently, contemplating the enormity of Albert Corrigan's final words. Finally, Jonathan turned to his Grandfather.

"How much of this did you know, Grandpa?"

"As much as I have already told you, Jonathan. I heard what Jennifer said and tried to persuade my father to intervene, but he refused."

Fifty Years After

Marcus paused, obviously wondering whether he should say more. Jonathan seemed about to speak when Marcus resumed.

"I have long suspected the truth but dare not allow it to be publically probed – the resultant scandal would be huge. It could destroy the Government and raise serious questions about the last Government, not to mention further questions about the role of the Police in the second half of the 20th century. I simply daren't do it."

"But what about justice for Janet and Mark and the two families. Presumably the brothers and sisters are still alive, even if the parents aren't. Surely they're entitled to receive justice? If Philip Stewart is a double murderer, should he continue to walk free, even if he's over 70?"

"In a perfect world. Jonathan, the answer is yes to your first question and no to your second – but it's not a perfect world, and there's no conclusive evidence to convict Philip Stewart (as much as I would like to) or his father, who is answering for his crimes before a much higher court than Her Majesty's Courts."

"So, we're going to allow the injustice to continue!" Jonathan commented bitterly.

Albert Corrigan reached out and took Jonathan's hand.

"I'll make you a promise, Jonathan. If you can find proof to substantiate what Marcus and I both think, I will make certain the case is reopened and a pardon is given to Mark. It won't bring him back to life, but it will clear his name. I will also personally ensure that Lord Little Wittering is brought to trial. I am even prepared to step down from the bench and lead the Prosecution myself. It would be a perfect way to end my career – finishing the trial that began it."

"How will I do that?" Jonathan asked. "The evidence has probably been destroyed and the case is so cold it's frozen solid!"

"I've kept in touch with the two families, and the original papers are still in storage. I can get you access to those and I will give you the addresses of the Brown and Smith siblings. I can also try to put you in touch with the female reporter from the Herald who covered the case. Like me, it was her first case. She's retired now, but is still alive and very active."

"If you and Grandma agree, Grandpa, and if Lord Corrigan will help me in the way he suggested, I'll do what I can. In any case I need to do more research if I'm going to write your biography. That trial was a key turning point in your life."

"Of course I'll let you. I could hardly stop you after all!" Marcus handed a USB key over to Jonathan. "That's the key to my personal file, which I promised you. There's only one condition."

"What's that, Grandpa?"

"You must not speak with the Earl of Little Wittering without first getting my permission."

Albert Corrigan nodded.

"I think that's right. The Stewart Gang still survives as far as I know and I do not want him alerted that his crimes are being reinvestigated until it's too late."

He wrote some numbers on a piece of paper and passed it to Jonathan.

"That's my phone number, Jonathan. I will be at home tomorrow morning. Ring me and I will give you the details you need."

"Thank you, Sir – Albert."

"Don't thank me too soon, Jonathan," Albert said, rising from his seat. "In the end you may come to regret that you ever embarked on this quest."

He paused to put his coat on and then shook both men's hands.

"It's been good to see you again Marcus, and to see you too Jonathan. However, I'd better leave now or it will be dark before I get home and my wife worries if I'm late."

Later, in his room, Jonathan pondered what he had just learnt about the Stewarts. He tried to Google Jack Stewart, but found nothing. When he Googled Philip he was luckier. He found out a little more and confirmation of what he already knew. More specifically he learnt that he had two brothers, one of whom was shot dead in Greenford in the 1980s and another, Timothy who had left the country to go to live in Malaga about the same time as his father. He also learned about the origin of Philip's title – Earl of Little Wittering which came about because of the words that Marcus had often used to tease him in the House of Commons.

Jonathan felt this added to the mystery, rather than resolving it. He sat, head in hands, at the side table in his room, thinking, with his laptop open before him. After a while he had an idea. He went to his email account, typed in an address and sent off a message.

"Harry could you do an urgent job for me? Jonathan"

The reply came back almost immediately.

"What sort of job?"

Jonathan responded.;

"Can you get into the Met's files and look for info on two people for me?"

Back came the reply.

"Certainly – it's a synch. Who are you after?"

"Jack Stewart and Philip Stewart."

Jonathan had to wait nearly fifteen minutes before Harry came back.

"So you're after the big time! I can get in – no problem – and I can try to find them. Remember I can't guarantee any results."

Jonathan responded immediately.

"I understand. Good luck and thanks for agreeing. Let me know if you find anything. Can you also find the original documents on the Mark Smith trial?"

Back came the reply.

"I'll do my best. I will create a file of anything I find and send it to you."

Fifty Years After

Jonathan smiled a satisfied smile and inserted the USB key in his computer. He quickly located the three entries he wanted and began to read what Sir Marcus had written about those early days with Evelyn. He found the missing Boxing day entry which confirmed what the two of them had said to each other earlier. He also found the entry about what happened when they discovered that Evelyn was pregnant. Their parents were both shocked and angered and both of them were thrashed by their fathers and ordered to leave school. Marcus was forced to begin work in his father's office and they were married after the minimum period of three weeks required to register for a marriage in Britain. He was especially touched by the dairy entry about the birth of his father. Marcus had written:

October 20 1960
Our son, Martin, was born today. It was a terrible birth. Poor Evelyn screamed again and again at the pain and the labour went on for ten hours before he was finally delivered. Later the doctor called me into his office and told me that it was unlikely that Evelyn would be able to conceive again and that, if she did, it would be very dangerous. He told me that I had to use a Johnny. I told Evelyn this and she was distraught. She had always wanted to have lots of children, she said. "Still," she said, brightening up, "If I have to have only one child, at least he's a boy." The baby is fit and well and both will be home in a day or two.

Jonathan became aware of a presence behind him and turned around to see his grandmother's smiling eyes.

"Typical man," she said. "He couldn't be bothered to record Martin's birth weight!"

"What was it, Gran?"

"He was 8 pounds 6 ounces."

"That wasn't too big," Jonathan commented.

"It was big enough for me!" Evelyn answered feelingly.

Fifty Years After

Evelyn looked at her grandson, thinking how alike physically and unalike in every other way that he was to her son.

"I've come to tell you your family are back," she said.

"How did you get on with Lord Corrigan?" she asked.

"I learnt a lot," Jonathan replied. "Much of what he told me came as a surprise. He's going to help me research this case thoroughly and Grandpa has agreed that I should do it too. They think that the actual murderer was Philip Stewart but there's no proof. I've got to try to find the proof."

"Good luck in that, Son," Evelyn said. "It might be easier to find a needle in a haystack."

"I know, Grandma, but I'm going to try. I think the families deserve it and the spirits of Janet and Mark deserve to be allowed to be at peace and their murderer deserves to be punished, however old he is."

"Bravo, son!" Evelyn said. "I expected nothing less of you."

"Gran," said Jonathan after a long pause, "Can I ask you a question?"

"Yes, of course! What is it?"

"Two or three times now you've called me 'son'. I'm not your son; I'm your **grand**son. Why have you done that?"

Evelyn was silent for a moment.

"I think they call it a Freudian slip, Jonathan. I've come to look on you as a son since you've been here. You're like Martin's younger brother that he never had. I'm sorry if I embarrassed you."

"Not at all, Grandma. I quite like the idea of you being my second mother. I just wondered why you said it, that's all."

7. Philip Stewart, M.P.

October 1966:
Philip Stewart sighed with content at the new nameplate on his office door. It read simply "Philip Stewart, MP". It had taken months of scheming and campaigning to achieve, but it had finally been done, and Philip Stewart was the new Labour MP for the staunchly Tory constituency of Marchfield West. No one had expected him to win there. There had been no competition from Labour Party heavyweights for the seat, which required an unheard of 12.5% swing to take. But he had done it! In fact, he had exceeded the required swing by an additional 5%.

He thought back to his selection interview. There had been two other candidates; both local activists, one of whom was a North London Borough Councillor. He dismissed both as lightweights. However, despite being shortlisted, neither turned up for the final interview. One was involved in a motor accident and was in hospital with serious chest injuries from being thrown against the steering wheel in a hit and run accident. Sadly, he learnt that the man later died. He remembered to send flowers to the funeral. The other, the Councillor, unaccountably in the morning realised he had an unbreakable appointment that night. His memory, apparently, was prodded into life by a phone call late the previous evening.

Despite the absence of any opposition, the small selection committee still insisted on doing a full interview, including a 15 minutes long speech, which he had cribbed from a copy of one made by Keir Hardie and which he updated. The key fact was that he told them that they would win the seat, which he saw, they doubted, and that he would work hard for them, which, he thought, they should have doubted. The most difficult moment came when he was asked questions. Two, in particular gave him trouble. They were asked by one of the members, a friend and sponsor of the injured candidate.

"You are known to be the son of an industrialist and a company director of one of your father's companies. Why are you in the Labour Party?"

"Why indeed?" he thought.

The real answer was that the Tories wouldn't have him. His application had been blocked by the Greenways – father and son. Philip really hated Marcus Greenway. He always seemed to get in his way when he was trying to do something. He had taken that girl from under his nose and knocked her up – just as he had intended to do – but he had been frightfully moralising about it – the hypocritical Wanker. Then there was the last time he and Marcus had met and talked, when he made an offer that Marcus Greenway could not refuse – thus putting him and his sainted father on the Stewart payroll along with so much of the rest of the Establishment of North London. Was he grateful? Far from it – he had had the cheek to tell him he never wanted to see Philip, much less talk to him, again. Well that was all right by Philip Stewart. He reckoned that he had enough to destroy Marcus Greenway if he chose, and he would make certain that Marcus was constantly reminded of it. However, that did not stop the Greenways preventing his becoming a Tory. Never mind – they probably regretted it now, he reflected.

"I asked why are you in the Party?"

Philip came out of his musing.

"I do apologise. I joined the Party because I saw the error of my ways. Capitalism is wrong and cannot be justified because it allows a tiny few to batten on the backs of the workers."

"I see," the man had said, "and what have you done since you joined us to help restore social justice and spread the wealth held by the few to the many who are without?"

Fifty Years After

Philip ground his teeth quietly.

"I have made many donations to the Party. I've joined a Union – the GMB – and I've ensured my father pays our work force more."

"But."

The Chairman cut off the man.

"That's enough Bill. You only had two questions. Allow the rest a chance."

The man shut up – much to Philip's relief.

An hour later Philip was the candidate. Three hours later he was talking to his father, Jack, about Bill's attitude and questions. One month later the General Committee was told of the unfortunate death of Bill through a sudden violent attack of food poisoning. Philip, of course, sent his condolences to Bill's widow, attended the funeral and paid for a wreath.

The campaign was a doddle. The Tories did not expect to lose the seat and scarcely bothered to campaign. Neither did anyone else. Philip did some desultory leafleting and a little canvassing, stitching on a cosmetic smile and kissing one or two babies. The main effort took place on or about Election Day, when a whole lot of strange things happened. Ballot papers and boxes went missing, only to turn up later, full of votes – most of them being for Philip. Voters turned up at polling stations, only to find it was the wrong station or that they had already voted. Other voters, known to be supporters of the Conservative candidate, met various difficulties that caused them to give up on the idea of voting. There was a car accident near one polling station in a solidly Conservative area that blocked the access roads up for hours. A house caught fire at peak voting time near another polling station in a Conservative area. And so it went on. Incidents occurred, which, taken singly, were just unlucky. However, taken together, they suggested something more sinister.

Fifty Years After

The Labour activists could not understand how their campaign with such limited resources produced such an amazing result. The pundits were also astonished and were discussing its possible causes all night long after the result was declared. Philip simply put it down to the Stewart Family Organisation and plenty of money put in the right places. No one bribed any voters – that would be undemocratic and a cause to set the election result aside. However, the money did a lot of other things not covered by Election Law, which ensured his eventual victory.

Philip's Conservative opponent had been a leading member of the Party and a member of the Shadow Cabinet. After recovering from his initial shock at the scale of his defeat, Frank Witherspoon began to hear of the various incidents that had marred polling day in Marchfield West. He took his concerns to Sir Walter Greenway. Sir Walter was the Chairman of the Marchfield West Conservative Association. He studied the papers that Frank showed him before answering his question.

"I would seriously advise you to do nothing Frank. It certainly looks very suspicious, I agree, but there are three reasons for just shrugging your shoulders and walking away. The first is that it sounds like sour grapes from a bad loser. The second is that Labour voters, having won against all odds will flock to the polling station in overwhelming numbers to keep their man in Parliament. The third is simple self-protection."

Sir Walter paused, noting Frank's confusion at this statement.

"What do you know about Jack Stewart, Philip Stewart's father?"

"He's a very successful local businessman," Frank replied.

"And what is his business exactly?"

"He builds houses and also buys houses to let out. Most of them are probably unfit for human occupation, so he buys them cheaply and charges high rents to desperate (mainly black) workers."

"That's true," Sir Walter said, "but he does an even more lucrative side line in drugs, money laundering, 'insurance' (also known as protection) and, according to strong rumour, the occasional wages heist. I gather he and his sons are equally ruthless in stepping on anyone who makes things difficult for them."

Frank looked aghast.

"What are the Police doing about it?"

"Taking his cash, as far as I know."

"So, there's nothing we can do?"

Sir Walter shook his head.

"You could accept an offer of a company directorship in his legitimate building company. I think I can put a bit of discrete pressure on Jack Stewart to buy you out."

And that, Philip reflected, resolved the matter. Frank Witherspoon was offered and accepted a directorship in Stewart and Sons, Building Corporation, and thereby joined Sir Walter on Jack Stewart's payroll. Walter Greenway, who could have caused trouble for Philip over the election irregularities, remained surprisingly silent. It was felt that there should be a formal enquiry into the complaints, especially as the local newspaper, the North London Herald took them up. As a result, there was a brief enquiry, headed by Sir Walter, but he found nothing amiss and confirmed the result. Philip was successfully in Parliament, partly because he received the blessing of his sworn enemies – the Greenways.

Jack arranged a victory party for his son at one of the local pubs. The leading members of the local Labour Party and local Union officials attended, as did some of the local Council officials. The Conservative Mayor and the Leader of the Conservative dominated North London Council, however, declined his invitation, as did the Greenways. At the end of the party, Philip made a speech.

"Ladies and Gentlemen," he began, "we have made a new beginning for Marchfield West. The tired Tory Party and its burnt out former MP have been swept away. A new day has born for the oppressed workers of North London. I pledge myself to work tirelessly on their behalf, but also on behalf of all small businesses in this constituency, because they provide work for the unemployed and put money in people's pockets, which enables them to improve their lives and those of others when they go out and spend it."

He looked around at his followers, who clapped and cheered his words, smiling in triumph and then concluded by promising to help everyone who wanted help and ensure there was law and order in Marchfield. Again cheering interrupted his speech. He continued, more quietly, to thank his father and brothers for their help and support. The Stewart family were very close knit, and, since the untimely death of his mother, Philip had grown very close to his father and brothers. He concluded his speech by proposing a toast to them.

As the toast was being drunk, Jack leaned over towards his son and whispered in his ear.

"Remember how much your election has cost me. I expect a return, Son."

"Don't worry, Dad," the new MP replied. "My advice and help to the poor and needy will come at a cost. Those I help may get what they want but find the cost of my help makes them poorer and needier than they were before."

"That's my boy," Jack said contentedly. "You're a chip off the old block."

8. The Hacker

January 5 2010
His friends knew Harry Mackintosh as "The Hacker." The title made him chuckle, since he alone knew how false it was. True, he had done hacking and had the equipment and the skill to do so, but he had stopped doing it seriously when he fell victim to a hacker and discovered just how devastating it can be for the victim. He got his nickname after he gave up hacking for real when one of his friends asked if he could hack the files of the Metropolitan Police and acquire some information about car chases in London. When he handed the required information over everyone assumed he had gained it by hacking. He did nothing to correct this story since it protected his real source - his father, who was a Sergeant at the Met.

Before asking his father for help, Harry Googled the names he was given by Jonathan. He read the article that Jonathan had read and realised that he was skating on very thin ice. He Googled the Smith Trial and began to wonder just what his friend was up to and what he was getting himself into. He found his father resting in front of the television.

"Dad," he said. "Do you remember how you got some information for me once?"

"Sure, Son," his father replied, "It was about car chases I seem to remember."

"That's right – and everyone thought I'd got it by hacking the Met's computers."

"What do you want this time? And who do you want it for?"

"Jonathan Greenway, the Prime Minister's grandson, contacted me. He asked me if I could find information on Jack and Philip Stewart, the Stewart family, and the original police files on the Janet Brown Murder case of 1961."

Harry's father looked startled.

"That's really heavy stuff, Son. Why is Jonathan interested? His grandfather could order the Met to allow the Home Secretary access?"

"I rang him back to ask him that before coming down, Dad."

"What did he say?"

"He said he had been commissioned by his grandfather and Lord Corrigan, to whom apparently Jonathan had spoken, to investigate the Murder Case and the Trial and see if there are grounds to reopen it with a new defendant."

"And he's after the Stewarts?"

"It appears so, yes, Dad."

Harry's father studied his fingernails intently, an action he always did when he was thinking hard, before replying.

"This is no ordinary request for a file, Harry. It's very dangerous. The Stewart Gang was very violent. You're going to be playing with fire mingled with petrol and dynamite if you get entangled with them. If I do this for you must be very careful and keep shtum."

Harry nodded.

"That's not good enough," his father said seriously. "I want to hear you speak the words."

"I promise, Dad, that I will do exactly as you say."

"Very well. I'll see what I can do, but it may take a day or two. Let Jonathan know that."

"Yes, Dad."

"Good – now bugger off and let me watch TV in peace!"

Meanwhile, Jonathan had also been busy. Albert Corrigan had kept his word, and Jonathan wrote to all four Brown and Smith Siblings to ask if they would help him in his search for new evidence. He then, on an impulse, started looking for evidence of the Jurors' names. He found that

Fifty Years After

the information he was seeking was denied to him, and he turned once more to Harry, who sighed, and used his old hacking skills, trying to get into the Jury records of the Old Bailey trials in 1961. He failed, but decided to attempt a brave alternative. Harry put an advertisement in most of the major newspapers and on Facebook, using a false name and an accommodation address. He asked if anyone who had served on the Jury, which tried the Janet Brown murder case could get in touch with him. He did not expect to get any response and was surprised when, a week later, a man wrote to him.

"My name is Wilfred Martins. I was a joiner's mate before I retired fifteen years ago. I was one of the members of the Jury that found Mark Smith guilty of the murder. I was unhappy with what went on in the Jury Room before the verdict. We were all shocked at the sentence, and, even more so when it was actually carried out. I would be happy to talk with you......."

He then gave an address and telephone number, which Jonathan immediately used to make contact with him. As a result, Jonathan organised a programme of visits and interviews spreading through early February 2010, allowing him enough time to study whatever documents Harry managed to secure from the Metropolitan Police. In the meantime, while he waited for Harry, he continued to work his way through Sir Marcus's open and secret diaries and, with the written backing of Sir Marcus, he wrote to Cambridge University, asking them to suspend his course until October 2010, when he would repeat his Year 2. He was pleased when the University accepted his request. He also used Google to discover an additional piece of information – what happened to D I Buchan. He found that the Detective Inspector had retired eighteen years after The Smith Case, avoiding an investigation that had begun into illegal contacts between the police in North London

Fifty Years After

and the Stewart Family. He died of Cancer in 1996, aged 70.

Harry finally made contact with Jonathan on January 15th, having been given a large package of papers in a heavily sealed A3 sized envelope the day before by his father. He appeared at Sir Marcus's home two days later. Jonathan asked what was in the package.

"I don't honestly know," Harry confessed. My contact gave me the papers sealed in the way you see them and told me not to read them, or even look at them, and certainly not to discuss them with you."

"I see," said Jonathan, who did not understand what Harry's father's reasons were.

"What are you up to, Jonathan? I heard you've taken temporary absence from Cambridge. Why?"

"I am trying to right an injustice by bringing a multiple murderer to book and clearing the name of an innocent man wrongly convicted and executed for one of this man's murders."

"You're obviously referring to Janet Brown and Mark Smith. But, if Mark didn't do it, then who did?"

"There were only three people on the scene of the murder. One was the victim and one was the one chosen to carry the can. It doesn't leave many alternatives, does it Harry?"

"You must mean Philip Stewart, the Earl of Little Wittering! But you'll never get a Jury to convict him!"

"Never say 'never', Harry! We can at least try. It's better to try and fail rather than not try at all."

Harry smiled at his friend's enthusiasm and watched as Jonathan put the package away carefully with his other papers – the Diary and the USB key, the book on the trial, and some notes sent him by Lord Corrigan. Then the two of them left the house to go into the neighbouring village to share a drink in the local pub and exchange gossip about their university friends and acquaintances.

9. The Trial Revisited

January 29 2010.

Jonathan carefully opened the envelope and withdrew the contents, laying the papers out in different piles on his desk. Once this task was completed he discovered he had five files, some of which surprised him. He took a tear off book of A4 pages and wrote the following title headings, one on each sheet, and placed each sheet on top of its appropriate pile. The piles were then headed as follows:

1. The original Smith/Brown case files;
2. The Jack Stewart File;
3. The Philip Stewart File;
4. The Stewart Family File;
5. The Alasdair Buchan File.

Having done this, he placed each file into an A4 sized hard cover folder for protection, and put the last four files into his suitcase and locked it, placing the key on a chain which he always wore around his neck. It held a St. Christopher medallion, given him by his mother to celebrate his 18th birthday.

Jonathan opened the original police file and read the first paper, which was the arrest statement by PC Adams. What he saw there startled him. Certain passages were highlighted with a red highlighter pen. Jonathan wondered why. He went back to his account of the Smith Trial and compared the documents that he found in the file with the evidence presented in Court. Something immediately became clear to him. Two statements – the ones made by P C Adams and that made by the forensic scientist had been altered from the statements originally made to the police. As he studied the changes, all deletions from the original documents, two things became clear. The first was that all the deletions were favourable to Mark Smith and tended to support the version of events that Marcus had told him was Mark's story. The second point was that these changes were ordered by Inspector Buchan. Having read the original documents, he then read the amended ones. The forensic report appeared to have been written by the same hand, but the arrest report raised suspicions in Jonathan's mind as to whether the report was written by PC Adams. He read again the evidence that the Policeman had presented in Court and wondered what pressure had been brought on Constable Adams to present the evidence that he did present. There was no mistaking the import of what had been done. The original report suggested that Mark had been an innocent victim of what the Americans called a frame up. The amended report suggested that Mark was the murderer. This gave Jonathan pause to think.

The second paper was Inspector Buchan's report of his interview of Mark. He remembered the evidence given by the Inspector at the trial and saw that the report corresponded closely. However, one aspect of the report disturbed Jonathan, who was used to the tight rules regarding such interviews in 2010. The exact wording of the first paragraph, not referred to in Court, went as follows:

"P C Adams, who said he had arrested him on suspicion of the rape and murder of a young white girl, brought Mark Smith into me. I ordered Smith's clothes to be removed and sent for analysis and then interviewed him. He complained that he was cold, as a result of the fact that he was naked. I told him that we had better get on with it quickly. He refused to budge on the story he had given to P C Adams when he was arrested and so I left the interview room, leaving four officers in there with him. When I returned an hour later, his body was bruised in a number of places and he complained that he had been both beaten and sexually assaulted by my men. I asked him if he wanted to make a formal complaint, but he declined.

We then continued his interview, but he did not change his story."

Mark's story about how he had known Janet for six months, and had been going out with her for all that time, and had frequently made love together, then followed. He repeated the story of his interrupted tryst and what he called the attack on him by Philip Stewart.

Jonathan then read the exact words that Mark Smith had spoken to Inspector Buchan, words which had never been fully repeated in the Court, and he felt that he began to understand what had actually happened that day and why it had occurred. Janet Brown and Mark were lovers and were going to get married a few weeks later. He described how they had met and how their relationship had developed despite the disapproval of all four parents. He then explained how Philip had become involved, stalking Janet, and described the incident between Philip and himself on Christmas Eve 1959, before describing, in identical terms to those used by the Constable, the events leading up to the murder of Janet. He described how their love making was interrupted by Philip who dragged him off Janet, kicked and punched him and knocked him out. He recovered consciousness and found a gun in his hands and Janet lying, shot dead, beside a tree.

His statement ended with these poignant words that tore at Jonathan's heart strings.

"Janet was the only girl I've ever loved and I wanted to share my life with her. As far as I'm concerned my life is over. There's nothing left for me to live for."

It was signed "Mark Smith" and dated 26th April 1961.
    "You poor sods!" Jonathan breathed. He wiped a tear for the two doomed lovers from his eyes and added, under

his breath, "I'll get justice and vengeance for you both, I swear it, whatever the cost."

Jonathan knew that the Inspector had revealed little of this statement and that Sir Walter Greenway had not referred to the details – details that might have influenced enough of the Jury to prevent a guilty verdict. He wondered why he and, especially Albert Corrigan, had failed to mention it. It was almost as though everything in Mark's favour was either ignored or downplayed and that Mark himself did not care. At least, Jonathan, reflected, he understood Mark's attitude now.

The next document in the pile was the forensic report, where Jonathan found the same evidence of tampering, with two versions of the report – a fuller one, highlighted as P C Adams' report had been highlighted, and a shorter one, presented to the Court. James Arthur had written fully and extensively but was ordered to delete anything from the report that favoured the defence.

The last document was the interview notes of Philip Stewart's interview. There was nothing new in this document, but Jonathan was interested to note that the notes stated that Sir Walter Greenway was present with his son, Marcus, making notes. Jonathan read this last document, before closing the file and trying to sort out the turmoil of his thoughts. "No wonder Harry described it as 'dynamite'!" he thought. He took out a sheet of paper and began to write.

- Two documents were deliberately altered on D I Buchan's express direction to remove evidence helpful to the defence. The documents presented to the Court reflected these changes.
- Mark and Janet had been lovers for six months and intended to marry.
- Janet was pregnant and probably realised it.

Fifty Years After

- The forensic evidence actually supported Mark's account rather than Philip's, which was, effectively, presented to the Court as the true account.
- Mark was devastated by Janet's death and did not want to live. He probably welcomed the sentence, despite his shock on hearing the actual words of condemnation uttered by the judge and seeing the dreaded black cap on the judge's head.

Jonathan put down his pen and read what he had written. What should he do now? He did not know. The file confirmed what Lord Corrigan suspected. However, Jonathan also knew he had no right to be in possession of it. Stamped across the top of each document were the words, "Closed until June 23rd 2061." He could not legally get access to the file, and his mere possession of it, he thought, probably constituted a criminal offence for which he could be sent to prison.

"I need advice," he said aloud, as he reached for Lord Corrigan's card and dialled the number on it. Albert Corrigan answered after two minutes.

"Lord Corrigan speaking. How can I help you?"

"Albert, it's Jonathan Greenway. I need to speak to you urgently and privately. When can we meet?"

Albert heard the urgency and sensed the fear in Jonathan's voice. He spoke gently to the young man.

"Have you found something out, Jonathan?"

"I have learned something, Albert, but I don't know what to do. I don't want to talk over the phone. I need to meet you."

"I think you're wise not to talk over the phone, Jonathan. Will the day after tomorrow at 11 do? Come to my Chambers at the Central Criminal Court. I'm not in Court then, so we'll have plenty of time to talk."

Jonathan agreed with relief, put the phone down, and turned to the other four folders.

10. The Stewart and Buchan files.

January 29 2010
With a sigh, Jonathan unlocked and placed the trial folder in his case. He removed the folder on Jack Stewart, which seemed to be largely full of police intelligence reports. Nothing of Jack's character came through the terse notes, dates and codes, which outlined what was obviously the career of a senior criminal. However, among the mass of dates, code numbers and statistics, two or three individual crime reports emerged. One was a complaint from a Greenford shopkeeper that Jack's "family" had been trying to collect protection money from the shops in the High Street. A second linked Jack Stewart with a gangland drive by killing in Marchfield, while a third strongly suggested that he was running a group of prostitutes in North London. There was a common factor in all three reports, Jonathan noted. This was a heavy stamp containing the letters NFA in thick capitals. Jonathan had not met these initials before, but, on checking them on Google, found they meant No Further Action. He noticed that D I Buchan had signed all three notes.

Finally, he found a log of a phone call made by Inspector Buchan to Jack Stewart three days before Jack left the country to go to live in Malaga. The final paper in the file was a report from an undercover policeman who had been involved with the Stewart Gang. It was dated two days before Alasdair's phone call and offered to provide firm evidence of the involvement of all four Stewart men in serious crimes. The paper listed examples of fraud, violence, and several murders, protection and vice rackets and money laundering. The paper concluded with a chilling comment: no further action was taken because of the disappearance of the Police Officer and witnesses concerned and the fact that Jack Stewart left the country to

Fifty Years After

live permanently in Spain outside of the Extradition Zone. Inspector Buchan signed it.

It seemed that Philip's brother, Frederick took over the leadership of the Gang in London, answering to his father in Malaga, until his murder in a gangland shoot out a few years later. No one was arrested or tried for the crime, and Timothy assisted Frederick, until his father's death in 1980, when he disappeared. It was reported that he had travelled on holiday to Kenya, but he was subsequently reported to be in Malaga. No one knew who was administering the Gang in North London, but there were continual reports of low-level activities, and it was believed that Philip Stewart retained his links with the Gang and with his brother, Timothy.

The papers about Philip Stewart added little to what he had already learnt from other sources. Its chief value is that added specifics to what were otherwise generalised allegations, lacking firm evidence to back them. However, again, Jonathan noted that D I Buchan had intervened on a number of occasions to thwart an investigation that offered to produce clear results in the attempt to bring Philip to book. On other occasions, the complaint was mysteriously withdrawn, or the complainant simply disappeared.

Jonathan put the files away with a worried frown. He wondered what he had got involved with and belatedly understood the reason why Harry's father was concerned about what Jonathan was getting involved in. Finally, he opened the folder on Alasdair Buchan. He realised that the Inspector was central to the Stewart story and the Brown/Smith double tragedy. He gained nothing particular from what he found there, but did pick up a lot of what he would call "noise" in other circumstances. It was clear that the Inspector had close links with the Stewart family. Jonathan could not tell whether these were established before the Smith/Brown Murder Trial or came about after it. He suspected that Alasdair Buchan was already enmeshed in the net of corruption before April 1961. If so, he thought, it was tragic that Mark Smith should have fallen into his hands, when there were so many other officers available to take the case. In fact, Jonathan was sure that Police protocol, even then, would have ensured that D I Buchan refused to take the case because of his connections with the family of the chief witness. The fact that he did not do that was, to Jonathan's mind, yet another reason why the trial was unfair. He noted that his colleagues became increasingly concerned about D I Buchan's behaviour and, eventually, he was told he had a choice. He could either go through the disciplinary procedure, which would lead to his probable dismissal from the force and possible prosecution, or, he could protect his pension rights, and take early retirement. D I Buchan needed no second hint. He took early retirement and went to spend his declining years in Malaga, courtesy of Jack Stewart and Sons, Jonathan surmised.

Jonathan put away the folders, ensuring that the suitcase was securely locked and placed behind his clothes in his wardrobe, and turned back to Marcus' USB diary. Here, too, he found hints as to the real occupation and source of wealth of Philip Stewart. It was clear to Jonathan that Marcus suspected that Philip used a mixture of coercion and bribery to end the strikes, which so troubled the Labour Government of which he was a part in the late 1990s. When Marcus became Prime Minister he inherited a big file of complaints against Philip Stewart. These ranged from simple cases of corruption to possible cases of murder. Marcus also referred to the petition for a reopening of the Smith Trial.

Jonathan imagined his grandfather sighing heavily as he typed those words into his diary. He looked in the file to find what Sir Marcus did about it. He found the answer about five entries later.

Fifty Years After

"I have decided that I can do nothing about Lord Philip of Little Wittering. It would seem to the public that I was pursuing a personal vendetta against him. Dad and I stopped him becoming a Conservative Party member because of his questionable activities and doubts we had about his role in the Mark Smith Trial."

Jonathan sat up startled. Had his grandfather really written that? He read the passage again. There was no doubt about it. Sir Marcus claimed that Sir Walter and he entertained doubts about Philip's role in the trial. He wondered what the nature of these doubts was and decided to ask his grandfather when he next saw him. All this, added to what he had already learned from his Grandfather, caused him grave concern.

Jonathan recalled the words that were almost a chorus line for the American Watergate Crisis.

"What did he know and when did he know it?" were questions US Senators asked about President Nixon.

Jonathan found himself repeating the question about Sir Marcus and the Smith Trial.

"What did Sir Marcus know about Philip Stewart's role in the murder and when did he know it?"

Jonathan was very conscious that he had been left during the week in splendid isolation at the Prime Minister's country residence of Chequers, to which Sir Marcus and Lady Evelyn Greenway returned on Friday night, remaining there until Monday morning. Jonathan realised that he needed to talk to someone before he went up to London to see Lord Corrigan. He knew he could not discuss this with his Grandfather and so he rang Evelyn's mobile. She answered promptly, as she always did.

"Jonathan, how lovely to hear from you, and what a surprise!"

"I thought I needed to talk to you Gran."

"That's all right. Marcus is at a Cabinet meeting and I've no one bothering me at the moment. What's worrying you, Son?"

"Nothing I feel it's safe to talk about over an open line like this. You never know who might be listening."

Lady Evelyn was silent at the other end of the line.

"Did you hear me, Grandma?"

"Yes, Jonathan. I'm sorry; I was just thinking what to say. Is this about what I think it's about?"

"It's about something that happened in the past, during the last century, Grandma."

"In North London and Central London?"

"Yes, Grandma."

"And you've found out something that's disturbed you and you want to share it with me. Is that right?"

"Yes, Grandma."

"You wish to meet with me face to face I presume."

"Yes Grandma. I have some papers to show you too."

Evelyn was silent for a second time, taking longer to answer this time as she thought about a way out of this situation. Eventually she asked another question.

"Jonathan is this intended to be a tete a tete or a ménage a trois?"

"Just the two of us Grandma, and it should be tomorrow, because I have to see someone else in London, who is very important, about the same issue in two days' time."

"All right, Son. I've just remembered that my favourite local charity has a Bring and Buy sale tomorrow in the village. I'll come down this evening and return to Downing Street tomorrow evening. You can come back with me and travel to your meeting from here, and go back to Buckinghamshire with us on Friday afternoon."

"Thank you, Gran. I'll tell Jenkins to expect you tonight."

Fifty Years After

Jonathan closed his phone, and went to find the Butler, before going out for a walk to try to put his thoughts in order before meeting his grandmother.

First he focussed on Detective Inspector Buchan. It was clear to him that Inspector Buchan suppressed any evidence in favour of Mark Smith. He wondered whether Albert Corrigan was aware of this but, after a moment's reflection, decided it was unlikely. He would certainly have protested to the trial judge had he known. The important question was why did the Inspector do this? Was he in hock to the Stewart family? If so – why were the Stewarts apparently so anxious to send Mark Smith to the scaffold?

That question brought the figure of Philip Stewart front and centre of Jonathan's thoughts. Did Philip murder Janet? If he did, what was his reason and why did he seek to implicate Mark? Jonathan did not feel that a single punch two years earlier was a strong enough motivation for a double murder.

Then there came the vexed question of the Greenway involvement. He knew there was history between Philip Stewart and Marcus Greenway – but how serious was this, how far back did it go, and was the trial a factor in it? Why was Sir Marcus apparently so anxious to downplay his involvement in the trial, and what was the role of his father, Sir Walter?

Jonathan's mind drifted back to the Stewarts, as he mooched along a path in the estate. How was it that the Stewart Gang appeared to get away with murder (literally) and virtually every other crime for fifty years, virtually unchecked? Did they help secure Philip's staggering election victory and was Philip's alleged corrupt practices pay back for services rendered to him by the Gang? As he thought along these lines, a line from Lloyd Weber's Evita came to him. "How is it that those who oppose you are cut up, stepped on or simply disappear?" Plainly it was a question for Philip Stewart to answer – but he knew he was unlikely to get the chance to hear his answer outside of a law court, in view of his grandfather's instruction to avoid contact with the Peer.

The more he thought about this, the more he realised that something was missing from this picture. Jonathan felt it was a key element in the puzzle. If Philip murdered Janet, he needed to find a reason for his action. If Janet was the target, then the involvement of Mark may have been serendipitous – a lucky break – enabling him to escape the fatal consequences of his act by pushing it on to someone else. The answer, he was sure would be found with Janet's story. However, Janet was dead, shot by Mark Smith or Philip Stewart. Jonathan could only hope that Janet's sister could help shed some light on Janet's story. He realised suddenly that he had no idea what Mark and Janet looked like, and hoped that one or other sibling might give him a photo of the two young lovers.

Jonathan ended his musing and retraced his steps to the house, arriving shortly before the official car carrying his grandmother swept up to the front door of the house. Jonathan was surprised to see her so soon, until he looked at his watch and at the rapidly darkening sky and realised just how long he had been out on his walk.

Evelyn and Jonathan did not meet until they sat down together for dinner. They ate swiftly and silently, not wishing to discuss the issue that had brought Evelyn back so suddenly to the house with the domestic staff present. Once the meal was over, Evelyn ordered the Butler to serve coffee in the drawing room and made her way there, while Jonathan diverted via his bedroom, in order to fetch the folders. Once they were seated comfortably with the coffee pot and two cups, Evelyn opened the conversation.

"Well, young Jonathan, why have you summoned me at such haste from my dear husband's side."

"Grandma, you asked to be kept abreast of my researches into the Smith/Brown Murder Trial."

"Yes," she said encouragingly.

"I have received a number of important papers which contain vital new evidence in the Smith – Brown Case. I am due to discuss these with Lord Corrigan the day after tomorrow, but I wanted to share my concerns with you first and hear what you feel about it all."

"I'm happy to listen and share my thoughts with you, Jonathan. What have you discovered?"

Jonathan opened his case and took out the Smith/Brown folder. He handed it to his Grandmother, who opened it and began to read. Her eyes opened wide when she saw the heading on the top of each page.

"How did you get this, Jonathan? This file is supposed to be closed for another fifty years!"

"Don't ask, Grandma. I have my contacts and my means. If I want something, I can usually get it."

Jonathan sipped his coffee as Evelyn read the papers, turning the pages and looking graver as she did so. Once she finished, she went back to the beginning and read them all a second time. Finally, she returned the folder to Jonathan and began to speak.

"There is no mistaking the import of these papers, Jonathan, or the risks that you are running in simply possessing them. This file makes it clear that the trial of Mark Smith was rigged against him from the outset of the investigation. It seems that D I Buchan was determined to destroy Mark Smith for some reason."

She sighed.

"It also shows that my beloved husband lied over his contacts with Philip Stewart. I'm not sure what that means,

Fifty Years After

but I'm aware that he has been reluctant to talk about this case and refused to allow it to be reopened two years ago."

"It gets worse, Grandma. I have files on the various members of the Stewart family, which shows constant complaints about crimes they were involved in, ranging from simple fraud and drug running all the way up to murder. However, all attempts to investigate the complaints were blocked by the same D I Buchan."

Evelyn looked very grave.

"It would seem that Inspector Buchan was in the pay of the Stewart family and was trying to protect them. But what was he protecting them from in the Smith Trial?"

"I can only think that Philip Stewart murdered Janet Brown," Jonathan answered.

Evelyn stirred her coffee thoughtfully.

"I agree, but I don't understand why he would do it? What did he have to gain from it? And why did he implicate Mark Smith?"

"Mark was black and Janet was white. Philip apparently could not bear that."

"There's certainly evidence of that in the Trial transcript, Jonathan. However, that's not a reason for killing Janet. Had he killed Mark, racism would be an adequate explanation. But it doesn't work for Janet. There has to be another answer."

"I know, Grandma, and that's why I have an appointment to meet Janet's sister in two weeks' time."

"Who else are you meeting apart from her and Lord Corrigan?"

"One of Mark's brothers and a member of the Jury that convicted Mark."

"You might get more information from them. You will need to, because you can't use the information from files you have no right to have in your possession."

"I'm hoping that Lord Corrigan may find a way," he said.

Fifty Years After

"He's a wily bird," Evelyn conceded, "and he has good personal reasons to reverse that verdict. However," she paused and stared directly at Jonathan, "there's another reason why you want to talk to me isn't there?"

Jonathan nodded.

"What is it?" she insisted.

"What did he know and when did he know it?" Jonathan murmured tonelessly.

"What did you say?"

"I was quoting the words of the Watergate Committee about Richard Nixon. What did he know and when did he know it?"

"I thought that's what you said! But why did you say it?"

"I believe that Grandfather and Great Grandfather also knew more about what really happened than they were prepared to admit and that this may explain why Grandfather seems so reluctant to deal with the corruption and criminality associated with the career of Philip Stewart."

"So, what are you asking me to do?"

"I need advice, Gran."

"Go on."

"Do you agree with me that Mark Smith was a victim of injustice and that his execution was an act of judicial murder?"

"I do, Jonathan."

"Do we have a duty to try to right the wrong?"

"Now we know for sure that there was a wrong done, then I agree we must do our best to ensure it's put right."

"Do you agree that Philip Stewart was the most likely murderer and that he framed Mark Smith for the crime?"

"Yes."

"And that makes him a double murderer?"

"Oh yes, certainly."

Fifty Years After

"Should he be brought to justice, even though it won't bring Mark back to life and the crimes were committed fifty years ago?"

"Yes, I think he should be."

Jonathan paused dramatically, before swallowing heavily and continuing.

"Finally, Grandma, if Grandpa was involved in some way in this act of injustice, should I back off and leave it alone?"

Evelyn took longer to answer and her face showed the conflict in her mind and how troubled she felt. Finally, almost reluctantly, she spoke.

"I think Marcus knows more than he's let on and that he's lied about his role in the trial. I think there are serious questions that he needs to answer and that the truth may damage his political career, if not actually end it."

Evelyn paused, looked at her hands, sighed, and continued, looking directly into Jonathan's eyes.

"However, I do not think that any problems for Marcus balance against the burden that both the Smith and Brown families have carried for half a century. We have a duty to see that justice prevails, whatever the personal cost to us all. Marcus will have to look after his own interests and I will have to look after him."

Evelyn looked sternly at Jonathan and concluded in a strong and determined voice.

"You and Albert Corrigan must do what you both know is right."

Evelyn studied Jonathan's face, saw the conflict in his eyes but also the determined line of his jaw. She knew then that, whatever the personal cost to the family, her grandson would pursue his crusade to the ultimate conclusion. She also knew that she would support him, whatever suffering it cost her. "Noblesse oblige," she thought.

Fifty Years After

Jonathan stood up, walked over to his Grandmother, and embraced her. He saw the tears in her eyes and offered her his handkerchief to wipe them as he spoke.

"Thank you, Grandma. I wish I hadn't started this – but, having done so, if I stop here, I am becoming complicit in the same act of injustice, albeit fifty years later."

Jonathan gathered his folders up and returned them to his case. The two stood up and wished each other good night.

"I will have to go to the W I do tomorrow morning, since that was my cover for coming here. I don't intend to talk to Marcus about what you have discovered and I would suggest that you don't either. It's too early for that. Confirm your story with definite evidence of wrongdoing. Then we'll both talk to him."

"Yes, Grandma."

"In the meantime, be ready to leave for London after lunch tomorrow," she said as she headed for the door.

"Yes, Grandma," Jonathan replied.

Lady Evelyn opened the door, and turned back to face Jonathan.

"And thank you so much for telling me."

With that, she closed the door and left Jonathan alone in the room.

Jonathan finished his brandy, placed the cups and glass on a tray for Jenkins to collect, picked up his case, and switching off the light, also left the drawing room and went upstairs to his room, relieved that, at last, he could see his way forward.

11. Stewart versus Greenway

The 1970s.
Six months after Philip Stewart's staggering election triumph in the General Election of 1966, Marcus Greenway joined him in the House of Commons on the opposing benches. The newly elected Conservative MP for Marchfield East died suddenly from an illness contracted on his holiday abroad. Marcus won the resultant by election.

Oddly, in view of the growing hostility between Marcus and Philip, his father secured the election of Marcus, following a conversation with Jack Stewart.

"I want my son to sit in Parliament for the other Marchfield seat," Walter told Jack.

"Why are you telling me?" Jack asked. "I don't fix elections or nominations, especially for the Tory Party."

Sir Walter Greenway stared straight into the eyes of Jack Stewart for several seconds before he answered Jack's question.

"I know you too well Jack Stewart to take that question seriously! I know exactly what went on in Marchfield West. I've seen the complaints and kicked them into the long grass for you."

Jack smiled.

"I know that some of my friends went a little too far in their enthusiasm to support my son's campaign. I would be surprised if they felt any enthusiasm to get involved in the campaign of another Labour candidate."

"They might feel enthusiasm for Frederick," Sir Walter pointed out.

Jack laughed.

"One politician in the family is enough, Sir Walter, as you will find. Philip turns my head with his arguments."

Fifty Years After

"I know," Sir Walter said with pointed emphasis. "I well remember how he comported himself during all the stages of the Mark Smith Trial."

Sir Walter paused, before dropping his voice and speaking in a menacing tone to Jack.

"And, Jack, we both know the truth of that little tale, don't we? And I'm sure neither of us would want that to get into the public domain!"

Jack glared at Sir Walter and was equally menacing in his reply.

"Are you trying to threaten me, Sir Walter, because I would not advise it? It's a very unhealthy thing to do and often has fatal consequences for the perpetrator."

Sir Walter smiled. He had Jack Stewart rattled, and he knew it. He decided to turn the knife.

"I'm not trying to threaten you or Philip, Jack. I'm merely stating the facts, as we both know them. I'm sure you don't need me to spell them out to you, certainly not in a public place like this café."

"You don't need to spell out anything, Sir Walter. I trusted you to do a job and you did it well. It's in your interest as much as it's in mine to allow that murder and the trial to rest in peace and obscurity."

"You needn't worry on that score, Jack. I have got the files on the trial and the murder closed for 100 years, so they won't surface until 2061, by which time you and I will have probably provided fertiliser to generations of plants!"

Jack laughed.

"That's fine, Sir Walter. So long as we both remember that we need each other, all will be well. Of course, the fact that our two sons hate each other for some reason will prevent any suggestion of a deal between us!"

Sir Walter nodded his agreement, rose, and left the Café, satisfied that there would be no great difficulty in Marcus emerging as the winner of the by election, as, in due course, he did. Jack Stewart grinned maliciously at Sir Walter's retreating back, saying to himself, "I've got you where I want you, you slippery bastard, and you know it! You'll no doubt wriggle and wriggle, but you'll never get off my hook, and neither will your precious son." He took a sheet of paper and wrote a note to Alasdair Buchan.

"Dear Alasdair,
I've just had a chat with Sir Walter Greenway. I fear he's getting jumpy. If he tries to seek an opportunity to reopen either the Mark Smith trial and police investigation files or the file on the Election of my son, please let me know at once. I will take the necessary steps to ensure that a correct attitude to these files is reinstated."
Ever yours
Jack."

He folded it, enveloped, addressed and stamped it, before leaving the café and dropping the envelope into the nearest post box. Two days later D I Buchan opened and read the note, before ripping it up and throwing it into the fire in his office.

"Anything important, Boss?" his sergeant asked.

"No, Tom," Alasdair answered, "Just another nutter airing his views on who was Jack the Ripper!"

Marcus enjoyed the election campaign. He discovered that he was a natural canvasser and really enjoyed the cut and thrust of the candidates' debates as well as the (often colourful) language he met on the doorstep. It was inevitable that there would be a low turn-out, especially as the campaign itself was low key and it was clear it would have little impact on the situation within Parliament, where Labour Prime Minister, Henry Turner, had a comfortable majority. As a result, Marcus did relatively well, achieving a slight swing, on a lower turnout and a reduced numerical majority, but a bigger share of the vote. His family were all seated in the Visitors' Gallery when he took his seat.

Fifty Years After

The other Members of Parliament, from all Parties, quickly came to realise that there was something very personal going on between the two North London MPs. Marcus never missed an opportunity to respond to speeches by Philip, who equally answered his speeches. However, it was Marcus who first drew blood, as his catchphrase, "I think I hear a little wittering from the honourable member opposite," quickly caught on. Whenever Marcus rose to speak in a debate, MPs on both sides of the house would shout out the words, "Little Wittering". Marcus used to grin when this happened, but Philip hated it and showed it. That, of course, only made Marcus do it even more.

Ten years after he was elected Philip was promoted to the Cabinet as Minister for Trade and Industry. The Conservative Leader of the Opposition, Francis Maudling, called Marcus into his office in the House of Commons to speak to him.

"How are you enjoying your stay with us, young man?" he asked.

"I'm enjoying it very much, Leader," Marcus replied.

"Call me Francis," the Leader of the Opposition instructed.

Marcus nodded and waited to hear what Francis Maudling wanted.

"I have watched your performances in Commons debates and received reports about your work rate, Marcus, and I'm very impressed. As a result, I've decided to promote you to the Shadow Cabinet when I reshuffle it during the Summer Recess. We've all enjoyed your run-ins with Philip Stewart. Now he's a Minister I feel it's only right to level things up for you. So I'm going to offer you the portfolio of Trade and Industry in the Shadow Cabinet. Will you accept?"

"Of course, Francis. I will enjoy holding Philip Stewart to account."

Fifty Years After

"I'm sure you will, Marcus," Francis said, rising and offering his hand. Marcus shook it, and, smiling his thanks, left the office, passing another future shadow minister who was waiting outside the door.

At first Philip's tenure of his ministry was relatively uncontroversial and the exchanges between the two rivals at the Dispatch Box were decidedly tame. Philip would announce a new deal or a new contract, and Marcus would find a technicality to criticise the "little wittering" he heard from the opposite bench. He did not forget to use his catchphrase at every available opportunity – since he knew that MPs on both sides of the House expected it and enjoyed it. However, even Marcus was forced, with great reluctance, to agree that Philip was doing surprisingly well. That situation lasted until the winter of 1978 and the Great Steal Workers' Strike against Philip's attempt to remove some Trades Union perks and powers.

Philip presented his bill to the Cabinet, with the Prime Minister's support. However, there was considerable concern expressed about the wisdom of proceeding with it. The Home Secretary, a former Union official, was especially concerned.

"The Unions won't like it, Philip, and we could well have a 'Winter of Discontent, marked by widespread strike action, which would damage our chances in the Election next year," he said.

"I agree with your aspirations, Philip," the Chancellor said, "but I feel that this bill will achieve little in practical terms to limit the power of Union leaders and merely anger them by attempting it."

Only Philip's friend and confidant, the Defence Minister, supported him.

"I think it's a moderate bill and sends a warning to our Union friends that, if they persist in acting in the way they are doing, we could really crack down on them," he said.

Fifty Years After

The Prime Minister asked for other contributions, but none were forth coming.

"I think we should go with this Bill," he said in conclusion. "I asked Philip to prepare a measure to fire a warning shot across the bows of the big unions, and I think this does exactly that."

He called a vote, and the majority of the Cabinet voted "Yes" with just three who abstained. No one voted against, despite the reservations some had expressed. Philip was given leave to introduce the bill to the House of Commons, where it was given a lukewarm reception. Philip noticed that not even Marcus Greenway could find any enthusiasm either for it or against it. Two months later, the bill completed its stages in both Houses of Parliament and emerged into law virtually unchanged. However, by the time the bill had become law, Philip became aware that the true battle had only just begun. He received dozens of union deputations during the progress of the bill and hundreds of letters from Union members urging him to drop it. He ignored them and pressed on, thinking that, once the bill was law, the opposition would end. He could not have been more wrong. In the week after the bill received the Royal Assent, thousands of Trade Unionists took part in marches against the Act right across the country. The largest was organised by what used to be called the Triple Alliance, consisting of the Dockers; the Transport Workers; and the Coal Miners – and it was held in London. The marchers marched from Hyde Park Corner to Westminster and tried to lobby Philip, but he was pointedly absent. He was, in fact, in North London, talking to his father.

"Dad," he said. "We're family, and I've always helped you when I can. Now I need your help. This dispute with the unions could ruin me."

Fifty Years After

"You're a fool, Philip," Jack told him. "You know enough about our workers to know how they would react to your law. What on earth made you do it?"

"The Prime Minister told me to," Philip answered in the tone of the small boy, who caught out in wrongdoing, tries to blame someone else for what he did.

"He presumably appointed you because of your knowledge of industry and industrial workers, Philip. You should have warned him not to do it."

"It's happened, Dad," Philip said shortly. "Now I need the help of the firm."

"We can't organise 10,000 motor accidents, Philip! Not even my poodle, Alasdair Buchan could hush that up!"

"I don't want 10,000 accidents, Dad. I need one. Mike Bush is the leader of the noisiest Union – the only one balloting on strike action. He needs a lesson."

"Do you mean, the leader of the steel workers?" Jack asked.

"Yes, Dad. They'll the ones who'll go on strike. I can buy out the other leaders However, Mike Bush is incorruptible."

Jack nodded.

"You're getting too keen on these violent solutions to your problems, Philip. I don't like it and, eventually, it will destroy you. However, on this occasion, and this occasion only, I'll see what I can do. It will take a little time though, and you've got to be patient."

The Steel Workers' strike broke out in early November 1978 and ran on for three months. During that time there were many violent confrontations between the Police and Union, in the course of which there were a large number of injuries, some of which were serious, and, unfortunately, also some deaths. Philip watched the developing situation, and arranged for large sums of money to be paid by the Stewart gang to specifically identified Union leaders of interest and influence. Slowly, the strike began to break down. Philip made no concessions to a politically

Fifty Years After

motivated strike. In this he received the full backing of the Prime Minister and all Parties in the House of Commons. Marcus even called a truce in his attacks on his opposite number during the strike. But then things changed dramatically.

In late December 1978 Jack Stewart left the country to live in Malaga. Three months later Inspector Buchan retired and went to join Jack in Malaga.

Philip had an intern working with him, a Politics graduate named Daphne Bright. On February 9th, 1979, she was in the office when the phone rang. She answered it because Philip was absent. It was a male voice on the phone.

"Is Mr Stewart there?" he asked.

"No," she replied. "I'm his intern. He's away from the office for the day. I can take a message for him."

"H'mm," the voice at the other end sounded doubtful. "It seems I have no choice. Tell him there's been an incident at a picket line in Bradford. A driver lost control of his car as it passed a picket line. Unfortunately, the vehicle ploughed into the pickets and four people were killed and another eight injured."

"That sounds very serious. Mr Stewart will be very concerned."

"It's all right, Darling. Just tell him that among the dead was Mike Bush. You'll find that his anger will subside."

"So that's the message," Daphne summarised. "A car ploughed into a Union picket line in Bradford, killing four people, including Mike Bush, and injuring another eight. Is that right?"

"That's right, Darling."

Daphne kept her temper. She hated men she didn't know and, in this case, had never met, calling her 'Darling'.

"What's your name?"

There was a startled pause. The person on the phone had obviously not expected to be asked to give his name.

"Tell Philip my name is Mack," he finally said.

"Mack who?"

"Just Mack."

The line went dead.

When Philip returned, Daphne reported to him about the phone call.

"A man called Mack rang you, Mr Stewart. He wanted to talk to you, but I told him that you were not available. Eventually he agreed to ask me to pass a message to you."

"What is the message?"

"There was an incident in Bradford where a driver lost control of his car, which crashed into a Steel Workers' Union picket, killing four people and injuring another eight."

"That's shocking," said Philip. "Please send my regards and best wishes to the injured and the relatives of the dead. Was that the whole message?"

"No," Daphne said. "He asked me to tell you that Mike Bush was one of the dead."

Philip's face brightened momentarily, but then darkened again.

"It's a pity," he said. "He was a great man."

"And you're a liar," Daphne thought.

Later that day she visited Marcus in his Westminster office. Marcus showed her to a seat before returning to his seat behind his desk and sitting down.

"What can I do for you Miss, err?"

"Miss Bright, Daphne Bright, call me Daphne."

"That's fine, Daphne. What can I do for you?"

"I'm an intern working with Mr Stewart. You know, he's the Minister for Industry."

"Yes, I know who he is, Daphne," Marcus said kindly. "What has he done now?"

Fifty Years After

"He's been giving money to the strikers to give up their strike and seemed both pleased and unsurprised when I told him that the national leader of the Steelworkers' Union was killed when a car crashed into a picket line in Bradford."

"Can you substantiate that?"

"Oh yes. I can give you the names of people who received money, when and how much."

Marcus gave Daphne a notepad and she spent the next hour ransacking her memory and writing down the details of the bribes Philip paid. Before she left, Daphne asked Marcus not to use her name, however he used the information she had given him, and he agreed.

After Daphne left his office, Marcus studied the list of names and addresses and found his list of Union officers. He rang the Union head offices and obtained the phone numbers of the officials he had listed. When he rang the men involved he found that most were still angry at the way Philip had treated them, and they were happy to confirm the truth of Daphne's story. The news of Philip's reaction to the death of Mike Bush came as no surprise to Marcus. He was already aware of dark rumours swirling around the person of the Minister. He had a list of a number of suspicious or unexplained deaths of people who had criticised or opposed Philip's rise or his projects, and whose deaths were both sudden and opportune for him. Mike Bush was merely the latest. Marcus was determined that he would be the last, if he had anything to do with it, and began to think of a written question for the minister and his stinging supplementary.

Marcus got his chance to ask his question much more quickly than he expected. The death of Mike Bush caused the strike to swiftly cave in on itself and collapse, with no person there to drive it. Philip appeared in the House to announce that the Steel Workers had abandoned their

Fifty Years After

strike, and he claimed that this justified his decision to stand firm. Then he sat down and Marcus got to his feet.

"I wish to congratulate the Minister on his success," he began, "but I am concerned about the number of allegations I have heard concerning substantial cash sweeteners to local union leaders either to prevent them joining the strike or to encourage them to abandon it. Whereas, I agree, that the Minister is entitled to take whatever steps he feels necessary, within the law, to bring a strike to an end, I wonder where the money for all these cash payments came from and who authorised them."

Philip was furious. He suspected that he had been betrayed and guessed who the traitor was. "Daphne will pay for this," he said to himself grimly. However, he put on his public face for Marcus and smiled serenely.

"I authorised the payments, and all were in the guise of welfare payments towards the cost of dependent relatives of strikers – wives and children, etc. I made the payments from my own pocket, as a gesture of good will."

"I bet you did," Marcus thought.

"I believe that the tragic death of the Strike Leader, Mike Bush was a major cause of the collapse of the strike and I congratulate the Minister on his good fortune that such a terrible accident should have occurred when it did. Our thoughts, of course, are with his family, and the families of all the victims. However, does he agree that it seems to be very dangerous to oppose, criticise or attempt to thwart him in any endeavour he's involved in? The list of fatalities among this class of people is growing by the year!"

There was uproar at this question and The Speaker ruled it out of order. Philip glared at Marcus and Marcus smiled serenely back at him as he apologised to the Speaker and sat down. However, the point had been made, and his challenge was on all the news broadcasts that evening and in the newspapers next day.

Fifty Years After

That evening a number of events happened in consequence of Marcus's question. Jack rang an ailing Sir Walter from his exile in Malaga, to ask what Marcus was playing at and to remind Sir Walter of the deal they had struck.

"I'm sorry, Jack," replied Sir Walter, "that issue is out of my hands. I've only a few weeks to live according to the doctor and I've no energy for the quarrels of ancient rivals. I'm sure you're the same. I believe we should leave them to it and let Parliament sort them out."

Jack Stewart, who died a few weeks after Sir Walter in the winter of 1979/80, agreed. Then the two men talked of other things, effectively, sorting out all the remaining issues between them while they still could. Marcus received the plaudits of his colleagues and his leader noted him as a future Minister once the expected Election was fought and won. Philip returned to his office in an angry mood and summoned Daphne.

"You gave the list of names to Marcus Greenway didn't you?" he shouted at her.

Daphne was taken aback. She had never seen him so angry. She looked into his eyes, and suddenly felt afraid. She had heard stories about this man's attitude to women from other female staffers in the House of Commons. She had always dismissed them, but now she was not so sure.

"I didn't talk to him," she said feebly.

"I don't believe you," Philip stormed. "You had to have told him. No one else knew, or, if they did, would not have spoken to Marcus Greenway. It had to be you."

Daphne sat silently, but her red face gave her away. Philip stood up and leaned menacingly on his desk facing her.

"You're a traitor and a liar, Daphne. I can't trust you and don't need you. Take your bags, clear your desk and get out of my office."

He moved to the door, turning back to add a parting shot.

Fifty Years After

"I will be back in fifteen minutes. I expect this office to be empty. Do not bother seeking a place with any other Minister. I'm going to make certain that you won't get one."

With that, he left, slamming the door.

Daphne, frightened by Philip's vehemence and his reputation for violence, swiftly gathered her possessions together, jammed them into her bag, took her coat, and fled from the office ten minutes later. Philip returned five minutes after she left, saw the office was empty and picked up Daphne's keys from where she had left them on her desk.

"Good riddance, Bitch," he breathed. "No one betrays Philip Stewart and gets away with it!"

Next morning, Daphne rang Marcus Greenway, told him what had happened, and accepted his invitation to become his paid personal private secretary, dealing with his constituency affairs. Three weeks later, the Prime Minister called a General Election. Seven weeks later, a new Government was formed. Eight weeks later, Marcus Greenway took up his role as Secretary of State for Trade and Industry, with Daphne as a personal assistant, and a discredited Philip Stewart as his Shadow. The Labour Leader thought it would be sad to break up such an enjoyable partnership of opposites. However, neutral observers among press and political pundits thought that Philip Stewart was lucky to survive because it was widely felt that his handling of the strike had been a major factor in the Government's defeat.

12. Lord Albert Corrigan

February 1st 2010

Jonathan entered Albert's Chambers at 11 am precisely on February 1st. He was always meticulous over timing and was punctual to the second, much to Albert's surprise. Albert looked up and saw that Jonathan was carrying four A4 sized folders under his arm. He waved Jonathan to a chair and closed the file that was open before him and which he had been studying.

"I'm sorry if I'm interrupting you, Albert. I know your work is far more important than mine and I'm extremely grateful to you for agreeing to see me at such short notice."

Albert smiled at his young visitor.

"Don't worry, Jonathan. I've plenty of time for you today. This file contains social worker reports on a paedophiliac murderer who was convicted last week and I have to sentence next week. I will read it up tomorrow. Today is about another convicted murderer – one who was hanged fifty years ago."

Albert stood up and walked over to his drinks cabinet and took out two brandy glasses and a bottle of Napoleon Brandy.

"Drink?" he asked, pouring one for himself.

Jonathan nodded. Albert filled the second glass and pushed it across the table. Jonathan took it and sipped his brandy, drawing his chair up to the desk as he did so. Albert smiled at him and leaned back in his chair, waiting for Jonathan to begin. After all, this meeting was at his request. When Jonathan remained silent, Albert spoke to him.

"What have you done since we last met, Jonathan?"

"I've arranged an appointment next week with one of the surviving jurors from the Mark Smith Jury, and in the following week, I'm meeting first Mark's younger brother and later Janet's sister."

"That's good, but I doubt it's the reason you wanted to talk to me."

It was Jonathan's turn to smile.

"You're a lawyer, Albert, and you keep on the right hand side of the law. I'm not, and I have friends in low places, who often follow the left hand path, if you know what I mean!"

"I understand where you're coming from, even if I don't necessarily approve, Jonathan."

"I have a friend at Uni. His nickname is the Hacker – and I'm sure you understand why, Albert."

"He is one of those annoying young men and women who force their way into other people's computer files and effectively steal them. Is that who he is?"

"Sort of, Albert. At least, he used to be. He stopped some time ago when his own computer was hacked and he realised just how much damage and how much suffering it causes. However, he boasted that he was able to hack into the Metropolitan Police files, and I asked him to do that for me,"

Albert looked aghast.

"You didn't ask him to do that, surely? It's against the Law."

"I'm afraid I did, Albert."

"Of course, he refused."

"No. He did exactly as I asked."

"What did you ask for?"

"I asked for three things: the police and trial files on the Brown/Smith Case; the files on Jack Stewart and Philip Stewart; and the file on the Stewart Gang. My informant also accessed the file on D I Buchan."

"I presume the files you are carrying represent the result of this illegal activity. Is that correct?"

"Absolutely."

"And you want to make me a partner in your crime by reading them?"

"Yes."

"Has anyone else seen these?"

"My friend, let's call him Tom, handed me a bulky A3 sized brown envelope, tightly sealed and unaddressed, together with some advice. Don't show anyone else and be very careful."

"And have you followed this advice?"

"Partly, Albert. I've been very careful. I arranged the papers and put them in the folders you see and kept them in a locked suitcase in my wardrobe."

"But you've not kept them to yourself, have you?"

"No, Albert. I felt that I had to show them to one other person."

"Who was that person?"

"Lady Evelyn Greenway."

Albert relaxed. The young man opposite him may be reckless, but he was no fool.

"Well, my young friend, what have you found from your researches?"

"I know who killed Janet Brown and how the trial was rigged. I know that the Stewart Gang corrupted Alasdair Buchan and made him a part of the plot against Mark. I also know that my Grandfather and Great Grandfather were involved in some way, perhaps unwittingly."

"That's a big list, Jonathan. Did you get all this from the files?"

"Most of it. Some I got from the trial transcript and USB key Granddad gave me."

Albert studied the face of his young visitor and realised that Jonathan was a very troubled young man. He softened the stern judgelike expression he had assumed hitherto, and smiled gently at Jonathan.

"All right, lad. It's your party. You play it the way you want."

Jonathan grinned.

Fifty Years After

"I hoped you'd say that, Albert. I'm going to show you the files in the reverse order to the order in which I studied them, beginning with the one I didn't ask for – the file on D I Buchan."

Jonathan handed a slim Blue folder over to Albert, who opened it, and began to read the pages. At first he looked puzzled, wondering why Jonathan had bothered to show him these papers. Then, as the picture of the policeman's true involvement with the Stewart family began to unfold, his puzzled expression changed to one of anger.

"There's no getting away from the import of these papers, Jonathan. Detective Inspector Alasdair Buchan had two employers – the Home Secretary and Jack Stewart. It appears that he valued Jack Stewart's cause more than the Law's cause."

He paused and then leant forward to emphasise his words.

"This file was never hacked from a computer. This was a confidential paper file. Your friend Tom could only have got hold of this in one way – one of three police officers at the Met."

"If you say so, Albert. I can only say 'no comment' or, in American terms, 'plead the 5th Amendment.'"

Albert smiled grimly at this comment.

"You might have to, Jonathan, if this ever gets out."

Albert closed the folder and accepted a further folder, the Jack and Philip Stewart file. It was the thickest of the four, and Jonathan had put it in a red folder. Once again Albert ploughed through it, reading every page, sometimes two or three times, before going on to the next. As he read, old habits resurrected themselves, and he took a yellow lawyer's notepad, and began to write notes, listing the crimes alleged against the two men and the number of times investigations into their activities were halted due to an intervention by Alasdair Buchan.

Fifty Years After

"Murder, trafficking, drugs, money laundering, burglary, rape, protection rackets – was there nothing this gang didn't engage in?"

"It would seem not, Albert," Jonathan responded.

"And every time an enquiry began to make progress, it was stopped by order of D I Buchan. Finally, when everything was in place to arrest and charge Jack Stewart, Buchan tipped him off and enabled him to flee the country to live on the Costa del Crime."

Jonathan could hear the anger despite the restraint that Lord Corrigan was showing.

"I see why Tom's contact warned you to be careful, Jonathan. I agree. You're playing with fire here. It would be less dangerous, possibly, to face an angry King Cobra while naked and unarmed, than to come up against this mob."

Albert closed the second folder, and placed it on top of the first, with a troubled expression. Wordlessly, Jonathan passed him a third, thinner file, in a green folder. Albert read through it quite quickly before closing it in turn and placing it on top of the other three.

"This adds a little to the other file," he commented. "Most specifically, it shows the Gang is still in business, run by the missing brother from exile in Malaga and possibly, though not certainly, administered by Lord Stewart of Little Wittering, with whom I shared a drink last night in the Commons Bar."

Albert poured another glass of brandy for himself and Jonathan, and pushed his chair back, leaning in it with his hands on his head.

"I've had enough of reading for a moment. I suspect I know what the other blue folder contains, and we'll discuss that after lunch. For the moment, let's look at the Stewarts. What do you make of them, Jonathan?"

"I believe that they were and are a major gang of criminals, responsible for most of the major, and many of the minor, crimes in North London. They have been shielded from prosecution by buying the services of well-placed Police Officers, most especially Alasdair Buchan. There are hints that my Great Grandfather was also on their payroll."

"Did you notice that the MP defeated by Philip in 1966 became a director of a legitimate Stewart company?"

"I did, Albert. I also read the press cuttings about my Grandfather's challenge to Philip Stewart to explain how and why so many people who had made life difficult for him ended up dead or crippled following an attack or a car crash."

"So, the Gang and Philip Stewart, its de facto leader, is able to do what it wants, Jonathan, largely due to police corruption."

The two men sat silently, sipping brandy and thinking about what had been said. Eventually Lord Corrigan broke the silence.

"You think that Philip Stewart murdered Janet Brown and framed Mark Smith. Am I right, Jonathan?"

"Yes, Albert."

"I presume the remaining file adds key information that led you to this conclusion."

"No comment, Albert."

Jonathan grinned.

"I want you to make that judgement yourself, when you've seen the evidence."

"Touché, Jonathan," Albert Corrigan responded with a grin. "I deserved that."

He paused before standing up.

"Now let's go and get some lunch. But first, we'll lock your folders away in my filing cabinet."

Having secured the four folders, Albert led Jonathan to a restaurant between the Old Bailey and St Paul's Cathedral. He told Jonathan that it served good food at reasonable prices and also had a good wine cellar. Once seated, they

Fifty Years After

ordered their lunch. Albert ordered beef steak and supporting vegetables. Jonathan, a vegetarian, ordered a soya bake and supporting vegetables. Albert selected a bottle of Burgundy from the wine list, and the two men settled down to lunch.

"You were Mark Smith's lawyer, Albert, so you must have met and talked to him many times in the run up to the trial and in the three weeks between his conviction and execution."

Albert nodded.

"I guess I had at least ten sessions with him, including the one on the eve of his execution, when I had to tell him that the Home Secretary had rejected our plea for clemency."

"What was he really like? Tell me about him."

Albert sat quietly, eating and collecting his thoughts, before trying to answer Jonathan's question. Finally, he asked Jonathan a question.

"What do you know about the West Indian community in London, Jonathan?"

Before Jonathan could answer, Albert added a correction.

"I'm old fashioned, Jonathan. I should call them Afro-Caribbeans."

"I know a little, Albert. My girlfriend, Belinda, is a third generation Afro-Caribbean. Her Grandparents were born in Jamaica and came to England in the 1950s and her parents were both born here, as she was. She calls herself British and Jamaican (sometimes) but she's never been to Jamaica. We're hoping to have a holiday there in the summer."

Albert smiled.

"You're the reverse of Mark and Janet – but, of course, it's much easier now."

"We still get odd looks, sometimes, when we're out together, especially in the villages and small towns. No one cares in London, of course!"

"It was much worse in 1961 – but we'll come back to that in a minute."

Albert paused again, to sip some wine and cut up his steak into smaller portions.

"What do you know about the 'Empire Windrush'?"

"Nothing," Jonathan admitted.

"It was a ship," Albert explained. "In 1956 it travelled from Kingston Jamaica to Southampton with a ship load of Jamaican passengers, en route for London, to work in the hospitals and on the buses. Both services were having trouble in recruiting workers, and the London County Council launched a recruiting drive in Jamaica. The passengers included men, women and children. Among them was a family of five: Winfred and Abraham Smith, and their three sons – Mark (aged 13), Luke (aged 8) and Matthew (aged 5). Winfred worked as a nurse in Chase Farm Hospital and Abraham joined London Transport as a bus conductor. The three boys went to school. Mark left school at 15, without any qualifications, and became an apprentice at a printing company. Apprenticeships lasted five years and so, of course, he never completed it. However, I spoke to his employers, and they thought very highly of him. He worked hard, never complained, and was capable at his job. They were devastated when he was arrested and charged, and even more so at the outcome of the trial."

"How did he meet Janet?"

"By accident. Janet and he both attended the North London bonfire in Marchfield Park and were standing close together, but apart, when a lout fired a rocket into the part of the crowd where they were. They both bent down at the same time and their heads knocked together. On standing up, they looked at each other, apologised to each other, and Mark took Janet to a nearby pub and bought her a drink. Women never bought drinks in those days. They accompanied men and the men did the buying – although

Fifty Years After

the women sometimes passed money to the men to do it for them."

"It's much easier today – and better," Jonathan commented.

"Indeed!" Albert agreed.

"It all grew from there," he continued. "They discovered that they liked each other and began to go out together, meeting several times a week. Janet worked in a clothes shop incidentally."

"What was Mark like as a person?" Jonathan asked.

"He was rather shy and very quiet. I found him very reluctant to speak, except about Janet, whom he obviously loved deeply. Her death, especially in that violent way, affected him much more deeply than the predicament he was in."

"Was he a violent man?"

"I don't think so. True, he admitted that he punched Philip Stewart on the chin when he met him in the street on Christmas Eve in 1959. Philip had used some very unpleasant racial epithets, apparently. I'm not going to repeat them. Mark was, naturally, upset, and hit Philip, before walking away."

"How did the relationship with Janet unfold?"

"It developed quite quickly. However, both of them found it to be difficult, because they could not take their future partner home. Neither set of parents approved of mixed marriages. Mark's brothers were really too young to understand what was going on, and he did not feel that he could trust them with knowledge about Janet. He feared they would tell his parents and Winfred and Abraham would order him not to see Janet. That would have put him in a very difficult position. He loved Janet – but did he love her enough to disobey his parents and possibly be disowned by them? Janet had the same problem, but she was able, apparently, to confide in her sister, Jennifer. Sadly, Jennifer never confided in me, although I understand that she did speak to Marcus. She confirmed that the two enjoyed a very close physical relationship."

"Did Mark and Janet have sex?"

"They began dating in November 1960 and first had sex in February 1961. Mark told me it was very cold making love in the open in February! Their lovemaking continued on a regular basis, always in the Park under the trees, until Janet was murdered in April 1961."

"Did Mark know that Janet was pregnant?"

"No, and I'm not sure that she did either. However, Mark told me that the two of them talked as they made their way to their favourite tree that final day, and that Janet told him that she had something special to tell him after they had made love. Apparently that was their practice – make love first and talk afterwards."

"So you think she was going to tell Mark that she was pregnant. Is that right, Albert?"

"I think so, Jonathan. But what I do know was that Mark was going to marry her. He planned to take her away to Gretna Green and marry her there, and then come back to present their parents with a fait accompli. They could then accept them or reject them."

By now they were well into the sweet course.

"How did Mark react to Janet's death?"

"He was first bewildered and then devastated. He never recovered from it, and wanted to be with her."

"Do you mean that he wanted to die?"

"Oh, yes, certainly. He refused to give evidence and tried to stop me appealing on his behalf. When I told him of the Home Secretary's decision, he was actually relieved."

"Did he say anything?"

"Yes. You need to understand that Mark was an Evangelical Christian and he asked to see the Chaplain after I left and his family came and went. He spent his last night in prayer with the Chaplain. To me he said, 'I'm innocent and God will not send me to Hell. Instead I shall be with Janet and there will be no more racialism and no more suffering and death. I know the rope will hurt me,

Fifty Years After

but it will only be for a moment – and then it's all over. I don't want to live without Janet and at least I know that, this way, I will be with her forever.' Then he stopped, brushed the tears from his eyes and continued, looking straight into my eyes. 'I want you to promise me something, Albert.' 'What?' I asked. 'Promise me that you will never give up on us. One day, I know, because my God has told me, the truth will be told. Please tell it for me and then we can both be at peace.' He stopped again, as the tears came back. His final words to me were, 'When I've been exonerated, have my body removed from this place and have me reburied alongside Janet.'"

Jonathan noticed that Albert's voice seemed to choke as he said this, and he could see that the old man's eyes were glistening. He felt the same in his own eyes as he reached over and took Albert's hands.

"We will exonerate him between us, and we will have his body exhumed and reburied with his life partner," he said earnestly.

"Yes we will," said Albert, as he swallowed the last of the Burgundy and made to rise from his seat. "Now let's get back to my office and study that fourth folder of yours."

On their return, Albert made some coffee and put the coffee pot, sugar bowl, jug and cups on a side table. He told Jonathan to help himself, as he unlocked his cupboard and took out the blue fourth folder, carried it over to his desk and opened it. What he found inside caused him to experience a series of shocks, as he read the file with mounting anger.

"Why did the Home Secretary close this file for 100 years?" he asked the room. "Only royal files and especially sensitive government files warrant that degree of protection."

"I was surprised as well," Jonathan admitted.

Fifty Years After

Albert studied the Home Secretary's signature ordering the closure.

"That's Henry Taylor's signature. Taylor was a close friend of your Great Grandfather. I guess Sir Walter persuaded him to do it. I cannot think of anyone else with sufficient clout with the Home Secretary to be able to do it."

Albert looked at Jonathan with compassion.

"I'm afraid, young man, if there was a plot, it looks as though your Great Grandfather and possibly your Grandfather was involved in it."

"I'm fully aware of the possibility, Albert. That's why I showed Grandma the files before this meeting."

Albert nodded absently as he turned to the first page of the file – PC Adams' report.

"My God!" Albert said, as he read the first report. "If I hadn't seen this, I would not have believed it possible." He looked up and spoke to Jonathan.

"Have you touched this file in any way, other than reading it? Did you mark the excised passages?"

"No, Albert. The file is exactly as it came to me, except for the hole punches to put the papers in the folder."

"That's what I thought," Albert said between gritted teeth. "I never saw this version. I was sent the expurgated version."

"I think the signature on that version is a forgery. I studied it intently through a magnifying glass and was able to spot significant differences between that signature and the original. The actual handwriting on the second report is also a copy. It's close, but it's not exact."

"So PC Adams was unaware of the alterations made to his report? And he made no objection in court when he was presented with the copy."

Albert stood up and went to a display cabinet in the corner of the office. As Jonathan watched him, he took a replica handgun from the cabinet and placed it in one of his jacket pockets, which bulged with the weight of it. Jonathan looked surprised. Albert explained.

"Look at my left hand pocket, Jonathan. How does it look?"

"It's flat."

"And the right hand one?"

"Is bulging."

"That's where I put the gun."

Albert withdrew the model gun and placed it back in the cabinet.

"It belonged to my son, who left it here one day when he visited me. I've always meant to take it back, but never quite got around to it. Can you draw any conclusion from the experiment we have just conducted?"

Jonathan's face looked blank.

"Think of the excised portion of PC Adams' report."

Jonathan tried to think what it said – and finally, admitted defeat and picked the folder up to re-read the report. That's when the light dawned.

"Mark Smith did not have a gun. If he had had one, it would have shown in a bulge in his pocket."

"Exactly. And if Mark did not have a gun?"

"He probably did not shoot Janet."

Albert gave Jonathan an admiring glance.

"I'm glad you put it that way. Most people would have said 'he didn't shoot her'."

"He could have seized the gun from someone else – Philip Stewart for instance and shot her with it – but I think it's highly unlikely."

"So do I, Jonathan. The second excision is important too. Remember the Constable, who seems to have been a very observant fellow, commented that the couple's clothes were neatly folded and piled. The prosecution claim was that Mark forced himself on Janet, stripped her, raped her and then killed her. The Constable's report proves that did not happen."

"How?"

"Would an intended rapist, stripping a struggling girl, have bothered to fold her clothes neatly and put them in a neat pile?"

"No. He wouldn't have time."

"Exactly. These two took their time and removed each other's clothes (or their own) and took care that they did not get too dirty or damaged. This was no rape attempt. It was consensual sex. In other words, P C Adams confirmed Mark's story. It's no wonder they doctored the evidence – the bastards!"

Albert's anger grew as he read the pathologist's report.

"Again, anything favourable to Mark has been excised. Put together, in their original form, I could have got Mark acquitted of the charge. In their edited form, the two documents pointed clearly to Mark as a rapist and murderer. I would guess that D I Buchan knew exactly what he was doing and whom he was protecting. There's one very significant fact in the excised sections, apart from the obvious lack of injuries to the vagina due to forced entry and the fact that Janet was pregnant."

"What is that, Albert?"

"The injuries to her face and buttocks, which appear to have been inflicted a day or so before. I wonder who did that? Perhaps her sister can shed some light on it?"

Albert read through the rest of the file, noting the presence of the two Greenways at Philip's interview, and ending with the sombre death certificate for Mark Smith. He closed the file with a sigh and pushed it away from him.

"Is that enough to force a reopening of the case?" Jonathan asked.

"It's enough to get the verdict set aside as unsafe if we could use it, but, unfortunately, we can't!"

"Why not?"

"Because you and I should not have the file at all. We're both committing a crime by even touching it."

He smiled at Jonathan's suddenly worried face.

Fifty Years After

"Don't worry, lad. I won't tell on you! But I'm going to keep all four folders here under lock and key. I will, when you give me a key to open the case, use it to get the present Home Secretary to release the original documents. Then we can get the case reheard and end the Stewart Gang's career."

"And possibly, that of my Grandfather."

"I'm very much afraid so, Jonathan. Remember I did try to warn you. I think he let you follow this up knowing that the files were locked beyond your reach, and not knowing exactly how resourceful and determined you are. He's been very foolish – because you are exactly the same type of character as him."

"What do you mean by a key, Albert?"

"I need a fresh piece of evidence from one of your three witnesses, which will enable me to get some leverage on the Home Secretary and the Chief Justice. I also need it before the summer, because I am planning to retire in July and then will lose some of my clout."

"I will try my best, Albert."

"I know you will and I think you will succeed."

Albert and Jonathan stood up simultaneously. As Jonathan was putting on his coat, Albert spoke to him.

"You said you showed Evelyn these documents. What did she say?"

"She said a gross act of injustice had been performed and we have to act to put it right or become part of that act. She is aware that Granddad could well be affected, but feels that it is a risk that has to be taken."

"That's what I expected of her. It's also my opinion. Between us, Jonathan, we will bring this case to a final closure. Good luck Lad, and take care. The Stewarts are a very dangerous family and it's foolhardy to offend them so long as they are free. I don't want to be involved in yet another murder case."

"I'll be very careful, Albert. You can be sure of that."

13. Wilfred Martens

February 8 2010
Seven days after his conference with Lord Corrigan, Jonathan travelled by the Dockland Light Railway to Stratford to meet up with Wilfred Martins, the eighty year old man who had responded to Harry's advertisement. Wilfred lived in sheltered accommodation in West Ham, and Jonathan travelled to talk to him there. He rang the bell of the main door of a nineteenth century townhouse that had obviously been converted into a privately run old people's home, because the name of the proprietor was over the door. He noticed it had been renamed the Laurels. Its old name was still clearly evident within the Masonry. It had been named Mafeking Mansion, which, Jonathan reckoned, dated it to the beginning of the twentieth century.

Jonathan was taken to Wilfred's room, where he found a spritely, but fragile looking, elderly man waiting for him, seated in a wheelchair, with three sealed brown envelopes on a small table beside him. He welcomed Jonathan and waved him to a chair, asking the woman who had brought him in if she would get Jonathan a cup of tea. She agreed and bustled out of the room, leaving them to it, only to return about ten minutes later to place a tray containing a small tea pot, a tea cup and saucer, a small milk jug and a sugar bowl on the table between Wilfred and Jonathan, who had been engaging in small talk while waiting for her return. Jonathan poured out his tea and smiled at Wilfred.

"It was good of you to break your oath of silence and answer my friend's advert," he began.
    "No problem, Son," Wilfred whispered. I've wanted to right the wrong I did fifty years ago for a long time. I'm glad that I can do it before I die."

Fifty Years After

Wilfred paused, coughed several times, drank some water, and continued. Jonathan had to lean forward to hear his whispered words.

'You said your name was Jonathan Greenway. Does that mean you're related to Walter Greenway, the Barrister?"

"I'm his great grandson, and Sir Marcus Greenway is my grandfather."

"My God, there's a turn up for the book! Fancy a Greenway wanting to hear the truth! Miracles will never cease!"

"I understand your comment, especially now I have learned much of what went on in that trial, and have guessed at much of it. I'm not engaged in double dealing. I'm simply trying to get long delayed justice for Janet Brown and Mark Smith."

"You're not shitting me are you?"

"Certainly not!" Jonathan answered. I'm as straight as a dye."

Wilfred relaxed in his chair.

"Why don't you tell me your story?" Jonathan said.

"I was one of twelve white men selected for the jury. I was actually only 30 at the time and the youngest of the twelve. It was my first time on jury service and I was excited to be trying a murder case. It was a strange one, though, because it was all over almost before it began. Most of us felt that the Defence Lawyer did a good job and that there was considerable doubt whether Mark Smith was guilty. I suspect that, if we had been allowed to debate and choose freely, the jury would have been split 8 to 4 for not guilty."

"So how come you unanimously found him guilty within 20 minutes?"

"That's the shame of it," Wilfred answered. When we got into the Jury Room, one of the Jurors, named Matthew Allbright, handed us each an envelope. It was plain and sealed with sellatape, as you can see."

"What was in the envelope?"

"A card, with instructions and 10 new £5 notes."

"What were the instructions?"

"We were told when we were sent out to elect a foreman and decide our verdict, to elect Matthew Allbright as Foreman and vote the way he did, whatever we might feel as individuals. If we did, a second envelope would be given us, with a thank you card and gift of the same size as the first."

"So you were each offered £100 to elect this man and do what he said. Is that right?"

"It was. You must remember £100 was a lot of money in those days. It was about ten weeks' wages for most of us."

"I see," Jonathan responded. "And. presumably you did as you were told."

"Yes. We elected Matthew Allbright and waited to hear what he would tell us. We didn't have to wait long. 'Well everyone,' he said. 'I'm sure we all want to get home quickly, so let's find the bastard guilty and that's the end of it.' 'But, if we do that, they'll hang him,' one of the jurors said. 'No they won't,' Allbright replied. 'He's only 18, so they'll just put him in prison.'"

"And so you found him guilty?"

"Yes."

"Even though you thought he was innocent?"

"Yes."

"And you got a shock when he was condemned to death?"

"We all did."

Jonathan drank his tea, allowing the clearly uncomfortable Wilfred to relax, before resuming.

"Why have you decided to talk now?"

"I want to put the record straight before I die. I don't have much time left," he said, coughing violently.

Jonathan poured him a glass of water and passed it to him. Wilfred drank it slowly and the coughing subsided.

Fifty Years After

"I'm dying from lung cancer," he said. "I smoked too many cigarettes I'm afraid." He tried to laugh, but ended up in another coughing fit.

"Finally, the spasm passed, and Wilfred was able to continue.

"Three of us felt that we were being offered blood money, and felt bad about taking it. The other two tried to return the money to Matthew Allbright. Both disappeared soon afterwards. One man has never been found, but the other's body was found floating in the Thames. Apparently he had gone for a walk beside the river and fallen in. He couldn't swim, and he drowned. That was the official story any way."

"I see," said Jonathan, shuddering inwardly. "And what did you do?"

"I was a coward, I'm afraid. I kept the money in the envelopes the notes came in, unopened, and put them in a safe place. They are the ones on the table. I want you to take them and give them to that defence Barrister unopened as evidence of what went on."

"Are you prepared to make a statement?"

"I've already done that." Wilfred handed the third sealed envelope to Jonathan.

"This contains a notarised statement which I made last week in front of my solicitor. I got him to draw up a will for me at the same time."

Jonathan thanked him as he placed the three sealed envelopes in his bag.

"I've two more things to say to you, Son, before you go."

"What are they Wilfred?"

"The first is a warning that I'm not likely to be able to give evidence at any new trial – much as I would like to. My doctor told me I have only a few weeks to live."

"I understand, Wilfred. I will tell Lord Corrigan so."

"The second is some advice. Don't stray near riverbanks if you're going to pursue the real killer. He's very dangerous, as my two jury colleagues found to their cost."

"I can safely promise you that, Wilfred. That's why I've kept well clear of anyone connected to the Stewarts."

"Very wise, and I can see you've already picked up my drift. All I can say is good luck. Go and get the bastard. And when you've got him, throw him in prison and chuck away the key."

"I'll do my best, Wilfred. Meanwhile, you take care. We need brave and upright men like you to stick around for as long as they can."

Wilfred smiled, shook his hand, and waved Jonathan goodbye.

Six weeks later, Wilfred was found dead in his room. Albert, who had visited him to thank him and reassure him that he would ensure that justice would be done, during that time, was told that he had a smile on his face when he was found.

14. Luke Smith

February 10 2010

Jonathan met Luke Smith in a café in Oxford Street. He was 62 years old but looked younger. He was smartly dressed in a dark, two-piece suit and a white shirt and matching tie. His glasses gave him an intelligent look, which proved to be truthful. Jonathan shook his hand and sat down at his table, ordering coffee and scones. He found that Luke was not entirely happy to see him.

"So you're Jonathan Greenway?" he asked.

"Yes, I am," replied Jonathan. "Sadly I can't be blamed for my name."

"Greenway is not a name that is popular in my family," Luke pointed out.

Jonathan nodded.

"I have read the papers of the trial, and I can understand that my family did you and Mark no favours whatsoever. If I were you I would order me to leave without any further ado and not darken your paths further."

"I considered doing that," Luke admitted. "But, I must admit, I'm curious. First of all, who exactly are you?"

"I'm a 20 year old I T undergraduate from Cambridge. I have an Afro-Caribbean girlfriend called Belinda, whom I love very much and hope to marry when we both leave Uni. I am the grandson of Sir Marcus Greenway, and the great grandson of Sir Walter Greenway."

Luke's hostile expression softened after this recitation.

"What are you trying to do?"

"I'm trying to right a wrong in which my family sadly played no small part. I'm trying to bring justice to a young teenage girl who was vilely murdered and to her lover who was not only judicially murdered, but whose name was eternally smeared as a rapist and murderer."

Jonathan paused to draw breath.

Fifty Years After

"I also believe that the person who raped and murdered her is still alive and enjoying a position of great privilege and wealth that is entirely undeserved. I intend to help bring that man to justice, clear Mark's name and retrieve his body so that he can be buried alongside his intended life partner and the mother of his unborn child."

"I didn't know she was pregnant, and I don't think he did either."

"I'm sure he didn't. We only learned it a month ago, and it appears she was intending to tell him on the day she was killed."

Luke relaxed.

"You realise, don't you, that you may destroy your grandfather as well as Janet and Mark's killer?"

"Yes, I do – but it's a risk I have to take."

"And you're prepared to take that risk?"

"I am, and so is his wife, my Grandmother."

Luke offered Jonathan his hand. Jonathan took it and shook it.

"What can I do to help you?"

Jonathan smiled.

"Tell me as much as you can about Mark, Janet and the two families, and, if you have any, let me have a photo of Mark and Janet."

Luke reached down and opened the bag he had brought with him. He drew out a small photograph album and gave it to Jonathan.

"I thought, if you were genuine, that you would ask to see the principals in the tragedy and so I had some reprints made of photographs that we took in and around 1959 to 1961. I have labelled them with the dates and names. You can look at them later on. My card is stuck on the front cover, and you can ring me if anything is unclear."

"Thank you, Luke. That's more than I could have possibly expected."

Luke nodded, and began to speak.

Fifty Years After

"I never met Janet, although we both met her sister and brother after the double tragedy of the murder and the trial and execution of my brother for a crime we all knew he did not commit. The attempt, first to get a reprieve, and, subsequently, to get a retrial and an exoneration, as well as the punishment of the real murderer, brought us close together, despite our obvious differences. Matthew and Tom became friends, went to the same university, and went into business together. Sadly, they were both killed attending a meeting in the Twin Towers on 9/11. As a result, Jennifer and I are left to carry on the fight alone."

"Not any longer, Luke. At least three of us are supporting you."

Luke nodded his appreciation, and continued.

"Matthew and Tom were both too young to know much about what was going on between Janet and Mark. I will leave Jennifer to tell her side of the story since I know that you are visiting her in two days' time. She, incidentally, has contributed some of the photos. She also has other material for you, which she has not given to anyone else."

"How do you know all that?" Jonathan asked.

"Because we spoke to one another on the phone after you contacted us to exchange notes. Had we felt that you were a fake, we would have both made an excuse to miss your meetings with us. As it was, we decided that you seemed genuine."

"I am genuine, believe me."

"I do believe you now I've met you face to face," Luke said hastily.

Jonathan was mollified by this and allowed Luke to continue.

"Mark was very quiet about his romance, and I only learnt about it from him two days before the day of the murder. He told me then because he was planning to run away with her. The two of them knew that neither set of parents would approve their marrying each other, and so they were intending to elope to Gretna Green the following week and get married there. Mark and Janet had everything planned. They had even bought their rail tickets and booked rooms in an inn in the village where they would stay."

"Why do you think he told you this and did he show you the tickets?"

"Not only did he show me them; I still have them and the receipt for the room they booked. I've put them in the album for you."

"So, Janet and Mark were very much in love. Is that what you're saying?"

"Mark thought the sun shone out of her backside. That's the truth. Jennifer told me later that Janet thought the same about Mark. They never quarrelled and, according to Mark, tended to finish one another's sentences for each other."

Luke fell silent for a minute and then resumed, speaking slowly, for emphasis.

"Mark could never have wished to hurt Janet. He would no more do that than he would deliberately hurt our mother or me. She meant the world to him, and he was totally devastated by her death."

"Did you see him after he was arrested?"

"I went to see Mark with my Mother while he was awaiting trial once, and saw him alone three days before his execution, before he knew it was going to happen."

"How was he?"

"It was very strange," Luke answered, after a moment's thought. "He was totally calm. I would have panicked had it been me, but he was almost fatalistic about it all. He expected to be found guilty, even though he always maintained that he was innocent, and was only upset that he had been unable to protect Janet from her killer. He felt he deserved to die for his failure and, in any case, had no wish to live without Janet beside him."

"Albert Corrigan said the same to me," Jonathan commented.

"There was one other thing he said to me before I left him that last time."

"What was that?"

"He told me that he expected to hang within the following few days and that he welcomed death. It would reunite him with his beloved and would not hurt too much. It would be very quick, he told me, and said I was not to worry. However, he made me promise to do my utmost to get his name cleared, to get the real killer punished, and to have his body removed from where it would be buried in the prison and rebury him with Janet. I promised, and, later, so did Jennifer."

"That's what we are trying to do," Jonathan responded.

They both rose at the same time. Jonathan reached for his wallet, but Luke stopped him.

"No, Jonathan. I will pay for us both. I cannot say how relieved I am that someone is really listening to us at last. I know Jennifer will feel the same way. The photo album is yours but the tickets, and hotel booking are for the Court."

"I understand, Luke, and, thank you."

Jonathan left Luke paying the café bill and left the café to take a taxi back to Downing Street, where he was staying with his Grandparents. He felt he was making progress.

15. Greenway versus Stewart

1980 - 2010

Following the General Election, the roles and positions in the House of the two rivals were reversed. It was now Philip's role to challenge, and Marcus's role to fend off the challenge. However, it became immediately clear to the watchers on both sides of the Chamber that Philip was not up to the job. He clearly hated the role of Opposition and was unable to think quickly enough on his feet when Marcus countered his question with a political riposte that left him flatfooted and almost gasping for breath. Philip would have preferred the insult epithet of "little Wittering" to the apparently sympathetic, but highly superior, smile that Marcus gave him when he tripped up on a supplementary question. That smile said to Philip, "You're simply not intelligent enough to catch me like I used to catch you. Just accept it, and stop trying." That's what Philip thought that Marcus was saying to him, and that's what Marcus intended him to think.

Meanwhile, unknown to Philip, Marcus had instructed Daphne to keep contact with Philip's numerous interns.

"I particularly want to know if he's still handing out bribes and taking them, as well as making fraudulent expenses claims. If you hear of any violence either ordered by him, carried out by him, or condoned by him; I would like to hear as many details as you can gather on it."

"Why are you doing this, Sir Marcus," Daphne asked.

(Marcus had been knighted in the New Year's Honours List two years earlier for his services to charity.)

"The man is a criminal, and he must be brought to justice. However, to convict him will be very difficult because of the very nature of the offences he commits and the people who obey his orders. So I have to have so much evidence

Fifty Years After

that the weight of the paper alone will sink a ship before I can successfully lay charges against hm."

Daphne nodded, and, over the months, she brought snippets of evidence that, by themselves meant very little, but taken in context presented a coherent and persuasive picture of a master criminal in day-to-day charge of a criminal organisation. Slowly, the picture built up. Daphne was very careful not to be seen to be asking questions. She knew enough of Philip's potential for violence to take extreme care to be distanced from apparent hostility towards the man. Sir Marcus, she noticed, adopted the same tactics, except for the formalised hostility in the House of Commons.

Philip, however, was no ordinary criminal. He had a sixth sense of danger – either present and real or potential and threatening. He had that sense now. Something was wrong, but he did not know what it was or where the danger, if there was any danger, lay. He knew that Marcus Greenway was his lifetime enemy. Only he and Marcus knew the depth and extent of that enmity. The other MPs thought it was just an amusing rivalry; a sort of display put on by the two men for their amusement. Although some of them did notice that the two men never drank together in the Commons Bar or spoke to each other except across the dispatch box. That, they knew, was very unusual. However, no one spoke about it.

Philip wondered about Marcus, but decided that he had done enough to keep that particular troublemaker silent. He knew that it was simply too dangerous for Marcus to try anything against him. Was it perhaps the siblings of the two lovers involved in the Brown/Smith Murder Trial? He knew the brothers and sisters of the young couple hated him. He wondered if they suspected the truth or whether they were still trying to find out the truth. Philip cursed the fact that he had been obliged to give evidence at the trial.

Fifty Years After

His life had never been quite the same since. Philip resented the fact that the death of a black teenaged man, hanged at the State's expense, should cause such continued discussion. "It was 50 years ago, for God's sake", he thought. "It has to be them," he thought as he picked up the phone.

Philip's instincts for self-preservation had always been strong. He had felt this sense of uneasiness once before, shortly after Labour lost the General Election and he lost his post and the salary and other perks that went with it. Then it was another rival. In this case the rival was one he could not see, and therefore one who was much more dangerous than Marcus Greenway, whom he saw every day. He had launched an investigation, using the Family Organisation, and he had eventually discovered that a rival gang leader was plotting to invade his Gang's territory in North London. Philip was not going to stand for that, and he issued orders that the offending gang leader should be wiped out. The man had died in a hail of bullets, following a carefully set up ambush, in Greenford. When the Police started to investigate the incident, someone whispered to the Officer in charge of the investigation, "This is the Stewart family at work. Steer clear." He heeded the call, and the investigation died.

Marcus was unaware that Philip had effectively instigated a turf war in North London. Daphne did not pick it up, and it was only when the Home Secretary called him aside after a Cabinet meeting to ask him what he knew about an inter gang war that seemed to be raging north of the Thames that he found out. By this stage, the victims included Philip's oldest brother and the leader of the Greenford-based gang that had intruded on the Stewarts' territory, together with at least six others, evenly split between the two sides.

Fifty Years After

"The Police seem unable to deal with it, Marcus," the Home Secretary told him. "Is there anything you can do, in view of your local knowledge of the area?"

"I can try, Bob," Marcus replied. "However, I can't promise anything."

That's good enough for me, Marcus. Let me know how you get on."

Next morning, Marcus asked Philip to meet him in his office. However, Philip Stewart felt offended to be summoned to visit Marcus Greenway like a naughty schoolboy reporting to one of the Prefects for punishment. That had happened to him at school. In that case, Marcus had humiliated him in front of the other prefects. It was in early January 1960, and the fact that Marcus had defeated him over Evelyn only made it worse. It took time for Philip to swallow his pride and speak to Marcus's assistant, Daphne (of all people!) to make an appointment.

They met the week after Marcus had requested the meeting. Philip walked into Marcus's office, pulled up a chair, and sat down facing Marcus without saying a word. Marcus pushed an empty glass and a half empty bottle of dry sherry across the table to him, and sat down opposite him. Philip pointedly ignored it.

"I'm glad you came, Philip. I need to talk to you about events in North London; events which affect people living just to the south of our constituencies."

"So it's Philip, today, is it Marcus. Not 'Little Wittering'?"

"I'm being very serious, Philip. Bob Wilton asked me to see you and see if, together, we can stop the senseless slaughter in Greenford."

"So, you're the mouthpiece of the Home Secretary now, are you?"

"Yes, Philip."

"Why do you think I might have some say over what happens in Greenford?"

Marcus banged his hand on his desk.

"Philip, neither you nor I are stupid. You and I both know that the Stewart name is synonymous with murder, drugs dealing, pimping, money laundering, protection rackets, and a variety of other crimes – too numerous to mention. I understand it's already cost the life of your brother, Frederick. How many more do you want to die?"

"The Young Gang have been interfering in our affairs, trying to take over our territory. We have to stop them."

"What are you, Philip? Are you one of Her Majesty's Shadow Ministers or are you simply another murderous Gang Leader?"

"What sort of question is that, Marcus? You know exactly what I am. You always have done. You also know what the consequences of crossing me would be for you, and especially for Evelyn."

Marcus poured himself a sherry and downed it at a gulp.

"Philip, I have not invited you here to listen to threats. I want you to end the slaughter that's causing so much trouble and grief in North London. I want you to meet the leaders of the two groups and negotiate an end to hostilities."

"And if I don't agree?"

"You may find the Police become very active in investigating the Stewart Gang."

"So now you're threatening me?"

Marcus sighed heavily.

"Philip, so far eight people have died and twelve people have been injured in shooting incidents because of this 'war'. Of those twelve, at least six had nothing to do with the conflict, and two of them were children on their way to school. This has to stop."

"What are you suggesting? Or are you merely lecturing me?"

"Philip, between us, we represent all the people of Marchfield. Together, we can call the 'official' leaders of the two gangs to my office and negotiate an end to

Fifty Years After

hostilities. If we can do that, the Police will let sleeping dogs lie."

Philip reluctantly agreed, and a month later, the two MPs hosted two gangland leaders and killers at a peace conference and hammered out a deal that agreed two distinctive territories and laid down a rule that known gang members should stay out of each other's territory. The deal worked, and the killings came to an end, to the relief of everyone involved. Eventually, the Home Secretary stopped Marcus in one of the House of Commons corridors and congratulated him.

"I don't know what you did, but it seems to have worked. Peace has broken out in North London. No one has died or been injured for over three months."

"I did some straight talking to Philip Stewart and then Philip and I knocked some heads together. It seems to have worked."

A few years later their positions were reversed. Philip returned to ministerial office following Labour's victory in the 1988 General Election. However, the unions began a series of strikes against the Government's austerity policies and Philip resorted to his familiar tactics of bribery and coercion to break them, although being much more careful over who he used as go-betweens. He lost office in the reshuffle, which followed the second Labour victory five years later. Marcus, meanwhile, was promoted to Shadow Chancellor. Philip and Marcus were no longer directly opposed to each other, but the old rivalry continued until Philip lost his seat in the Labour defeat in 2002, when Marcus was appointed Chancellor by Prime Minister Maudling.

Sir Marcus and Lady Evelyn moved into 11 Downing Street and away from the Commons rivalry with Philip Stewart, who was reshuffled out of the Shadow Cabinet by a Leader of the Opposition, who had finally grown tired of

Fifty Years After

the constant complaints about his financial dealings and his attitude to women. Marcus was now swamped by the detailed financial papers that outlined proposals that might or might not improve the economy and he had no time to pursue his enquiries into Philip's continued criminal dealings. Daphne continued to feed him information, which he filed, but his interest had waned, especially following the veiled warning, which Philip had given him. He had no wish to be responsible for any harm coming to Evelyn.

The Conservatives won a snap General Election in 2004 and three years later Prime Minister Maudling suddenly announced his retirement from politics. The Conservatives organised a swift leadership election. Marcus threw his hat into the ring and spent six weeks chasing around the country, addressing Party meetings and appealing for their support. After two ballots, Marcus became Conservative Party Leader, and, next day, Prime Minister. He allowed himself six months to get into the saddle and then called a snap General Election. He knew that a financial crisis was in the offing and wanted to secure his own majority before it broke. He appointed his friend, Marion Barlow, the former Foreign Secretary, to the Chancellorship, and the two people worked together to try to steer the country through the crisis they both knew was coming.

Crisis had already hit Philip Stewart. For once, the Stewart Gang's campaigning let him down and a public who had become increasingly angry at being asked to pay for their MP's help, turned against him, and voted him out in 2002. The retiring Labour Leader wanted to keep his services and elevated him to the Lords. He asked to be given an Earldom, which was an exceptional honour, not usually given to a former junior minister. A few eyes were raised at this, but a donation or two to a number of nominated charities, oiled the way for the new peer. Philip took the title "Little Wittering" as a way of sticking two fingers up

Fifty Years After

to the new Prime Minister. In the Lords he continued to criticise the Government and its Leader with as much enthusiasm as he had in the Commons. However, their Lordships did not appreciate their new colleague's aggression. As a result, Philip felt increasingly that he had been shunted into a dead end.

It was when Philip was in this mood of despondency that the prickling sense that warned him that he was in difficulties came on him. He sat in his office in the Palace of Westminster, reading his copy of 'the Guardian'. He worked through the news stories without much interest, ignored the sports stories. Tottenham Hotspur, his football team, had not played a match that night. He had no reason to look at the Sports Section. However, his eyes wondered to the advertisements and one shouted out at him.

"If you served on the jury, which tried Mark Smith for the murder of Janet Brown in 1961, we would like to speak with you. Please contact Harry Smith on (a mobile phone number followed) and leave us your number. We will get in touch with you."

Philip phoned the number and spoke to the answer phone.

"My name is Philip Green. I was a member of the Mark Smith Trial Jury and voted happily for the murderer's condemnation. I was pleased when he was sentenced to death and even more when he was executed. What do you want to know? My number is (he quoted a mobile number)."

There was no reply. This worried Philip, and he reviewed the possible suspects, concluding that the most likely was Luke Smith, the younger brother of Mark. He telephoned one of his henchmen and instructed him to make contact with Luke and keep him under surveillance. This man sat in the café when Jonathan met Luke. He watched, but did not hear the exchange, but noticed that a book passed

Fifty Years After

between the two men. He followed the visitor out of the café, but lost him. He rang Philip to make his report.

"I followed Luke Smith as you requested. He met a young man in a café. I think he was about 20. Luke passed an object, possibly a book, to him and the two engaged in a long conversation, before he left the café and got into a black limousine that looked like a Government car. I don't know where they went."

"I don't think that the youngster was the man we're looking for. However, I wonder what he was up to. Leave the finding of him to me. You should keep Luke under surveillance. We're looking for a white man aged between 70 and 90."

"All right, Boss."

Philip sat and pondered what he had learnt. Something was certainly going on and he was certain it involved that wretched murder trial from which he seemed never to be able to shake himself free. He noted the Government car and guessed its destination was likely to be Downing Street. "It's Marcus Greenway again," he thought. He decided to pay a surprise visit to Chequers, where he could speak with the Prime Minister in complete secrecy.

16. Jennifer Brown

February 12 2010
Jonathan recognised Jennifer as soon as he entered the café. She was seated, with her back to the wall, in the corner of the café, as far from the window as she could get. He smiled and waved to the neatly dressed, young looking, woman who had to be in her sixties. Her hair was blond. Jonathan realised that she dyed it. It was neatly combed into what would have passed for fashionable twenty years earlier. She was obviously waiting for him, as her eyes searched every man who entered the café. Jonathan stopped at the counter and ordered, paid for, and received a coffee and croissant, before crossing the floor of the café and joining the woman sitting in the corner over a long since emptied cup of coffee.

Jonathan reached the table, put his cup and plate down, placed the bag he was carrying on the floor, sat down and introduced himself to the woman.

"Hello. You must be Jennifer Brown. I'm Jonathan Greenway. I'm delighted to meet you and sorry to have kept you waiting. The trains were all over the place this morning. Would you like me to get you another coffee?"

Jennifer smiled at the earnest, neatly but casually dressed young man, who had thus addressed her.

"Hello Jonathan. I'm pleased you made it and of course I forgive you for being a bit late. I was actually late myself. You're right. I'm Jennifer, but no longer Brown. I'm Jennifer Foster – Mrs Jennifer Foster. I'm married with three children. All three are married with children of their own. So I'm a grandmother now. And yes, I would like another cup of coffee – but don't think you have to pay for it. I will give you the money."

She reached for her purse. Jonathan shook his head.

"No, Jennifer. I hope I can call you that."

She smiled.

"Of course you can, so long as I can call you Jonathan."

"That's fine then. But as for the coffee - it's my treat. I was late and kept you waiting. The least I can do is to buy you a drink!"

He returned with her coffee and they got down to business.

"You probably wonder why I contacted you?" Jonathan began, but she cut him short.

"No, Jonathan. I already know. You met Luke two days ago and he rang me after the meeting to reassure me that you genuinely want to help us get justice for Janet and Mark. Had he judged you otherwise, as he told you, I would have made an excuse not to meet you. We've been disappointed too many times over the last fifty years to bear to be disappointed again."

"I know you have, Jennifer, and I also know why. I can guarantee that it won't happen this time. We almost have enough to act as it is – but Albert thinks we need more. We both hope that you might be able to give us what we need to prise the case open."

A man, sitting at the next table, sat up sharply and laid down his paper momentarily to stare at the two of them before apparently resuming his crossword.

"What do you want to know? How can I help you, Jonathan? It was a long time ago. Surely there is no new evidence available that can assist us in a new trial, and I don't see that I have any that's relevant."

Jonathan smiled.

"My girlfriend is studying for a law degree. I'm on my way to see her after this meeting. I haven't seen her for over a month and she must be suspecting that I'm meeting other women!"

"And she would be right, wouldn't she, Jonathan? Because that's exactly what you're doing now!"

Jennifer smiled as she said this, and Jonathan was momentarily nonplussed. He did not know how to respond

Fifty Years After

truthfully without offending her. Jennifer laughed as she read his confused mind.

"You've a face like an open book, Jonathan," she said. "You're wondering how to tell me that you're not interested in that way in an old woman of 64 without offending me, aren't you?"

He nodded; relieved he was free of the need to reply to her sally.

"You should understand that only the young are concerned about age. When you reach a certain age, we no longer care. Indeed, some of us actually take pride that we've reached certain landmarks."

She paused, before continuing decisively.

"What were you going to tell me about your girlfriend? Does she have a name?"

"She's called Belinda."

"How old is she and is she nice?"

"She's 20 and very nice. Like me, she's in her second year at Uni. I've temporarily suspended my second year, and am intending to return to Cambridge next October. I'm reading IT incidentally."

"So are two of my grandsons," Jennifer commented. "One of them is at Cambridge. He's in his first year. I'll give you his name and college address so you can look him up when you return. I shall be relieved that a responsible young man is keeping an eye on him. The young can get so wild nowadays, especially when they're away from home for the first time."

Jonathan finished his croissant and sipped his coffee meditatively.

"Tell me about Janet. What sort of girl was she? Thank you for her photo, incidentally. I've studied it and believe I know a little about her. It's surprising what you can learn from a photo."

Jonathan remembered how he had opened the album when he got into the car outside the café two days before. The

Fifty Years After

first photo was of a smiling, petite and very pretty, dark haired girl. Her hair had what was then a fashionable wet look, and it was obvious that she took a lot of time over her appearance and her hair. She was neatly dressed in skirt and jumper and looked a very obvious 18. He remembered, too, the second photo – one of her and Mark together. Mark was slightly older than Janet, but then he knew that already. He was dressed in a suit and tie, and was very neatly turned out. He was clean-shaven and his hair was neatly maintained. They were holding hands and were obviously deeply in love. When he saw that photo, any doubts that Jonathan might have harboured about Mark's innocence were finally swept away. Mark could not have murdered Janet. At the worst the two of them might have had a suicide pact if their parents' opposition to their liaison had driven them to desperation. But, murder? "No way!" he had thought.

Jonathan returned to the present. Jennifer had noticed his sudden lack of attention.

"A penny for your thoughts," she said.

"I'm sorry. You must think me very rude. I was just thinking of the photographs I saw of Janet and of Janet and Mark together."

He bent down and retrieved an oblong parcel from his bag.

"I had the photo of the two of them enlarged and framed as a gift for you. I have one for Luke as well."

He gave the parcel to Jennifer, who smiled her thanks.

"There was really no need, Jonathan. What you are doing for us is thanks enough. But thank you."

She reached down for her bag and took a smaller package from it, replacing the package with the parcel that Jonathan had given her.

"Please take this in exchange. Don't open it here, but I think it may be what you're looking for. I'll explain in a minute."

Fifty Years After

Jonathan looked puzzled, but thanked her, accepted the parcel, and placed it in his bag, which he then zipped up, and moved to a more secure position under the table, between their legs. He noticed that Jennifer did the same.

"You know that Janet left school at 15, don't you," Jennifer began. "Most girls did in those days. She had no qualifications – but that didn't really matter. No one expected working class girls like us to stay on at school, take exams and go to University. We were expected to get a job, get married, have kids and get out from under our parents' feet as soon as possible. So, Janet went to work in a local dress shop. She enjoyed her job, and bought some nice clothes. She bought me a lovely red dress (red was always my favourite colour) that last Christmas. She was so happy – and she had her first boyfriend."

Jonathan saw a tear come in to Jennifer's eyes, and he gave her his handkerchief to wipe them.

"The first time I wore that dress was at her funeral," she explained. "Mum thought it was wrong of me to wear red and not black, but I said that Janet had bought it for me and she would want me to wear it in her honour."

"I understand, and I understand your Mother's position as well. How did she react to Mark?"

"She never met him. Janet knew that Mum and Dad would never accept him as a boyfriend or a husband because of..." she faltered and Jonathan finished her sentence.

"Because he was black."

"Yes, exactly. Apparently Mark's parents had similar feelings about Janet, because she was white. So the two used to meet secretly. I think that added to the thrill of it all for them."

"When did you first know about Janet and Mark?"

"It was on Christmas Eve. We shared a bedroom, and we always tried to catch our Mum or Dad out when he or she put our stockings on our bed. We never succeeded, but we kept each other awake by talking. She told me all about

Mark that night. She swore me to secrecy first and then told me how they met by accident on Bonfire Night."

"Did she tell you what he was like?"

"What do you mean?"

"Did she describe his appearance?"

"Oh, I thought you meant what he was like as a lover!"

"That, too, if you like."

"She said he was a little older than her, dark skinned. She avoided using the word 'black', and had a body to die for. He was very handsome, kind, and always dressed to kill. She loved him and she knew he loved her – but they hadn't had sex."

"Did she tell you where they met?"

"Oh yes – they met in the Park. Apparently they had found a secluded spot where the trees both hid them from sight and protected them from the weather. They used to meet after work. Mark worked in a printing company."

"When did they first make love?"

"On St. Valentine's day. After that they often made love together."

"Did Janet know that she was pregnant?"

Jennifer looked surprised.

"How do you know that? It was never mentioned in the trial."

Jonathan took both their empty cups and went to the counter to get another coffee for them both and a plate of assorted muffins. He returned to the table and placed them between them, together with several sugar packs. He sat down and picked up a muffin, put two lots of sugar in his cup, stirred it, and began to drink, before answering her question.

"Jennifer, you must just accept that I know. I cannot and must not, at this moment, tell you how I know – but do understand that I've seen conclusive proof that Janet was pregnant, and had been for about a month, when she was murdered."

Jennifer studied Jonathan's serious face, and nodded her understanding.

"You're right, Jonathan, both about the fact and the timing. She was planning to tell Mark the day she was killed. She had known for about a week and had persuaded Mark that they should run away together and get married and hope that we would all accept it as a fact when they returned."

"She was right about that, incidentally. Luke told me that Mark had bought the tickets and booked a room for them in Gretna so they could meet the residence qualifications."

Jennifer nodded.

"Luke did tell me, and that's why none of us, either we four kids, or our four parents, ever thought that Mark could have killed Janet – whatever the evidence appeared to say."

"Thank you, Jennifer. You've been very helpful. You've filled in most of the gaps for me. But there's one important one remaining."

"What's that?"

"Did Janet and Mark have a fight a day or two before she was killed?"

Jennifer looked shocked.

"Certainly not!" she answered. "Whoever gave you that idea?"

"I heard that she had received injuries to her face a day or two before the fatal incident. I wondered who could have inflicted them."

"I see," Jennifer said, suddenly looking almost furtive, and, Jonathan sensed, afraid.

"There are things that are not safe to mention in public, as you know, and, indeed, have already practised when I asked you how you knew about Janet's pregnancy. Just accept that I have good reasons to know that it wasn't Mark. I know who assaulted my sister and I know why he did it. I also know exactly what he did to her and what he said to her. You will too, I promise you, very soon."

Jennifer looked pointedly at the floor, and Jonathan suddenly understood. The answer that he wanted lay in the packet she had given him. He reached inside his pocket, found his wallet, and, ignoring Jennifer's sudden negative reaction as she thought he was offering to pay her for the information, took out a piece of paper and began to write. When he had finished, he slid the paper and pen over to her.

"Does the parcel contain something especially relevant and personal to Janet?"

Jennifer nodded and began to write a reply.

"She began to keep a diary after she met Mark. The first entry was Nov 5 1960 and the last the day before she died. That's what I've given you. It contains a detailed description of the assault on her."

She slid the paper back. Jonathan read it and put it in his wallet. He nodded to show he both understood and thanked her before opening his phone and ringing for a taxi to pick them up.

The two finished their coffees and muffins, put on their coats, picked up their bags and went outside to wait for their taxi. The other man followed them unobtrusively and overheard their last exchange before they got into their taxi.

"You seem to understand Mark and Janet, and you have no problems with the fact that they were different races," Jennifer observed.

"We live in different times, Jennifer. I count myself to be fortunate that it is so, because Belinda is black – just like Mark. We experience some hostility when we're together – especially from people, if you'll forgive the expression, of your age. However, most people, especially of our age, find it to be perfectly natural."

Fifty Years After

"So," Jennifer commented, "Mark and Janet, Jonathan and Belinda. It's strange how history repeats itself!"

"I hope it doesn't repeat itself exactly," Jonathan said with a shudder, crossing himself as he did so.

At that point the taxi arrived. Jonathan left the taxi at Euston and Jennifer refused to let him pay the fare, insisting that she was probably better able to pay than Jonathan was, and wanted to do so. Jennifer presented her cheek to Jonathan, who kissed her farewell, with the words, "Look after that photo and I'll see you in Court, probably in the autumn."

Meanwhile, the man who had watched them, made a phone call, as a result of which, he made his way to the underground and took a tube train to Westminster.

Fifty Years After

Part Two

Preparing the Case (February to April 2010)

What did he know and when did he know it?
(Watergate Senate Committee 1974)

Fifty Years After

17. Cambridge

February 12 2010
Jonathan arrived at Cambridge Railway Station at about the same time as the man, who had watched Jonathan's meeting with Jennifer so carefully, but also so unobtrusively, arrived at the Palace of Westminster, to be directed to Lord Stewart's office.

Philip greeted him with little ceremony.
"Well, Bert. What have you got to report?"
The man called Bert sat down, not waiting for Philip to invite him, and lit up a cigarette, also uninvited. Philip ignored the pointed rudeness because Bert was his best undercover operative. It was Bert who had tipped him off about the Young Gang's incursion into their territory. He waited for Bert to speak. Bert took his time, puffing a number of smoke rings into the office air. Finally, he spoke.
"I've been following the woman you asked me to shadow for a number of days. She does very little out of the ordinary. Since I've monitored her movements, her outdoor activities seem to consist of the occasional church function, accompanying her husband to the bowling green, and acting as an unpaid nanny for her grandchildren."
Bert paused for effect.
"At least they did until today."
Philip, who had looked bored, suddenly became alert.
"What happened today?"
"She walked to a rather swish café in Knightsbridge, where she lives with her husband, and ordered a coffee and sat drinking it slowly."
"Are you saying she was waiting for someone?"
"Yes, and, eventually, he came. He apologised for being late."
"Who is he?"

"He's a university student from Cambridge. In his early 20s. He's studying IT, He's on leave from his course for some reason. He has a black girlfriend, also at Cambridge, but studying law."

"Do they have names?"

"His name is Jonathan Greenway."

Despite himself, Philip reacted in a startled way to this statement.

"Did you say Greenway?"

"Yes, Boss."

"You're sure of this?"

"Absolutely, Boss."

"You couldn't have misheard?"

"No chance, Boss."

"I see," Philip mused. "Did you catch the girlfriend's name?"

"Just her Christian name – Belinda."

"So he's having a relationship with a black law student at Cambridge University called Belinda. She shouldn't be hard to find. He should be fairly easy to track down as well."

"No problem if that's what you want me to do, Boss."

"One thing at a time, Bert. What did Jonathan and Jennifer Brown talk about?"

"Her name's Foster, Boss. She's married with three children and a number of grandchildren."

"Fine," Philip commented. "What did they talk about?"

"The Mark Smith Trial."

"Why?" Philip asked. He felt alarmed for the first time as his previously vague fears of danger began to assume a very definite shape and name.

"Jonathan Greenway is working with the two families and others to force a retrial. He was looking for information which would unlock the case."

"And has he got any?" Philip asked.

He hoped that the secure lock his father and the father of Marcus had put on the Court papers had not been breached.

"I don't know, Boss – but he did surprise Jennifer."

"How?"

"He knew that Janet was pregnant. Jennifer thought that she was the only other person who knew and asked him how he knew about it."

"What did he say?"

"He told her he could not tell her his source but his information was certain."

"I see," Philip said.

"The clever sod!" he thought. "This Greenway needs some watching and perhaps teaching a lesson about the dangers of crossing the Stewarts."

Philip resumed his questioning.

"Did this Jonathan get what he wanted?"

"Most of it. She gave him a detailed account of the relationship between Mark and Janet and told him that the two were planning to elope. Mark told him that he already knew and had definite evidence that that's what the two planned."

"Damn!" Philip said to himself. "Why didn't I search his clothes when he was out for the count?"

"Is that all?" Philip asked.

"No, there was one thing more – but I don't know the full account of it, because they stopped talking and the last bit was written down."

"What did he ask?"

"Whether Mark had had a fight with Janet a day or two before he killed her?"

"Is that the way he asked?" said Philip, feeling a sudden surge of relief.

"No, Boss. Those were my words. He said 'before she was killed'."

This was bad, Philip thought, very bad.

"Did anything change hands?"

"Yes, Boss. They gave each other a package. He told her that he had given her a framed enlarged photo of the couple and she gave him an unidentified book sized and shaped package and told him to be careful how he opened it."

"I bet that was a diary of some sort," Philip thought with growing concern.

"Was that the end of the conversation?"

"Yes. They left together in a taxi. She said that the relationship between him and his girlfriend was a mirror image of that between Mark and Janet, and that history was repeating itself. Jonathan said he hoped it wouldn't repeat itself exactly."

"You've just spoken your own fate and that of your girlfriend," Philip thought.

Philip smiled thinly at his agent.

"Thank you, Bert. That was a very succinct report; much better than most of the reports I received from civil servants when I was a minister."

"What do you want me to do now, Boss?"

"Two things:
1. I want to know exactly who this Jonathan Greenway is and what his relationship is with the Greenway Clan.
2. I want to know the full name and whereabouts of this Belinda girl and her pattern of movements."

"What are you planning, Boss?"

"Let's say that I agree with Jennifer Foster. I think history should repeat itself, especially if that young fool cannot be persuaded to cease meddling in our affairs."

"Cherchez la Femme, eh?" said Bert, who prided himself on his general knowledge. "So I'm off to University – and not <u>any</u> old University – Cambridge! I am going up in the World!"

"Don't be stupid!" snapped Philip. "Keep a low profile. Book into one of the Cambridge hotels and snoop around until you've got the information I need. Then come back here and report to me."

Fifty Years After

"OK, Boss. It looks like we're going to have a bit of excitement soon."

He turned to go.

"One final thing before you go, Bert."

"Yes, Boss?"

"You said this Jonathan Greenway was in his low 20s. How was he physically?"

Bert searched his mind, recalling the image he had of the young man.

"He was very fit. I think he plays sport, Boss, and possibly lifts weights. I wouldn't want to tackle him. Also, he seemed very confident and I would suggest, very determined."

"I see," Philip mused. "I must find a way to meet him."

He turned to Bert.

"You said that he had suspended his course?"

"Yes, Boss."

"That means he's not staying at the University. Try to find out where he's staying."

"Yes, Boss. So – you want to know who Jonathan Greenway is, whether he's related to Sir Marcus Greenway and you want to know where he's currently staying. You want to know his girlfriend's full name and what her regular movements are. Is that right?"

"Yes, Bert. And I think I need that information urgently." Philip paused as another thought struck him.

"He called a taxi. Did he say where he was going?"

"He's gone to Cambridge to see his girlfriend. He told Jennifer that when they first met and he told the taxi driver to take him to Euston and Jennifer to her home. Do you want me to return to shadow Jennifer afterwards, Boss?"

"No, Bert. If you can locate this Jonathan character, it would be better if you shadowed him."

Bert acknowledged the instructions, and left Philip's office, to head home, pack an overnight bag, and set out to catch a train to Cambridge.

Fifty Years After

Jonathan, meanwhile, was walking through the busy streets of Cambridge towards Belinda's college, which was, like most of the Cambridge Colleges, on the outskirts of the city. It took him about forty-five minutes, since he was not in a hurry, and he needed time to absorb fully what he had read in Janet's diary. He thought he now had the full story – or at least the full story of the murder. He knew who the murderer was and why the murder had been committed. He knew (and had evidence) how the Jury had been corrupted and also knew how the evidence had been doctored. He knew what Mark and Janet intended to do had they lived and why Mark made no attempt at defending himself. He was also aware of the true nature, methods and the extent of the danger to himself (and, by extension, to Belinda) that the murderer presented. He determined that he would persuade Belinda to accompany him back to Chequers for her own safety until the murderer was arrested.

He had reached this point when he turned into the grounds of Belinda's college and walked up to the second floor, where she had her study bedroom. He knocked confidently on her door, and fell into the outstretched arms of a joyful and surprised Belinda when the door opened. It was some time before he could speak to her, since, as he had told Jennifer earlier, they had not met since before Christmas, and they had a lot of loving to make up. Later, lying naked together, in Belinda's bed, they started to talk.

"I tried to phone you this morning," she said accusingly. "I needed your help, but you didn't reply. Who were you with? I hope it wasn't another woman!"

"It was, actually," he replied, waiting for her to hit him.

She didn't hit him, but she did glare at him accusingly.

"Did she keep her clothes on?" she asked.

"Of yes," I assure you, Darling. We were both fully clothed all the time. We were also totally in the public."

"So, it was a first date, then?"

Fifty Years After

Jonathan wondered how long to continue to tease her before she threw him out of her room and threw his clothes after him. He decided not to risk it.

"It was a sort of first date, Darling – but not what you are imagining. For a start – she was over 60 and it was a business meeting; not a romantic one."

She did slap him then.

"I don't know why I love you, Darling. You're always teasing me. One day I will throw you out of my room naked and lock the door after you."

"And keep my clothes?" Jonathan asked.

"Oh no – I'll throw them out of the window and then all the girls can admire you as you go out to collect them and put them on. With any luck the Janitor will pick them up before you can get down there and you will have to walk back to your college dressed in someone's academic gown only!"

"You wouldn't dare, Darling," Jonathan said, laughing.

"Try me, Darling," Belinda replied, also laughing.

"What did you?" they both began together, and then both stopped.

"Ladies first," Jonathan said.

"What did you talk about?" Belinda asked.

"You know I'm working for Lord Corrigan to try to get evidence to reopen the Smith Trial?"

"Yes, Darling."

"Well, I've met an old man who was a member of the trial jury, who gave me two sealed brown envelopes containing money; the brother of Mark Smith, who gave me an album of photos of Janet, Mark and their families, together with two return tickets to Gretna Green and a booking for two for a room in Gretna Green; and today, I met the sister of Janet Brown, who gave me Janet's diary."

Belinda giggled.

"I think I should throw your clothes out of the window for allowing me to think that you had been with another girl."

"I could always lock you out of your room, you know, Darling. You're naked too, you know!"

"It's a girls' college, Darling. Naked girls don't get noticed as much as naked boys; at least, not by most of us!"

They both laughed before Jonathan became very serious.

"Enough of the joking. I'm sleeping here with you tonight. So can you go down and book me into dinner?"

Belinda looked startled and began to get dressed.

"That's very forward of you! How do you know I want to share my bed with you tonight? I've got an important seminar tomorrow."

She left the room, closing the door firmly. Jonathan heard her footsteps walking away down the corridor and dressed himself. Once dressed, he read Janet's final diary entry for the second time. There was no mistaking its import, he thought.

At that moment, the door opened, and Belinda returned. She looked disappointed to see that Jonathan was now fully clothed.

"Since you have invited yourself to stay the night, I expected you to be ready to rip my clothes off and make mad, passionate love to me again," she complained.

"We'll do that tonight, Darling," Jonathan promised. "It will be a sleepover with a difference – no sleep, but little talking either. Only action – and lots of it!"

"Promises, promises," Belinda grumbled. "Still," she added brightly, "If you manage even part of that agenda it will be an interesting night!"

They both laughed.

"How about some coffee?" Jonathan asked. "You know me – lovemaking; then coffee drinking; then work!"

"Yes, oh great Lord and Master; your humble and obedient slave humbly and obediently meets your every desire," she laughed, as she switched her kettle on and washed up a couple of mugs.

Later, as Jonathan promised, after coffee, they turned to work.

"You said you rang me because you wanted help. What with, Darling?"

"I have to present a seminar paper and I wanted your help in writing it."

"I'm not a lawyer, Darling," Jonathan pointed out. "My comments would be based on common sense, not a knowledge of the law."

"I think you could help me with this seminar, Darling," Belinda answered. "The title is 'An analysis of a past trial and a discussion of the issues it raises.' I'm planning to discuss the Mark Smith trial, since it involves your family directly, and I know you've been researching it."

"That may be more complicated than you realise, Darling. I will explain it all to you later, but probably, in view of what you've just told me, after the seminar."

"So you can't help me then?"

"I didn't say that, Darling. But I will have to be very careful what I tell you and what you tell them. One foolish word and the whole effort to get the case reopened and the real murderer brought to justice could be jeopardised and both you and I could be in real danger."

Jonathan paused, before adding in a grave tone.

"I think, he said, "that we're both already in grave danger. That's why I've come here. I'm taking you away after your seminar to a place of safety for a while, until the murderer is under lock and key. I've got the tickets already. You're coming with me down to Buckinghamshire, but you must not let anyone know."

"I can't just run away. The University will send me down."

"No they won't, because Lord Corrigan or Sir Marcus Greenway (or both) will inform the University that you are required in London for a while on a matter of real national emergency. That's how I got my course suspended until next year. We will do the same with yours. And you'll be involved in a historic trial!"

"I will have to pack my stuff. Otherwise, I'll be running around the house in Buckinghamshire stark naked!"

"Jonathan grinned.

"I would enjoy that, Darling. However, it doesn't quite fit the dress code of the house where you're going to stay!"

She slapped his face again and grinned at him.

"All right," she said. "Read my paper, while I pack a suitcase."

She handed Jonathan two sheets of word processed A4, and bustled about packing her clothes, while Jonathan sat down to read what she had written.

It proved to be a brief, but accurate, account of the trial. However, it ended with the words: "Why is this trial important?"

"It's not finished," Jonathan commented.

"I know. That's why I was trying to ring you. It seems a simple case. It lasted less than 6 hours. Mark Smith offered no defence and Albert Corrigan was left scraping the barrel in his attempt to save him."

"You will understand exactly what was going on when I tell you the true, hidden story. However, I can suggest a number of issues for you, from the transcript of the trial, which you have admirably summarised."

"What are they, Darling," Belinda asked eagerly, her pen in her hand ready to make notes.

"I will list them for you, Darling," Jonathan answered. "First, why did the jury not understand the significance of the fact that the gun was in the wrong hand? Second, even on the basis of Philip Stewart's evidence, Mark did not intend to kill Janet. So why wasn't the charge manslaughter? Third, why were the judge, the appeal court and the Home Secretary apparently anxious to hang a man who was technically still a child? Fourth, had Mark been

Fifty Years After

white and Janet been black, would the result have been different? Fifth, why didn't Mark testify in his own defence and why didn't Albert put him in the witness box. Finally, consider this statement of Lord Corrigan's – 'The Jury were hostile to Mark from the first. It was clear to me that Sir Walter would tear him apart under cross-examination. He was famous for it. I knew I couldn't save his life, but I could, at least, leave him a little dignity.' That should be enough to keep your fellow students happy."

Belinda smiled and leaning over, kissed him.

"Thank you, Darling. I knew I could rely on you. You can go back to your book and I will finish this before we go down to dinner. Then, after coffee you can rip all my clothes off and have your wicked way with me!"

"Is that a promise, Darling?"

"That's a promise, Darling."

"Then I will take you up on it, Darling!"

"Good – I can't wait. By the way, what's the book, Darling?"

"It's Janet Brown's Diary from November 5th 1960 to April 25th, 1961."

Belinda looked surprised, but realised that she should say nothing, as she returned to her laptop and began typing.

Jonathan watched her type, occasionally making life difficult for her by nuzzling her neck or stroking her back under her blouse. She told him off gently, but actually enjoyed his being there too much to complain about what in other circumstances she would have called sexual harassment. Later they had dinner in the college refectory, followed by coffee in Belinda's room. Then Jonathan kept his promise in full, and Belinda did not complain any more.

18. Return to Buckinghamshire

February 13/14 2010

Next morning, Belinda brought breakfast up for Jonathan. Breakfast, in this case, consisted of two pieces of cold toast and a cold hard-boiled egg, which he supplemented with a cup of coffee. They left the college at 10 am, and took a taxi to the station, where they left their luggage in a left luggage locker, before returning to the City Centre and the University Law department for Belinda's midday seminar. Bert left his home at 10 am and made his way to Euston Station, aiming to catch a train to Cambridge at about midday. As Bert entered his train, so Belinda and Jonathan entered the seminar room.

Belinda introduced Jonathan to her tutor, explaining who he was and why he was there.

"Interesting," the tutor commented. "Will you tell us how far you've got?"

Jonathan smiled.

"If I were you and you were me, and I asked you that question, sir, how would you answer?"

"I would say, 'no', because any information I gave here could leak out and prejudice my chances."

"That's exactly my position, sir. However, irregular though it is, I would like to chair this session as a sort of facilitator of a tribunal trying to find evidence to establish a new trial."

The tutor sat back and smiled. He could sit back and relax for once, with someone else taking the strain.

"Fine by me," he said.

The students arrived in dribs and drabs as usual. Belinda expressed some annoyance at this and had to be calmed down by Jonathan. When they were all present the tutor opened the session, introducing Jonathan and explaining what he was doing. Belinda read her paper and a long

Fifty Years After

discussion followed. At the end Jonathan warned the students to keep silent about what they had heard. After the students had left the tutor congratulated Jonathan and Belinda and expressed the hope that the visit had been useful.

Jonathan smiled.

"Only insofar as they confirmed what I've already done," Jonathan admitted.

"Well, confirmation is always a good thing," the tutor concluded. "Well done Miss Thompson. I'll look forward to your next essay."

"I'm afraid that won't be for a long time, Sir. Belinda is suspending her course until next year for her own safety and security and that of those around her until after the actual murderer and his followers are all safely behind bars awaiting trial. This is the last you're going to see of her until October."

"Well, take care, young Belinda. I shall follow your story with interest and look forward to a first-hand account when you return."

They all shook hands, and both left the building, hailing a taxi, and travelling to the station in time to catch a London train at about 1.30. Settling into the taxi, they buckled their seat belts, and sat back as the taxi drew away from the kerb for the short trip to the station. Belinda expressed her disappointment at Jonathan's choice of transportation.

"I thought, oh Great Lord and Master, that you were going to ride away with me on the back of your horse!"

Jonathan grinned as he thought of an appropriate answer.

"The horse looked at the extra weight involved. He decided he didn't like the idea, and pretended to be lame."

Belinda leaned forward and slapped him gently across the face.

The driver heard the exchange with a grin and saw Belinda slap Jonathan in his mirror.

Fifty Years After

"Behave yourselves, you two," he said in mock severity. "I can't have fighting in the back of the taxi!"

Belinda took him seriously.

"Don't worry, driver," she said. "It's a standing joke between us. Jonathan teases me about my weight and I slap him. Afterwards we kiss and make up."

The driver looked back and grinned at them.

"I thought it was it was something like that, Miss," he said. "You let him get off too lightly though. When you get him home you should pull his trousers down and smack his bottom."

"He would like that," Belinda said ruefully. "Do you think I'm fat, driver?"

"Not at all, Miss," the driver said diplomatically. "I don't like thin girls, like the models, all skin and bone. It's not healthy."

"You see, Darling," she said triumphantly. "The driver agrees with me. I'm not fat!"

"I love you just the way you are, Darling," Jonathan replied. "However, I'll stick a cushion inside my trousers when we get home just in case!"

All three laughed at this as the taxi turned left into the road that leads to Cambridge Railway Station, passing Bert as he walked around the corner in the other direction, unseen by the couple in the taxi.

Two minutes later the taxi drew up outside the main entrance of the station and Jonathan and Belinda got out. Jonathan paid the driver and spoke earnestly to him before they left him.

"Thank you for an enjoyable ride, driver. It's a pity I don't know your name."

The driver took a card from his pocket and gave it to Jonathan.

"The name's Bob, sir, Bob Walker. That's my card. Next time you're coming to Cambridge give me a ring. I'll collect you from the station."

Jonathan put the card in his pocket.

Fifty Years After

"My name's Jonathan Greenway."

The driver looked surprised at this.

"You're not related to…"

"The Prime Minister, Yes."

Jonathan completed his sentence for him.

"This is Belinda, my girlfriend. We're students at the University."

"I thought you were," Bob said.

"You may be asked by someone – probably a man, although it could be a woman, about us. He or she will probably pretend to be a police officer. He or she won't be – but pretend to be taken in. Tell him or her our names and tell him or her that we asked you what was the easiest way to get a train from here to Glasgow."

Bob was surprised.

"Why Glasgow?"

"It's in Scotland."

"I know that, Jonathan – but why are you going there? I would go to Edinburgh if I wanted a romantic weekend with my girlfriend."

"You can get a local train from Glasgow to Gretna Green."

Bob laughed.

"So you're pretending to elope are you? Surely that's old hat?"

"It is," Jonathan agreed, "but the people I suspect are interested are old fashioned enough to believe that if a white boy wants to marry a black girl that's what they must do! So they'll believe it."

Jonathan gave Bob a £10 note as a tip, which Bob pocketed with a smile of gratitude.

"Don't worry, Son. By the time I've finished with them, they'll probably be booking a round trip to the North Pole!"

"Thank you, Bob," Belinda said. "And thank you for the advice. I'm going to try it tonight!" she added with a grin.

Fifty Years After

"You do that, Miss," Bob said grinning through the car window as he pulled away.

The two entered the station, collected their luggage, and went onto the platform where the London train was due in ten minutes. The platform was relatively crowded and all the seats were taken, so they stood, leaning against the wall of the station building, with their bags around their feet, talking idly until the train arrived.

Bert, meanwhile, made his way from the station into the town. He saw the taxi carrying Jonathan and Belinda pass him at the corner of Station Road and the main road into the city. He vaguely noticed that there were two young people in the back, but took no notice. There were a lot of young people in Cambridge by definition. He felt he had plenty of time and it was a relatively pleasant day. The wind was little more than a breeze and the sun was shining – although there was little heat even out of the shade. Eventually, he found a hotel near the city centre, checked in, unpacked his bag, and went down to the restaurant for lunch. "What's the point of stinting yourself when you know the boss will pay?" he thought. Having eaten lunch, Bert walked around the city centre, looking at the shops and picking up a map from the Information Office. In the evening he returned to his hotel, had a drink in the bar, ate dinner, and went to his room, to plan how he would set out to locate Belinda and Jonathan Greenway on the following day.

Bert's two targets boarded the train for London, entering a First Class carriage and taking their seats, having first placed their luggage in the racks above their heads. They were alone, as Jonathan intended.

"You Greenways do enjoy your comforts," Belinda observed. "I'm a Greenford girl. I never thought I would travel First Class!"

Fifty Years After

Jonathan's tone was sombre as opposed to Belinda's lightness.

"It's not about comfort, Darling," he said. "It's about secrecy and security. I guessed we would be alone and I needed to talk to you about this case."

Belinda nodded.

"I know, Darling," she said. "Just ignore my sense of humour."

Jonathan kissed her and then began to speak.

"I want you to imagine, Darling, that our ethnicities are reversed. You're a white girl and I'm a black boy. You're 18 and walking in the Park alone. I'm older than you, armed with a gun, and stalking you with the aim of raping you. What would I wear?"

Belinda thought about this before answering.

"I've never met an intended rapist, so I don't know the uniform! However, I guess you would wear trousers and some sort of pullover. Possibly the pullover would be over a T Shirt."

"OK – where would I keep the gun?"

"In your trouser pocket. Remember the famous film line – 'Is that a gun in your pocket or are you pleased to see me?'"

They both laughed.

"You're right, of course, Darling. However, suppose I'm wearing a suit and tie, where would I put the gun?"

"Definitely in a jacket pocket, probably on the side of the hand which you would use to fire it."

"All right so far. We've got to a secluded point under trees. That's where I'm going to strip you naked and rape you. What do I do with your clothes?"

"You would rip them off me, possibly damaging them and throw them onto the ground."

"What about my own?"

"I doubt that you would strip off entirely. You wouldn't have time. I think you'd simply take down your trousers and pants and, if you are wearing a suit, your jacket as well, and throw them on top of my clothes."

"I agree. Now listen to what P C Adams found at the scene of the crime. First he met Janet and Mark earlier on, walking hand in hand, and spoke to them. He made no mention of seeing any suspicious bulges in Mark's suit. In those days he would certainly not have hesitated in searching Mark (a black man) if he had any reason to suspect he might be carrying a weapon. Next, both Janet and Mark were completely naked when he found them later. Finally, all their clothes were neatly folded and piled up, including Mark's tie. What do you make of it now?"

"Janet and Mark took their clothes off themselves, unhurriedly, and Janet was the one who folded them and placed them in a neat pile. They were having consensual sex."

"And the gun?"

"Mark did not have a gun."

"Had Janet been raped by Mark, would there not have been evidence of the rape on her vagina or the area around it?"

"Not necessarily, Jonathan. However, there can be signs of bruising where the victim was forced. There may be other signs of a struggle as well."

"There was no evidence of physical damage to Janet's body apart from the entry points of the two bullets which killed her and some bruising on her face and behind from an earlier assault."

"It links in with the other facts, Jonathan. Janet was not raped."

"What about the earlier bruising?"

"It's probably not related – but would require proper investigation."

"Finally, had Mark been tied up, would there have been evidence of it?"

"Certainly. The bonds, even with a soft material like a tie, would have left bruising on the wrists, especially if the binding was of recent origin."

"There was no reference to evidence of binding in the Pathologist's report."

Fifty Years After

Belinda was confused.

"I've read the same transcripts that you've read. I don't recall seeing the evidence you've just described. Where does it come from?"

"It came from the original arresting officer's report and pathologist's report. The pathologist also reported that Janet was in the early stages of pregnancy. But these parts of the report were excised on the orders of D I Buchan."

"My God," Belinda breathed. "Can you prove this?"

"Yes."

"How?"

"I've seen a copy of the original police file."

"Why don't you present it to the Court of Appeal?"

"Because it is closed until 2061."

"That's unusual isn't it?" Belinda asked.

"Very unusual. It was closed by order of the Home Secretary."

"The same Home Secretary who rejected Mark's appeal for clemency?"

"Yes."

"What have you done with the file?"

"Lord Corrigan has it in his safe."

"I think that's very wise."

"Together with evidence that links Philip Stewart with organised crime and establishes that he is probably the leader of the Stewart Gang that's still operating in North London. D I Buchan was on their payroll."

Belinda looked very grave.

"It seems as though Mark Smith was the patsy for Philip's crime. But why would Philip murder Janet? That's the question you asked the Seminar. What's your answer?"

"Racism," Jonathan answered.

"Can you prove it?"

"Yes – I've got the proof with me and I will let you read it on the trip out from Paddington."

"Where are we going to, Jonathan?"

Fifty Years After

"Dalton. That reminds me, I've got to make a call. Let me do it now and you need to ring one of your law class friends, the gabbiest, and tell her to mislead any questioner as to our whereabouts. We've gone to Gretna Green to get married."

"OK. I'll do that."

Jonathan made a brief phone call to Chequers.

"Jenkins," he said, "It's Jonathan Greenway. I'm on my way back from Cambridge with my girlfriend, Belinda Thompson. Could you ask Hawkins to take a car and meet us at Dalton Railway Station at about 3.30? I'm not sure what time the train arrives. We're travelling from Paddington. He knows my mobile number, and he should ring me to confirm the time."

Belinda heard a faint acknowledgement as she waited for her friend to answer. Jonathan put his phone away as hers came to life.

"Hi Carole," Belinda said. "It's Belinda. I'm phoning to ask you to do something for me. I'm leaving College for a while. Jonathan's grandfather has asked me to suspend my course until next autumn. Could you go to my room? I left it unlocked. Remove all the things I've left there and look after them for me. Use the coffee and biscuits, etc."

"Of course, Belinda. Don't worry."

"One other thing. Someone may come snooping around asking about Jonathan and me. Tell them that we've gone to get married in Gretna Green and that we're going on a tour of the Highlands and Islands of Scotland afterwards before breaking the news to our relatives. It may be our only chance. We may be poor as church mice after Jonathan's Mum and Dad find out he's married a black girl."

"Don't worry, Belinda. I'm cool about that. But you're not really in trouble are you?"

"No comment," Belinda replied. "But, if by being 'in trouble' you're asking am I pregnant, the answer is no."

Fifty Years After

"That's cool," Carole commented. Don't worry, Belinda. I'll cover your backs. It's a pity we can't do the kidnap though!"

"If someone does talk to you about us, tell him or her about the plan, and see what the reaction is. I'll phone you again in a day or two. Bye."

"What kidnap plan are you talking about?" Jonathan asked.

"I was supposed to invite you up for the Rag Ball in two weeks' time. Once you were in my room, the other girls were going to rush in, overpower you, strip you, tie you up, and hold you for ransom."

"Cool!" Jonathan muttered. "I would have enjoyed that! Were you part of the plot?"

"Of course, Darling. I suggested it!"

"Well, you'll have to do it next year – but, of course, you'll lose the advantage of surprise."

"I'll arrange it when the time comes, but it will not be at the Rag Ball, because you will be prepared for it then."

They both laughed.

They looked up as a conductor came up to them to check their tickets. Satisfied, he wished them a comfortable journey, and moved on. Jonathan turned back to the trial.

"After showing the files to Albert and leaving them with him, I spoke with one of the original members of the jury. He was probably the last of them still alive. He doesn't have long to live and he wanted to get things off his chest."

"What did he say?"

"He presented me with three envelopes. One was a sworn affidavit, which he had drawn up for Lord Corrigan and me. The other two were envelopes he was given at the trial. He had never opened them, but he knew they contained two payments of £50 and an instruction to elect a particular person foreman and find Mark guilty. I understand that the named individual was a member of the

Stewart Gang and that two other jurors returned the money with a protest about what had happened. Both died in 'accidents' shortly after doing so."

"That's jury rigging, and enough in itself to annul the verdict," Belinda observed. "Does Lord Corrigan know about it?"

"Not yet. He's coming down to join us for a conference at the weekend. That's when I intend to update him on the jury fixing and the outcome of my interviews with Luke and Jennifer."

"What did you learn from them?"

Jonathan explained what had happened during his meetings with Luke and Jennifer.

Belinda sat silently absorbing the information that Mark had given her and comparing it with what she had read that morning and the discussion that had followed her reading. Jonathan let her think undisturbed, watching the flat Cambridgeshire countryside roll past the train. She remained silent for nearly half an hour before she spoke again.

"Jonathan," she asked. "Have you spoken to your Grandparents about this?"

"Yes, Darling," he replied. "Sir Marcus authorised me to see if I could find new evidence to justify a petition to set aside the verdict."

"What about Lady Evelyn?"

"She has seen the police files."

"What did she and Lord Corrigan say?"

"Both agreed with me. There has been a massive injustice here and a murderer is still at large unpunished. We have a duty to bring this, somehow, to the notice of the court, whatever the personal cost."

"What do you mean, Jonathan?"

Belinda always called him Jonathan when she was being especially serious.

"We all three think that Sir Marcus knows a lot more about this case than he is prepared to admit. We also think

Fifty Years After

that Sir Walter knew more of the truth as well and that, between them, they've managed to block any attempt at reopening the case for some reason. Sir Walter began it and continued it until his death and Sir Marcus has continued it since then. If that's true, and Lord Stewart is the murderer as we all think, the resulting trial could destroy Sir Marcus as well as Lord Stewart."

"And Lady Evelyn agrees with this decision, despite the potential cost?"

"She does, Belinda. She told me that we have no choice and that Sir Marcus will have to take whatever comes as a consequence."

"Your Grandmother's a brave woman, Darling. I don't think I could do the same if you were in that position. I'd like to think I could – but I'm sure I couldn't. I'm looking forward to meeting her."

"Both of them will love you, Darling. I'm not sure of my father's attitude though. I don't get on well with him, and neither does my Grandfather. The rest of the family will be fine though. We should announce our engagement before we return to college in October."

This surprised Belinda.

"Hold on, Darling. Haven't you forgotten something?"

"What, Darling?"

"Aren't you supposed to ask me if I'm prepared to marry you first, before announcing our engagement? I might say, 'no' after all, Darling."

Jonathan looked contrite.

"I'm sorry, Darling. Of course you're right."

He left his seat and knelt in front of her.

"Will you forgive me and will you marry me?"

"Of course I'll forgive you, after I've followed Bob's advice and smacked your bum tonight because of your presumption. And, yes, I'll marry you – although I'm not sure you deserve to have me."

Jonathan smiled, stood up and, taking her in his arms, kissed her.

Fifty Years After

They did not resume their conversation until after they arrived at Euston Station. They were much too busy doing other things to talk. On the underground between Euston and Paddington, it was simply too crowded and too noisy for them to talk. As a result, it was only when they were seated on the train from Paddington, again in First Class, that the conversation continued after Jonathan had rung through to confirm their expected arrival time at Dalton. Having done this, he took down his bag, and extracted a small manuscript book from it. He handed the book to Belinda.

"This is your reading material for this part of our journey. You are the first person, other than Jennifer and me to read this."

Belinda nodded, opened the book, and began to read it. Jonathan watched her, spotting the changes of emotion in her face as she read Janet's words and Mark's letters to her, which she had clipped into her diary. She took the photograph of the couple out and kept it in her sight as she read. At one point she looked up.

"Her writing was very neat and you can see she was very young – but you can also see from the dairy, the photo, and the letters that they were very much in love. It's terrible reading this knowing what happened to the two of them and that Mark was accused, found guilty, and hanged for her murder. He would have no more murdered her than I would murder you!"

Jonathan nodded.

"That's what I thought too. I also thought how lucky we are that we don't have the problems they had because of their relationship."

Belinda nodded and returned to her reading.

She reached the end of the diary shortly before the train arrived at Dalton. When she handed the book back to Jonathan, he saw there were tears in her eyes as well as a flash of anger.

Fifty Years After

"Knowing this, Jonathan Darling, how were you able to be so restrained in the Seminar this morning?"

The train began slowing down and the tannoy announced that they were approaching Dalton. Jonathan took down their bags from the luggage rack.

"It was simple, Darling. I could not afford to mention what I knew and the diary just has to remain a secret. It is our ultimate weapon. However, I think it removes all possible doubt as to the real murderer and also provides a motive for him."

They both stood up as the train halted. Jonathan opened the door and lifted out the bags. He looked around to see if anyone was following them, but there was no evidence of pursuit. Sighing with relief, he found a luggage trolley, placed the bags on it, and escorted Belinda to the barrier, handing their tickets to the official on duty as they passed. Outside of the station Belinda saw a large black limousine waiting for them. Jonathan walked up to it and the driver came to meet him.

"Thank you, Hawkins," Jonathan said, as the driver took their bags and placed them in the boot of the car before opening the rear passenger side door and helping them in.

"I'm glad you got here safely, sir, and I'm pleased to meet you, Miss."

"My name's Belinda," she responded. "What should I call you?"

"Everyone calls me Hawkins, Miss."

"Thank you, Hawkins," she said. "Where are we going?"

"Where going to Chequers, the Prime Minister's country residence, Miss. That's where Jonathan has been staying since Christmas. I gather you're going to stay here too. So I'll be your driver whenever you want to go out."

Belinda turned to Jonathan.

"Why didn't you tell me?" she asked. "Now I understand your comment about the dress code!"

"I didn't want the secret to leak out even accidentally. I've brought you here because your life may be in danger."

"That sounds very dramatic, Darling," Belinda responded. "Are you sure you're not exaggerating?"

"I've not exaggerated anything. The Stewart Gang are involved in every type of crime. The number of dead victims is very lengthy. Philip Stewart is almost certainly their leader, since his father and one of his brothers are both dead and the other brother is living in Spain. He'll probably know about me by now and he'll certainly know about you very shortly after he's identified me. Once he's done that you would be a soft target living in Cambridge and going out to lectures daily. Kidnapping you would be a doddle. He would then use you to shut me up and he may finally decide to kill you. At Chequers we are both completely safe. I suspect that Philip Stewart will soon discover where we are living. But it won't help him, even if he does – because here we can get the entire British Army to protect us if necessary."

Belinda was satisfied by this response and sat quietly, watching the countryside pass them until they entered the gates of the Chequers Estate and safety. Hawkins halted the car outside the door of the great house. A chambermaid collected their baggage and took it to their room where Belinda was surprised to discover that the Chambermaid unpacked her bags and put her clothes away in the wardrobe and chest of drawers.

Jonathan took her out for a walk in the grounds, safe behind the outer walls that divided them from the outside world. Belinda was surprised how empty the house was.

"Where is everyone?" She asked. "Are we alone here?"

"Grandmother and Grandfather will be back tomorrow afternoon."

"When is Lord Corrigan arriving?"

"He and the Attorney General are coming for lunch on Sunday, after which we are all going to have a case conference and I'll reveal the evidence we have collected."

After their walk, they returned to the house and went to their room where they relaxed, watching television and enjoying the comfort of safety. Following dinner, they returned to their room and Belinda carried out her threat to "punish" Jonathan for his teasing of her that she had made that afternoon in the taxi, before the two retired to bed and somewhat more conventional sexual activity. Eventually they slept. At about the same time, back in Cambridge, Bert switched off the light in his room and retired to bed. He knew he had a busy day ahead of him.

19. Decisions

February 15/16 2010

Next morning, in Cambridge, Bert got up early, bathed, dressed, had breakfast and went out into the city, looking for the University's Law Department. He found the fact that the University's departments were scattered across the city rather confusing, but, after a couple of hours and asking several different people for directions, he found the building and entered it. A student challenged him and he introduced himself.

"I'm Detective Sergeant Mulgrave, Cambridgeshire CID, and I'm looking for a student named Belinda."

"She's not here this morning," the student, a young man, said, but I can get you someone who knows her well if you'll wait here."

Bert agreed and, ten minutes later, Carole came down into the entrance hall. She walked up to him and introduced herself.

"Sergeant Mulgrave, I'm Carole Green. What can I do for you?"

"I'm looking for a female student named Belinda."

"I'm her friend. She's not here at the moment. Belinda travelled with her boyfriend to Scotland. I believe that they plan to get married there."

Bert felt that the entrance hall was too public a place for the sort of conversation he wanted to have, so he suggested that they should go to a café and have a coffee. Carole agreed, and the two made their way to a coffee shop near the Law department. They talked over coffee and cakes, which Bert noticed that she enjoyed.

"What has Belinda done?" Carole asked.

"We're investigating a drugs ring, and we think she may be involved," Bert invented.

"She's not involved in drugs, and, apart from me and the guys in the law department, the only other person she knows is her boyfriend – Jonathan Greenway. He's the grandson of the Prime Minister and so unlikely to be involved in drug dealing."

"What's her full name?"

"Belinda Thompson."

"Where is she at the moment?"

"She's in Scotland, getting married."

"Why?"

"Belinda's black and Jonathan's white and their parents have made difficulties for them – so they decided to run away and get married."

"I see," said Bert, doubting the truth of what she was saying. "When's she due back?"

"Two weeks' time. She's got to be here for Rag Week since we plan to take Jonathan hostage at the Rag Dance to raise funds for our charities."

Bert was interested.

"What do you plan to do?"

"Belinda was going to lure Jonathan to her room and we were going to rush him, strip him and tie him up."

Bert laughed.

"That's sounds a good idea. But you could make it even better."

"How?"

"Kidnap Belinda as well and keep them both as hostages. I'll help you. I have a white van/caravan, and I can put them inside and keep them there until their ransom has been paid. All you have to do is ring me on this number," he handed her a card, "and carry the two of them downstairs to my van. I'll do the rest."

"Thanks for the idea. It's a good one. We'll get on with planning it and get back to you. Now, if you'll excuse me, I have a lecture to go to."

Bert felt ecstatic. He had got to first base in one easy step. He returned to his hotel and checked out before returning to London.

Fifty Years After

In Buckinghamshire, Jonathan and Belinda got up late and had a late breakfast before going to the workroom to photocopy enough copies of Janet's diary for each person at the conference. In addition, they made copies of the Juror's affidavit. Once this work was completed, they worked together on a statement from Jonathan outlining the results of his investigation. In addition to this, they included a photo of the two victims and an additional photo of the two envelopes. They started to put these into folders for each participant when they were disturbed by a phone call for Jonathan.

Philip Stewart left his office and drove down to Buckinghamshire, arriving at the gate of the estate at about 12.30. The police on duty stopped him.

"I'm Lord Stewart of Little Wittering. The P.M. is not expecting me, but I hope he will be able to see me for half an hour."

"He's not here. He's in his constituency at a function. However, his grandson is here if you wish to see him and he can pass on a message to Sir Marcus for you."

He rang through to Jonathan who agreed to meet Philip in the small reception room near the entrance hall.

Jonathan left Belinda to continue assembling the folders, and made his way down to the Reception Room, where he found Philip Stewart waiting for him. He walked over to him and shook Philip's hand.

"Good afternoon Lord Philip. I'm Jonathan Greenway. I'm the grandson of Sir Marcus Greenway."

"So this is the trouble-maker!" Philip thought. He studied the boy and thought, "He's just like his grandfather was at that age."

He smiled at Jonathan.

"I'm pleased to meet you, young man. You look just like Sir Marcus did when he was your age. I expect you will be as famous as your grandfather one day."

Fifty Years After

"Thank you, Lord Philip. I hope you're right. But, what can I do for you. I'm afraid my grandfather is not due back until this evening. My grandmother is with him – so I'm the only Greenway here."

Jonathan studied the rather plump, below average height figure of his grandfather's nemesis, thinking, "So this is the face of evil! He doesn't seem that dangerous. He's overweight and has a health problem."

Philip decided this was a good opportunity to get to know his enemy – although he felt that was too strong a term for this young and insipid looking student.

"I understand that you are a student at Cambridge University. What are you reading?"

"I'm a second year Information Technology (IT) student."

"Why are you here and not in Cambridge? After all, it's term time."

"I'm undertaking a project for my Grandfather and I'm on leave until next October."

"That's very interesting. Is it an IT based project?"

"Sort of," Jonathan lied. "I'm looking at the possibility of developing IT controlled irrigation on the estate farm."

"Interesting," said Philip, who did not believe a word of it.

"Are you single or are you in a relationship with someone?"

"Nothing serious, Lord Philip. I find I prefer the company of men to that of women, but my friend Harry is not so sure as I am. So I'm waiting for him to come out."

"He's good, this one," Philip thought. "I wonder how much of what he's said is actually true."

Jonathan was becoming tired of this fencing and so he decided to cut it short.

"While it's interesting talking to you, Lord Philip, I don't think you came here to ask about me and my future. Why did you come here?"

"That's more like the real Jonathan Greenway, I feel sure," Philip thought.

"I wanted to talk to Sir Marcus."

"As I said, Sir Marcus and Lady Evelyn are not here. Can I take a message for them?"

"Not a message you would like," Philip thought.

"Tell him that Philip Stewart called on him to talk to him about the past and remind him of our previous conversations."

Jonathan pretended to be mystified.

"Philip Stewart called on him to talk about the past and remind him of past conversations. Is that it?"

"Yes."

"I don't understand it – do you think **he** will?"

"I'm certain of it. If you get the wording right – he will understand it."

"Fine. I've enjoyed talking to you. Unfortunately, I'm very busy at the moment, so I'll have to love you and leave you, as we used to say at Harrow."

"I'm an old Etonian myself," Philip said, as he turned to leave, "So I wouldn't know that saying."

"We all have our problems", said the former Harrovian as he showed Philip out of the room and returned up the stairs.

Philip left the house with mixed feelings. He felt that he had met his enemy, but failed to understand him. "I mustn't underestimate him. I wonder how Bert has got on tracking down the girlfriend he denies having," he thought. The police officer on duty at the gate opened the gate for him and saluted as he left, taking the road back to London.

Jonathan returned to Belinda equally confused. He now knew what Philip looked like, but he felt he mustn't underestimate the peer. Back in the workroom, he found that Belinda had finished assembling the files, so they went down to lunch, before asking Hawkins to drive them to a jewellers' in the nearby town. Here they spent a pleasant hour choosing an engagement ring for Belinda, settling finally on a plain band with a large single diamond in a gold clasp. Belinda fell in love with it immediately, and looked forward to showing Evelyn first and her mother and her friends as soon as it was safe to do it later. They returned to the house in time for afternoon tea and the chance to welcome Jonathan's Grandparents and Daphne, Sir Marcus's assistant, to the house. Marcus and Evelyn welcomed Belinda and Evelyn was especially interested in seeing her ring. She put her arm around Belinda's shoulder and led her away.

Sir Marcus asked if Jonathan had made any progress.

"Yes, Granddad," he replied. "I shall update you all on Sunday afternoon. I think we may have done enough to open this case up."

"That's good," Sir Marcus said.

Jonathan felt that Marcus was somewhat surprised by his announcement and possibly somewhat perturbed. His next statement seemed to worry his grandfather more.

"Philip Stewart was here, Granddad. He wanted to see you, but I saw him for you. He tried to pump me but I told him nothing."

"What did he want?"

"Apparently he wanted to remind you of previous conversations between you."

"I see," Sir Marcus replied. "Thank you, Grandson. I'm going to have a bath and will see you at dinner."

Sir Marcus went up to his room and Jonathan went out into the hall where he found Daphne unloading files. He went up to her.

"Daphne, I'm Jonathan, Sir Marcus's grandson."

"Yes, I know about you and what you're doing. I also know that Sir Marcus seems worried about it."

"Really?"

"Yes, he's been gathering information about what Philip Stewart has been doing – but seems reluctant to pursue any thing."

"Interesting," he mused, "I wonder why"

"I don't know," Daphne responded, "and, at the moment don't care. My problem is shifting all the Prime Minister's papers from the car. Would you care to help?"

He nodded and helped her move the files into the office before they went to their rooms where Jonathan waited for Belinda to come and join him before they went down to dinner.

Saturday was a rest day for Belinda, who spent time exploring her new surroundings, and for Daphne, who acted as combined guide and escort. Jonathan, however, was busy meeting his grandparents. In the morning he spent time with Evelyn, updating her on what he had achieved and learned, and the questions that still needed to be answered. He showed her his exhibits and she was especially interested in Janet's diary and the photo album. Looking at the photo of the young couple together, holding hands and, heads together, smiling shyly at the camera, she commented that the youngsters deserved better and deserved to be avenged in the one case and justified in the other.

"It will come at a cost, though, Grandma," Jonathan warned.

"I know, Son," Evelyn answered.

"And, are you prepared to pay it, Grandma?"

"Yes, Son. I know it will be hard, especially for Marcus. But they deserve it and demand it after all these years."

In the afternoon, Jonathan knocked diffidently at the door of his grandfather's study. Invited to enter, he did so, and was waved to a seat by his smiling grandfather.

Fifty Years After

"Jonathan, what a delightful surprise! I assumed you would be spending time with your new fiancée."

"Belinda is spending time with Daphne, who's showing her around the estate and the house. I gather they're having girl talk, and it was made clear that I was not welcome to join them!"

"So, you've come to annoy your old grandfather. Is that it?"

"I wouldn't put it that way, Grandpa – but if you insist."

Marcus laughed.

"She's a lovely girl isn't she? I am looking forward to getting to know her better.

However, I already think you've made a good choice and approve absolutely."

"Thank you Grandpa. I think she's a smashing girl and a very intelligent one, which my parents will appreciate."

"Don't be so sure about your father, Jonathan. He has some strange ideas – strange for this era at least. Your mother will certainly approve of her. When do you intend to tell them?"

"When all this is over, Grandpa. We can't really go anywhere until Philip Stewart is either under lock and key or publically freed from all suspicion."

"You're right, Jonathan, especially now he's seen you. I'm annoyed about that. I should have foreseen it and allowed for the possibility."

Sir Marcus poured Jonathan a glass of his favourite brandy, and settled down in a comfortable chair opposite him, with his own glass in his hand.

"What are you doing, Grandpa?"

"I'm writing a speech I have to deliver in the House on Monday on the conflict in Afghanistan. Would you like to read it?"

Jonathan nodded and Sir Marcus handed several sheets of typescript over to him to read. Jonathan perused the document carefully, sipping his brandy as he read them,

Fifty Years After

and laying the sheets of paper carefully on the coffee table as he did so. Eventually, he laid the last paper down, placed his glass on the table, and looked at his Grandfather.

"Do you want my honest opinion, Grandpa?"

"Of course! Why else would I show the papers to you?"

"Are our troops being successful or actually facing defeat, Grandpa?"

"To be honest, I'm not sure, Jonathan. It's actually somewhere between the two."

"Your report is too pessimistic. It looks as though we're losing, Grandpa. All you will do is discourage our troops and their supporters and encourage the Stop the War Coalition. You need to emphasis our successes and minimise our failures."

"I've always been told I'm too honest. I tend to see the difficulties rather than the successes and my speeches have always reflected this."

"You need a good speechwriter, Grandpa. Let me have a go at amending this for you."

Sir Marcus nodded and, having reassembled the papers, gave them to Jonathan.

"Let me have them at lunchtime tomorrow. You can finish it while your Grandma and I are at church."

"I'll do that happily, Grandpa. But can you answer a question for me?"

"What's that?"

"What did Philip Stewart's message mean?"

Sir Marcus was silent. His face clouded at this question. He wondered how to answer it. Jonathan thought he had gone too far and that Sir Marcus would order him to leave the room. However, he was wrong, because Sir Marcus chose to answer his question.

"I have felt for a long time that Philip was not the innocent that he affected to be. I should have acted much sooner, but I was afraid that he would hurt Evelyn. He certainly threatened it. Now I'm afraid for you and Belinda. He's met you and I'm sure he knows about her. I don't know what to do about him – but I know I must do something."

"I know and can almost prove that Philip murdered Janet and framed Mark. Sadly, I think that Great Grandpa persuaded the Home Secretary to put the trial files beyond our reach."

"Despite that, you've managed to prove that Philip killed Mark?"

"Tomorrow I'll tell you how I got access to the police files and what they showed. I also managed to get new documents and to talk with surviving relatives of the couple and the last surviving juror before he died. I know, now, what happened and why, and how it was covered up. I lack one thing – and you have that, Grandpa, according to your assistant, Daphne."

"What do I have that you need, Jonathan? You only have to ask and I'll ensure that you'll get it."

"Daphne told me that you have a file of crimes proved or alleged against Philip Stewart. Could I have it to add to the file I've already assembled against him?"

Marcus nodded.

"Tell Daphne I asked her to let you have it. She'll be delighted to give it to you, I know. She fears that I'll do nothing with it, and she's probably right! She'll know that you'll do something with it."

Sir Marcus poured Jonathan another drink. The two of them shared a final drink as Sir Marcus relaxed.

"You've taken a weight off my mind, Jonathan. I can leave my speech and Philip's future to you and concentrate on my papers. If your work is good I may have a job for you, assuming I have a future after this."

"I'm sure you'll have a future, Granddad. Everyone can make one mistake, especially when they're young. I'm sure they'll forgive you. You weren't directly responsible for what happened to those two, whatever you knew and whatever you did with that knowledge."

"Thank you, grandson. I only wish that your father shared your attitude."

Jonathan laughed.

"That's because he went to Eton, Granddad. You forget that I went to Harrow!"

They both laughed and Jonathan, rose, took the speech, and left Marcus to his papers.

After leaving his grandfather's study, Jonathan looked for Daphne, whom he eventually caught as she entered the Hall with Belinda.

"Daphne," he said, "Sir Marcus asked me to ask you to give me the Philip Stewart File."

"Really!" she replied. "I never expected to hear that. How did you manage it? You must be very persuasive."

"He is very persuasive," Belinda, interrupted. "He could charm the hind legs off a donkey."

"Do you need them now?" she asked. "Only I'm showing Belinda around and we were looking forward to having a girlie talk about men we know over a cup of tea and some cakes."

"Does that include me?" Jonathan asked.

"For cakes and tea, or as a subject of the talks?" Daphne responded.

Belinda answered for them both.

"You have to get your own tea and cakes and have to leave me to decide whether I'm going to talk about your weird and wonderful ways, Darling!"

Jonathan laughed.

"No, Daphne, there's no hurry. I'm going to rewrite Granddad's speech on Afghanistan for him, so you can give the file to Belinda. She can review and summarise the contents for tomorrow afternoon's meeting."

Daphne looked at Belinda in surprise.

"Your fiancé's a marvel, Belinda! I've tried to get Sir Marcus to beef up his speech for some time without success. If you want a second opinion show me your revised text when you've completed it."

Fifty Years After

Jonathan kissed Belinda and thanked Daphne, saying he would take her up on her offer, before leaving them to go to his room.

In London, Philip was on the phone to Malaga as Bert entered his office to report on his visit to Cambridge.

"OK, Tim. I'm definitely coming to the wedding. Family's important to me and your daughter deserves to have us all there on her big day."

Bert heard the muffled sound of Timothy Stewart's reply and Philip's laughter in response.

"All right Tim, I know what you mean. You've got a big day tomorrow. I hope you pull the job off. I've got to leave you now because someone's just come into my office. Talk to you tomorrow."

He put down the phone and the smile left his face, to be replaced by a frown as he looked at his agent.

"Well, Bert. What did you find out in Cambridge?"

"The male target is named Jonathan Greenway. He's the grandson of the Prime Minister and a student at Cambridge University. I understand he's studying IT in his second year, but is currently on leave from his studies for some reason. The female target is named Belinda Thompson. She's a black woman and a student of law in her second year. She and Jonathan are what they call 'an item'. I met one of her friends, who told me that the two had left Cambridge together to go to Scotland where they intend to get married. She expects them back in Cambridge in two weeks for their Rag Week. Apparently they plan to kidnap Jonathan, strip him and tie him up, in order to hold him as hostage. I persuaded them to carry on with the plan but to include Belinda as a second hostage and that I would take care of the hostages for them."

"So, you plan to return to Cambridge in two weeks' time to capture them and bring them to me, is that it?" Philip asked, his quietness masking his anger.

"Yes, Boss."

Fifty Years After

"Then you're a fool, Bert! The girl you spoke to has deceived you. Jonathan Greenway is at Chequers and I assume that Belinda Thompson is with him. I met him there yesterday. I talked to him, and he lied to me almost consistently. He's a very persuasive liar and a very determined young man. He looks harmless – but you already know that. So, he's very dangerous."

Bert looked crestfallen. He prided himself on his work and the thought that he had been completely bamboozled by a mere girl humiliated him more than any words that Philip could say to him.

"What do you want me to do, Boss? Should I go back to Cambridge and deal with the girl? I could teach her quite a lesson about the consequences of playing with the big boys. I would enjoy that, but I don't think she would!"

"You can do that after we've disposed of young Greenway and Thompson. When they're no longer around, you can do what you like with the girl who tricked you."

"Fine, Boss. How do we dispose of the Thompson/Greenway Couple?"

Philip was silent for five minutes as he thought about the question. Bert watched him nervously. He knew that his Boss had a short but extremely violent and unpleasant way of dealing with employees who failed him.

"You will take a team of four men and your partner to Buckinghamshire as well as the white camper van and your car. Keep the team and the camper van in a safe, but hidden parking space until you have the couple. Using the car, you and your assistant should keep a covert observation of the main gate. The moment you see the couple leave, call the van, follow them in the car and trap them against the van, seize them, bind them, place them in the van and drive them to the coast to the boat, and then come and get me."

"Should we strip them and dump their clothes before we reach the boat?"

"Obviously," Philip snapped.

Fifty Years After

"OK, Boss. Are we following the normal rules of engagement – this meeting didn't happen and no contact until we have them under our control?"

"Absolutely. I'll pay you when you deliver."

Bert nodded and left the office to ring his nominated mission companions and arrange for them to leave London two days later.

That evening, Jonathan, Daphne, and Belinda sat together, working silently. Belinda reviewed the mass of papers in the Philip Stewart file with Daphne, assembling them together in a thematic way and cataloguing them before writing a report for the meeting on the following afternoon, while Jonathan worked on Marcus's speech. Jonathan completed his first draft of the speech and handed it to Daphne, who read it through and marked a few sections in red.

"It's good, Jonathan," she said. "It's much better than Sir Marcus's original draft or his usual style, but I've marked three sentences which contain errors. If you make the corrections I've suggested, it will be fine."

"Thank you, Daphne. How are you two getting on?"

"We've completed the arranging and cataloguing. We've now got to write the report and do the photocopying."

Jonathan returned to his work, but was almost immediately disturbed when his mobile phone rang. It was Albert Corrigan.

"Hello Albert. What can I do for you?"

"What are we doing tomorrow and what do I need to do before I come down there?"

"I'm going to introduce the new evidence I've collected and explain how it relates to the case. Obviously I'm not going to go through it on the phone."

"Obviously."

"However, we've prepared a dossier of photocopies of the documents and photographs for each person at the conference – Sir Marcus, Lady Evelyn, Daphne, Me,

Fifty Years After

Belinda, you and the Attorney General (seven copies). I would be grateful if you could get seven copies of the four files I gave you to add to the seven dossiers."

"I'll do that, Jonathan. But, I must stress that you need to take great care until we get the 100 years' embargo lifted. No one should take the photocopied files away with them."

"I understand that, Albert, and we will recover the copies. You, however, will take all the originals because I think my role ends at tomorrow's conference."

Albert chuckled.

"You would think that, Jonathan! But I'll still need your help. I need an assistant and a young pair of legs."

"My fiancée, Belinda, is reading Law at Cambridge. She's here with me. I've taken her away from Cambridge for the time being. She'll be your assistant and I'll be your legs."

"That sounds like a plan, Jonathan. I'll see you tomorrow."

Albert turned off his phone and Jonathan resumed his speech writing.

They worked late into the night, and resumed after breakfast next morning. Jonathan left Belinda and Daphne to complete the assembling of the seven dossiers, while he ensured that the originals of the documents were assembled in his case file, in a sensible order. He realised that he lacked the time needed to prepare a written statement, but was happy that he had finished his task for Sir Marcus. He printed the revised speech, collated the pages and stapled them together before placing them in an A4 envelope. His grandparents returned from the local church service at midday. Sir Marcus went to his study and Jonathan went to find him there. He was admitted after his soft knock. Sir Marcus was pleased to see him.

"Good morning, Jonathan" he said cheerfully. "Have you completed your task?"

"I have Granddad," Jonathan replied, equally cheerfully.

He handed Sir Marcus the envelope.

"I have cleared it with Daphne, who made me correct three sentences which contained errors of fact. Otherwise, it is as I drafted it."

Sir Marcus smiled at Jonathan and opened a new brandy bottle, from which he poured two glasses. As they drank, he opened the envelope and extracted the speech within. He read it as Jonathan watched him. At the end, he put the speech down and smiled at his grandson.

"Well done, Jonathan. You've done a brilliant job. I'm going to add you to my team, as a speechwriter. You do a much better job than I do."

"Thank you, Granddad."

"We'll have the meeting this afternoon in the small Reception Room on the first floor. It used to be the room where the gentlemen withdrew after dinner to take port. It should be big enough to hold seven of us; but not so big as to make us look ridiculous."

The phone rang on Sir Marcus's desk. Sir Marcus answered it. He listened in silence for a minute before speaking.

"All right, tell them to come through to the house. I will meet them in the Hall."

He put the phone down and spoke to Jonathan.

"That was the gate. Lord Corrigan and William Cosgrave, the Attorney General, have arrived. Let's go down to the Hall to meet them."

The two men left the room and made their way down to the Hall. Jonathan greeted the two men and, with his grandfather's permission, whisked Albert away to the workroom where Belinda and Daphne had just finished assembling the dossiers. Albert greeted them and congratulated Belinda and Jonathan on their engagement. He picked up one of the dossiers and flicked through the

Fifty Years After

documents in it. His eyes opened wide as he saw what the dossier contained.

"How did you get this?" he asked Jonathan, as he held the photocopy of Janet's diary.

"From Jennifer Foster, her sister," Jonathan replied simply. "The photos came from Luke Smith, Mark's brother. The envelopes came from the last surviving Juror. The other files were gathered together by Daphne at my Grandfather's request."

"You've obviously all been very busy," Albert said. "Well done!"

Albert took seven files from his bag and gave them to Daphne and Belinda to add to their dossiers. He also added seven transcripts of the 1961 trial.

"Can I see the originals of these documents?" he asked Jonathan.

"Certainly," Jonathan responded.

He unlocked and opened a brief case, which was on the floor. He began by presenting the affidavit to Albert, who read it with raised eyebrows.

"Before seeing the Police File, that would have surprised me," he commented. "But nothing surprises me now in this case."

He followed this with the two envelopes. Albert turned them over in his hand.

"I see that you have not opened them," he said with approval.

"The recipient had declined to open them and I felt that I should do the same. I know what's in them and I feel they should be opened under a camera and in the presence of you all."

"Very good," Albert said.

Albert turned over the pages of the photo album with idle curiosity, but was much more interested in the diary and its contents.

"I can see that this document is the evidence we've been looking for. Does it answer the question about who attacked Janet before the fatal assault?"

"Yes. The assailant is named and the assault fully described and the reason given."

"It would appear from what I've seen of the diary's contents and the photos that Mark's version of events receives some backing," Albert said cautiously. "I think the Juror's evidence is enough to overturn the verdict. We will have to see if the rest of the evidence is enough to convict Philip Stewart."

"We met the other day, by the way," Jonathan said.

"Damn!" Albert commented. "That's the last thing I wanted. You didn't tell him anything important did you?"

"Absolutely nothing. I lied – that's all. Belinda told me her friend had texted her and told her a man had been snooping about looking for us in Cambridge. She told him we'd gone to Scotland to elope."

"How did she come up with that idea?"

"Belinda and I suggested it."

"Well, it was a good try, but all you've done is make her a target for Philip's murderous entourage." He turned to Belinda. "Warn your friend, Belinda, to take care of herself and avoid any further contact with the man she spoke to."

"Yes, Lord Corrigan," Belinda replied.

"My name's Albert," Albert said. "I've told Jonathan to call me that, and I want you to do so too – especially if you're going to be my assistant in the retrial."

At that moment they heard a gong boom downstairs.

"That's the call for lunch," Jonathan said. "We must go down quickly or the cook will shoot us. We won't have to wait for Philip Stewart to get around to it."

"That's not funny, Darling," Belinda commented, as they left the room.

20. Case Conference

February 16 2010
After lunch they all assembled in the small Reception Room, where they found that the staff had provided a tray of cups and saucers, milk and sugar, spoons, a coffee urn and plates of cakes and biscuits. They had arranged the chairs into a circle and a large folder was placed on each chair. While they each poured themselves coffee, Jonathan opened his brief case and laid a series of documents on the table, to which Albert added four A4 folders, obviously containing additional papers. Jonathan checked that everything was there, and in the order that he wanted, and was satisfied. He nodded at Sir Marcus, who called the meeting to order and formally introduced everyone before handing over to Jonathan.

Jonathan looked around at them all.
"I am the son of Martin Greenway, Sir Marcus and Lady Evelyn's only son. I was in my second year as an IT student at Cambridge before this case caused me to suspend my studies until next autumn. Belinda and I have only just become engaged. She is also in her second year, only reading law. She has also suspended her course until the autumn."

He smiled at them.
"I have to tell you that none of our parents yet know that we have become engaged and plan to marry when we leave Cambridge. In fact, they don't even know that we know each other!"

"You've both got a couple of very interesting conversations ahead, then," Albert commented to general laughter. "Good luck!"

"Thank you very much for that, Albert!" Jonathan and Belinda said, to even more laughter.

Jonathan let the laughter die down before continuing.

Fifty Years After

"My family came here for Christmas and I got here before everyone else, having travelled here independently from my parents and brothers. Having arrived, I found myself at a loose end, and decided to find out more about the career of my esteemed Grandfather, whom I had last seen as a 10 year old boy. He has definitely gone up the ladder since then!"

Once again the group laughed. Sir Marcus nodded.

"In the course of doing so, I found out about the Mark Smith Trial and my grandfather's role in it. As I read about it something did not seem quite right. I didn't know what – it just felt wrong."

"Interesting," said Lord Corrigan. "You may not be reading law, but you would make a good lawyer. You've possibly chosen the wrong career Jonathan."

"I don't need to study law, Albert. I'm marrying a lawyer. Can you imagine what would happen if we were both lawyers? We would have endless case conferences!"

Once again the group laughed.

"When we went down for dinner that evening I asked Granddad about Philip Stewart and the Smith Trial. It wasn't a popular request, and it was Grandma who told me about him."

Jonathan then reviewed the series of conversations he had over Christmas and their outcomes. Jonathan looked around at them and noticed that they were listening intently. The light-hearted mood, which he had induced by his opening remarks, had gone.

"Last Thursday morning, Belinda was giving a paper at a seminar. She had prepared a paper on the Smith trial partly because of the family connection. I attended the seminar and acted as facilitator for the discussion afterwards. We asked the students to consider what issues they would feel necessary to bring before a conference such as this. You have a copy of the trial transcript," Jonathan picked up and waved his copy, "in your pack, but

Belinda is going to read her paper to you as a reminder of what happened in June 1961."

Belinda stood up, picked up and read her paper to them before sitting down again.

"Well done, Belinda," Albert said after she had seated herself. "That was a masterly summary. That is exactly what happened in the courtroom and what the prosecution claimed. I ought to explain a few things that you haven't covered or couldn't have known from the transcript. First it was my first case, and I made a number of mistakes. I would have handled the trial very differently, even with the evidence we had then, if I were conducting the defence now. Secondly, I sensed the hostility of the jury to the defendant. I knew the case was lost as soon as the trial began. I also knew that Walter Greenway would destroy Mark if he went into the witness box. He did not want to give evidence and I saw little point in his doing so. He was almost certainly going to die. I wanted, at least, to leave him a little dignity."

Jonathan continued his review.

"I was given the task of finding new evidence and I realised that there were only two possible witnesses – the siblings of the two victims. I considered by now that Mark was as much a victim as Janet. I considered that the same person murdered both of them. The difference being that one was illegally murdered by the murderer's own hand, and the public hangman legally murdered the other."

"That's a very harsh judgement," said William Cosgrave, "and you are pre-empting the decision of this case conference."

"No I'm not, Mr Cosgrave. I'm telling you what I thought at that time."

"Fair enough. Incidentally, call me William."

Jonathan nodded and continued, outlining how he had made contact with Luke and Jennifer, before coming to the issue of the police files.

Fifty Years After

"I then did something, which I knew was illegal. I contacted a friend of mine who is in my department and has a reputation as a hacker. His chief claim to fame is that he could hack into Metropolitan Police files. I asked him if he could access and download the original case file and also any files on the Stewarts"

William Cosgrave theatrically put his hands over his ears.

"I don't want to hear this," he said. "Marcus, did you know that your Grandson did this and do you approve?"

"The answer is 'no' and 'no', William. But if you ask whether I am surprised, the answer is again, 'no', because it's exactly what I would have done in his position. What did you find?"

"My friend whom we'll call Tom. It isn't his real name incidentally, but I don't want to have to visit him in Belmarsh if William suddenly got very efficient!"

Again they laughed.

"Tom came round to see me with a large sealed A3 envelope. He told me that he hadn't hacked the files. Instead he'd asked someone with contacts to gather the material I wanted. He was given the file in the sealed envelope and told not to open it, but to give it to me still sealed and to warn me to take great care."

"That was very wise advice," Albert commented.

"I opened the envelope and found four separate files in it. You have copies of each file in your pack. They were the three I had asked for – the original case documents; the Stewart family File and a file on Philip Stewart, as well as a file I hadn't asked for, since I didn't realise how important it would be – a file on D I Buchan."

"Your informant acquired all these for you?" an incredulous William Cosgrave asked.

"Indeed," said Jonathan gravely. "But Tom did something else, too, entirely off his own bat. He appealed for anyone who had been on the Smith Trial Jury to get in touch with us. One person did and I will come to that later."

Fifty Years After

Jonathan poured himself some coffee and drank some of it as his audience found the four files that he referred to.

"I opened the trial file first. It shocked me to the core. I've heard accusations of police corruption, but I never believed it until I opened this file and discovered exactly what Alasdair Buchan did in this case. The first surprise I had was the discovery that the file was closed for 100 years. I thought that was very unusual, especially as the order was signed by the Home Secretary – the same Home Secretary, who had rejected Albert's appeal for clemency for Mark."

"That is certainly very unusual," William conceded, looking at Albert, who nodded. "One wonders why this case was considered so important that it should be closed for so long."

"I think that Walter Greenway leant on the Home Secretary. They were good friends," Albert commented. "Of course, why Walter would do that is open to conjecture."

"Unfortunately," Jonathan answered, "the Stewart family file makes it more than clear that Sir Walter had been bought by the Stewarts and was on the Stewart payroll."

"Impossible," Sir Marcus commented. My father knew about the poor relationship between Philip Stewart and me. He would never have gone behind my back and taken money from Philip's father."

"I've read the files, Darling," Evelyn said. "Jonathan showed them to me after he read them. I'm afraid the evidence is clear. Jack Stewart used Walter on several occasions to ensure that his gang was able to act with almost impunity. He and D I Buchan blocked any enquiry that seemed to be getting too close to them."

Sir Marcus opened the Stewart file and looked through it with sombre eyes, eventually sighing heavily and nodding his agreement. Jonathan, understanding Sir Marcus's trauma, waited for him to show he agreed before continuing.

"I will return to the Stewart file, to which Granddad has added a lot of additional material later."

Jonathan paused, picked up a biscuit and put it in his mouth, and then continued with his presentation.

"When I opened the file, I understood why it had been so tightly sealed. It was clear that the arresting officer's report and the report of the Forensic scientist had been altered in order to remove evidence favourable to the defence. The original reports were never presented to the court or the defence. The doctored reports were used, and one of those – the arresting officer's – was clearly a forgery. D I Buchan ordered the alterations. Please read the four reports. Notice especially the highlighted sections, which were removed. The reports have not been amended by me – they are in the state in which I found them."

Jonathan waited as the group read the various documents, noting their shock as they did so.

"I never saw the original documents," Albert confirmed. "Had I done so, I would have conducted the defence very differently."

"In itself," William Cosgrave commented, it's enough to order a retrial, on the grounds that the evidence was contaminated, resulting in a mistrial. However," he cautioned, "we first have to get the closure order lifted and the original copies of these papers in our hands."

Jonathan let them read the papers in the file before resuming.

"There is one other point of interest in the case files. Mark's interview by D I Buchan was conducted with Mark stripped naked and subject to a beating by his interrogators. That would also disqualify any statement he made, since it was made under duress. However, he never varied his story or admitted anything – despite the pressure put on him. That is significant. However, we now come to another significant, but previously unknown, fact.

Fifty Years After

"Commentators who have written about this trial have always expressed surprise at how quickly the jury returned a guilty verdict. Albert may have been inexperienced, but he put up a spirited defence and did enough to cast a reasonable level of doubt on the prosecution's case. He also questioned the basis of the charge of Capital Murder on the evidence presented by Philip Stewart. If one believed Stewart's story, the real charge should have been manslaughter – not murder, since Janet's death was the result of a tragic accident. Despite this, the Jury were convinced and returned a verdict of guilty of murder within such a short time that they could not even have discussed the evidence, such as it was. So how did it happen?"

"How did it happen?" asked William Cosgrave.

"I went to visit Wilfred Martins – the youngest of the jurors and the only one still alive. I was just in time because he is dying of lung cancer. He knows he is dying and is troubled about his role in the trial. He wanted to put things right before he died and responded to Tom's advertisement as though it was a gift from the Almighty Himself."

"Herself," Belinda murmured.

Jonathan stuck his tongue out at her, and the rest laughed at him as Belinda grinned back at him.

"Wilfred made a sworn affidavit with a solicitor the day before my visit. He knew he was dying and would never make it to court for the retrial, and he wanted his voice to be heard. This is what he wrote.

"My name is Wilfred Martins. I am of sound mind, but I am dying from lung cancer and I want my story to be written down in a form in which it can be presented to a court of law. I was on the jury that tried Mark Smith for the murder of Janet Brown in June 1961. On the second morning we were all given brown envelopes by one of the jurors. His name was Matthew Allbright. I never opened my envelope, but the other jurors did. The envelope contained 10 new £5 notes and a note. The note read 'Elect

Matthew Allbright as Foreman and vote as he tells you and there will be another £50 for you.' When we retired to consider our verdict, we elected Matthew Allbright and he told us to vote guilty. One of the jurors pointed out that Mark Smith would be hanged if he were found guilty of shooting Janet Brown. Matthew Allbright told us that he had been assured that the judge would not sentence him to death. We voted guilty and we were given a second envelope. This contained another £50 and a second note, which simply said 'Thank you.' I have never opened my envelopes because I considered it to be blood money. They are the two envelopes, in their original form, which I have given (will give) to Jonathan Greenway so he can give them to the Court. Two other jurors tried to give their money back to Matthew Allbright. One disappeared and has never been seen since. The other was found floating in the Thames."

"The document is signed Wilfred Martins and witnessed by two solicitors. A copy is in your file. The original is in my hand."

"What do we know of Matthew Allbright?" William asked.

"He became an employee of Jack Stewart's on the first day of the trial and remained in his employ until he retired 25 years later. He died in 1998." Albert answered.

"This is enough in itself to persuade a court to declare the 1961 trial a mistrial," William said.

The other two lawyers – Albert and Marcus – agreed.

"Do you have anything else?" William asked.

"Luke Smith gave me a photograph album, showing photos of the couple and of their families. This showed that the two were very much in love and helps to substantiate Mark's story. In addition, he gave me two return railway tickets from London to Gretna Green and a confirmed hotel booking in Gretna Green for Mark and Janet dated the week after the murder. So it's clear that Mark and Janet planned to run away together."

"Yes, I agree that you could make that point," William said.

William Cosgrave paused and looked around the group.

"I congratulate you, Jonathan. I'm not sure that I approve of all your methods, but you have certainly gathered enough evidence to get the verdict set aside and a formal pardon given to Mark Smith. What you haven't done, however, is to provide anything to tie Philip Stewart to the crime."

"I agree, Jonathan," Albert said. "Do you have anything else?"

"I have," Jonathan answered. "However, let me first finish dealing with Wilfred's story. William, here are the two envelopes. You can see they are still tightly sealed. Here is a paper knife and Daphne has a camera. We want you to open the envelopes and take out the contents while Daphne films you doing it for the court."

William Cosgrave agreed and slit the envelope open, taking out the cards and banknotes and confirming that they were as Wilfred had described them in his affidavit.

Daphne stood up and walked into the middle of the circle. She paused, and then pointed to the pile of papers she and Belinda had assembled the previous evening.

"That contains a list of Philip Stewart's crimes and suspected crimes over the years. It includes several murders, drug dealing, protection rackets, prostitution and many rapes. He seemed to see women as trophies, as Lady Evelyn said earlier. We are there only for his pleasure."

She sat down with tears in her eyes. Jonathan stood up again.

"The final document is quite lengthy. It is the last document in your pack. Jennifer Foster who found it after Janet's death among her personal effects gave it to me. She did not give it to the police. Janet told her about her pregnancy and the assault on her by Philip Stewart the night before her fatal visit to the park. It recounts in her

Fifty Years After

words, Mark's letters and photos the story of Mark and Janet's love affair. It is, in short, Janet's diary from November 1960 until the night before her death in April 1961. I'm going to adjourn this meeting for 60 minutes to allow you to read it."

It was a very sombre group who returned to the Reception Room from the various places they had scattered to for their private reading of Janet's diary. It was William Cosgrave who took over the direction of the meeting when it resumed.

"I would first like to thank Jonathan, Daphne and Belinda for the work they have done; work which has forced this case open and enabled us to redress a long injustice. Even though, sadly, we can't bring Janet and Mark back to life, we can reunite them in death, enable them at last to rest in peace, and give back to Mark his good name. I think the rest of us should give them a round of applause."

The remaining four clapped them politely.

"You should also thank your nefarious friend Tom," William added, "but don't say that I said so! I can't be seen to be condoning hacking or acquiring information by other means just as illegal. I would like to be able to say that I'm surprised that Albert helped cover you lot up, but I'm not really surprised. Judges have always been the worst offenders when it comes to sticking to the letter of the law!"

Albert Corrigan laughed.

"I'm only a judge for another month, as you know William, so I'll have to change my ways again then, won't I?"

"No comment, Albert," William replied. "Now, let us get on with the serious discussion: where do we go from here? I'm welcome to suggestions from you three by the way," he said, looking at Jonathan, Daphne and Belinda.

Fifty Years After

"The most important first step is to get the embargo on the files lifted and to secure the originals before they can be doctored further to remove the evidence," Albert pointed out.

"You and I will go to see the Home Secretary tomorrow, Albert, show him the evidence we have and get him to (a) lift the embargo and (b) order the Metropolitan Police to hand the files over to us in our presence untampered with."

"I agree, William. Once we've got them, we can use these files and the evidence from Wilfred Martins to get an appeal court judge to declare a mistrial."

"What will you do then?" Sir Marcus asked. "Ask for a royal pardon for Mark Smith and leave it like that?"

William Cosgrave smiled.

"We can't do that Prime Minister. I know you've refused to allow a public enquiry to be held into this case several times, but you can no longer do that. It was a very simple case in essence. Three people were involved. One was shot dead – either accidentally or deliberately. One was a witness and the third was the killer. If we exonerate Mark Smith, then Philip Stewart was the killer. The diary and his record show motive and predisposition to violence and the ultimate form of violence. We cannot let him remain free to kill again. In any case, I suspect we have two young people with us in this room who are probably already in his sights. Isn't that so, Jonathan and Belinda?"

"Philip Stewart and I have already met down here," Jonathan commented.

"And someone pretending to be a policeman asked my friend, Carole, about us. She told him that we had gone to Scotland."

"I told him a string of lies as well," Jonathan added.

"That probably makes three potential victims," William concluded. "We know that Philip Stewart does not forgive those who cross or oppose him."

"So," Albert concluded, "We first get the original trial set aside, and then we get Mark officially pardoned. I suppose that, after that, we arrest Philip Stewart and begin a new prosecution with a trial later in the year. Do you agree William?"

"Yes, I do agree, Albert. It will again be at the Central Criminal Court. Meanwhile, I will inform the Master at Arms so that the police can enter Lord Stewart's rooms at Westminster to search them and arrest him when the time comes."

"I will speak personally to Joanna Macdonald, the Labour Leader, to inform her what is about to happen and why, and advise her to say nothing to Lord Stewart by way of a warning and to make no comment after the arrest," added Marcus.

William Cosgrave stood up.

"If you will excuse me, Jonathan. I will, with your permission, keep the dossier which you so kindly prepared for me and, Daphne, I would be grateful if you emailed your film to me."

Daphne nodded her agreement.

"You need to give me your address William," she said.

"Sir Marcus will give you my email address, Daphne. Could you get the film across to me this evening?"

"Of course, William."

"Good." He turned to face Jonathan.

"You have done a masterly job in assembling the evidence, but your job is over, and it's dangerous for you and Belinda to keep these documents in your possession. Pack them up, put them in your brief case, lock it and give the case and the key to Lord Corrigan. He will pass them on to the new Investigating Officer. I will speak with the Chief Commissioner and ask that an officer from outside the Metropolitan Police should carry out the investigation; both of the original murder and the subsequent cover up. You two may have to give evidence to him or her, of course, and you will certainly both have to give evidence at the trial."

"They will both be working for me, William," Albert said, "as part of the Prosecution team. I intend to conduct the Prosecution. That's why I've retired."

"I know that, Albert, and I fully understand your reasons. It's not my role to advise you on your tactics, but I would suggest that young Belinda reads Janet's diary into the court records. She is nearly of the right age to be Janet, and, at least, will understand how Janet felt when she was writing."

"I agree," Albert said, watching the two gather up and place the various documents in the brief case.

"There's one other thing, Prime Minister," William said.

"What's that," Sir Marcus asked.

"You need to take steps to secure the safety of your grandson and granddaughter elect. They need the protection of armed police officers and must not leave the grounds of this estate unaccompanied and preferably not on foot. They were anonymous hitherto, and did not warrant special treatment. It's clear that Philip Stewart already knows about them and will be taking steps to silence them. That appears to be his way. We must prevent that."

"I will ask the diplomatic squad to provide 24 hours support by two armed officers and instruct Hawkins to act as their driver whenever they wish to go out. They're young people, we can't expect them to remain cooped up here, not even for their own protection!"

"And you should instruct your gate people not to give any stranger enquiring after them any information, and there must be no more visits from outside of this group or their families permitted to them in the house under any circumstances."

"Don't worry, William. I will stay here and supervise things until this is all over. You will need to arrange a housekeeper for Number 10. I will remain here and protect my future great grandchildren," Evelyn said.

Belinda pretended to look shocked.

"Lady Evelyn is it a Greenway habit to make assumptions? Your grandson wanted to talk about our wedding before he'd even proposed to me and known that I would say yes. Now you assume I'm going to have a baby, before I even know whether I'm pregnant. Indeed, what makes you think we've had sex? I'm a good girl!"

They all laughed at this, and, on that note, the case conference finished.

21. Kidnap

March 1 2010

It took longer than William Cosgrove anticipated. It took over a week to arrange a meeting with the Lord Chief Justice and the Home Secretary. When eventually the four people met, the Judge and the senior politician were harder to convince than the two lawyers expected.

"All this happened fifty years ago," the Home Secretary commented. "There have been a number of requests for us to reopen the case – but no clear reason acceptable in law has ever been given. What's different now?"

"There is new evidence," Albert Corrigan explained.

"What sort of evidence?" Lord Black, the Lord Chief Justice asked.

"We have evidence of jury tampering and also of interference with key evidence, all designed to convict the defendant."

John Francis, the Home Secretary looked sceptical.

"We often hear tales of evidence tampering and jury rigging – but you can't possibly establish hard evidence of that after all this time."

Albert opened his brief case and removed three documents. He passed them to Lord Black and John Francis.

"These are photocopies, but we have the original of the third document and the other two are in police files which we need your permission to retrieve."

Albert went on to explain the three documents.

"The first was the original report made by the Constable who arrested Mark Smith. You will see that D I Buchan, the investigating officer, ordered the Constable to remove the highlighted sections. It was the expunged document that was presented in Court."

The two men read the document with raised eyebrows.

Fifty Years After

"The second document has been similarly treated. It is the forensic report."

Again, the two men were presented with the doctored original.

"You can see that the changes were all to the disadvantage of the defendant," William commented.

The two men nodded.

"The third document is an affidavit sworn by one of the jury a few weeks before his recent death of Cancer. We opened the envelopes he referred to and the contents were as he recounted. We filmed the opening for the court."

Lord Black and John Francis studied the three documents intently.

"Are you satisfied as to their provenance?" Lord Black asked William Cosgrave.

"Yes, My Lord," William answered.

"You're the Government's legal officer, what do you advise?"

"I believe that you should refer this case to the Court of Appeal and seek a declaration of a mistrial."

Albert spoke after William.

"We also want the Home Secretary to rescind the 100 years' closure rule on the original case documents from which the first two documents were taken. We need legal access to them (a) so that we can ensure they are not destroyed, and (b) so the police and courts can mount a new case."

"Why was the case file closed for so long?" John Francis asked.

"Because your predecessor ordered it," Albert answered.

"I will lift the order," John said. "There's no justification for it in law and it seems part of a cover up."

John Francis drafted an instruction to the Metropolitan Police Record Department to release the four files that Albert and William wanted to Albert and William. Once it was typed and printed, he signed the paper and gave it to William Cosgrave.

"What else do you need?" Lord Black asked.

"We need a new police investigation, conducted by a senior member of a different Police Force, and covering both the original murder, the trial and the subsequent cover up," Albert answered.

"I agree," William added.

"I think you're right," Lord Black commented. "I think I know the ideal person – Detective Superintendent Julia Donaldson of Surrey Police. She has a good reputation and is a fine detective with a nose for criminality. She seems to be able to positively smell it! What's more, once on the track of a criminal, she doesn't give up easily. Do you have an alternative suspect, incidentally?"

"Yes," Albert Corrigan said.

"Can I ask who?"

"You may. There were only two possible suspects – Mark Smith, who was hanged for the crime, and Philip Stewart, the chief witness. We have good reason to suspect that Philip murdered Janet Brown and framed Mark Smith."

"I see," said John Francis. "Well that's going to open a can of worms! Good luck, gentlemen!"

With that the meeting ended, and the two men went with the letter of authorisation to the Records Office. Albert was not really surprised to notice the amazing speed with which the four files were located. He wondered if the officer on duty was the contact used by Harry the Hacker to secure the original files.

"I've been expecting someone to come to ask for these files," the officer, Sergeant Mackintosh, explained. "I've known for a while the explosive nature of the contents and I've kept a very close eye on them. I can assure you that they have not been interfered with."

Albert and William checked the Files, particularly the murder case file, and found that the Sergeant was correct.

Fifty Years After

It had not been interfered with. Albert took control of the files, putting them in his brief case. Both men sighed with relief. The most difficult hurdle had been successfully negotiated.

The next step was to assemble a case file for the appeal court, which set a date four weeks later for the hearing. This occupied William Cosgrave and Albert Corrigan for the rest of the month.

Meanwhile, Daphne and Evelyn were beginning to lose patience with Marcus. Far from acting with the expedition necessary to prevent Philip Stewart from fleeing once he suspected that the game was up, he did nothing. Despite his avowed dislike of his rival, he seemed very reluctant to begin the process of bringing him to justice. Neither his wife nor his assistant could understand why. Eventually, it was Evelyn who travelled up to London to tackle her husband.

"Marcus, when are you going to talk to Joanna about Philip Stewart?"

"When I get round to it, Darling. I have a lot to do, you know. Philip Stewart has waited 50 years to face justice. He can wait for a week or two longer."

"No, he can't, Marcus. It's almost as though you're afraid of him. What has he got over you?"

"Nothing, Darling,"

Evelyn knew he was lying and was worried.

"Whatever the cost, Darling, that monster must be stopped. He will only be stopped when he's behind bars and his gang is shut down."

"I know, Darling. I will do it tomorrow."

"No you won't Darling. You'll do it now."

Evelyn picked up the phone on Marcus's desk, found his list of phone numbers and rang one of them. A female voice answered.

"Hello Joanna, it's Evelyn Greenway calling. My husband wants to talk to you."

Fifty Years After

Evelyn passed the phone over to Marcus; ignoring the glare that he gave her.

"Hello Joanna," he said between gritted teeth. "I need to speak to you in private. Could you come to my office in the Commons tomorrow morning?"

"Certainly Prime Minister. What time do you suggest?"

"Would 11 am suit you?" he asked.

"Of course, Prime Minister," she replied. "I will see you then."

She put down the phone.

"Don't ever do that to me again, Darling," Marcus said to his wife.

Evelyn smiled.

Bert and his team arrived outside the estate two days after the case conference. Bert divided the team into two and set up an ambush outside of the Chequers grounds, using their car and campervan. He ordered that the two should be seized, handcuffed, thrown into the van, drugged, stripped and driven to Shoreham and held on the "Lucky Lady" awaiting Philip's inspection and further orders. They agreed to the plan and took up their ambush positions, but nothing happened. The team waited for a week before Bert lost patience and asked the officers at the gate where the two were. They told him that they had gone to Cambridge for the Rag Week Dance and Bert took his team to that city.

Jonathan and Belinda were bored. There was nothing to excite them locally. Their work on the Smith Case was, for the moment, done. Evelyn was good company, but she was about 70. There was only so much you could see in and around the house and grounds. They dared not go for a walk outside of the gates. Hawkins took them out on a number of occasions, but there was not much he could find, especially in March, to entertain them. In the end they emailed their tutors in Cambridge, asking them to email them work. Their surprised tutors were pleased to oblige and so the two self-suspended students became distance learners.

In Cambridge, meanwhile, the absence of their star student and his feisty girlfriend saddened the students who knew them. Two of them, Michael Harding and Emma Jackson, students with a vague similarity to the missing students, decided they would be them for the Rag Ball. Like Jonathan and Belinda, they were considered to be an item and so when the Rag Ball organisers decided to play along and declare them the King and Queen of the Ball, they were delighted to act the part of their two friends, unaware that their friends' enemies were watching them. Once the ball was over, slightly the worse for drink, the couple began to make their way back to their college. Suddenly they were both seized and hoods were pulled down over their heads. Their arms were grabbed and pinioned behind their backs and they felt the cold steel of the handcuffs on their wrists before they were each lifted bodily and thrown into the back of the white vehicle that had suddenly appeared and stopped beside them before they were attacked. As they lay, winded, face down on the floor, they felt the sharp prick of a needle in their behinds, and knew no more.

The news of their disappearance broke next day and an intensive police search began which only ended when Bert walked into his local police station the following day. The duty sergeant looked up as he entered.
"What can I do for you Sir?" he asked.
"I wish to talk to someone about the two missing Cambridge students," Bert replied.
"Do you have information as to their whereabouts, Sir?"
"I've got a damned good idea where they are, Sergeant. Just let me talk to one of the officers in charge of the case."

"One of my officers will show you to an interview room and we'll get you some tea will I get one of the Cambridgeshire detectives to come down here."

Bert waited impatiently for over two hours until two detectives entered the room and introduced themselves as Cambridgeshire police officers – an inspector and a sergeant. They sat down opposite Bert and asked him what he knew.

"My name is Bert Campion and I am a P A to Lord Philip Stewart. He is the one who ordered the kidnap and my team carried it out."

The two officers looked startled.

"Why did Lord Stewart order their kidnap?" the Inspector asked.

"He wanted us to kidnap the Prime Minister's grandson and his girlfriend who have been making a nuisance of themselves. We thought the two students were them because they performed the role we were informed the two targets would be carrying out."

"I see," said the Inspector. "So the kidnap was a mistake, was it?"

"Yes."

"Does Lord Philip know?"

"Yes. They were stripped and chained up in his yacht "The Lucky Lady" and I took him down to inspect them."

"And he realised that you were wrong?" asked the inspector.

"Yes, he had seen Jonathan Greenway before and knew the prisoner wasn't him."

"Assuming you'd got the right people, what was he planning to do with them?"

"He was going to torture them and then drown them in the Channel."

Both officers looked sceptical.

Fifty Years After

"You do realise, Mr Campion, that these are serious accusations to bring against a Peer of the Realm, don't you?" the Sergeant said.

"I do, and they're the truth, Sergeant."

"OK. So what did Lord Philip decide to do with the two students you kidnapped?"

"The same as if they were his targets. Later he changed his mind and said the boys could what they liked with them."

"You told the duty Sergeant that you knew where they are," the inspector said, "where do you think they are and why?"

"My men have had some contact with a white slave trader who lives in Le Havre. My bet is that they've gone there. You should get the French police to search for them."

In London, Marcus finally held his meeting with Joanna Macdonald, the Labour Leader of the Opposition. Joanna met Marcus in his special office. She entered warily. The invitation was unexpected. She was not aware of any major crisis and, as a result, the sudden invitation was unexpected. She wondered what it was all about. Sir Marcus was immaculately dressed as usual, but, studying his face carefully as he offered her coffee, she sensed that there was strain behind his eyes. She waited for him to speak. After all, it was his meeting.

Eventually, after five minutes, he did so.

"I'm glad you could come, Joanna. There's a very delicate matter I have to raise with you."

Joanna smiled and decided to tease the obviously tense man in front of her.

"What's up, Marcus. Has one of your MPs failed to keep his trousers zipped up again?"

Marcus smiled sadly.

"I wish it were as simple as that, Joanna."

Fifty Years After

He paused. He was hoping to avoid this conversation and had been pitchforked into it by Evelyn. He was wondering where to start.

"What do you know about North London, Joanna?"

"It's north of the Thames," she ventured. "That's about all. I'm a Lancashire lass and my constituency is in Manchester, remember."

"Yes. I know. You've a very large majority, but not over us – over the Lib Dems."

"Indeed I have. I think your candidate knows every person who voted for him by name!"

They both laughed at the (all too accurate) picture she painted of Conservative hopes in her seat.

"If I can summarise for you, North London has been blighted by a major criminal gang for decades. It's headed by a family just as dangerous, but less well known, as the Kray brothers were."

"Who are the family?"

"I'm going to come to that in a minute, Joanna."

"Okay, Marcus. It's your meeting, after all."

"Thank you, Joanna."

Marcus sipped his coffee before resuming.

"Have you heard of the Mark Smith case?"

"No."

"It is an old case. It dates from 1961 when a young Afro Caribbean man named Mark Smith was hanged for raping and shooting to death a young white girl named Janet Brown in a park in Marchfield."

"I see. I don't approve of the death penalty, but I know that was the law then. Did he actually do it?"

"He denied it, but there was an eyewitness who gave evidence against him and this was backed by the forensic evidence."

"So it was an open and shut case. Poor Janet, and poor Mark! However, why are you talking to me about it now? It's not your style to engage in idle gossip about the past, Marcus."

Fifty Years After

"My grandson has been very busy researching this case and has unearthed new evidence that suggests that the evidence was rigged and the jury was bribed to find Mark guilty. The Home Secretary also seems to have been involved because he caused a stir by refusing to commute the sentence since the defendant was only 18 at the time. The age of majority then was 21."

Joanna nodded.

"I've heard of such miscarriages of justice, so I'm not surprised, but I am doubly sad for the two people involved."

She looked searchingly at Marcus.

"You seem very disturbed by this case, Marcus. Were you involved in it by any chance?"

"My father was the prosecutor and the chief witness was my old enemy, Philip Stewart."

Joanna looked startled, and tried to hide her instant reaction by burying her face in her coffee cup and picking up a biscuit.

"What are you telling me, Marcus?"

"There's no easy way to put this, Joanna. I know he's a senior member of your Party, but, if the appeal court decides that the original verdict was wrong and that Mark did not murder his girlfriend, and the evidence certainly points that way, then Philip Stewart automatically becomes the chief suspect and will be arrested and put on trial for murder."

Joanna suddenly saw the connection that linked the question Marcus asked her about North London with the issue of the trial.

"Are you saying that he's also connected with this North London gang you referred to?"

"He's almost certainly the leader of the gang, Joanna. The new investigation will undoubtedly bring that out. They have been covered up by the use of bribes among senior officers of the Metropolitan Police. As a result, the new investigation is being conducted by another force."

Fifty Years After

Joanna looked grave, but her mind was racing as she tried to grapple with the disastrous potential of what the Prime Minister was telling her.

"What do you want me to do?" she asked at length.

"Nothing for the moment. It is vital that no action is taken against Lord Stewart and that nothing is said to Lord Stewart that could give him warning. However, when the police are ready, they will need to be able to search his Westminster office. The Master at Arms will certainly contact you before he authorises the search. I am simply asking you to give your permission and not to raise it at Question Time. Calm your Shadow Cabinet's reactions down and also try to keep your MPs calm. We'll all have to keep calm, I suspect, because I have a feeling that we may all be engulfed in another scandal. Fortunately, so far, the press has not become involved. When it happens, my advice is that you should respond to press enquiries with the words, 'no comment'."

Joanna was stunned.

"Can I share this with the Shadow Cabinet?"

"I would prefer that you don't, at least, not until after he's been arrested. Then you'll have to. As a member of the Privy Council you may have to advise the Queen to strip him of his peerage. We can't have murderers in the House of Peers."

Joanna smiled at this.

"At one stage, Marcus, you couldn't be a Lord unless you were a murderer!"

"Fortunately, we've progressed a little since the Wars of the Roses, Joanna."

They both laughed and Joanna got up and offered Marcus her hand. He took it and shook it.

"Thank you for briefing me, Marcus."

"Thank you, for being so understanding, Joanna."

Albert Corrigan was meeting with Julia Donaldson in his chambers. She came up from Guildford that morning to take over the Smith/Brown Case. She was surprised when

Fifty Years After

the Chief Constable of Surrey Police called her to his office.

"Julia," he said to her, "I have a special mission for you. I'm not sure of the ins and outs of the case, except that it's a delicate one that requires tact, determination and self-discipline. You have these qualities and they are why Lord Corrigan asked for you. The Chief Constable of the Met agreed with the request and will make office space available for you at Scotland Yard."

"What's this all about, Sir," Julia asked.

"As far as I can make out it's almost a cold case. Back in 1961 a young black man was hanged for killing a young white woman. Both were teenagers and they had been in a relationship. He is alleged to have raped her and shot her dead when she objected (or something like that). There was an eye witness and the forensic evidence backed his story."

"It seems like it was an open and shut case," Julia commented. "So, what do I have to investigate?"

"I don't know, if I'm totally honest with you, Julia. I was told of certain irregularities in the trial and possible cover-ups after it. You will have to get to the bottom of it. I suggest that you go up to Town tomorrow and meet with Lord Corrigan."

"Do you mean Lord Albert Corrigan, the Master of the Rolls, Sir?"

"Yes, Julia, except that he's now announced his impending retirement. He's due to retire at Easter."

So it was that Julia Donaldson arrived at Albert's Chambers, was offered a seat and a sherry and handed a large dossier of papers. She looked surprised.

"Lord Corrigan, I was told I was to investigate a rather obscure, very straightforward murder. It was the sort of murder that's sadly too common. It's what we in the police call 'a domestic', except that it's an extreme form of the genre."

Fifty Years After

"Please call me Albert because we're going to work together on this case. I've retired in order to prosecute the actual murderer. I was the defence barrister in the original trial. It was my first case and I lost it. I'm determined to get justice for the two victims involved."

"I thought there was only one victim – the girl," Julia commented.

"I'm including the boy who was hanged. I believe that we've established his innocence of the charge and shown that the trial was both rigged and corrupted by the family of the real murderer, the chief witness, Philip Stewart."

"I know that name," Julia said, "but I'm not sure where I've heard it."

"He is an ex MP, an ex minister, and is now a member of the House of Lords."

Julia slapped her hand on Albert's desk.

"Of course! I knew I knew the name. He's Lord Stewart of Little Wittering."

Albert nodded.

"It would take a long time for me to go through the papers with you. Instead I've prepared a summary to guide you through the dossier. I've got to go into court now, and I'll be there until 4.30. You can use this office. The coffee urn is there for you, as is the biscuit tin. Help yourself. Be sure to get some lunch and spend the time studying the dossier. I'll answer any questions you have when I return this afternoon."

Julia nodded and thanked him. Albert put on his robes and wig and left the room, leaving the Superintendent there. She moved over to Albert's desk, poured herself another coffee, opened the dossier and began to read. As she read the first paper – Police Constable Adam's arrest report her eyes opened wide and she realised she had a major problem on her hands. She picked up the phone and rang the Chief Constable of Surrey, who answered.

"I've met Lord Corrigan, Sir, and have begun to read the papers related to this case. I now think I understand why I'm here, and I also realise that I'm probably going to be here for a long time. I may even need two or three of our guys to help conduct the investigation."

"Take as long as you need, Superintendent Donaldson. If you need help, you only have to ask and I'll ensure you get what you need."

"Thank you, Sir."

Julia put down the phone and continued to read the lengthy dossier with mounting concern.

Philip rang Evelyn's mobile. Evelyn answered quickly.

"What can I do for you, Philip?" she asked.

"I want to talk to your grandson and his girlfriend," he said simply.

"Belinda is his fiancée," Evelyn corrected. "They got engaged earlier this month."

"Give them my congratulations," he said dryly. "Can you give me their telephone number?"

"No, but I can go and speak to them."

"Are they up here in London, then?"

"No, we're in Buckinghamshire."

"I thought you were with Sir Marcus."

"He doesn't need me to be there. We have a staff in Downing Street who will ensure that he's properly looked after. I've got two twenty year old lovebirds in my house. I'm here to ensure that nothing untoward happens between them or to them."

"Can I come down and speak to them?"

"What about?"

"I have a proposition to put to them."

"You can always try. I'll tell them to expect you tomorrow afternoon."

Lord Corrigan returned to his office with a sigh. "Thank God it's Friday," he thought. Entering the room, he removed and hung up his gown and put his wig away before looking over to where Julia was sitting at his desk, writing notes on one of his yellow legal pads. She looked up as he entered.

"How's it going?"

"I think you've got enough fresh evidence to force a retrial and sufficient to justify an arrest warrant against Lord Philip Stewart," Julia answered. "However, I'm not so sure we have sufficient to charge and convict him of the murder of Janet Brown, although we can certainly get him on other offences."

"And the cover up?"

"That's a very murky picture. It looks as though the Greenways were up to their necks in it. So too was Inspector Buchan – but I suspect that other Police Officers and possibly other politicians are also involved."

"What do you plan to do?"

"First, I want to re-examine all the new witnesses. Except for Wilfred Martins, who, I understand, passed away in any case, none of the statements are acceptable in court. I also want to know the provenance of these documents. I think I need to talk first to your young assistant – Jonathan Greenway. It's odd how the name recurs."

"He's the grandson of Sir Marcus Greenway."

"Ah," she said. "I understand now. However, does he realise how much trouble his grandfather may be in?"

"He realises that," Albert said grimly.

"But he still goes on?"

"He feels he has no choice. I think he wishes he hadn't got involved – but having done so, he feels that, if he stopped now, he would be an accomplice in a crime."

"He's right of course," Julia commented. "But very few 20 year olds would think that way. He must be a remarkable young man. I'm looking forward to meeting him and his girlfriend."

"Belinda is his fiancée," Albert corrected. "They became engaged last month."

"When shall we visit them?"

Fifty Years After

"I will drive you down tomorrow morning," Albert said.

Julia agreed, and, packing up the papers to take with her, she left the room and set off to drive back to her home in Coulsdon, just outside of London.

Jonathan and Belinda, meanwhile, were quietly in Buckinghamshire, resuming their university studies, working on Marcus's biography, and taking the occasional car ride with Evelyn and Hawkins and walking in the grounds. Jonathan also taught Evelyn to play poker and discovered that she and Belinda were better at cards than he was. In these ways, the days merged into one another as the month rolled quietly on. Belinda received a text message from Carole, which told her that Michael and Emma had gone missing after being them at the Rag Ball. Belinda was very upset at this and told Jonathan. He was equally upset, but, as he said to her, "There's nothing we can do about it. We were plainly the intended targets, so we can't go out looking for them without running the risk of being kidnapped and probably killed ourselves. It's almost certainly the work of the Stewart Gang."

"The Lucky Lady" meanwhile berthed in Le Havre harbour. Tom rang his friend, Jacques, who walked down to inspect the cargo. Jim and Tom had taken the two prisoners to the shower room just before the boat berthed and scrubbed them down. They oiled their skins and shaved off all their body hair. Having got their prisoners' bodies clean and shining, with no part hidden by unwanted body hair, their jailors took them back to their cell and chained them up again. Tom accompanied Jacques to the cell and allowed him to examine the two prisoners. He put his fingers in their mouths and other orifices and produced an erection in Michael as well as an orgasm in Emma. He pronounced himself satisfied and began to haggle.

"Are they virgins?" he asked.

"As far as I know," Tom replied.

"English?"

"Yes."

"Aged 20?"

"Yes."

"Okay. I'll give you 1000 Euros for each."

"That's not enough. How about 10000 Euros each?"

"Certainly not, Tom. Do you want to ruin me? 2000 Euros each."

"There are five of us. Give us each 1000 Euros and you can have them."

"5000 Euros for the two seems fair to me. I'll agree."

They shook hands on the deal.

"Okay. They're yours. When do you want to collect them?"

"After dark tonight. Do they have any clothes or jewellery?"

"No, we stripped them naked and threw everything into a skip on a building site on the way down. Probably the British police have them now – but they certainly don't!"

"I prefer it that way, Tom. It gives us greater control over them. See you tonight with the cash. Have them ready for me."

Albert met Julia at Waterloo Station and drove her down to the Estate, arriving at the gate at 11 am. They were admitted at once and were met by Evelyn as they entered the house.

"Lady Evelyn," Albert explained, "This is Superintendent Donaldson of the Surrey Police. She has taken over the Stewart Case and wishes to talk to your two charges about it."

Evelyn smiled at Julia.

"Good morning, Superintendent. It's good to see you and to know that something is happening at last in this case. It's been so long. My grandson and his fiancée are upstairs, resting after taking a long walk through the estate. Lord Corrigan will take you into the small Reception Room, and I will collect and bring Jonathan and Belinda to you."

Fifty Years After

Philip woke up late, tired after his round trip, and, after breakfast, left the family home in North London and drove west towards Buckinghamshire.

Jonathan and Belinda entered the small Reception Room and were introduced to Julia by Albert.

"Julia, this is Jonathan Greenway, the grandson of the Prime Minister, and this is his fiancée, Belinda Thompson. These are the two who were instrumental in gathering the material you have in your file."

"Belinda and Jonathan, this is Superintendent Julia Donaldson. She's from Surrey Police and is now in charge of the investigation. She wants to ask you some questions and take statements from you."

"Thank you, Albert."

Julia looked at the young man sitting opposite her, straight backed and with a pleasant, but determined, look on his face. "It would be easy to underestimate this one," she thought. "However, it would be very dangerous. This young man is honest and straightforward. I don't think he's easily scared off."

"How did you get involved in this?" she asked.

Jonathan explained how he'd come across the case while researching his grandfather's life, found out more about it, and felt that there was something odd about it.

"So, you began to investigate?"

"That's right, Superintendent. My grandfather and Lord Corrigan told me that, if I could get new evidence, they would see if they could get the case reopened."

"And that's what you did?"

"Yes."

Julia pointed to the papers in her brief case.

"Did you gather all this?"

"Not all of it. Some came from work by Sir Marcus's assistant – Daphne."

"What did you collect and how did you do it?"

"First I got copies of the Police Files on the Brown Murder Case, the Stewart Family Gang, Philip Stewart and D I Buchan. I asked a friend of mine if he could secure the first three and he added the fourth."

Julia showed Jonathan the four files.

"Were these the files?"

"Yes, Superintendent."

Julia pointed to the Martins Affidavit and the two envelopes.

"My friend put an advert in the paper and Wilfred Martins answered it. I went to see him and he told me the story of the bribes, before giving me the two unopened envelopes and the affidavit. He told me he didn't have long to live. We opened the envelopes in the presence of the Attorney General. We videoed it for the courts."

Jonathan pointed to the photograph album, the railway tickets and the receipt from the hotel.

"They were given to me by Luke, Mark Smith's brother and Janet's diary and its contents came from Jennifer Foster, Janet's sister."

Julia wrote this all down in approved statement form and asked Jonathan to read it and sign it. As he was doing this, she spoke with Belinda, who described how they had photocopied the documents and assembled the dossiers and how Daphne had added the extra Stewart files. This information was put into the correct legal form and signed. Julia finished with them by asking for and receiving Luke and Jennifer's addresses and phone numbers.

"I will go to see them and get statements from them over the next two days," she said. "However, thank you for all the work you've done. You've exposed a major scandal and helped get justice for two people, even though it was too late for one of them."

"Albert told us that Mark didn't want to live after his fiancée died," Belinda commented.

"Luke confirmed it to me," Jonathan added. "However, Mark also asked for two things to be done – the real killer

Fifty Years After

to be punished and his name cleared, and his body to be moved from its burial place in the prison and reburied with Janet."

"That will be done, I promise you, and you all will be present at the funeral," Julia said.

Jonathan phoned through to the kitchen to see if there were refreshments available for the two visitors now that their work was complete. A distant voice promised that they would be brought up, and he put the phone down, only for it to ring again. It was Evelyn.

"I have Lord Stewart down here with a proposition for you. Are you free to come down?"

Albert shook his head.

"Don't go down. The less you see of Philip Stewart the better."

"I agree," Julia said. "You should keep away from him. You know too much!"

Jonathan spoke to Evelyn.

"Grandma, I'm feeling a bit faint, after the long walk I had this morning. I don't feel up to another long conversation. Tell Lord Stewart I will be available sometime next week if he really wants to see me."

A male voice came on the phone.

"I'm sorry to trouble you Jonathan, but it's rather urgent. I have a vacancy in one of my companies for the two of you and I wanted to offer you both jobs – you as an IT consultant and your fiancée as a legal advisor. We'll pay the rest of your fees and a £20000 retainer to both of you."

Jonathan put his hand over the phone and turned to Belinda.

"He's trying to bribe us. He's offered us both jobs, he wants to pay the rest of our fees and a £20000 retainer to both of us."

He returned to the phone.

"It's a very generous offer, Lord Stewart, but sadly I don't think I could take you up on it."

"Don't slam the door shut on it young man. You won't get a better offer anywhere else."

"We'll think about it and come back to you in a couple of days," Jonathan promised.

He put the phone down.

"Well done!" Julia and Albert said. "You've turned down something in excess of £30000 each", Julia added. "He must have been desperate."

"He is," Jonathan said. "He's afraid of us and wants to silence us in one way or another."

Evelyn felt very proud of Jonathan and Belinda as she escorted Philip to his car. She had heard the offer and Jonathan's reply. "Both like and unlike Marcus," she thought. "Marcus is like rubber, he bends with the wind, but holds firm in the end. Jonathan is like steel. He doesn't bend at all."

Evelyn joined the others in the small Reception Room. She noticed that the staff had served refreshments and asked how this had been arranged (since she had forgotten to order it by the time Philip arrived and it was too late).

"I ordered them, Grandma," Jonathan answered.

"Thank you, Jonathan," Evelyn responded. "Have you done everything you need to do, Superintendent?" she continued.

"Yes, Lady Greenway," Julia answered. "Your grandson and his fiancée have been very lucid and very helpful."

Belinda interrupted.

"You haven't got everything, Superintendent Donaldson."

"What have I missed, Belinda," Julia asked.

"There are two missing students from Cambridge."

"Yes, I know about them. However, it's not my case."

"It is," Jonathan said, supporting Belinda.

Julia was surprised by his vehemence.

"Why is it my case?" she asked.

"Because the two students were pretending to be Jonathan and me," Belinda explained. "My friend, Carole Green, told the man who asked questions about us that we would be at the Rag Ball and that some students were plotting to kidnap us and hold us to ransom. I think that Philip Stewart ordered his men to snatch us, and they took Michael and Emma by mistake."

"I see," said Julia, and she did see, vaguely. "But why can't the local police deal with it as they would do normally? There are no questions about the activities of the Cambridgeshire Police."

"Because they're likely to arrest Philip Stewart and you probably don't want that to happen too quickly," Jonathan said.

Albert and Julia exchanged glances.

"I will send out a confidential memo to all police forces that any information regarding Philip Stewart should come to my desk and that no approach and no arrest should be made without my prior approval," Julia said.

The Cambridge Inspector left the interview room and put a call through to Interpol requesting a police search of Le Havre for "The Lucky Lady". When he returned, he informed Bert that he was under arrest and would be returning with him to Cambridge to make a formal statement and be charged with kidnapping Emma and Michael.

"I would like to make a deal with you, Inspector," Bert said.

"What sort of deal?"

"Immunity from prosecution in return for testifying against Philip Stewart and members of the Stewart Gang."

The Inspector thought about this.

"That's a London problem," he said, "Not a Cambridge one. However, I will let the London Police know about your offer."

Bert went white suddenly.

"No, Inspector," he said. "Please don't do that. Tell Lord Albert Corrigan, the Master of the Rolls. He put me inside once, and I trust him. He will let the appropriate officer know. Meanwhile, it would be better if the world thought I was dead – run over perhaps by a hit and run driver."

The Inspector wondered about this.

"Does anyone have Lord Corrigan's phone number?" he asked.

Eventually someone found his mobile number and the Inspector rang it.

"I have a man here, Lord Corrigan. He told us that he kidnapped the two missing students and that Lord Stewart ordered it. He asked me to tell you and also tell you that, in exchange for immunity from prosecution, he's prepared to spill the beans over the Stewart Gang. He wants me to announce that he has been killed in a hit and run accident. What do you want me to do?"

"Accept the offer and take the man to Cambridge. Put him in a safe place there and follow his suggestion about announcing his death. The police officer currently investigating Lord Stewart, Superintendent Donaldson of the Surrey Police will come up and see him in a day or two."

"You're a very lucky chap, Albert Campion, because Lord Corrigan has asked me to accept your offer and take you to Cambridge and keep you in a safe place until you can be interviewed by the new officer investigating the Stewart Gang – Superintendent Donaldson."

"Is he from London?"

"No, the Superintendent is from Surrey."

"Good," Bert said, as he was led away to the Police Van.

That afternoon Jacques kept a close eye on the harbour and the boat. He noticed that the number of police cars in the area had grown and was still growing, and that there was a pattern. Basically it looked as though the police were quietly sealing the harbour area off. No one was stopping pedestrians, but he noticed that police were putting up signs diverting motorists away from the harbour area and stopping and searching vehicles leaving the harbour. Jacques walked through the incipient police cordon down to the beach and along to the harbour. He looked out to sea and saw two police boats were anchored a short way off the harbour entrance.

"They must know about 'the Lucky Lady'," he guessed.

He walked smartly away and decided to call the deal off. However, he made no effort to contact Tom to warn him.

The raid went in at 6 pm. There was no resistance and the five men were all arrested. The two prisoners were found, released, and taken to hospital. The families were informed and flown over to console their offspring. The five prisoners were taken to a French prison and charged with kidnapping and trafficking. The Cambridgeshire Police were informed and asked to send officers over to collect the prisoners or to extradite and collect them. Two days later, files relating to the case came to the notice of Julia Donaldson in London.

22. The new Police Team

April 2010
The first week of April was Holy Week and Julia decided to take the opportunity to wrap up the loose ends of the Smith Case and organise her team of three detectives to begin to explore the more difficult part of her mandate. She decided to move her office out of Scotland Yard and return to her home base in South London. She spoke to her friend, the Lewisham Borough Commander, and acquired a suite of four offices in Lewisham Police Station for her team to work from. It had the advantage of being easily accessible to central and north London because of its proximity to Lewisham Railway Station and the Dockland Light Railway. Once they had settled in, she called them together for a planning conference.

Her second in command was an experienced Detective Sergeant from Yorkshire – Thomas Skinner. She knew him well, having worked with him for twenty years. In addition, she had a young Welsh Detective Constable – Gethin Jones. She had been impressed by his enthusiasm and dedication to his work. The third member of her team was another Detective Constable – Susan Godfrey, from Dorking in Surrey. She was an aspiring Sergeant and had made a number of successful arrests. She briefed them on the magnitude and scope of their task.

"We've got an apparently long dead and buried open and shut murder case. It took place in 1961 and featured two 18-year-old people. One was a white girl, named Janet Brown. She worked as a milliner. The other was an Afro Caribbean youth, named Mark Smith. He was an apprentice printer. They were going out together and had been for about five and a half months when it is alleged that Mark raped Janet and then shot her to death. The main witness was another young man, a 20-year-old white man named Philip Stewart. He claimed that Mark Smith tried to

Fifty Years After

shoot him, but shot the girl instead. Forensics supported Stewart's story, and Smith was convicted. His appeal was rejected and his appeal for clemency also rejected. He was hanged in July 1961. As I said, on the face of it, it's an open and shut case. The defendant did not give evidence and the Jury reached its unanimous verdict in 20 minutes. The whole trial lasted just under six hours.

"However, there has always been some dissatisfaction over the verdict and a number of attempts have been made to get a retrial or a ruling of a mistrial. All have failed. One of the reasons for that was that the same Home Secretary who refused to show clemency to Mark Smith ordered the case files to be closed until 2061. However, 'Cometh the hour, cometh the man,' so they say. A 20 year old man, the grandson of Sir Marcus Greenway, who incidentally was the assistant to the Prosecutor (his father) in the 1961 trial, was determined to discover the true story behind the trial. Somehow he managed to get hold of the original case files. I don't know how. I've asked him and he's not been very forthcoming about it! However, the file shows that the trial was effectively rigged against the defendant. Two key documents – the arrest report and the forensic report were doctored to exclude evidence favourable to the defendant by order of the officer in charge of the case, one D I Buchan. In addition, young Greenway managed to speak to the only surviving Juror who gave him evidence that someone bribed the jury to find the defendant guilty. Lastly, Jonathan was given the diary of the murdered girl, which ended on the day before her death. That diary also backs the defendant's account of events and gives us the basis to charge Philip Stewart with murder once the old verdict is swept away."

Julia looked around at the stunned police officers.

"That's our first task, Lady and Gentlemen. I have a huge file of documents here and I have asked a copy of the file to be placed in each of your offices. It is strictly confidential. I do not want a Stewart equivalent to young Jonathan Greenway gaining access to it! I've interviewed Jonathan and his charming fiancée, but we need to interview his two sources. That's what we're going to do tomorrow. You two men are going to interview and get a statement from Luke Smith (that's Mark's brother) and Susan and I will talk with Jennifer Foster (Janet's sister). Once we've got those statements in the bag we'll meet to prepare the papers for the Appeal Court."

They all nodded.

"That's when the hard part begins. We have to bring Philip Stewart and the Stewart Gang to book. We also have to find out who's been protecting them and who's been receiving payments from them. That job begins as soon as we've finished the first half. It will be unpleasant because we'll be investigating our London Colleagues and possibly also senior political figures. I've had a hint that this could include the most senior – the Prime Minister. We have to be objective and fair, but also determined. The Stewart Gang has terrorised north London for fifty years. Our job is to end the terror and put them all behind bars. Do any of you feel unable to do this?"

Julia looked at each in turn. They all shook their heads.

"Right, then; Gethin and Thomas, once you have finished with Luke and we've done the paper work for the appeal court, you have an urgent date in Cambridge. You are going to debrief one Albert Campion. He claims he was a fixer for Philip Stewart and organised the recent kidnap of the two Cambridge Students. He gave us the information, which enabled us to rescue them and arrest their kidnappers. They will be brought back to London in due time and Susan and I will interview them. You, however, will get as much information from Campion as you can. He's asked for immunity from prosecution in return for shopping the Stewart Gang. We've got to make sure that it's a worthwhile deal for us. He could be the key, which enables us to unlock the Stewart Gang.

"Are there any questions?"

"Just one, Ma'am," said Thomas. "What is the deadline for this investigation?"

"For the Retrial – this week. I want to get the old verdict cleared out of the way as soon as possible so that we can take Philip Stewart out of circulation. For the rest, we'll take as long as it takes."

"By Philip Stewart, do you mean Lord Philip Stewart, Ma'am?" Susan asked.

"Yes, Susan."

Julia paused.

"We could be together for a long time working on this. I suggest we drop the ranks. I'm Julia. Let's address each other by our first names, not our ranks."

They all agreed to this and went to their individual offices to study their files. Julia phoned each one in turn to check that the intercom she had asked the local force to establish between the four offices worked. She was pleased to find that it did.

They returned to Julia's office at 4 pm, to consider where they were and where they were going. This was to be the invariable pattern for the investigation. Albert Corrigan joined them, as was also to be the pattern.

"What do you three think about our case now?" Julia asked.

"I think, Julia, that you have all you need to get a review and to get the trial verdict annulled," Thomas said.

"I think you've got enough to ask for an arrest and search warrant for Lord Stewart," Susan added.

"One step at a time, Albert cautioned. "We don't want to have an extradition battle on our hands or another vanished peer."

"I agree," Julia said. "We mustn't get ahead of ourselves."

"I think we're going to need either more help or more luck to deal with the Stewart Gang," Thomas said. "Once we start probing there we'll have the press on our backs at once."

"Incidentally," Albert commented, "talking about the Press. There was a young reporter at the 1961 trial. She worked for the local North London Herald and actually interviewed both Mark Smith and Philip Stewart after the trial. She was heavily criticised at the time, I remember, for talking to a man who was facing the gallows. However, I suggested it in the hope that, if he told his story, it might stir up the public to demand a stay of execution. It didn't work, but it's worth talking to the reporter if you can find her."

"What was her name, Albert?" Julia asked.

"I think it was Juliet Stevens. I'll check my files, but I'm almost sure that was her name. Of course, she's probably married now and known as something completely different, like Jennifer Foster is."

"I'll see if we can trace her," Julia said. "That's a nice job for you, Gethin. Find her and interview her. Try and get her original notes if you can. Most reporters keep their notes, especially if it's one of the first big stories they've covered."

Julia suddenly had a thought.

"When you do the interviews tomorrow try to get other examples of the writing of both Janet Brown and Mark Smith. We may need to establish the authenticity of the diary and letters further then the verbal evidence will do. See if the siblings have kept any other letters or perhaps school exercise books. Anything that can be definitely traced to one or the other that can be used for comparison."

They nodded. She turned to Albert.

"Albert, since you are going to be our barrister and prosecutor, do you have anything to add?"

"Not really. I'm sure you've already said this, but we need to have three watchwords in our investigation – caution, accuracy and secrecy. The longer we can keep moving in the dark, the better for us. At a certain point this

Fifty Years After

case is going to explode into the light. That's when our troubles will begin. At the moment no one knows that Philip Stewart is under investigation and no one knows that the Prime Minister's very future is at risk. I want that situation to remain as long as possible."

"We all agree with that, Albert," Julia concluded. "Now, she added brightly, "I've heard there are some good pubs in Lewisham. Let's go and check the intelligence."

Next morning the two men visited Luke in his home and took his statement. They covered the same ground that Luke had covered with Jonathan. Once the statement was fully written down, Luke signed it. Gethin raised the question of other evidence of Mark's writing.

"I do have a cardboard box of his belongings, which you can take and go through. After the trial let me have them back."

"Of course, Luke," Thomas said. "We will only use what we need to establish the fact the letters in Janet's diary were written by him. Of course, if we find anything else that helps us understand Mark or helps establish Philip's guilt, we'll use that as well. We will bring the rest back to you."

"Thank you, Sergeant," Luke said. "Thank you all especially for taking Mark's case seriously at last."

They acknowledged Luke's thanks and made their way back to their base.

Meanwhile Julia and Susan were talking to Jennifer. They went through the evidence that Jennifer gave to Jonathan and put it down in the usual form as a statement, which Jennifer signed. Then they turned to the question of other evidence.

"What happened to Janet's possessions after her death?" Julia asked.

"After Dad died, I gathered together her clothes and gave them to a charity shop. I found her diary and other books and her 'toys'. I still have some in the loft."

Fifty Years After

"What I need is an exercise book or something similar with her name on and in which she has written. It is to establish that the handwriting is her own."

Jennifer left them, climbed the stairs and they heard her open up the loft. A few minutes later she descended the stairs and entered the living room clutching two school exercise books.

"These were Janet's last English books. They should establish her writing for you, Superintendent."

Julia thanked Jennifer for her help, and the two police officers stood up to leave. However, Jennifer stopped them with a final question.

"When will you take this case to court, Superintendent? We've been waiting 50 years. Our Mums and Dads are dead and so are our brothers and sister."

"I understand that, Jennifer. We don't know the exact dates yet, but the plan is to try to get the verdict reversed first and then arrest Philip Stewart and charge him with the murder. Later we will put him on trial and then set out to smash the Stewart Gang once and for all. My guess is that stage 1 will be later this month and stage 2 in October. "

"Thank God," Jennifer breathed, "and thank you. It's good that we have a police team that we can actually trust for once."

Back at the office, the team prepared to split up. Julia collected the exercise books handed to them by Luke and Jennifer and arranged to spend the rest of the week with Susan and Albert preparing the papers for the first trial. Albert told them that he wanted to bring Belinda in on the meetings as she was going to act as his assistant during the trials. Julia reluctantly agreed. She did not like amateurs being involved in police investigations or trial preparation, even if they were trainee lawyers. At least, she thought, it was better than having Jonathan Greenway, an IT student and a complete amateur being further involved.

"Will you be bringing her here?" Julia asked Albert. "She's basically restricted to the Chequers estate for her own protection. I'm not prepared to relocate this office to Buckinghamshire for her benefit. Indeed, I feel that the files we have gathered should remain here now they've arrived here."

"I'm going to ask Jonathan and Belinda to record a reading of the diary and letters for the court and I shall be using Jonathan as my runner and Belinda as my organiser and note taker. I will go down and collect her tomorrow morning and will house her with me overnight until we have finished. In the meantime, it is useful for Jonathan Greenway to act as a distraction to Philip Stewart by keeping him doing his studies in Buckinghamshire. Philip has convinced himself that Jonathan is his real enemy and will not believe that he's not directly involved in the case anymore."

"Fair enough, Albert. In that case we will begin work at 2 pm tomorrow. Meanwhile Thomas and Gethin are travelling to Cambridge to debrief Campion. They will stay in a hotel in the city until they have finished the debrief and then we will know what we've got."

"What about Emma and Michael?" Albert asked. "When do you plan to take statements from them and from their five assailants?"

"The two kidnap victims have been flown back to UK and are in hospital in Cambridge. The Cambridge Police will handle their interviews when they are fit enough and pass the statements down to us. The five assailants are subject to an extradition procedure. When they are shipped back to us we will hold them in the cells here and interview them ourselves before transferring them to Cambridge."

Albert nodded his agreement and left the meeting. Once he reached his house, he rang Evelyn and asked her to warn Belinda to be ready for him to collect her the following morning and to pack and bring an overnight bag with her because she will sleep over in his house while they were working on the papers.

Fifty Years After

"What about Jonathan?" Evelyn asked, anticipating objections from her grandson.

"Tell him that he is not needed at this stage and is safer staying with you. Belinda will never be out of my sight and I will bring her back as soon as the work is completed."

Philip, meanwhile, knew nothing of the arrest of his men in France or of the defection of Bert. He knew that Jonathan was a very dangerous opponent, despite his youth, and was still thinking about how he could neutralise him like he had neutralised his grandfather and great grandfather. Concentrating on his iconic opponent, Philip was totally unaware of the real danger creeping up on him in the persons of the four Surrey Police Officers, Albert and Belinda, Daphne and Bert. His usually alert and effective danger recognition instincts had been redirected and, as a result, the real danger eluded him as it crept up on him. Later that day, Philip began to hear a rumour that Bert had been killed in a car crash and that 'The Lucky Lady" had sunk in the English Channel with the loss of all on board. As he was brooding over his perceived misfortune in running into yet another Greenway in the latter years of his life, just as he felt that he had gained mastery over his oldest rival at last, the phone rang. He picked it up and was surprised to hear the voice of his young opponent.

"Lord Philip," Jonathan began, "It's Jonathan Greenway. I'm sorry to bother you when you must be very busy with political papers, but I need your help."

Philip smiled.

"So the little wanker has his price after all!" he thought. "I left the baited hook in the water and he has bitten after all. I guessed he would. These pampered and privileged Greenways are all the same. They make a pretence in public of sobriety and ethical perfection, but, in private, they're on the grab, just like the rest of us."

Fifty Years After

"Hello, Jonathan. Don't worry about disturbing me. I'm always at the disposal of your Grandfather's family. How can I help you?"

"Belinda and I have been commissioned by my Grandfather to write his biography. That's why we've been given time off University – but it's all very confidential at the moment. Grandfather is afraid that, if the story leaked, people will think he's contemplating resignation and retirement. The fact is that it is Grandma who has persuaded him to do something he doesn't want to do – write his life story."

"Evelyn would!" Philip responded with relief, as the light began to dawn on him and the figure of young Jonathan Greenway became suddenly less menacing. "How can I help?"

"We've got to the trial of Mark Smith for the murder of Janet Brown. Granddad was involved in that and I know what his role was and I also have the transcript of the trial. I've talked to Mark's brother and Janet's sister so I know something about those two. Of course, I've also talked to you and Granddad. However, something Granddad said puzzles me and I wondered whether you could shed light on it?"

Despite himself, Philip was intrigued. "What has the little wanker stumbled on?" he thought.

"What's the problem, and how can I help?"

"The trial transcript notes that, at a certain point, Jennifer Brown left the court and Granddad followed her out. I know what they said to each other because I've asked them both about it and their accounts tally. Jennifer told Granddad that Mark and Janet were lovers. Granddad told Sir Walter what Jennifer had told him and asked whether he should pass the information on to Albert Corrigan. Sir Walter refused and said that it was not his job to help the defence if they had not found out this information for themselves."

"I see," Philip commented. "What are you asking me?"

"Sir Walter had a duty as a servant of the court to make any new information available to the court. He chose not to do so. It occurred to me that he might have had some contact with either you or some other member of your family before the trial. I know that he and Granddad were present when you were interviewed by Inspector Buchan."

"How does he know that?" Philip wondered. He decided not to arouse Jonathan's suspicions by asking the question. Instead he decided to confirm the fact as though it was of no importance.

"They were there in an observing capacity. After all, they were the Prosecution team and I was their chief witness." He paused to let this sink in, and then continued. "I'm not sure about contacts between my Dad and Sir Walter. I didn't have any, but I think they became friends afterwards and I know that Sir Walter became legal advisor to my Dad."

"Was there any contact before the trial?"

"I don't think so, Jonathan, but, honestly, I don't know. I was only 20 at the time. That's your age now. How much do you know about what your father is doing or who he's seeing?"

"Virtually nothing," Jonathan said ruefully.

"I'm sorry that I can't give you more help, Jonathan. I would love to see the manuscript of the book when it's completed, and, if there's any other way I can help you, don't hesitate to ring me. Your Granddad and I have had an interesting relationship, as everyone knows!"

"Thank you, Lord Philip," Jonathan concluded. "I may take you up on that."

"I'm Philip, Jonathan," Philip said. "I will be at your disposal if you need me. Good luck with the book!"

Philip put the phone down with a greater sense of satisfaction than Jonathan did. He felt that, at last, he knew what Jonathan was up to. It all made sense, and, he felt that he had misunderstood the situation and badly over reacted.

Fifty Years After

"I'm getting too old for this game," he thought.

Jonathan turned to Belinda, who had been working with him on the book; and was sitting beside him during the conversation.

"I've learnt nothing concrete," he confessed, "but I feel that Philip Stewart was speaking the truth. Plainly there was a link between Jack Stewart and Sir Walter Greenway, but when it started will have to remain a matter of conjecture."

"Will you miss me tomorrow night, Darling?" Belinda asked. "Albert Corrigan is coming to collect me tomorrow morning and I will be staying with him overnight."

"Of course I'll miss you," Jonathan replied. "We'll just have to make up for it tonight, won't we?"

Belinda giggled and changed the subject.

"What will you do when I'm away in London?"

"I'm going to try to crack Granddad's secret cipher. You know, the one of the closed file within the file. There has to be a reason why it is specially encrypted. I think the reason is the answer to the question we've been asking."

"What did Sir Marcus know and when did he know it?" Belinda quoted.

"So far it is a question that he has chosen to evade or obscure the answer to," Jonathan concluded.

"Good luck, Darling," Belinda said, and meant it. She knew that he had been trying to crack the code for over a month without success. "If anyone can do it, you can!"

"The annoying thing, Darling, is that it has to be simple or else he could not have remembered it. There's no record in his open diary for instance. It has to be a combination of letters, capitals, numbers and symbols. I've gone through all the obvious ones – things connected with Mark Smith, Janet Brown, Philip Stewart, Sir Walter and Grandma – but nothing has worked. I've obviously missed a trick, but I don't know where."

"I'm a law student; not an IT student, Darling. But, just as you used your common sense to work through the legal documents in this case, perhaps I can do the same for your code. You said you've tried all the names and dates connected with the individuals in this case?"

"Yes, Darling, and none work."

"Have you tried to combine names and dates?"

Jonathan looked at Belinda in surprise, before jumping up, pulling her to her feet and crushing her lips to his. Eventually he spoke.

"Darling, you're a genius! That's it! You must be right! I'll follow that up tomorrow."

He began to unbutton her dress.

"Meanwhile, let's practise for tonight."

She giggled again, and reached for his trouser button and zip.

Later, before dressing for dinner, they sat together, enjoying the warmth of their bodies, watching Sir Marcus meeting President Kent on the lawn of the White House. Sir Marcus had used the Easter Recess to travel to America, to meet the President, address the US Congress and speak to the United Nations. A number of senior ministers travelled with him and, as Jonathan and Belinda knew, he hoped to come back with some significant trading deals. In a hotel in Cambridge, Gethin and Thomas were watching the same news broadcast before going down to dinner and a very liquid aperitif. Next morning, they planned to begin the debriefing of Albert Campion.

Next morning was Maundy Thursday. The Queen was in Cambridge that day, performing the Maundy Ceremony. As a result, many of the roads were closed and Gethin and Thomas decided it would be quicker and certainly easier to walk to the main Police Station. They arrived there after a brisk walk in the spring sunshine at 10.30 and were greeted by the desk Sergeant.

"Your client's in the cells waiting for you, gentlemen. Do you want him brought up to an interview room and do you want the duty solicitor called?"

Fifty Years After

"I hope he won't request it," Thomas answered. "However, you'd better have one on tap. Incidentally, for the record, I'm D S Thomas Skinner and this is D C Gethin Jones. We're both from the Surrey Police and this enquiry is in connection with what we term Operation Thunderbolt."

The Sergeant nodded and sent one of the duty constables to fetch Albert Campion while he phoned the duty solicitor and the two visitors were served tea and biscuits. Thomas and Gethin waited for the solicitor to appear before going down to the interview room. The duty solicitor was a young woman. She introduced herself to the two detectives, who invited her to take a seat.

"My name is Mary Scott. I'm the duty solicitor. I gather you want me to sit in on an interview with a suspect. Can you tell me what this is all about?"

"Certainly, Miss Scott," Thomas replied. "The interviewee is not a suspect but technically an informant. His name is Albert Campion and he organised and orchestrated the kidnap of the two Cambridge students."

"Allegedly," Mary corrected.

"No, actually," Thomas corrected her. "He has already confessed to this and gave the Cambridge police the information they needed to enable the French police to mount their rescue operation."

"I see, Mr., I'm sorry but I don't know your names."

"I'm D S Jenkins and this is D C Jones. We're from the Surrey Police concerned in Operation Thunderbolt."

"What's that?"

"We're investigating the Stewart Gang from North London. Albert Campion is a confessed senior operative of the Gang and offered to give us information about their activities in exchange for a promise of immunity from prosecution. We're here to debrief him, but we feel that a solicitor should be present to ensure that the law is followed."

"Okay, D S Skinner. I understand. You want me to be a witness and, if required, an advisor to Mr Campion. Is that it?"

"Exactly, Miss Scott."

She stood up, followed by the two men.

"All right then," she said. "Let's go."

Albert Corrigan arrived at the Estate gate at about the same time as the two Surrey detectives were talking to Mary Scott. He drove up to the house, greeted Evelyn with a kiss and met Belinda and Jonathan in the hall. Belinda was wearing a grey coat and hat and clutching an overnight bag as instructed. Jonathan was trying and failing to look organised and in control. Instead, he just looked anxious.

"Don't worry, Darling, I'll be quite all right. You'll just have to ask Grandma to give you a hot water bottle for company tonight," Belinda said with a smile on her face and in her eyes.

"I promise you that I will look after her, Jonathan," Albert said. "I won't let the wicked peer get near her!"

Jonathan kissed Belinda and said goodbye. Lady Evelyn smiled at Albert, who smiled back.

"These youngsters," she said to Albert, "seem to think that one day is an eternity."

"It is when you're in love, Lady Greenway," Albert replied. "Have you forgotten how it was with you and Sir Marcus when you first met?"

Evelyn grinned.

"No, Lord Corrigan, I haven't forgotten. How could I? We were much worse than these two!"

She turned to Belinda and Jonathan who were locked in each other's arms, almost glued together by their lips.

"Put her down, Jonathan," she commanded. "I don't want you to eat her! I think Lord Corrigan needs her help. That's why he's come to collect her."

The two lovers separated, both looking shame faced.

Fifty Years After

"I'll see you tomorrow, Darling," Belinda said to Jonathan. "Good luck with the encryption."

"Until tomorrow, Darling," Jonathan replied, reluctantly letting her go. "Take care."

Albert put his hand behind Belinda's back and steered her out of the Hall and down the steps. He took her bag and put it in the back seat of the car before opening the passenger side front door and guiding Belinda into her seat. He made sure she had buckled her seat belt before he got into the driver's seat, buckled up and started the engine. They both waved as the car drew away. Evelyn and Jonathan watched them go.

"What are you going to do now, Son?" she asked.

"I'm taking a break from study, Grandma. Instead, as Belinda said, I'm going to have a final go at cracking Grandpa's code, the one that covers that very secret file. Belinda's given me the clue that I've been struggling to find that may enable me to crack it."

"I'm going to take the dogs for a walk. When I return I shall be in my sitting room. I have a lot of letters to write. If you need me, give me a ring on the internal phone. Otherwise, I'll see you at lunch."

"Yes, Grandma."

The two separated. Jonathan went back up the stairs to his room and his laptop. Evelyn put her coat on, summoned the dogs – two terriers – and set off for her walk.

Philip Stewart, feeling relieved that the threat he had perceived to be hanging over him was lifted, sat in his office, reading Parliamentary papers and preparing a speech which he wanted to make on the Government's latest Education Reform Bill, to which he was opposed. Philip wanted to see the Government restore the old apprenticeship scheme and was planning to move an amendment requiring it to do just that. As he worked, he had the television on in the background and heard

Fifty Years After

confirmation that Albert Campion had been killed in a car crash in Cambridge.

"That will teach him to leave women alone," he said to the room.

Philip assumed that Bert had gone back to Cambridge to follow up his previous contact with Carole Green. He decided that he would ask Martha, his latest female assistant, a 21 year old postgraduate politics student from Reading University, to buy a condolence card and send it to Bert's brother, Bob.

"I suppose I'd better do the same for the five men who died when my boat blew up," he thought and mentally added that to his list of things to do.

In Cambridge the two detectives and the solicitor entered the interview room to meet Albert Campion who was sitting at the table, smoking a cigarette and looking at an empty teacup. The uniformed Constable who had been keeping an eye on him, stood up as the interviewing team entered the room, nodded to Thomas and left the room. Thomas switched on the tape recorder and introduced the team to Albert Campion.

"Please confirm your name, Mr Campion and give me your age, address and occupation."

"I'm Albert James Campion of 197, High Street, Greenford. I'm an office supervisor and have been working for many years as an assistant to Lord Philip Stewart."

"I understand that you have offered to help us in exchange for a guarantee of immunity from prosecution. Is that correct Mr Campion?"

"Yes, Sergeant."

"I have to be honest with you. I can't give you such a guarantee. Such matters are way above my pay grade, but I can promise that Superintendent Donaldson, the head of our team, will refer this interview to the DPP with her recommendation that you be offered such a guarantee.

Fifty Years After

This assumes, of course, that you follow through with your promise to help us as much as you can."

"I understand that, Sergeant Skinner, and can I say that I'm glad you're from Surrey and not from North London."

"Why's that, Mr Campion?" Gethin asked.

"Because Lord Stewart owns most of the police in North London, and everything I told them would go straight to him. My life would then be counted in hours, not even days. Lord Stewart does not like traitors."

The two officers nodded to show they understood and Thomas resumed his questions.

"I understand that you surrendered to the Police and assisted them in the rescue of Michael Harding and Emma Jackson, two students from Cambridge University. Would you tell us about that?"

Bert described how the two students were kidnapped and taken to Shoreham.

"Why did you wait for Lord Stewart?" Gethin asked.

"He intended to take them out to sea and interrogate them under torture to see what they knew before throwing them into the English Channel."

"Didn't you think that was wrong?" Gethin asked.

"It was not in my job description to think and dangerous to challenge Lord Stewart, Constable Jones."

"Carry on, Albert."

"Call me Bert, Sergeant. I feel uncomfortable with Albert."

"Very well, Bert. Carry on with your story."

"When we got down to Shoreham, Lord Stewart realised that we had got the wrong students. He was very angry and told the team to throw the kids into the Channel or leave them on a French beach to die of exposure. It was March and they were naked remember. Then we left."

"What happened to the boat?"

"They set sail immediately."

"And you?" Thomas asked.

"I drove Lord Stewart back to London. He fumed for an hour and then mellowed. He decided he could use the two students as bait to catch his real prey and phoned an order to the team not to kill them for 24 hours. Then he started talking and told me the details of what he planned for Jonathan and Belinda."

"Which were?"

"He intended to have fun with them, Sergeant."

"What was his definition of fun, Bert?"

Bert gave a detailed description of Philip's plans to torture and kill Jonathan and Belinda.

"What did you say?"

"I said nothing. It is not wise to disagree with Lord Stewart. Instead I dropped him in London and went home. Next morning, I rang the Cambridge Police and informed them where I thought they would find the students."

Gethin interrupted.

"I gather you directed them to Le Havre. That surprises me in view of what you've just told us. Why did you do that?"

"I know my men, Constable Jones. The leader, Tom Barton, has been with the organisation for many years and has contacts on the continent with people involved in running prostitution rackets. Lord Stewart gave them carte blanche as to what they did with the two prisoners, so long as they disposed of them."

"You used the word 'disposed'," Thomas pointed out. "Was that your word or Lord Stewart's?"

"Lord Stewart regularly used the term. It means 'kill in some unspecified way'. I guessed that Tom would not want to destroy the two kids when he could make money from them. He had a contact in Le Havre and I suspected that he would take the boat there and try to sell them."

Mary looked uncomfortable.

"What was the intention of the sale?" she asked. Then remembering that it was not her job to ask questions, she

Fifty Years After

apologised to the two officers, who reassured her. Bert answered.

"They would have been sold into prostitution somewhere on the Continent."

"Both of them?" Gethin asked, surprised.

"Constable, you may not realise it, but boys are every bit as desirable as sex workers as girls. In some cases, they are considered to be more valuable. Girls are easy to buy, but boys are less common and are much harder to come by. I promise you, they would have sold those two for a good price."

Thomas gathered together his papers.

"Bert, we're going to break now for lunch. After lunch I want to talk to you about Mike Bush. Is that all right with you?"

"Yes, Sergeant."

"Do you want to have this young lady present to advise and support you?"

"It's not really necessary, Sergeant. I'm not going to try to hide anything from you."

Mary picked up her yellow notepad and put it in her bag with relief. She stood up and spoke to Bert.

"If you need me Bert, this is my telephone number."

She passed him a card.

"Ask the desk to telephone me and I will return."

Jonathan was feeling depressed. He tried all morning to break Marcus's code, using different combinations of names connected with the Mark Smith trial, but none worked. He was about to give up the struggle, when he heard the lunch gong in the Hall and, switching off his laptop with relief, came down the stairs to join Evelyn for lunch. Evelyn was cheerful as usual. Over soup she asked him how he had managed.

"So far I've achieved nothing, Grandma. I've tried every combination of names and numbers I can think of connected with the trial – and each has been a dead end."

"Perhaps you're being too clever, Son. Marcus has always been bright – but he's certainly not as clever as you are. Think away from the trial. I don't suppose that was the most important event in his life – even though it may seem so to you."

"It was fairly important, Grandma," Jonathan pointed out.

The staff came in and cleared away the soup dishes before serving them the main course of roast beef and vegetables. The Butler poured them each a glass of pinot noir. Then they left them on their own. Evelyn resumed the conversation.

"If you were creating a code to protect something, what would you do?"

"I'd choose something very easy to remember."

"And what would that be?"

"Someone or something very important to me."

"And who would that be?" Evelyn asked with a twinkle in her eyes.

"Belinda, of course," Jonathan smiled. "And, of course, you Grandma."

"You need a number, so what are the most important numbers in your life?"

"That's easy. It was my first date with Belinda."

"When was that?"

"27th October, 2008."

Evelyn laughed at the promptness of the reply.

"I bet you even know the time," she said.

"It was 3.35. I met her in a café in Cambridge after a lecture."

"So, then, if you were devising a code, what would you chose?"

Jonathan thought for a moment.

"Belinda.08" he said.

"But I've tried combinations like that, and they don't work," he added.

"You've forgotten your other chief influence – me," Evelyn pointed out.

Jonathan thought about this for a few minutes as he tackled his roast beef.

"Believe.08," he said finally.

"Very good, Jonathan. I think you've got it," Evelyn said with a smile. "If you haven't worked it out yet, I think I have!"

Evelyn picked up her wine glass and drank a deep draft with an air of triumph, caused partly by Jonathan's obvious confusion. She let him struggle as the Butler entered the dining room to refill their glasses and order the staff to clear the table and serve the sweet, an apple pie made from local apples and cream. Evelyn thanked the Butler and asked him to serve coffee in the drawing room. The Butler bowed and left. Evelyn turned to Jonathan.

"Well, Son. Have you solved it yet?"

"No, Grandma," Jonathan confessed.

"Shame on you!" she chided him playfully. I'm just an ignorant old woman, but I've worked out the code. You're a future university professor and an IT expert – but you haven't!"

"You'll have to help me, Grandma," Jonathan admitted.

"Who are the two most important influences in your Granddad's life?"

"You're one, obviously, I suppose the other must be his father or mother."

Evelyn shook her head.

"Important influences don't have to be positive. Influences are things that help determine our attitudes and actions. They can be negative as well as positive."

"Yes, I can see that, Grandma. But where does it get us?"

"Be patient, Son. The trouble with the younger generation is that you're always in a hurry! Let me enjoy teasing you for a while."

"You're being cruel, Grandma," Jonathan complained as he put his spoon down and sipped his wine, while looking reproachfully at her.

Evelyn laughed.

"Do you use that hang dog look to get your own way with Belinda?" she asked.

Jonathan smiled.

"Sometimes," he admitted.

"Marcus does the same," Evelyn told him.

Evelyn finished her slice of apple pie and washed it down with the last of the wine. However, she kept her spoon in her hand, and used it as a pointer."

"Who is the most important negative influence on Marcus?" Evelyn asked.

Jonathan thought about this for some time. He debated the claims of Walter and Martin Greenway and decided that neither was important enough. It was then that the truth struck him like a lightning bolt.

"I've been a fool," he began.

"I know," Evelyn interrupted. "You've been debating the choice between what I might call Greenway father and Greenway son, haven't you?"

"Yes, Grandma."

"And neither are right?"

"No Grandma."

"So, who is the winner?"

"Philip Stewart."

"Of course it's Philip Stewart, you ninny," Evelyn said. "Now make up Marcus's code word in the same way as you made your own."

Jonathan thought for a moment.

"He first went out with you at Christmas 1959, didn't he, Grandma?"

Evelyn nodded, pleased that he was thinking along her lines.

"The first three letters of his first name are Phi and yours are Eve. However, Phieve is a horrible combination and Pheve is, if anything, even worse!"

Fifty Years After

Jonathan continued to think, and Evelyn watched him, fascinated. She began to see why Belinda loved him so much. He reached out for a sheet of paper and a pen. Evelyn saw what he was doing and suggested that they go to the Drawing Room for coffee and that he would find what he needed there. Once there, she watched, drinking her coffee, as Jonathan forgot all about coffee and became totally absorbed in writing and crossing out, letters and numbers. Finally, after fifteen minutes, he put the pen down and smiled.

"I should say Eureka," he said, "but it's been done before!"

He handed Evelyn a sheet of paper, covered with crossings out, but with one combination standing.

"Is that it?" he asked anxiously.

She read the code.

"Steve.1959."

She smiled at him.

"That's what I think it is anyway. Drink your coffee and then we'll go and try it."

Twenty minutes later, the two of them were sitting before Jonathan's laptop. Jonathan put the memory stick back in, put in the first code, Evelyn59, to call up the file, and selected the closed file. Asked for the password, he typed in Steve.1959 and the file opened up to him. Together they listened to the contents in silence. Both were shocked but not surprised at what they heard. Both had half expected this answer to their 'What' and 'When' question. However, it did not make the discovery any easier for either of them.

Lady Evelyn's earlier gaiety was replaced by a grave expression, mirroring that on Jonathan's face.

"You will have to ring Superintendent Donaldson and inform her, Son," Evelyn said gently. "I know this will probably destroy Marcus's career, but we have no choice."

Fifty Years After

Jonathan sighed heavily. He had not wanted it to come to this, and he wished Belinda were with them to share their distress. He picked up his phone, searched for and found the card that Julia had given him, and rang the number printed on it. A female voice answered almost immediately.

"Superintendent Julia Donaldson, Surrey Police, speaking. How can I help you?"

"Superintendent Donaldson, It's Jonathan Greenway. I'm speaking to you from Chequers. I need urgently to speak to you. Do you have a minute?"

In Cambridge, the two detectives resumed their conversation with Albert Campion after lunch.

"I hope you had a good lunch, Bert," Thomas began.

"Thank you, Sergeant. I did. They serve good food in this nick."

"That's very good, Bert. So you feel relaxed and able to answer more questions, do you?"

"Certainly, Sergeant."

"Before we move on to Mike Bush, there are two things to tie up from this morning. Are you happy to be here without Miss Scott?"

"Yes, Sergeant."

"Is there anything you can think of that you haven't told us about the kidnaps?"

"Only one thing, Sergeant. We were originally outside the Prime Minister's country residence, hoping to kidnap his grandson and his grandson's girlfriend while they were out walking. The men on the gate told us they'd gone to Cambridge for the Rag Ball. That's why we went there."

"Okay. Now, tell me about Mike Bush."

"There isn't a lot to tell you, Sergeant. I'd only been with Mr Stewart (as he was then) for a couple of years when the Great Steel Strike happened. I spent most of the strike travelling around the country with bags of banknotes, paying off local union leaders, to stop them striking. Most took the cash and the strike slowly crumbled."

"How much did you give the union leaders?"

"It was usually a Grand. A few got a bit more, perhaps 5 Grand."

"Do you have the names?"

"While I was waiting for you to come up here I wrote down as many names, dates and figures as I can. I also know of one or two other side lines Lord Stewart favoured." Bert handed a notebook to Gethin. "It's all down in there."

Gethin took the book and began to study the contents, as Thomas continued the questioning.

"Did you attempt to bribe Mike Bush?"

"No – we knew we couldn't bribe him. He had a political agenda and would not be diverted."

"Whose idea was it to kill him?"

"That was Philip Stewart."

"What was your role?"

"I was instructed to talk to one of the company's drivers and ask him to meet Philip Stewart."

"And did he?"

"Of course, Sergeant. No one would refuse an instruction to see Philip Stewart! To do so was a death sentence. Unless you were actually dying, refusing to see him when summoned caused you to become a dead man walking."

"What was the driver's name?"

"We knew him as Mack."

"So Mack went to see Philip Stewart, received his instructions and staged an accident that killed Mike Bush and ended the strike. Is that correct?"

"Yes, Sergeant. It's a technique I gather that Lord Stewart used quite often. I talked to some older gang members (they're dead now) but they told me that he ordered the deaths of two people who opposed his nomination as an MP and two members of the Jury at that murder trial - you know the one where the black lad killed the white girl? Apparently they refused to take the money they were offered to find the black guy guilty."

"Are you sure of this?"

"It was before my time – but that's what I was told. I heard there were others too, but I can't swear to it."

"So you weren't really surprised when you heard Lord Stewart order the drowning of the two innocent students?"

"I wasn't surprised, but I was shocked. They were both blindfolded and could not know who had kidnapped them or given evidence against Lord Stewart. They could have been released without fear."

"So why do you think Lord Stewart ordered these two murders?"

"I think he was angry that he had been tricked and thought they conspired with the two students he wanted in order to deceive us."

"I see," Thomas said.

Thomas turned to Gethin.

"What have you got there, Gethin?"

"A whole list of crimes, Sarge. They include bribery of police officers and politicians, including the present Prime Minister apparently, and at least one Home Secretary."

"That was one I heard of," Bert interrupted. "It was the Home Secretary who had the Black Lad hanged. That was done by Philip's Dad – Jack, who was a real bastard."

"Other crimes include drugs dealing, prostitution and people trafficking, money laundering, and a number of other murders, mostly gang related. Apparently, they had a war with a rival gang from Greenford, which Marcus Greenway and Philip Stewart sorted out."

"Can you swear to the truth of all that?" Thomas asked Bert.

"Certainly," Bert replied. "I've indicated what I knew and what I was told."

"There were four Stewarts," Thomas said. "Who did what?"

Fifty Years After

"I understand that old man Stewart (Jack) founded the gang and was forced to leave the country in 1979. His son, Frederick took over the leadership, until he was killed in a shoot-out with the Young Gang in 1982. His other son, Timothy is in Malaga, where he looks after the Gang's affairs on the Costa del Sol. The present leader is Lord Philip Stewart."

"Would you swear to that?"

"Absolutely," Bert replied.

"Interview closed at 4 pm." Thomas said, and shut off the tape.

"Where are they keeping you?" Thomas asked.

"I'm in an open prison in the Fens," Bert replied.

"Do you feel safe there?"

"Yes."

"Good, then we'll leave you there. We'll write these interview notes up over the Easter weekend and include the information from the book you've given us and D C Jones will come up to see you with the written statement to sign. If you think of anything else before then, write it down and let Gethin have it when he visits you."

"Yes Sergeant."

"Thank you for helping us. We'll tell the Superintendent how cooperative you've been and she will inform the D P P. We'll let you know the outcome."

The two detectives left the Police Station and went to have dinner in the city before returning to their hotel for the night and checking out next morning for the trip back to Lewisham.

Albert Corrigan led Belinda into Julia's office just after lunch and they began the process of sorting out and collating the papers for the appeal. Albert explained to Belinda that it was largely a paper exercise, especially as; in this case, there would be no opposition from the other side.

"We need PC Adams' first and second statements and James Arthur's first and second reports," Julia began.

"I think you need the account of how Mark was interviewed as well," Belinda suggested diffidently.

"Why?" Julia asked.

"He was stripped naked and beaten up by the officers before D I Buchan spoke to him. Surely that was illegal even then?"

"It was," Julia conceded. "Okay. We'll include it, although it did not affect Mark's evidence and it was not referred to in the trial."

It was at this point that the meeting was interrupted when Julia's mobile phone rang. She spoke into it.

"Superintendent Julia Donaldson, Surrey Police, speaking. How can I help you?"

Belinda heard Jonathan's voice coming over the phone.

"Superintendent Donaldson, It's Jonathan Greenway. I'm speaking to you from Chequers. I need urgently to speak to you. Do you have a minute?"

"Yes, Jonathan. How can I help you?"

"I've found out something very important."

"Have you been sleuthing again?" Julia asked lightly.

"I've been I T'ing," Jonathan answered.

"What have you been investigating?" asked Julia, when she had worked out what Jonathan meant.

"A memory stick, but I do not want to say more over the phone."

Belinda sat up alert. She realised that Jonathan must have cracked the code. Julia and Albert looked at her curiously.

"Do you want me to come down and collect it from you?"

"I will make you a copy, yes, because Belinda and I need the original for the work we are doing."

"Very well. When do you want me to come down?"

"Can you come back with Belinda tomorrow?"

"You do realise that it's Good Friday, don't you? I usually go to Church on Good Friday."

"We have a church down here, Superintendent. I promise you that you will find the visit worthwhile."

"Very well then. I will see you tomorrow."

Julia shut off her phone and turned to Belinda.

"Do you know what this is about?"

"I have an idea, yes."

"Tell me."

"We are writing an official biography of Sir Marcus Greenway. He has given us his public diary and a secret diary on a memory stick. We have been able to access all but one file on that stick. They all contained the sort of detail that Sir Marcus would not want the public to read. One file, however, was doubly encrypted. We have been trying to find out what, if anything, Sir Marcus knew about the real truth behind the Mark Smith trial and execution. Jonathan thought that the hidden file might tell us and I agreed with him. Jonathan was going to try to crack the hidden code today. My guess is that he succeeded and that we were right."

"I see," Julia said, looking at Albert, who nodded his agreement. "Well, that would certainly explain his sense of urgency and secrecy. We'll find out tomorrow."

They returned to the preparations for the appeal, adding the material relating to the bribing of the jury to it. Albert suggested adding the last diary entry, to explain the injuries noted in the autopsy. Julia agreed.

"We may need witnesses as to provenance," Albert said.

"Possibly," Julia, conceded. "I suggest that we ask Jonathan Greenway, Luke Smith and Jennifer Foster to attend as well as the solicitor who witnessed the affidavit from Wilfred Martins."

They all agreed on this and Albert undertook to write the summary of the case for the appeal court judges that evening, working with Belinda. Julia, who had intended to return home to Coulsdon for the Easter weekend, agreed to remain overnight in her Lewisham B and B, and they agreed to meet at 10 am next morning at Lewisham Police Station for the trip to Buckinghamshire. With that the case conference closed and Albert left with Belinda to start work, while Julia waited for a report from Thomas on his interview with Albert Campion. When he finally telephoned her with a brief summary of his findings, she told him that she would see him and Gethin after the Easter weekend, and wished them a good break. Finally, she sent Susan home with the same instruction and set off for a lonely dinner and an early night.

23. The Deadly File

April 2 2010
Albert drove Belinda and Julia to Buckinghamshire, arriving at the house at 1 pm. He noticed that Belinda was strangely silent during the journey. He knew that her phone had rung during the night and that she was talking on it for quite a long time. He asked her about it in the morning and she said that Jonathan had rung her, but she refused to discuss the call. Albert assumed they were missing one another. When they arrived at the house, Belinda seized her bag and ran into the Hall and up the stairs, looking for Jonathan. Albert and Julia joined Evelyn in the small Reception Room.

"When are you expecting Sir Marcus back from the USA, Lady Greenway?" Julia asked.

"He'll be back in London on Tuesday, and down here at the weekend, Superintendent," Evelyn replied.

Julia noticed that she was a little stiff in her replies, unlike her usual warm natured self. Like Albert, she wondered exactly what was in this file.

Jonathan and Belinda came down to join them after about half an hour. It was clear to Albert and Julia that Jonathan was upset and rattled and that Belinda shared his feelings. They realised that Jonathan had shown Belinda the file. What neither of them knew was that Jonathan and Belinda had discussed destroying both it and the book they were writing.

"Perhaps we should both go to jail for destroying evidence rather than let this smoking gun into the open," Jonathan said bitterly, and Belinda agreed.

Both were on the verge of tears, Albert thought. He wondered why.

Lunch was a dreary meal. Evelyn tried, and failed, to make light conversation. Belinda sat close to Jonathan and both picked at their food in silence. Julia and Albert tried to keep the atmosphere normal without success. It was with a sense of relief that they adjourned to the small Reception Room after the meal, to where Jonathan had brought his laptop. Coffee was served and Julia and Albert watched, coffee cup in hand, as Jonathan plugged in his laptop, switched it on, and plugged in the memory stick. Belinda stood closely by him, almost in a protective pose, Julia thought. Evelyn sat to one side. Jonathan fiddled with the volume control of his laptop, trying to make the sound loud enough for them all to hear. Eventually they all moved their chairs into a small circle around a small coffee table, on which Jonathan placed his laptop.

"This memory stick is part of Sir Marcus Greenway's diary," Jonathan explained in a flat and listless voice. "It contains items he considered too sensitive to be openly available. Much of it deals with political scandals and financial issues. Some relate to his investigation of Philip Stewart – which I am sure will be of interest to you Superintendent."

Julia nodded.

"All but one file is open once you know the encryption code. Granddad gave it to me and said Belinda and I could use the material to help us write his biography. However, there is one file that is doubly encrypted. Belinda and I have often felt that Granddad knew more about the Smith Case than he admitted to knowing. We both wondered if the answer lay in this file and when we found the hidden file, we were certain that it did. However, it was only yesterday afternoon, with Grandma's help, that I managed to break the code." He paused before whispering, "And now I wish I hadn't."

Belinda hugged him; and he pulled himself together.

"The first code is simple. He used Grandma's name and the year they met – hence Evelyn59."

Jonathan typed in the code and the file displayed its contents. Julia noted the code in her diary.

Fifty Years After

"The hidden code is similar. It incorporates the names of his greatest love and his greatest hate and the most important date in his life – the date he first talked to Grandma – December 24th 1959. The code contains the 1st 3 letters of the name Stewart and the first 3 letters of Evelyn, with the 3rd letter combining the 3rd of the 1st word and the 1st of the 2nd to form a new word. That is followed by the date. The code is Steve.1959."

Jonathan typed in the new code and the hidden file opened. Julia noted the code in her notebook.

"The file is an audio file and lasts for about fifteen minutes."

Jonathan activated the file and the voice of Sir Marcus spoke to them from the laptop.

"I have removed this entry from my diary with great difficulty, because it was difficult to remove the pages without leaving any trace. Luckily I always started a new diary entry on a new front page. This is what I wrote on the day before Mark's execution.

"The Trial of Mark Smith lasted one and a half days. I had my doubts about how fair it was as it was going on, but I was deeply disturbed when, having spoken to Jennifer, the sister of the murdered girl, who ran out of the court, I discovered that she knew that Mark and Janet were lovers and that Janet was pregnant by Mark. She also knew that he and she were planning to elope in the week after the murder. She told me that Philip Stewart had beaten her sister up and threatened to kill her if he caught her with what he called 'that nigger' again. She was apparently terrified that he would find them when she went out to meet Mark that day. I told Dad and he wasn't interested. He told me to stick to my job and let Mr Corrigan do his. It was his job to mount a defence, and not ours to help him.

Fifty Years After

"Of course, as everyone knows by now, Mark was found guilty in an incredibly short time by the Jury and condemned to death. He is due to die tomorrow morning, but I went to see him a week ago and he insisted that he was innocent of the murder, doesn't know who did kill Janet, and wanted to die to be with her. He said to me, 'Since I can't spend my life with her, at least I can spend my death with her.' I cried when he said that and swore I would find out the truth, so I went and found Philip Stewart. He was on his own, chasing after another girl. I caught up with him in the park, dragged him away and gave him a beating. I'm very strong when I'm angry. Then I said to him, 'Tell me the truth you bastard. You beat up, raped and later killed that girl didn't you – and now you're going to let an innocent man die for the crime you've committed.' He leered at me. 'You sanctimonious idiot,' he said. He was always good with words. 'Why do you care? All you Greenways are the same. You care only for yourselves. My Dad has bought your Dad – so you'd better keep your big trap shut. Of course I killed the bitch. She refused to let me have sex with her the previous day, When I stripped her clothes off her she attacked me so I hit her several times. I knocked the silly bitch back against the tree and took and disposed of all her clothes except for her tights, which I used to tie her up. When I'd done that I threw a bucket full of cold water over her to bring her round. Then I took my belt off and gave her a good beating on her arse and thighs before I fucked her hard – several times. Then I spoke to her

"'You belong to me, now, girl,' I said to her as I stood over her. She was leaning against the tree, with her legs spread out. "I've seen you with that black bastard. If I see you with him again, I've got a gun and I will shoot you dead. If I can't have you, he won't either." She said I would never dare. I warned her not to try me, or they would both die. She would die because I would shoot her and he would die because they would hang him for

Fifty Years After

shooting her. And that's exactly what I did when I found them together on April 26th. If you, Marcus Greenway, whisper even a hint of this to anyone, your precious Evelyn, the girl you stole from me and put up the spout, will die like she did and you will die like he will. I'll make certain of that. Trust me.'

"With that he struggled free of me and walked away, daring me to follow him. I let him go and hurried home to check that Evelyn was safe and to talk to my Dad. He shrugged his shoulders.
'I know that, Son,' he said. 'I'm only surprised that you don't!'
'But you've just prosecuted Mark Smith for a crime you say you knew all along he didn't commit!' I said aghast.
'I'm not the first and I won't be the last,' was his reply. 'The boy wants to die anyway, to be with his precious girlfriend – the romantic fool! I've asked the Home Secretary to give him his wish.'
'You've what!' I said, unable to believe what I'd just heard.
'You heard, son,' he replied. 'You've done agriculture. You know you sometimes have to cull animals when there are too many of them. Mark Smith is like that. There are too many of his sort over here. So his death doesn't matter.'

"There was nothing more I felt I could say. So I left him and did nothing for Evelyn's sake. Philip Stewart is a very dangerous man – much more dangerous than I realised. I dare not risk anything happening to my beloved Evelyn, and so I have let an innocent man go to his death on the gallows. I will have to live with that to the day I die, and I dare not say anything to anyone about it.

"Dad came into my room as I was writing the last sentence. I pushed the book away so he wouldn't see what

I was writing. He tried to console me. 'Sometimes it's necessary for the innocent to die so that others may live,' he said, quoting the Bible, in justification. 'Remember that Mark Smith was not one of us. He was a foreigner. He came here from Jamaica. He doesn't understand our laws. So he doesn't know any better.' I told Dad that that didn't justify what he had done and what he was doing. 'Be careful,' he warned me. 'The Stewarts own you and me and they also own this house. We have to do what they want and ensure that they survive. If they fall, so will we. We are inextricably tied to them.' With that he left me.

"That's what I wrote on July 14th 1961, the day before Mark Smith was hanged.

"Later Dad became a senior director in one of the Stewart businesses and used Stewart money to finance the growing wealth and status of the family. It was shortly after the trial that he became a judge, eventually, Lord Chief Justice. I understand it was Stewart money that paid for my by election campaign in 1966. I wish I could throw it back at them.

"If anyone listens to this tape and hears what I wrote back in July 1961, I hope you will understand me and, if you are from or related to, the Smith or Brown families, that you will forgive me.

"I am Marcus Greenway and today is August 24th 1982."

They sat listening in appalled silence. "What did he know and when did he know it?" They knew now without any doubt, and they also knew that this tape would destroy the Prime Minister and the Greenway family (as well as the Stewarts) if its contents were ever revealed.

"He was a fool," Julia breathed.

"You're right. He should never have spoken to Philip Stewart. Sometimes it's better not to know something," Albert commented.

"I didn't mean that, Albert," Julia said. "He should never have written this or recorded it. And if he did, he should have destroyed the tape, not encrypted it."

She smiled sadly at Evelyn, who was crying.

"I'm really sorry, Lady Evelyn, but you know what I must do."

"You have to take this tape, or, at least, the copy that my grandson gives you, but do try to spare him won't you?"

"I will do my best, Lady Evelyn. I promise you that, but it may be necessary to use it if Stewart refuses to admit what he did."

Julia turned to Jonathan and Belinda, both of whom were also looking strained and tearful.

"This must be difficult for you both, for different reasons. I can only say how sorry I am for you two as well, since you will both suffer if this becomes known. You've both been very brave when you were not directly affected by what you discovered. Now it's different. What do you expect me to do now and can you be brave enough to see it through?"

Jonathan said nothing. His water–filled eyes said it all. Belinda hugged him protectively and spoke over him.

"You must do your duty Superintendent. We both know that two families have been depending on us to get the truth for them. Their tragedy was much greater than ours will ever be. All we can lose is money, property, power, possessions and pride. We had little when we found each other and we have the brains and the ability to exist on what we earn from our own skills – and we have each other. No one can take that from us. The Smiths and Browns lost a brother, a sister, a daughter and a son. Those two people were irreplaceable. Their blood cries out for justice, as the Bible says. You have a duty to hear it."

Jonathan eventually spoke, struggling to be understood through his distress.

"This tape changes nothing, Superintendent. If anything it makes it even more important that you end the Stewart curse. Don't worry about us. We're survivors and we'll survive."

He turned the laptop off and removed the memory stick, giving it to Julia, who put it in an evidence bag and put it in her pocket.

"Please only use the sections of the file that bear on the case. We owe that to Sir Marcus. Remember, he's basically a decent man who was put in an impossible position."

Julia promised to do as he asked. Evelyn took the two visitors to her sitting room and Jonathan and Belinda left the house to go for a walk, hand in hand, in silence, each trying to come to terms with their new knowledge and their sense of grief.

"I wish I had never started this," Jonathan said, weeping silently.

"Shush, Darling," Belinda said to him, speaking to him like a mother to a young child. "I could have asked you to stop and I didn't. Those two victims of Philip Stewart's rage and lust deserve our help, because if we don't help them, they will never have rest. And – don't forget there was a third victim. Janet was pregnant, remember."

Part Three

The Philip Stewart trial (May to September 2010)

You shall be taken from hence to the place from whence you came and from thence to a place of execution where you shall be hanged by the neck until you be dead and may God have mercy upon your soul.
(Traditional words of sentencing in UK)

Fifty Years After

24. Appeal

9 April 2010

Sir Marcus Greenway returned from Washington immediately after Easter and began to prepare for the return of Parliament. Philip Stewart continued working on his speech for the House of Lords debate on the Second Reading of the Education Reform Bill. Belinda, Jonathan and Evelyn tried to recover from the shock of hearing Sir Marcus reading his confession on his computer. Julia and her team continued to work on collating evidence for the arrest and trial of the Stewart Gang. Gethin collected the statement sheets of their interview of Albert Campion and travelled to Cambridge for him to sign it. Bert handed Gethin a list of other crimes that he stated were due directly to the orders of Philip Stewart. Michael and Emma, the two kidnapped students, recovered from their ordeal, made statements to the police and returned to Cambridge University as heroes. The five kidnappers, meanwhile, were extradited from France and brought back to Cambridge via Lewisham in conditions of tight security, where they were individually interviewed and confirmed Bert's story. Finally, Bert was given immunity from prosecution, provided that he appeared as a witness for the Crown in the Stewart Gang trial.

Sir Marcus returned to Buckinghamshire for the weekend after his return from Washington. He sensed a change in the atmosphere as soon as he arrived. He left things alone until after dinner, when, over coffee, he asked what was wrong. Evelyn spoke for the three of them.

"Marcus, you've been a fool. We've heard your secret message. Why did you make the tape and why, having made it, didn't you destroy it?"

"I should have done so," Marcus confessed, but I thought I had protected it sufficiently until it was too late

Fifty Years After

to damage us but soon enough to rescue the reputation of the boy who died."

"You were much too late for that, Granddad," Jonathan said bitterly. "You knew the truth when he was still alive. You could and should have tried to save him."

"I know. I was wrong, grandson. I told my father and he silenced me just as effectively as Philip Stewart did. I tried to persuade him, but Sir Walter could never be persuaded to change his mind."

"What I find unforgivable is the attitude of Sir Walter," Belinda commented. "He knew that Mark was innocent but didn't care because Mark was black and Philip, who he knew was the real murderer, was white. You haven't treated me like that, and I know that you do see us as equal and are happy to have me as a granddaughter. But, I feel betrayed by that conversation and feel that you must act to end the long injustice"

"I have done that, Belinda. I allowed you and Jonathan to investigate the murder and made my diaries and my book on the trial available to you both."

"But, Granddad, you knew that the case file was embargoed for 100 years so you expected us to fail. You were not to know that I had my own sources of information, which enabled me to circumvent the embargo that Great Grandfather put on the files."

"That's true, Jonathan, but I did not rebuke you when you succeeded."

Sir Marcus walked to the window and looked over the garden, which was beginning to come back to life since the winter.

"I would that I had the power to bring those two young people back to life, like the plants do every year," he said.

He turned back to face them.

"What do you want me to do? Should I resign? Should I wait it out? Should I go to the Police and offer to give evidence, knowing that I would risk destroying you all?"

Fifty Years After

Belinda was silent. Jonathan looked at Evelyn, who spoke for them all.

"I don't think you should resign, Marcus. You need to stand tall. You were not part of the corruption of the trial. You twice tried to make your father change course, but, as a son, you were loyal to him. You never got on with him well and I know how difficult he was. You don't need to go to the police. They already have your file, and the Superintendent is a good woman, who is going to do her best to keep your file out of the court. So – yes, you should stand tall and see what happens. All three of us will support you and we know that you will support us."

Sir Marcus looked around at Belinda and Jonathan.

"Does Evelyn speak for you two as well?"

"She does," said Belinda. "We've spoken to her and agonised with her about this all week, and we are all in agreement."

"She's right," Jonathan confirmed. "We were devastated by your tape; but we've got used to the idea and we know that you were and are a good man, but you were put in an impossible position. Of course we support you."

Evelyn smiled suddenly.

"Now, Sir Marcus Greenway, you have another job to do. You have to organise an engagement party at once and a wedding in Scotland on November 5th."

"The engagement is easily done. I'll talk to Martin and to Belinda's parents and we'll have a party here in two weeks' time. But why a wedding in November in Scotland?"

"We have to ask the two lovebirds the answer to that one," Evelyn said.

Jonathan smiled sadly.

"We feel that we are the bearers of Janet and Mark's inheritance, and, because of that we want our wedding to reflect that. They met on November 5th 1960. That's when their romance began. They were going to get married in Gretna Green in May 1961. We want to make the journey

Fifty Years After

that was denied them, to stay in the same hotel and get married over the anvil, just as they planned but were unable to carry out."

"Do you agree, Belinda? After all, it's your special day!"

"Yes, Granddad. I hope you don't mind me calling you that. That's what I want. It feels right somehow. I feel the spirits of the two lovers will be there with us, especially if Philip Stewart is in prison."

"Very well then, family. The Greenways are a united team again!" Marcus concluded.

They all forced a smile and drank to Jonathan and Belinda's future marriage, after which Jonathan and Belinda left them to go to their room, leaving their Grandparents to come to terms with Marcus's guilt.

Two weeks later, the two surprised families gathered at Chequers and celebrated the engagement of their eldest children. They studied their new in laws and liked what they saw. Martin spent time with his father, trying to take advantage of the surprise gathering to rebuild the broken bridges between them. They were all surprised by the decision of the couple to marry in Scotland on Guy Fawkes Night. Jonathan and Belinda explained to them the reasons for their decision and told Belinda's parents the story of Janet and Mark. In the end, Belinda's father summed up the reaction of both families.

"It's your lives and your wedding, my dears. So, you must make the final decision. I suppose you'll be national celebrities by then anyway – if the trial you're talking about takes place this autumn."

Belinda's mother urged caution.

"This Philip Stewart sounds like a very dangerous man. You both need to be very careful my dears. We want to go to a wedding in Scotland, not a joint funeral!"

"We won't let any harm come to them, Mrs Thompson. Don't worry, we're taking care of both of them," Evelyn

Fifty Years After

said. "It's quite a challenge, though, keeping these two out of mischief – as I'm sure both you mothers know!"

They all laughed.

Marcus proposed a toast.

"I've known Jonathan since he first learned to walk. I've only known Belinda since early February. However, I like her as much as I like Jonathan. They're both lively and intelligent young people, who are courageous and have high moral standards, which they don't compromise. They're both a credit to you and you should be proud of them. Good luck to you both. Raise your glasses to Jonathan and Belinda."

They toasted the happy couple and then went in to dinner.

Two days later Jonathan and Belinda accompanied their Grandparents to Downing Street, so they were available to the Appeal Court. The case was heard in Westminster the following morning. Chief Justice, Lord Black, presided, supported by two judges – Lord Wilkinson and Lady Foster. Albert Corrigan entered the court, robed, and accompanied by Belinda and Jonathan. They sat on the left of the court, representing the petitioners and William Cosgrave, Attorney General, sat on the right, representing the Crown.

Albert opened the case.

"On June 21st, 1961, a young man was tried for the crime of the capital murder of a young woman. Both were aged 18. The young man was of Afro-Caribbean origin and is represented by his brother, Luke, who was just 14 when his brother was put on trial. The young woman was of English origin. Jennifer, her sister, represents her. Jennifer was also just 14 when the case opened. It lasted just three sessions and the young man was unanimously found guilty within 20 minutes and executed 3 weeks later when his appeal for clemency was rejected by the Home Secretary."

Fifty Years After

Albert turned to Belinda, who handed him two documents.

"On the surface, my lords and my lady. It was a straightforward case, but there have always been doubts about the verdict. The two young people sitting beside me have worked hard to investigate the background of this case, which has, to be fair, been well hidden. By various means, which, my lords and lady, you would not approve of, they managed to acquire a copy of the original police case documents. Two of them are in my hand, labelled 1 and 2. Both these documents purport to be the report of Police Constable Anthony Adams who was called to the scene of the crime and arrested the defendant, Mark Smith, whom he found kneeling, naked, beside the shot and naked body of the girl, Janet Brown. Document 2 was the document presented to the court that day, but document 1 was the original version of the report. Now, you will notice two points of difference between the two documents. The second is shorter than the first, and the handwriting and signature on the two documents is slightly different. The first expunging is about the fact that the Constable saw the two people half an hour before the murder and they were very happy together. They spoke to the Constable and he spoke to them. The second deletion included a description of the neatness of the clothing. These were factors, which supported Mark's story that he and Janet were in a relationship and that they had been engaged in consensual sex, and not a sexual assault."

Justice Foster asked Albert a question.

"You said that the second document was written in a different hand from the first. Who do you think wrote it?'

"It was the Inspector who ordered the changes, but I don't know who did the actual writing, My Lady."

"You were the defence counsel, I believe, Lord Corrigan," Justice Wilkinson said. "Why did you not raise this issue at the trial?"

Fifty Years After

"Because we never saw the first document until this year when I was shown it by Jonathan Greenway, My Lord."

Lord Black looked at his two colleagues, who nodded to him. He indicated that Albert should continue. Albert took another two documents from Belinda.

"We have a similar story with the Forensic report, which was also in the file. Document 3 is the original report and Document 4 is the report, which was presented to me and to the jury. The same process has occurred here. The parts of the report which supported the defendant have been carefully removed, once again on the orders of D I Buchan."

"What is known about D I Buchan?" Justice Wilkinson asked.

"I'm sorry, My Lord. I didn't expect that question. However, I can produce a document tomorrow which shows that D I Buchan was on the pay roll of the Stewart Building Construction Company of North London as a security advisor."

"I see," Justice Wilkinson said. "If we go on to tomorrow, I'll be happy to see your evidence. If not, I'll take it on advisement."

"There are other documents that we could use, but I do not want to prejudice any further trial by producing them here. So, if you will allow me, my Lords and my Lady, I will present just one more to you. This comes in several parts. The first is this document, which we call document 5."

Albert took the affidavit from Belinda."

"If you will excuse me, My Lords and My Lady, I am going to ask my assistant, Jonathan Greenway, to explain this item to you."

Lord Black gave his assent and Jonathan stood up.

"I was concerned that the Jury, which had been given reason to ponder the evidence by Lord Corrigan, took such a short time to reach a decision, and so we tried a long

Fifty Years After

shot. We took out an advertisement in the press asking for any juror from that trial who was still alive to contact us. Wilfred Martins was the youngest of the jurors and the last to survive, but he knew he was dying. He knew he would not live long enough to attend this hearing and so he swore this affidavit before a solicitor, who is willing to be present tomorrow if you wish him to confirm this. He stated that each juror was handed an envelope on the second morning containing a sum of money and instructions on who to elect as foreman. They were given a second envelope afterwards, also containing money and a card saying thank you. The total sum involved was £100, which I am told was equivalent to ten weeks' wages in 1961. This disturbed Wilfred, and, although he did as he was asked, treated the money as blood money and never opened the envelopes. He gave the envelopes to us and the video shows what happened when we opened them."

Albert looked up at the technician and nodded. They played the film of the opening.

"Do we know anything about Matthew Allbright?" Justice Foster asked.

"Yes, my Lady," Jonathan answered. "He became an employee of the Stewart Building Construction Company immediately after the 1961 trial."

"Is that your case?" Lord Black asked Albert.

"Yes, My Lord," Albert answered. "I believe that on this evidence, which is only part of what we have gathered, you have to order a retrial and dismiss the verdict as unsound."

"What is your opinion, Mr. Cosgrave?" Lord Black asked.

"The Crown has no objection, My Lord. We support this application."

"I don't think we need any more evidence," Lord Black said.

He looked at the other two judges, who nodded their agreement.

Fifty Years After

"Then we will withdraw and consider our decision."

The judges withdrew and returned ten minutes later.

"I regret that we have taken less time than the original jury," Lord Black said, "But I hope you won't object!"

He paused and smiled at them.

"You have made a strong presentation and I congratulate your young assistants, Lord Corrigan. They've obviously worked hard and done a good job, although I won't look too closely into their methods! Plainly, on the evidence presented, the original trial was flawed from the outset. The evidence was doctored to adversely affect the defence and the jury was plainly bribed, probably by orders of the Stewart family, which raises the question of the role of the chief witness, Philip Stewart in this crime. Is there a police investigation ongoing into this crime?"

Julia Donaldson stood up in her seat.

"Yes, My Lord. I'm Superintendent Donaldson of the Surrey Police. I'm investigating this and related cases and I have a warrant for the arrest of Philip Stewart which is simply waiting for the decision of this court and we will execute it."

"How soon will the arrest be made, Superintendent?"

"As soon as this afternoon, if the appeal is approved, My Lord."

"Very well. The decision of this court is to uphold the appeal. The verdict of the original trial in 1961 was plainly unsafe and I shall ask the Home Secretary to ask the Queen to issue a posthumous pardon to Mark Smith. Do you have any other petitions for this court?"

"Yes, My Lord," Albert responded. "Would you order that the body of Mark Smith be exhumed from Wormwood Scrubs Jail and issue an order that his body be reburied with the body of Janet Brown in the North London cemetery?"

"It is so ordered," Lord Black ruled.

Fifty Years After

The case and three months' work was over in an hour and a half. Justice had been partially done, and the rest would come later. Julia made a quick phone call, and then joined Albert, William and Albert's two young assistants, in a pub nearby to celebrate. Jennifer and Luke joined them. Noticed only by Julia, a woman in her late 60s followed them from the court to the pub and appeared to be watching the celebrating team. Julia wondered who she was and why she was there. She resolved to find out later.

Two hours later Gethin and Thomas knocked on the door of Lord Stewart's office in the House of Lords accompanied by the Master at Arms. Philip called on them to come in. He was surprised when the Master at Arms entered.

"Lord Stewart, these are two police officers. They are here with the knowledge and permission of the Leader of the Labour Party and the Lord Chancellor."

Philip was suddenly afraid, but he decided that he should present a bold front.

"What can I do for you gentlemen?"

"I am Detective Sergeant Thomas Skinner and this is Detective Constable Gethin Jones. You are Lord Philip Stewart?"

"I am," Philip replied.

"Lord Philip Stewart, I have a warrant for your arrest and I am here to serve it on you."

Philip looked shocked.

"What am I accused of?" he asked.

Thomas continued as though he had said nothing.

"Lord Philip Stewart I am arresting you for the murder of Janet Brown on April 26th 1961 in a park in Marchfield contrary to the common law. I am also arresting you on the charge of perjury at the trial of Mark Smith on June 21st and 22nd, 1961. You are not obliged to say anything, but your defence may be harmed if you decline to say anything now that you later rely on in court."

Gethin Jones handcuffed the peer. Philip was too shocked to say anything beyond a simple rejection of the charge.

"Is this some kind of joke? Mark Smith was executed for the murder of Janet Brown in 1961."

"It's no joke, My Lord. That verdict and sentence was set aside by the appeal court this morning and Mark Smith was pardoned this afternoon. His body is being dug up now and will be reburied in a special funeral in the same grave as that of Janet Brown as soon as it can be arranged. I am going to take you to our base in Lewisham Police Station. Constable Jones will search your office."

Philip Stewart began the first day of his new life as he was marched out of the House of Lords to a police car and from there to a police cell where he was stripped of his possessions and anything that he could use to harm himself with – including his tie, his belt and his shoe laces. He knew that that's where he would spend the night. That afternoon, in a specially orchestrated act by the two main party leaders, Philip Stewart's membership of the House of Lords was temporarily suspended, depending on the outcome of his trial.

25. Preparing for Trial

Summer 2010
Next morning the team reassembled in Julia's office, tired and dishevelled, having celebrated too long and too well the night before. There were two exceptions to the general hung over appearance of the team – Julia, and Albert, who arrived for the meeting accompanied by a tired looking Belinda and Jonathan. At Julia's request a large and very full coffee urn was brought to the office and plugged in and the three junior police officers and the two young assistants partook freely of the drug as the meeting progressed.

Julia, as team leader, opened the meeting.
  "Our task today is to begin the groundwork for Lord Stewart's trial. Yesterday went well, but, today, we have to deal with the media storm the pardon and the new arrest caused."
  "Is it that bad, Julia?" a plainly jaded Thomas asked.
  "The arrest is the lead story in every newspaper except the Daily Sport," Julia said. "It's been the first story of every news broadcast since 6 pm yesterday and was the subject of a, mostly ill informed, discussion on 'News Night' last night. This police station is already attracting a growing number of reporters and photographers."
  "We have scheduled a press conference for 3 pm this afternoon," Albert added.
  "In the meantime we have to crack on. Stewart has to be interviewed and charged in the next two days and we have a second interview to undertake as well."
  They all looked surprised. Julia explained.
  "While you lot were getting tanked last night I noticed an elderly woman had joined the edge of the party. I watched her and realised she was watching us. None of you noticed me go and talk to her, but I have arranged for her to come to the station this morning. She should be

Fifty Years After

arriving about now and you are going to interview her, Susan. I shall ask the two youngsters here to join you, since they will be interested to hear what she has to say."

Jonathan looked up sharply at this, shaking his head as he did so to clear the pounding of the alcohol induced headache.

"Who is she, Superintendent?" he asked.

"We have a rule, young Jonathan. In here it's Christian names, not ranks. I'm Julia."

"I'm sorry, Julia. I didn't know. But, who is she?"

"She is your young reporter from 1961 – Juliet Carter nee Stevens. Apparently she became a crime reporter for a Fleet Street daily following her coverage of the 1961 trial and execution and has retained an interest in the case since her retirement nine years ago. She looks up the court programmes as a matter of course and spotted the appeal. Of course she was interested since the case means as much to her as it does to you, so she came along, intrigued to find out what new evidence you had uncovered."

"Thomas and Gethin, once you've cleared your head from the excessive amounts of lager you both consumed, you're going to begin the interviewing of Philip Stewart. I'm going to lead a team of Lewisham officers to Stewart's house to conduct a search there. Albert is going to speak to the Press, accompanied by Jonathan and Belinda, since the reporters have been demanding to talk to them."

She turned to Jonathan and Belinda.

"Neither of you have ever faced a press conference before and no one has trained you in how to deal with them. Albert will guide you. Please only answer the questions that he allows you to answer and be careful not to go beyond what was said in court yesterday. Do not, under any circumstances, disclose the existence of Janet's diary or Sir Marcus's taped message."

"We'll be good, Julia," Jonathan said meekly. "We will keep to the script and do what Albert tells us to do."

Fifty Years After

"You must," Julia warned him. "We can't afford any adolescent style posturing or boasting. If you say too much you can jeopardise the trial."

"We understand, Julia," Belinda added. "Jonathan knows when to speak and when to keep his mouth shut."

"That's good to know, Belinda," Julia said.

Julia smiled encouragingly at the two lovers. Despite her dislike of amateur detectives interfering in police investigations, she admired the fact that they had forced open a case that had been glued tight and she had come to like them both.

"I have one more task for you two," she added.

"What's that, Julia?" Belinda asked.

"You have the transcript of Julia's diary. I want you two to rehearse reading it and the letters. I have arranged a professional camera team to go down to Buckinghamshire next Monday to film your reading of it for the trial. After that, subject to Albert's not needing you, you're free to do whatever you like. The rest of our investigation is strictly a police matter and, anyway, in the Stewart Gang case you have a family interest and can't be impartial."

Jonathan nodded at the reference to Walter and Marcus Greenway's involvement in the cover up of the Gang's activities.

"So it's thank you and good night, Jonathan and Belinda!" Jonathan commented.

"I'm afraid so, Jonathan," Julia said gently. "But remember, it is 'Thank you' – a very big one. We wouldn't be here if you two hadn't done what you've done."

She smiled at them.

"Now, Susan, take them away and go and talk to Juliet."

Once the three had left, Julia turned to the others.

"Gethin and Thomas, thank you for the good work you've done in Cambridge. We will add that to our file and begin work on preparing arrest warrants as soon as we've finished the work on preparing to charge Philip Stewart. I have the senior investigating officer from the Cambridge team coming here tomorrow to discuss how their work on the kidnap case overlaps with ours. We are not going to get directly involved in that case, but we'll have to discuss the issue of Philip Stewart's involvement."

"There's also the question of how much we charge Stewart with," Thomas observed. "Since he's the alleged gang leader he will be front and centre of any prosecution of the gang. Should we combine the Brown Murder trial with his other offences?"

"No," Albert said. "It would be much too complicated. The Janet Brown Case is a stand-alone. I believe that the Cambridge Kidnap is another stand-alone. I suggest that Philip Stewart's name is kept out of the Cambridge trial. He can be charged with complicity as part of the larger Stewart Gang case."

"I agree," Julia said.

"When you charge Philip Stewart with the murder of Janet Brown, how do you intend to deal with the effective murder of Mark Smith?" Albert asked her.

"We will charge him with two additional counts, Albert. One will be perverting the course of justice, and the other will be one of perjury."

"Good, I can handle that. Will he be charged under the current Act or the Act that was in force when the crimes were committed?"

There was a sharp intake of breath as the three Police Officers considered the implication of this question. Under the laws operating in 1961 Philip Stewart could be sentenced to death by hanging for shooting Janet to death.

"We will have to take legal advice on that, Albert. You know the law and legal precedent better than us. What do you think?" Julia said eventually.

"There's good precedent for applying the law as it was. The sentence was inflexible and inevitable – and the reappearance of the black cap would be a sensation, and may also shock Philip Stewart into cooperating with us on the second trial."

He paused before continuing.

"Of course, it's one thing to sentence him to death, and quite another to actually hang him. The first was mandatory under the laws operating in 1961, but the sentence is no longer carried out in this country since it was abolished in 1969. So the outcome would be clear legally. The judge would pass the sentence and the Home Secretary would commute it to life imprisonment and pass it back to the judge who would set a tariff, which could then be considered by the Appeal Court if either side requests it."

"It will, of course, reignite the debate on Capital Punishment," Thomas observed.

"Probably," Albert agreed.

The meeting then broke up as Thomas and Gethin made their way, via their offices, to the Interview Room, where Philip Stewart awaited them, accompanied by his lawyer and observed by a Lewisham Police Constable. Albert remained in Julia's office, examining once again all the documents they had assembled for the forthcoming trial, and Julia picked up a team of three local detectives and a warrant before setting off for Philip Stewart's home in North London.

Juliet Carter was another feisty seventy year old. Jonathan thought that she must have been a very beautiful young woman because her face, although now lined with age, still showed the classic lines that signify beauty in people of his age. She was neatly but fashionably dressed. Her hair, although now grey, showed evidence of the same care and attention that she had obviously given it all her life. The three of them sat down and Juliet smiled at them.

"You must be Jonathan and Belinda. I've heard a lot about you over the last few days."

Belinda blushed.

Fifty Years After

"I hope what you've heard are the good things we've done and not the bad ones," she said.

"I suspect there's been plenty of both!" Juliet laughed. "You needn't worry, when I first heard about you in connection with the Cambridge Kidnap Case, I went to Cambridge and started to root around. Old habits die hard! I discovered a friend of yours." She looked at her notes. "Her name was Carole Green. She told me a lot about you and introduced me to some of your friends. They also told me all about the Kidnap Plot – both the one to kidnap you, Jonathan, that they made, and the one that actually happened."

"I'm sure the first plot will still come about!" Jonathan commented. "I expect to end up naked, tied to a chair, in a girl student's study bedroom, waiting for my father or grandfather to ransom me."

"I have a horrible feeling I will be tied up beside him," Belinda added ruefully.

Juliet and Susan laughed.

"It will serve you both right!" Juliet said. "It's called the price of fame!"

She smiled at them and looked at Belinda's finger.

"I gather you are to be congratulated," she said. "When will the happy day be?"

"In November," Belinda answered. "In Scotland," she added.

Juliet shuddered.

"Scotland in November is cold," she said. "The world's your oyster and you've both got the power of a wealthy family behind you. Why not the Bahamas in the summer?"

Belinda repeated her explanation of their reasons.

"That's very romantic," Juliet said, "and quite a story in itself, Belinda. Whose idea was it?"

"It was mine, originally, but Jonathan agreed to it."

Juliet looked pensive and then smiled as an idea struck her.

"Have you heard of a proxy marriage?"

They shook their heads.

"It used to be used by kings and queens when they married before the days of quick transport. Someone would stand in for the missing partner and take the vows for him or her. You could do the same. The two of you could travel up to Scotland to get married for Mark and Janet. It would be a rehearsal for your wedding and a great media story."

"We'll think about it," Jonathan said cautiously.

"No, Darling," Belinda said enthusiastically. "We'll do it. We'll take Jennifer and Luke with us as witnesses and we'll stay in the hotel they were going to stay in."

"It looks as though we have a plan," Jonathan said with a sudden grin. "I presume that you will cover the story, Juliet."

"Of course!" she said. "It's my story. I will also interview the two of you this afternoon after the Press Conference and cover the Stewart Trial. The Smith Trial was my first big story. This will be my last one."

Susan coughed, and they turned to look at her, having forgotten that she was there.

"Can we get on with why you're here Mrs Carter?"

"Of course we can Constable Godfrey. Fire away."

"I understand that you talked to Mark Smith and Philip Stewart in the three weeks after the trial. Is that right?"

"Yes. I tried to get Mark's story told – but the paper wouldn't cover it. They told me it was old news and no one would be interested. You know the old saying that today's news is tomorrow's chip papers."

Susan nodded. The other two looked mystified.

"In the old days, before you two were born, fish and chip shops didn't use the nice hygienic paper they use today to wrap their wares up in. They used the unsold newspapers of the previous day," Juliet explained.

"Did you make any notes of the interviews and do you have them with you like Superintendent Donaldson asked?" Susan asked.

Fifty Years After

Juliet reached into the bag that lay on the floor in front of her and took out an old reporter's notebook.

"I've kept all my notebooks. I thought I'd write a book about my life one day – so I kept everything. It was easy to find this because it was, as I told you, my first case. I have notes of the trial and my interview notes. They're right at the beginning. Please tell the Superintendent that I want the notebook back (or a photocopy of its pages at least) after the trial."

Juliet handed the book to Susan, who placed it to one side.

"Do you have a copy of the articles you wrote?"

"I never wrote them. The Editor was not interested, as I told you. Instead I was sent to cover a burglary in Ponders End."

"We can assemble what you said to each other from your notes – but what were your impressions of the two young men?"

"I was very sorry for Mark Smith. I instinctively felt that he was an honest young man and in deep shock. He was plainly deeply in love with the murdered girl and unable to cope with the fact and manner of her death. He didn't seem to care that his own death was imminent or that it would also be, in its own way, violent. He said to me before I left him," She paused, searching her memory, "'I'm not afraid to die. I deserve to die because I failed to protect the girl I love and planned to marry. I know that I can't spend my life with her, but I can spend my death with her.' I thanked him and left the cell. I had to do so because I could feel the tears coming on."

"What about your interview with Philip Stewart?"

"He was a fish of a different order," Juliet commented. "He looked at me in a way I hate men doing. I felt that he was stripping me with his eyes. I couldn't help shuddering and wouldn't have liked to be alone with him in an isolated place like a park. I'm convinced that he would have stripped me in fact and raped me just for the hell of it. He repeated his story that he told in court, but somehow

Fifty Years After

I didn't believe him. I'd heard Mr Corrigan tear him apart, and his story simply didn't convince me. I couldn't understand how the jury was so easily convinced. Of course, I understand that now, but you will see I expressed that doubt in my notes.

"So Philip Stewart never changed his story. For instance, he never claimed to have had sex with Janet or to have shot her because she was sleeping with a black man?"

"Is that what you think?" Juliet said, her eyes suddenly shining. "Do you have any grounds for that?"

Susan mentally kicked herself. She thought that she was dealing with an elderly woman. She forgot that this was a retired successful crime reporter.

"That's of no consequence," Susan snapped, rather more abruptly than she intended. "I just wondered if his story had altered, that's all," she ended lamely.

"Fiddlesticks!" Juliet thought. "You've let something slip, Constable. I think you were not intended to say anything about what you now suspect or know happened."

"No, Officer," Juliet answered quietly. "He stuck exactly to the story he told in court."

Susan had been writing notes as Juliet answered her questions.

"I will write the notes up into statement form while you have coffee with my two friends here. You can arrange your trip to Scotland. Once I've finished, I'll read the statement back to you and you can change it if you wish. Then I'll ask you to sign it and you can go. Thank you for coming."

Downstairs, Gethin and Thomas were locked in battle with Philip Stewart and his family's barrister Charles Harris.

"Lord Stewart, you were arrested for the murder of Janet Brown and her earlier rape, as well as for causing the death, by legal means, of her lover, Mark Smith. PC Jones is going to read two documents to you. The first is the statement you made on April 28th 1961 to D I Alasdair

Fifty Years After

Buchan and the second is the transcript of the evidence you gave under oath at the Central Criminal Court on June 21st 1961."

Gethin read out the two documents slowly. Philip and Charles listened impassively. Thomas then resumed his questions, while Gethin took notes.

"Do you confirm that those were your words?"

"As far as I remember, yes, Sergeant. But I want to object to this questioning and to my arrest yesterday. That case was resolved in 1961. Mark Smith was found guilty of the murder and was hanged for it."

"The trial verdict was annulled yesterday by the Appeal Court and Mark Smith was pardoned by the Queen on the advice of the Home Secretary this morning. As a result, the case has been reopened."

"What about the Statute of Limitations, Sergeant? The murder occurred nearly 50 years ago."

"The Statute of Limitations does not apply to murder cases, as I'm sure Mr Harris will tell you."

The barrister nodded.

"So, do you wish to change anything or add anything to your statement?"

"Since it was the truth, I see no reason to change it."

"Did you know that Janet Brown complained that you had been stalking her in the days before she was murdered?"

"No Comment," Philip replied.

"Did you also know that she accused you of raping her and threatening to kill her if you saw her with Mark Smith again and that this happened on April 25th 1961, the day before she was murdered?"

"No comment."

"Did you follow Janet Brown and Mark Smith on April 26th 1961?"

"No comment."

"Did you drag Mark Smith off Janet Brown while they were making love and beat Mark Smith up, leaving him unconscious?"

"No comment."

"Did you then abuse Janet Brown verbally, telling her that you warned her what would happen if you found her with a black man?"

"No comment."

"Did you shoot Janet Brown as she lay on the ground, naked, killing her?"

"No comment."

"So you have nothing to say to these accusations?"

"I have nothing to say because I told you that I have nothing to add to my earlier statements, officer. They are the truth. The accusations represent a pack of lies. They are assertions, nothing more. Essentially they are the guesses of an over active imagination found in a 20 year old boy and girl anxious to make a name for themselves."

"Have you got all that Gethin?"

"Yes, Sarge."

"Would you read it back to Lord Stewart?"

Gethin looked at the paper in front of him.

"What is your full name please?"

Philip looked at Charles Harris, who nodded.

"My name is Philip Augustus Stewart, the Earl of Little Wittering."

"What's your date of birth?"

"27th of August, 1941."

"And your address?"

"16, Blenheim Park, Benfield."

"Thank you," Gethin said, as he filled in the details on the top of the statement, which he then began to read.

"I made a full and complete statement as to what I did and saw on April 26th, 1961, on April 28th, 1961. I do not see any need to add to that or the evidence that I gave in the Central Criminal Court during the trial of Mark Smith on June 21st, 1961. In both cases I told the truth, the whole truth and nothing but the truth as I said in the oath. D S Skinner has put certain accusations to me, and, in view of what I have already said above, I see no reason to comment on them. I object very strongly to the fact, manner and alleged cause of my arrest."

"Do you agree that what PC Jones has just read accurately reflects what you have said to us this morning?" Thomas asked.

Philip nodded.

"Let the tape note that the suspect nodded to confirm that he agreed with the statement," Thomas said formally. "Would you sign the statement please?"

Philip signed.

Having completed the interview, Gethin and Thomas escorted Philip and Charles out to the desk to face the duty sergeant who read out the charges.

"Philip Augustus Stewart, Earl of Little Wittering, you are charged that on April 26th, 1961, in Marchfield Park, you did shoot to death Janet Brown, contrary to the Common Law. You are also charged that on April 25th, 1961, in the same park, you did insert your penis into the body of Janet Brown without her consent, having assaulted her, knocked her down and stripped her naked, all without her consent. You are further charged that on June 21st, 1961, in the Central Criminal Court you did commit perjury by lying about your role in the murder of the said Janet Brown resulting in the unsafe conviction and execution of Mark Smith. Finally, you are charged with the manslaughter of the unborn child of Janet Brown and Mark Smith on April 26th, 1961, in the aforesaid park in Marchfield. Do you understand these charges?"

"I do, and I reject them utterly. I demand to see the Prime Minister, Sir Marcus Greenway."

"We will pass your request on to 10 Downing Street, but I have to advise you that the Prime Minister does not usually come down to see people charged with offences, however serious they are!" Thomas said mildly.

Still protesting his innocence, they led Philip away and placed him in a prison van, to be driven to Brixton Prison.

Fifty Years After

Hours later, now dressed in a prison uniform, he was informed that he was scheduled to appear in the local magistrate's court next morning to answer to the charges.

Julia and her team returned from North London just before 3 pm, loaded down with several cartons of documents and a laptop, which they added to the similar material seized from Philip's office the previous day. Following a hastily swallowed sandwich and a cup of tea, she joined Albert, Belinda and Jonathan and walked to the conference room, where the media representatives had already assembled and were impatiently waiting.

"Be careful, you two," Albert said again. "That lot in there are like a herd of lions, waiting to tear you to pieces and have you for dinner!"

"They can't be that bad!" Belinda protested.

"Don't be so sure, Belinda. Albert's been very mild about them!" Julia commented as she opened the door of the Conference Room.

Instantly the four appeared the hubbub within the room ceased and the camera bulbs started flashing, temporarily blinding Belinda and Jonathan, who had not expected it. They sat down and the Conference started with Julia reading a statement.

"On April 26th, 1961, a young woman and a young man were courting each other in a park in North London, pursued by another young man, who had a grudge against both of them. They innocently started to make love together, being unable to find a safer place because the boy was black and the girl was white and such things were not acceptable in the Britain of 1961. The young man, who followed them, tore them apart, beat up the boy, shot the girl twice and killed her, and placed the gun in the unconscious boy's hands. On June 22nd 1961 that boy was found guilty of the murder of his girlfriend and he was hanged on July 15th 1961. His body was given a felon's grave in Wormwood Scrubs Prison where he was hanged.

Fifty Years After

His girlfriend was buried near her home in Marchfield. Yesterday, in the Appeal Court, that verdict was set aside and, later, Her Majesty pardoned the young man. Yesterday also we arrested the other individual. Earlier today we charged Lord Stewart of Little Wittering with four charges: the murder of Janet Brown; the rape of Janet Brown; Perjury; and the murder of Janet's unborn child. We could also have charged him with stalking Janet for several days prior to the murder, but we can't do so because the trial will be held under the laws that applied in 1961, the Homicide Act of 1957 – and stalking was not a crime then. I expect that we will also have to drop the rape charge because of the Statute of Limitations. Lord Stewart has apparently denied all the charges. Later today, incidentally, Mark Smith's body is to be exhumed. It is intended to bury him in the same grave as Janet next week."

Julia sat down and a forest of hands went up. The BBC man spoke first.

"You said you were going to try Lord Stewart under the 1957 Homicide Act. This Act called for a person who used a gun to commit murder to be hanged. Do you intend to enforce that law in view of the fact that European Legislation prevents Capital Punishment being reintroduced?"

"That's up to the courts and the Home Secretary," Julia answered. "We don't make the laws, we just investigate breaches of the law and put those we think are guilty before the courts."

"I followed the appeal yesterday. Your team alleged very serious breaches of the law by the Prosecution in the Smith trial," the Daily Telegraph reporter said. "Who do you think was responsible?"

"No comment," Julia replied.

"Do you think it was the Stewart family?" the ITV reporter asked.

"Again, no comment."

"The Prosecutor in the case was the father of the present Prime Minister," a reporter from the Sun pointed out. "Were either of them responsible for the abuses you raised yesterday?"

"I don't know," Julia answered. "It's an issue that we will have to investigate."

"So there is an issue here?" the BBC man insisted.

"I haven't said that Mr Macdonald," Julia replied.

The questions continued to come on the issue of who was responsible for the abuses revealed in the original trial and Julia continued to fend them off. Finally, Albert took over.

"I was the defence barrister at that trial," he said, "and I intend to prosecute the case against Lord Philip, assisted by my two young friends here. There are serious issues connected with the way the police handled the evidence presented in the 1961 trial, but they are no longer an issue for the new trial. They may be an issue in a larger investigation, but that is a police matter and not one that we can speculate about."

The reporters turned their attention to Jonathan and Belinda.

"I understand that you're the grandson of the Prime Minister," a female reporter from the Daily Mirror pointed out. "What do you think about your family's role in this case?"

"I'm not sure that the family had a role, Miss," Jonathan answered. "Sir Walter was just doing his duty. Sir Marcus was helping his father."

"How and why did you get involved in this case?" the ITV man asked.

"It's a long story," Jonathan said, "but basically I wanted to know more about my Granddad and came across this case, read about it, and felt that there was something that didn't seem to be quite right about it. So I began to research it."

"Then Sir Marcus asked us if we would write his biography for him," Belinda added.

"How did you find the evidence that there was wrong doing in the preparation of the trial?" the reporter of the Times asked.

"We found a whistle blower."

"What do you mean, Jonathan?" the Sun Reporter asked.

"Someone tipped us off?"

"Someone from the police or from somewhere else?" the BBC reporter asked.

"It was someone who had cause to know what had happened and warned us. We were able to get access to the files and found out the truth of what the whistle blower told us," Jonathan explained.

"But you're not prepared to be any more specific. Is that it?" the reporter from the Daily Telegraph asked.

"Exactly," Jonathan said.

Julia intervened. She did not like the way the press reporters were homing in on the source of the leakage of the documents.

"I'm sorry, ladies and gentlemen. That's as much as we can cover today. We have other work to do. I will call another Conference when we have anything new to tell you."

With that she led them out.

"Thank you, Julia," Belinda said for them both. "We were close to getting trapped into saying something unwise there."

"I know," Julia said. "That's why I got you out of there. I know how to handle them, but you don't. Your friend won't thank you if you drop his father into it."

Jonathan smiled.

"Now you've got to speak with Juliet," Julia said, and then get ready for your big film premiere!"

After that we're going to Scotland for a wedding rehearsal," Belinda said.

"That's nice", Julia said, as she turned away from them to go back to her office.

Next day, Philip Stewart appeared before Belmarsh Magistrate's Court. Luke and Jennifer were both present, and so was Juliet, who introduced herself to them and asked them if they approved of her idea of a proxy marriage in Gretna Green with themselves as witnesses. Luke was reluctant, fearing a journalistic stunt.

"Belinda and Jonathan, who will act as the proxies, want to do this to enable your brother and sister to marry, as they intended, in the eyes of God. They are going to get married later in the year on November 5th in order to honour the memory of the doomed romance of Philip Stewart's two victims."

"So, it's not a journalistic stunt?" Luke insisted.

"No, although I suspect that the television companies will cover it, and the later wedding of the two youngsters. It would make great television and will link the public who see it with the two victims and their unborn child, all killed because of Philip's racist feelings of jealousy."

Hearing Juliet's answer, the two agreed to the idea, although Luke cynically suggested that it wouldn't do Juliet's career any harm either.

Juliet laughed.

"I retired nine years ago. I'm as passionately concerned about your siblings' fate as you are. That trial was my first case, just as it was Albert Corrigan's. I want to end as I began, by seeing justice for those two poor youngsters."

In court, they watched the very short proceedings as Philip confirmed his name and address and Albert Corrigan listed the charges.

"The charges were that Philip Stewart:
1. Murdered Janet Brown on April 26th, 1961 by shooting her twice;
2. Raped Janet Brown on April 25th, 1961;
3. Perverted the course of justice by committing perjury in the Central Criminal Court on June 21st 1961;

4. Committed manslaughter by killing the unborn child of Janet Brown on April 26th, 1961.

The Prosecution has decided to withdraw the Rape charge since it is covered by the Statute of Limitations and is out of time. We have also decided to withdraw the manslaughter charge, since Mr Stewart could have had no knowledge of Miss Brown's pregnancy."

"The charge sheet is amended to include only the murder and perjury charges, Mr Harris. Does your client understand?" the magistrate asked.

Charles Harris leant over the dock to whisper to Philip who, after a moment, nodded.

"He does. Your honour."

A discussion then ensued as to when the next stage of the process would take place. Finally, the magistrate and the two lawyers agreed the date.

"Lord Stewart, would you please stand?" the clerk to the court said.

Philip stood up.

"You will be remanded in custody in Belmarsh Prison until Monday June 7th when you will appear before this Court for the committal hearing."

With that, the magistrate stood up and left the court, and Philip was taken away, and escorted back to Belmarsh.

Luke took Jennifer and Juliet out to lunch and she spent the time finding out more about Mark and Janet and their brother and sister. She also learned, for the first time, about Janet's diary. She took their mobile numbers and agreed to ring them to fix up a time for the five of them to travel to Scotland.

Julia and Albert returned to Lewisham and, once there, discussed the preparation for the Committal Hearing.

"I'm leaving that to you, Albert," Julia said. "I've done my bit. You and your young assistants will have to prepare the evidence and the witnesses. My team are moving on to the Stewart Gang and the cover up. I've got Inspector Browning coming down here from Cambridge later this afternoon to discuss the Cambridge Kidnap Case and its links with Stewart."

Julia handed the Janet Brown Murder Case File to Albert.

"Don't forget that the film team will be in Buckinghamshire for the first half of next week to film the reading of Janet's diary. Make certain your youngsters are ready and able to do it and do it well. Tell them I will put them across my knee and smack their bottoms if they let me down! They're not too old for me to do it!"

"I'll let them know. Leave the Brown Case with me. Let me know when you need me for the Stewart Gang case."

That night, Albert phoned Jonathan and passed Julia's message on to him. He laughed at the threat.

"Tell Julia she will have to join the queue. My Grandmother has told us several times that she's going to tan our behinds. My father also has me on his list. So she's third on the smacking list!"

Albert laughed.

"I'm not surprised," he confessed. "Just be ready for next Monday. And don't tell Juliet too much. She looks like a fluffy old dear, but she has a mind that's as sharp as a razor. You won't get much past her."

Two days later Juliet came down to Chequers. Jonathan and Belinda met her outside the house and sat with her in the garden. It was a very warm day and Jonathan was stripped to the waist, revealing a brown and well-muscled body beneath his mop of blond hair. His dark blue walking shorts revealed a pair of well-developed thighs. Juliet thought she knew what had first attracted Belinda to the six feet tall Jonathan. Belinda, on the other hand, was shorter, at five feet six inches tall, and darker. Juliet knew

Fifty Years After

that Belinda described herself as black, but thought she was actually mixed race. She was dressed in a pair of shorts and a loose white t-shirt, which showed her figure to good effect. She wore her hair long and, that day, had it braided in African style. Juliet thought they made a fine couple and could see from the way they reacted to one another, they were very much in love.

A staff member brought out a jug of water and three glasses.
"I understand that next week you are tied up with a film crew. I have spoken to Luke and Jennifer and they have agreed to come with us to Gretna Green. Would you like me to arrange this for the week after next?"
"Would you?" Jonathan asked. "I've an address here," he said, passing a piece of paper across to Juliet. "It's the hotel where Janet and Mark were booked to stay. I feel that we should be booked in there. Tell them we need four rooms and explain why. I think we will need to be there for three nights."
Juliet agreed and said that she would make the booking and let them all know. She also agreed to arrange the details with the blacksmith.

"Now", she said, "tell me about your romance. When did you meet?"
"We met at a Freshers' Fair on October 7th 2008," Belinda said. "I looked at Jonathan and thought 'what a hunk!' and went over and talked to him. However, we first went out on a date together on October 20th when we went to have a coffee together. Everything went on from there."
Juliet noticed that Belinda ran her fingers possessively down Jonathan's naked chest. Belinda's hand stopped just above Jonathan's shorts and lingered there, suggesting her claim to ownership. Juliet thought the action was instinctive. Belinda was marking her territory in the presence of another female.

"Seeing him dressed like that, I know what you mean!" Juliet said, smiling as she noticed Jonathan blush.

"When Belinda came over to talk to me, I thought she was hot," Jonathan said, "and I was not going to miss the chance, so we left the Freshers' Fair together and went to get a coffee."

"The second years call the Freshers' Fair 'the meat market' and I certainly found a big bit of beef steak!" Belinda said. "We didn't join any clubs or societies, but we founded our own, with just two members, and we went on from there."

"I've looked you up on Google," Juliet admitted. "I know that Jonathan went to Harrow. Your Dad went to Eaton. Why did you go to Harrow?"

"Because he went to Eaton," Jonathan answered, and Juliet thought she understood.

"What about you, Belinda?"

"My parents could not afford to send me to public school so I went to the local Grammar School."

"How did you two become involved in the Smith murder case?"

Jonathan repeated his explanation.

"You said that you felt something was wrong about it," Juliet said. "What worried you?"

"Nothing specific. It was a gut feeling. I suppose I thought the trial was too short and that the Jury took too little time in reaching a verdict. That, of course, was after I read the trial transcript which I found in a book, which Granddad gave me when I told him I was interested in the trial."

"Are you reading Law at Cambridge?"

"I am," Belinda said, "but Jonathan isn't – he's reading I T. I knew about the case, though, because he told me when he first met me that his great grandfather was a barrister and became a high court judge."

"I gather you're both writing Jonathan's grandfather's biography. Who suggested that?"

"Lady Evelyn. She persuaded Grandpa to let us have his diary and, later, to have his secret diary, in which he wrote what he really thought about the other politicians in his Party and the other Parties."

"How did Belinda get involved in the investigation?"

Jonathan explained how he was worried about Belinda's safety and went to Cambridge to collect her and bring her to Chequers.

"I've been warned not to ask you details about the investigation, but could you tell me about your methods?"

"We worked together, pooling our ideas and knowledge, and using every resource, human and technological that was available to us. I think Google was one of our most valuable tools."

"That's fine, Jonathan. I'm sure I'll learn more from you when we travel to Scotland and while we're there. I've just one more question for you both before I go and have tea with your Grandma and let you either sunbathe to tan that magnificent body you have or go for a walk."

Jonathan blushed again and Belinda smiled.

"Am I right in thinking that you both feel very close to the murdered couple?"

Belinda looked at Jonathan, who nodded. She answered Juliet's question.

"I'm black and Jonathan's white. We get on well together and our parents approve of our marriage. Jonathan's Grandparents would buy us the earth if we asked for it. We're both 20 and we live in 2010. It was different for Janet and Mark. They were both 18, and Mark was black and Janet was white. They wanted what we want, but no one supported them. They only had each other for support. We have experienced a little racism. They experienced it every day of their lives together, and they died because of it. We make love together in comfort in a bed. They did it in the open under the trees, because they were not allowed to spend time together in each other's homes. Their parents all disapproved of their relationship. Finally, Janet was brutally murdered just as

Fifty Years After

she and Mark were about to strike out on their own, and he was caught in a net devised by Janet's murderer and trapped like a fox by a group of fox hounds in a court of law which saw only his black skin and killed him as well. Hanged as a common felon, his body was kept separate from that of his love in death just as they tried to keep them separate in life. I feel that we owe them something, and that's why we feel so close to them."

"That was a very long speech, Belinda, and a very moving one," Juliet said, brushing back the tears she felt in her own eyes and saw in Belinda's.

Jonathan and Belinda left Juliet to make her way to the house, walking off into the grounds, their arms wrapped around each other's waist, seeking solace in each other's company. Juliet watched them go, and then realised that Evelyn had walked out to join her.

"They're a remarkable pair of young people aren't they? I wish I had been like them when I was 20."

Juliet looked around and stared straight into Evelyn's eyes.

"Yes, they are. I find that young man's courage terrifying. Does he realise that he's risking everything you all hold dear in pursuing justice for this lost couple?"

"Oh yes, they both realise that. They know that they can both end up with just the clothes they're wearing – not that they're wearing very much today – if things go badly from here. They've already had to survive the threat of being kidnapped and murdered. But they're young, like we were once, and they're both determined to pursue this crusade to the bitter end, whatever that causes for them."

In Westminster, Sir Marcus Greenway had summoned Rufus, the Chairman of the Conservative Party, to see him in his House of Commons office. Rufus knocked and entered. Marcus, who was dictating a letter to a Constituent to Daphne, waved him to a seat, and asked Daphne to type the letters he had finished dictating and return to him later. Daphne took her mini recorder and left the room. Marcus offered sherry to his guest, but was refused. Rufus was known for his abruptness.

"What do you want to see me for, Marcus?" he asked.

"This is a highly confidential discussion, Rufus. I ask you to promise me that it will not go beyond the two of us, unless I tell you."

Mystified by the tone and content of the remark and Marcus's serious face, Rufus agreed.

"If that's how you want it, Marcus, naturally no one will learn of it through me."

Sir Marcus nodded.

"Fine, I hoped you would say that."

"So, Marcus, what's this all about?"

"You must be aware that Philip Stewart has been arrested."

"I am – but I'm not sure which of his many crimes it's for!"

"This is no joke, Rufus."

Rufus looked surprised at Marcus's suddenly sharp tone.

"He was arrested for murdering Janet Brown."

Rufus looked confused. He had not heard of a missing girl called Janet Brown on any of the news broadcasts.

"Who's Janet Brown?"

"She was an 18 year old girl, who was murdered in 1961."

"That's a long time ago."

"A man was wrongly convicted and hanged for it, but Philip certainly did it."

"What has this got to do with you and me?"

"I may have to resign because of it."

"Why?"

"Because I knew he was guilty before Mark Smith was hanged, but failed to stop the hanging, and am therefore complicit in the miscarriage of justice."

"How did you know?"

"Philip told me."

"And you think he will tell others, possibly the Court?"

"I think I may be obliged to tell the court myself, and then resign. My position would be untenable. We are there to make the law, and I tried to prevent the law doing its job."

"What did you do?"

"I told my father and he refused to do anything."

"Then it's not your fault."

"Yes it is. I refused three times to allow a public enquiry."

"It sounds bad, but you can survive it, and I think you should. If you resign, the Euro Sceptics will put up a candidate and ruin the country by taking us out of the European Union. Only you can hold the Party together on the issue. Do not resign unless you absolutely have to do so."

"I'm not sure that I can, Rufus."

"Have you spoken to your family?"

"Yes."

"What did they say?"

"What you've just said."

"Then you know what to do?"

"Yes, Rufus," Marcus sighed heavily. "I will do as you suggest."

The news of the arrest of a British Peer (a former minister) for murder caused a sensation and dominated the newspaper front pages and the news broadcasts in UK and across the world. In Malaga a British former ex-patriot, who was now a Spanish citizen picked up his copy of 'El Pais' and read about the arrest and impending trial for murder of Lord Stewart. The news came as a shock to him, particularly as he had been speaking on the phone to Lord Stewart only two weeks before and received no warning that such an event was possible. He put down the paper, and reached for his telephone book, hunting through his

Fifty Years After

list of British contacts. Finally, he found one and dialled a number. A male voice answered it.

"Is that Frank?" the man asked.

"Yes," the voice replied cautiously. "Who's that calling?"

"It's Tim," he said.

There was silence at the other end as Frank was obviously trying to work out who Tim was. Eventually he spoke.

"What can I do for you Tim?"

"Why has Phil been arrested and why didn't you stop it in the normal way?"

Frank's voice sounded more relaxed. He had obviously worked out who his caller was.

"It came as a surprise to us, and to him, Tim. Phil suspected that a Greenway kid was getting too nosey and too close to the family. He and his girlfriend, a black girl I believe, were trying to dig up the past and Phil was worried. He gave orders to rub them both out, but they were hidden away, and so he decided to kidnap and kill them when they came out from hiding. It didn't work, and they arrested him."

"For the kidnap plot?"

"No, it's rather odd. The five members of the kidnap team were arrested and are being held in Cambridge, but there was no reference to Philip in that case."

"So what's going on?"

"You won't believe this Tim, but they've resurrected an old case. Remember the 1961 murder of the white girl in Marchfield where Phil was a witness and a black guy was hanged?"

"I do, and I think the world was well rid of them! She was like a bitch on heat copulating with that black cunt in the fields like animals. Phil did us all a service. He should get a medal, not a prison sentence."

"You're right, but no one thinks like that today. It's not PC, Tim. The appeal court overturned the verdict and the

Fifty Years After

Queen pardoned the black guy. Phil has been charged with the murder and with perjury."

"I read that in the papers, Frank. What I don't understand is how you and Phil let it come to this. I thought you had the Old Bill under control."

"We still do with the Bill in North London, Tim. However, the Greenways brought in some new Filth from Surrey, headed by a woman. They're not even based in our area. They're south of the river somewhere."

"The cunning sods, Frank. It just goes to show that you can't trust the Old Bill or the Filth as you call them."

"What do you want us to do, Tim?"

"Keep your heads down for the moment. I'm going to fly over. I'll text you my flight and arrival time. Please arrange for a car to meet me."

"Don't worry, Tim. I'll do it myself."

"Thanks, Frank. I knew I could rely on you."

In Lewisham, Julia knew that she was in trouble. Looking at her augmented team and at the boxes of paper as well as the two computers that they had brought from the house in Marchfield Green as well as the office in Westminster, she realised that she needed more help.

"I will ask for some more people from Lewisham or one of the other South London boroughs," Julia told the team. "However, for the moment, it's all hands on deck I'm afraid, guys, including me. We'll just have to divide the files between us."

"I think you'll have to go wider than that, Julia," Thomas replied. "We need an officer who knows the names and the ground. Basically we need a police officer from North London."

"They're all under suspicion of colluding with the very people we're investigating, Tom," Julia pointed out.

"Can we find a relatively new and low ranking officer, who knows the people and the area, but is unknown to the gang?"

Julia sat silently, thinking. Eventually she answered Thomas.

"I will send Gethin when Sue gets back from Westminster." She turned to Gethin.

"Gethin?"

"Yes, Julia."

"I want you to go to North London and snoop around. Talk to the young detective constables there and try to find someone who has had no contacts with the Stewart Gang but has knowledge of them. Don't give anything away, but, if you find a suitable candidate, bring him or her back with you and I will talk to him or her."

"Yes, Julia."

"Okay, then. Let's get to work, guys."

In Buckinghamshire, Jonathan and Belinda had found a quiet place among the trees to practise their lines and to play with each other. Eventually Jonathan found the temptation too much, especially when Belinda started tickling him, and he began to pull off her t-shirt. Shortly afterwards they were both naked and in each other's arms.

"I've never made love in the open before," Belinda commented afterwards. "Now I know how Janet and Mark felt."

Evelyn and Juliet discussed what they termed 'the two youngsters' over a cup of coffee, sitting on the terrace overlooking the garden.

"I look on them like my own children, Juliet," Evelyn confessed. "They probably both get away with much too much, and, if anything happens either to them or to Marcus I've only got myself to blame. I could have stopped this from the beginning."

Juliet was both sympathetic and puzzled.

"Didn't you have children of your own, Lady Evelyn?" she asked.

Fifty Years After

"For goodness sake, less of the 'Lady'! I was Evelyn James before I married and Evelyn Greenway afterwards. Marcus only became a knight 20 years ago and I'm 67."

Juliet smiled.

"Okay, Evelyn. But what about your own children?"

"I have one son, Martin. He's 50. It was a very difficult birth and I was unable to have any other children as a result. There has always been tension between Marcus and him. I think Marcus blames him for what happened to me. It's unfair, of course. It wasn't Martin's fault. However, Marcus doesn't see it that way."

"So you see Jonathan as a sort of substitute, is that it?"

"You are very astute, Juliet. Jonathan has so much of the appearance of Marcus when I first knew him and has the character that I first believed Marcus had, that I see him as the son I wanted and never had."

"What about Belinda?"

"I love Belinda almost as much as he does and as much as I love Jonathan. Girls have always been few and far between in the Greenway family apparently – so Marcus loves her too. I stayed down here rather than spend time at Number 10 in order to look after them. Do take extra care of them when you're in Scotland. They're both too adventurous for their own good. They believe that the risks to them are over now that Philip Stewart is under lock and key. I think they're wrong. You must keep a very sharp eye on them. I will tell them to do what you tell them. Make certain they obey me and you."

Juliet looked at Evelyn with compassion and nodded.

"Don't worry, Evelyn. I'll make sure they return here intact and ready and able to annoy you even more."

"Thank you, Juliet. That's a comfort to me."

Evelyn stood up and Juliet followed her.

"I have to go to a Party cheese and wine in the nearby village. Would you care to come with me?"

"Certainly, Evelyn," Juliet replied, as the two walked away to where Hawkins was waiting with the car."

Fifty Years After

Charles Harris waited for Philip to be brought down to him in an interview room in Belmarsh Prison. Charles was wondering how he was going to handle this case. He had handled Stewart Family business for years and was fully aware that it was likely his client murdered the girl and lied about the boy. He was used to that, and found that judicious use of the Stewart Family fortune usually procured the desired result. He smiled at the English language's ability to use the same word with two opposite meanings. He was judicious in his use of the means to avoid a truly judicious verdict in Stewart Family cases. Charles knew some people would call him corrupt, and others would call him bent. He didn't care. They could call him what they liked. It kept his family fed and watered and kept him living in comfort. That's all that mattered to Charles.

Philip entered the room under the escort of a prison officer, who immediately withdrew. Philip sat down at the table opposite Charles, who thought it was strange seeing the usually dapper peer dressed in prison uniform.

"How's it going?" Charles asked.

"Once I got over the shock of being stripped and examined on arrival, it's been okay," Philip answered. "However, they've cut me off effectively from the outside world."

"How so?" Charles asked.

"I'm only allowed visits from you and family. They can't stop you visiting me, of course. But anyone else who visits me will be noted and followed up. It's too risky for them."

"Don't worry, I'll keep your links going with the family. Do you have any instructions in that regard?"

"Yes. I'm not certain that Albert Campion is actually dead. I wonder if he's grassing us up. Can you find out, and if he is," Philip smiled. "Well, you know what to do."

"I'll do that, Philip. Anything else?"

"Yes, get in contact with Timothy and warn him what's happened. Tell him that I won't be able to come to his daughter's wedding. That upsets me because family means everything to me and my niece acts as a substitute daughter to me."

Charles nodded.

"Philip, I don't usually bother with the truth as you know, but I always feel it's a good idea to know what the truth actually is. That way, I can plan on how to deal with what the opposition might throw at us. So what actually did happen on April 25th and 26th, 1961?

Philip grinned.

"I rid the world of two shits," he said.

"Explain."

"You know I like women, Charles."

Charles nodded, although 'Like' was not a word he would have chosen to describe Philip's obsession with, and his violent behaviour towards, women.

"I had seen Janet Brown several times. She was a good-looking bird, with long black hair, a good figure, nice bum and big tits – just the sort I like. So, I started following her, waiting for an opportunity to lay her, if you know what I mean?"

Charles nodded. He worked for Philip and took his money, but was often repelled by the coarseness of his language, especially on the issues of women and black people.

"On the second day I saw her meet up with this Nigger. I recognised him as the Wanker who punched me for no reason on Christmas Eve two years before."

"No reason?"

"Not really. He blocked my way when I was going home after dropping my Christmas present for Evelyn James – another bird I was chasing at the time. She refused to see me and I was angry. No bird refuses to see me! Anyway, this black bastard walks down the middle of the path and refuses to step aside for me so I told him to go back to Bongobongoland, and he hit me on the chin and calmly walked away."

"I see," Charles said, "and you hated him for it?"

"Yes, but I didn't know who he was or where he lived. If I did I suspect that his house might have caught fire."

Charles nodded.

"And Janet?"

"Who?"

"The girl you were following?"

"Oh. Yes. Was that her name? I had forgotten. She and he went into the Park, stripped off and copulated like the rutting animals they were under the trees. Next day I chased her down and cornered her by the same tree. I told her that I was going to do her and pushed her against the tree. She scratched my face and kicked me in the stomach, so I hit her hard on the chin, twice, knocking her head back against the tree trunk and knocking her down. While she was unconscious, I stripped her naked and used her tights to tie her hands behind her back. I chucked her clothes into the nearest rubbish bin and waited for her to recover consciousness."

"Why?"

"I wanted the Bitch to see my face and feel me inside her. I wanted to hurt her for what she had done to me."

"And did you?"

"Oh yes," Philip said, laughing at the memory. "She squirmed and screamed at me to stop, but I didn't – I did her properly and then I warned her. I told her that if I caught her with that Nigger wanker again I would kill her and him."

"And then?"

"I left her."

"Still tied up and naked?"

"Of course! You're too soft Charles. Why should I untie and dress the Bitch? She would only hit me again - no let her free herself and hunt her clothes! With any luck another man would find her naked and ready for him and have a go as well!"

Charles stared impassively at Philip, hiding his disgust. He was disgusted at Philip's callous attitude to the girl he had raped and later murdered and at himself for representing him.

"What did you do with her clothes?"

"I threw them in the rubbish bin – where I would have liked to put her, because that was all she was – rubbish!"

"What did you do then?"

"I waited until she freed herself and then followed her."

"Why?"

"I wanted to enjoy her humiliation as she tried to hide the fact that she was naked from other people that she met. Unfortunately, I forgot her coat and she didn't meet anyone."

"What happened on the 26th?"

"I followed her again. I had enjoyed myself on the 25th and thought I'd have a second helping. However, she was with the black guy, when I first saw her. I guessed where they would go and so went home and grabbed my father's gun. I knew it was loaded. I put it in my pocket and took a short cut to the Park, beating them to their favourite spot. I saw them talking to the Cop in the Park and then come to the tree and strip each other. I waited until he was lying on top of her and bonking her, and then I struck – because I knew it would hurt them both. I dragged him off her and knocked him out after kicking him in the balls. I was lucky because, like the girl the day before, he hit his head against a tree. I turned back to the girl who was trying to get up. I pushed her back down and took the gun from my pocket. 'I warned you, you bitch,' I said. 'You took no notice, and so you can have it,' and I shot her twice. I knew she was dead because of the way she slumped against the tree and didn't move so I moved over to the boy, intending to kill him as well. Then I had a better idea. If I killed them both, I thought, they would come looking for me, But, if I put the gun in his hand, and told the Cop I'd seen that he tried to shoot me and hit the girl instead, they would believe me because I was white and not him, because he was black. They would hang him and save me the bother. So, I put the gun in his hand and made him fire a third shot into the trees, and left him, to call the Cop. The rest you know already."

"Did your father know this?"

"Oh yes, because I told him when I got home that day."

"What did he do?"

"He called me a bloody fool, but he fixed it with Inspector Buchan and Walter Greenway. He paid them both to get the Nigger topped."

"You mean, of course, Mark Smith?"

"Did he have a name? I thought they were all the same! Do you give animals names?"

For a moment Charles was almost overwhelmed by his sense of repulsion at Philip's words and attitude. He had no concept of wrongdoing and no sense of contrition at his crime and the suffering he caused his immediate victims and their families. He almost walked out on Philip. However, two things stopped him. The first was the fact he needed the money, and the second was his own sense of self-preservation. It was dangerous to walk out on Philip Stewart, and a trapped and wounded lion is, perhaps, even more dangerous than one that is free and uninjured.

"Were there any witnesses to either incident?"

"None."

"Do you know of any evidence connecting you to Janet Brown or the alleged irregularities in the trial?"

Philip laughed. He remembered the meeting with Alasdair Buchan when the Inspector and his father had doctored the evidence. He also remembered being present at his father's meeting with Matthew Allbright, when the juror was bribed and given the envelopes to bribe the other jurors.

"One has to make assurance doubly sure," Jack Stewart had explained to his bemused son. "We cannot afford to take any chances."

Fifty Years After

"I don't think there was any evidence," Philip answered at length. "Being honest, of course we doctored the evidence and bribed the jury. What did you expect us to do?"

"Don't you feel at all contrite that you killed one person and was responsible for the deaths of two others?"

"Two?" Philip asked, puzzled. "Only one was hanged!"

"Janet was pregnant," Charles pointed out.

"Oh that!" Philip said. "That would have been a half cast, so the world was well shot of it. I did the world a service by ridding it of a whore who opened her legs for anyone; a randy Nigger who shouldn't have been here in the first place; and a half-breed, who would have probably lived on the social and grown up to be a criminal."

"Like you," Charles said impulsively, before he could stop himself.

Philip looked shocked.

"I'm not a criminal," he said. "I'm a peer of the realm with all the rights that an Earl has to provide a service for my people and to punish those who offend me."

Charles shook his head sadly as he gathered up his papers. Philip had given him nothing to work with. He looked at his client, trying to hide his disgust.

"One final thing, Philip. You know that this case is being pursued under the 1957 Homicide Act?"

"Yes."

"Do you know the significance of that?"

"Remind me."

"The mandatory sentence for causing a death by shooting was death by hanging. You can expect to be sentenced to death if you are found guilty."

Philip looked shocked.

"I thought they had abolished capital punishment."

"They have, and EU laws forbid its reintroduction, but you will still receive that sentence, because the judge will have no option under the law. However, the sentence will be commuted and then the judge will give you a tariff. If you want to breathe free air again, I suggest that you reconsider your attitude to your crime and to the three individuals whose lives you terminated suddenly by your actions."

Charles Harris stood up, pulled his chair back and walked away.

"I will see you in a day or two," he added as he stood aside to let the prison officer escort Philip back to his cell.

That weekend Sir Marcus joined Evelyn and the two lovers at his country retreat.

"How's the book going?" he asked

"Quite well, Granddad," Jonathan answered. "We've left the Smith Trial for the moment and we're working on your by election triumph in December 1966."

"That was one of the best moments of my life," Marcus recalled. "It was my first election campaign, and I enjoyed every minute of it. I always have enjoyed meeting people and you meet hundreds of ordinary people when you go out canvassing, and they always surprise you. I really enjoy the give and take on the doorstep."

"Do you still campaign in the same way, Granddad," Belinda asked.

Marcus smiled at her. He loved the way that she had adopted him already.

"I try to, Belinda," he said. "However, I can't do as much as I want to, because as Prime Minister and Party Leader I have to do so much for other candidates and much of my canvassing is in other parts of the country."

"I think that Jonathan should go into politics. I've tried to persuade you, haven't I Darling?"

"I'm much too honest for politics, Darling," Jonathan answered.

Evelyn laughed.

"I think you're too honest for politicians, yet alone politics!"

"How's your school work going?" Marcus asked.

Fifty Years After

"We're not at school, Granddad," Jonathan objected. "We're at Cambridge University!"

"Forgive my slip, Jonathan. I was never a University student. Anyway how's it going?"

"We're managing a few hours a day and the tutors seem to be happy with us – at least judging from the comments they send us," Belinda told him.

"I'm thinking of buying or renting a flat for you in London," Marcus told them. "The Philip Stewart Murder Trial may force me to resign as Prime Minister. If I resign, you will both have to move out of this house. I think you're reasonably safe now, but I will ensure that you have a security guard, whatever happens. London would also be more convenient for you – both for the trial and for your university work. And – while I'm still an MP – I can see you at Westminster, either in Downing Street or in my Westminster office."

Evelyn expressed her approval and the two of them agreed to accept Marcus's help in relocating.

On Monday, after Sir Marcus had returned to Westminster, the camera crew arrived at the house, accompanied by Albert Corrigan. Jonathan and Belinda watched with amazement as the technicians converted one of the stately drawing rooms into two small rooms, overcrowded with cheap furniture and fittings, in what was apparently a North London terraced house. When they were ready, they carried out a final run through of the entire diary, which took an hour and a half to read. The actual reading, which involved a simulation of Jonathan, as Mark, writing the letters that Mark wrote to Janet, and Belinda, as Janet, sticking the letters and photos in her diary and writing her entries, proved to be a lengthy procedure with several retakes of each section. The film crews tried to reduce the amount of stress on their two actors by mixing the filming of the individual scenes. In all, the process of filming took three days. The producer and editor filmed during the mornings, leaving Jonathan and Belinda free in the

Fifty Years After

afternoons, during which the editors edited what had been done in the morning. On Friday morning they screened the final production for Jonathan and Belinda, Evelyn and Albert, as well as Julia, who came down to see what had been achieved. Jonathan and Belinda left the room at the end in tears. Evelyn went after them to console them, and Julia and Albert were left with the production staff.

"You've done a good job," Julia told them. "With the supporting evidence of Jennifer Foster, as well as the graphical analysis of the diary and letters and the school exercise books of Janet and Mark, I think that will destroy any case that Charles Harris can put up. Those two kids did a fantastic job – do congratulate them for me and say I'm sorry that I had to put them through it."

She left to return to Lewisham and the film crew began to dismantle the set before they all adjourned for lunch, where the producer passed Julia's message on to the, by now recovered, couple.

Gethin spent the week in North London, apparently studying how the force dealt with motoring offences. He met over thirty Police Officers before finding the ideal candidate. Detective Constable Alfred Smith was 30 years old and was born and bred in North London. Naturally he was delighted to be working in North London. He quickly showed promise and was moved from the uniformed to the plain-clothes branch at the age of 25. Since then he had shown great skill with computers and he was known as their I T expert. However, this meant that he was largely unknown to the gang, which controlled all the serious crime in the area and so had not been approached by them. Indeed, he was anxious to use his skills to bring them to book. He was disappointed when his colleagues did not share his enthusiasm. He met Gethin over a pint in a pub in Marchfield.

"I know quite a lot about the Stewart Gang," he told Gethin. "I've been monitoring their activities for the last

Fifty Years After

three years and have compiled quite a dossier. It's all a waste of time though, because no one here seems to be interested."

Gethin sympathised.

"It's difficult when that happens. Did you ever watch 'The Untouchables'?"

"It's one of my favourite films," Alfred claimed. "I've often thought that we were in the same situation here with the Stewart Gang that the Chicago Police had with Al Capone."

"What do you think is the solution?"

"I think we need our own Elliot Ness, Gethin."

"Would you work with an Elliot Ness if you had one, Alfred?"

"Certainly."

Gethin bought them both a second pint and worked his way through it while they talked of other issues and watched the Football Championship Play offs on the big screen. As they talked, drank and watched, Gethin was thinking. Finally, he put his thoughts into words.

"There is an Elliot Ness, Alfred. She's called Julia Donaldson and is a Superintendent in the Surrey Police Force. I'm part of her special gang-busting squad and we're working from Lewisham Police Station to end the reign of the Stewart Gang and halt the bribery and corruption they've been using. I'm up here looking for someone with local knowledge to guide us through the tons of papers and computer files that we've seized. I think you're the guy. Will you join us?"

Alfred did not hesitate.

"Of course," he said.

On the following Monday, as the five were leaving for Scotland, Alfred Smith travelled to Lewisham where he met Julia, and joined the team, which now consisted of eleven officers.

Fifty Years After

At about the same time that Alfred set foot in Lewisham Police Station, an Airbus landed at Gatwick, at the end of a flight from Malaga. A tall man in his early 60s emerged from the plane, collected his luggage, and headed through immigration. As he was a Spanish citizen, he came through the EU and UK channel without challenge.

"Ah, Mr Dos Santos," the customs officer said in halting Spanish, "have you come for a particular purpose?"

"I've come to visit relatives and assist them with a little problem they have with their computers," Mr Dos Santos said in perfect Spanish.

"Good luck, and have a good time," the officer concluded as he waved him through.

The traveller walked through the Arrivals Lounge, looking for a familiar face. Eventually he saw the person he was seeking.

"Hi, Frank," he said. "You haven't changed a bit. It's good to see you."

He spoke perfect English albeit with a slight Spanish lilt to his natural Cockney accent.

Juliet met Luke and Jennifer at Dalton Station and drove them to Chequers, where she picked up Jonathan and Belinda. She had hired a small minibus for the journey since she thought they would be better and safer driving together than using the trains or driving in different vehicles. She and Luke shared the driving, and the other three sat at the back, talking quietly as they travelled north. They arrived at Gretna just after sunset and parked outside of the only hotel in the village at about 8 pm. They were expected and quickly accommodated, having taken up half of the available rooms.

The owner of the hotel, Jackie Campbell, was very happy to see them and, knowing roughly when to expect them, since Juliet had kept her informed by text as to their progress throughout the day, had prepared a traditional Scottish meal for them, before they went to bed early, tired

Fifty Years After

by their long journey. Next morning, they were up early, had a large breakfast, and went to see the blacksmith's cottage, the traditional place for eloping couples to marry.

"It's a strange request you're making," the blacksmith said, "but I understand why you're making it. So long as you take it seriously and do it properly, I don't see why we shouldn't do it. And, of course, I have no objection to doing the same for you two in reality in November, if that's what you really want."

"It is," said Belinda and Jonathan together.

"I'll talk to the Minister at the Kirk and she can bless your marriage when we do it afterwards and make it proper," he added.

"Do you object to a small camera crew covering this event?" Belinda asked. I know that Juliet thinks it would be a good thing.

"So long as they don't get in the way."

They discussed the time and agreed to carry out the ceremony at midday the following day before they returned to the hotel and spoke to Jackie about their own wedding in November when they would hire the whole hotel for three days. Jackie smiled and made the booking for them.

"I don't think we've ever had a Prime Minister staying here before," she commented. "Hamish, that's my husband's name, will be delighted when I tell him tonight when he gets back from Glasgow."

The wedding the following day was a very solemn and sombre affair. Jonathan wore a badge with Mark's face on it and Belinda wore one with Janet's face on it. The couple made their vows in the names of Mark and Janet, witnessed by a deeply moved Jennifer and Luke and recorded by a BBC Scotland camera crew. Following the wedding, they visited Fiona Macdonald; the local reformed church minister, who prayed for them and for the families of Mark and Janet. All seven people, accompanied by the camera crew, followed this up with a

Fifty Years After

celebration lunch at the hotel. At the end of the meal, Hamish drew Jonathan and Belinda aside.

"Could you come down and see me in my office later, when you've all finished?" he asked.

Two hours later the blacksmith and the minister left, saying they looked forward to seeing them all again in November, and Luke took Jennifer out with Juliet to drive around the local area. Mr and Mrs Campbell suggested that they should go to see Robert the Bruce's castle in Loch Maben. Jonathan and Belinda waved them off before they went down to see Hamish Campbell. He was pleased to see them and offered them whisky, which Jonathan accepted and Belinda declined. She accepted a glass of coke instead. Hamish opened the drawer of his desk and took out an old vanilla folder.

"When I heard what you two wanted to do it rang a bell in my mind. I was only 5 in 1961 and my Dad was the owner here. I remember him saying to Mum that she should cancel a booking that had been made and paid for. She asked why, and he said, 'Because the girl has been shot dead and the boy has been arrested for doing it.' We read about the trial, of course, because we felt we were involved. Then the boy was hanged, poor soul, and him only 18! I remember Mum cried her heart out the day he was hanged. It was almost as though he was her son. My Dad was a bit worried about it all because he didn't know what to do with the money. He wrote to the family (I know because he made a copy of the letter) and the boy's Dad replied. He told us to keep the money and give it to a charity in his son's name. That's what we did and we wrote and told him (again my Dad kept a copy of his letter) and we received a letter of thanks from the boy's Dad. He put all these documents in a file, together with the boy's original letter and the acknowledgement and a copy of the receipt. My Dad was meticulous in his book keeping. I'm just the same."

Jonathan and Belinda opened the file and saw that the contents were exactly as Hamish told them.

"What do you want us to do with them?" Jonathan asked.

"Take them back with you and give them to the Police who are investigating the crime," Hamish said.

"Thank you Mr. Campbell," Belinda said for them both. "We will do as you ask."

Next day they returned south. All five were content. Juliet was content because she had learnt a great deal more about the case and had also rounded out her profile of the couple at its epicentre. Luke and Jennifer were content because they thought they had brought their siblings finally together in the way that the two lovers had wished so many years before. Jonathan and Belinda just felt that they had gone a long way to giving Philip's victims the peace he had tried to deny them.

On the day after their return, Jonathan and Belinda travelled up to London by train and from there, travelled to Lewisham by the DLR. Julia was working in her office in Lewisham Police Station, continuing to struggle through piles of invoices and coded messages, when there was an almost shy knock at her door.

"Come in!" she called out.

She was surprised when Jonathan and Belinda entered.

"I thought you were safely out of the way in Scotland," Julia said.

"We got back yesterday," Jonathan explained, and decided we would come and see you today because we have a present for you."

"For me?" she said, surprised. "I didn't think you were going on a shopping expedition!"

"We weren't," Belinda answered, "And there aren't many shops in Gretna."

"We've brought you this," Jonathan said, producing a thin manila file.

"I thought I warned you against sleuthing," Julia said sternly.

"We weren't sleuthing, honest, Superintendent," Belinda said like a schoolgirl caught out in doing something naughty.

"We weren't looking for this," Jonathan added. "It found us, so to speak. The Hotel owner gave us the file and asked us to give it to you. It consists of correspondence between his Dad and Mark and Mark's Dad about Mark's booking, its cancellation and what he should do about the money. He kept copies of the letters he wrote; of the receipt he sent to Mark; and of the letters he received. It will enable you to do, what I think you call 'establish' the evidence that the two were planning to elope."

"I must have done something good in a former life!" Julia thought.

"You're right, Jonathan. It will help us complete the picture. Sometimes you have a stroke of luck like that in an investigation." She smiled sadly. "I could do with some in the Stewart family Investigation."

"If we can help, you know we're always willing, and we're moving to a flat in Blackheath in a week or two. Granddad has bought us a flat so that we are nearer you and nearer Cambridge," Jonathan explained.

"You might be able to help Alfred, our new computer expert, with Philip's computers," Julia said. "I'll tell him you're available."

26. The Opening Phase

Summer 2010

Timothy Stewart met the leaders of the Stewart Family Gang in their favourite pub in Marchfield. All of them were worried because of Philip's arrest and feared for their future. Timothy tried to reassure them.

"The Filth don't know anything about you lot," he told them. "My brother didn't keep any records that could identify any of you. He was too sharp for that. They can search his paper work as much as they like. They won't get anywhere, not unless someone spills the beans and I know none of you would dare do that."

He looked around at them challengingly, watching like a hawk to see if anyone tried to avoid his gaze. To his satisfaction, none did.

"You have to rebuild, but first, you have to lie a bit low," Timothy continued. "My job is to get you going again and then I'm returning to Spain. I run our franchise there. Frank will be in charge here,"

Frank nodded.

"Your job, Frank, is to deal with the current emergency. Phil wanted you to find and eliminate the Greenway kid and his black bitch. It's too late for that. They've done all the damage they could do. Later, perhaps, we'll kidnap them and deal with them like Phil intended: just to show others they shouldn't mess with us. But we won't do it yet. We've got to plug a possible leak. First we've got the five on trial in Cambridge. They've got to be silenced."

Some of the leaders objected.

"I don't mean you should kill them," Timothy added hastily. "I mean you should pay them to be silent – to take the rap for the team. Frank you need to visit Tom and find out how much their silence will cost us and then promise it to them. Be sure you keep your promise after they've gone down. We don't want them to start singing inside."

Fifty Years After

"Okay, Timothy. Anything else?"

"Yes. I've met Phil's brief. He says Phil thinks Albert Campion is still alive and singing like a canary. Unfortunately, he knows a lot about all of us. He's got to be found, if he's still alive, and brought back here. Frank and I will talk to him, and, if he's been a naughty boy and told stories out of school, we'll take him for a little walk."

"So that's our job – buy off the Cambridge 5 and bring Bert to you if he's still alive. Otherwise lie low," said one of the leaders.

"That's right," Timothy replied.

"What do we do about the Boss?" a third man asked.

"That's up to Charles Harris, his brief," Timothy answered. "We can't interfere."

"We could try to bribe the Jury," Frank suggested.

"Not possible," Timothy responded. "It's much more difficult now than it used to be and they'll be watching the jurors like hawks because of what happened last time."

"If we get a chance to kidnap those two nuisances, should we do it?" the second man asked.

"No – leave them to stew in their own juices," Timothy said. "Let him get his girl up the spout. That will give them enough to think about and persuade them to leave us alone until we're ready to deal with them properly."

"Do we run down all our normal undertakings – the prostitutes, drugs and protection services?" Frank asked.

"No, carry them on – we need the money. Don't try anything special for a while that's all, No bank heists and no spectacular killings."

They agreed to pass this instruction on to their members, bought another round of drinks and began to disperse. Next day Timothy Stewart became Fernando Dos Santos again and returned to Malaga after telling Frank to text him the moment Bert was taken so he could come back to UK for their 'little talk.'

Jonathan and Belinda moved out of the Buckinghamshire house and into a flat among the big houses on the Heath at

Fifty Years After

Blackheath. They spent their time during the summer months divided between furnishing their flat, continuing their studies, writing their book, and assisting the enquiry. Belinda worked with Albert preparing the case for the prosecution of Philip Stewart in the autumn. That included arranging for Hamish Campbell to be interviewed by Strathclyde Police. Jonathan worked with Alfred unscrambling the data from Philip's computers and placing the evidence of gang activities and Philip's role in the gang on computer, so that they could keep track of what they had discovered. Slowly they were unravelling the picture and coming to understand what a huge crime business they were investigating. The Gang was run in exactly the same way that Jack Stewart and Philip Stewart ran their legitimate businesses. The problem for the investigating team was that the two often overlapped and the lines between legitimate and criminal were often blurred. However, the eleven men and women continued to work patiently at it. With the help of Alfred, they also began to trace the webs of corrupt money dealings that linked the Gang with individual police officers and, more worrying still, links with the Greenway family and some senior politicians in both major Parties.

The trial of the Cambridge Five came and went in a morning. The five men pleaded guilty and offered no defence. Each was sent down for five years. There was no appeal and the kidnappers said nothing about the people who employed them. Unknown to the Police each man's bank account received a considerable donation the day after their trial ended. Timothy Stewart's plan had succeeded. However, search though they did, they found no evidence of Albert Campion's hiding place, and, finally, concluded that he had died, as the Police claimed, in a car accident.

Marcus and Evelyn enjoyed a quiet summer, although Marcus was often as tense as a coiled spring. Having

Fifty Years After

settled down Jonathan and Belinda in Blackheath and ensured that they were properly protected, they went on holiday and a belated golden wedding anniversary, spending two weeks in the middle of August in the Seychelles, a country that they had always wanted to visit, as guests of President Montgomery. On their return to Downing Street, Marcus found a letter posted in Malaga to him, marked Private and Confidential. He opened it and found a note inside composed of letters cut from a newspaper. The note read, "If Philip Stewart goes down; you will go down too." He passed it to the Police with the observation that he had declined five invitations from Philip Stewart to visit him in Belmarsh Prison for a chat. The Police did some research on newspapers available in Spain and decided that it was made up from letters from the Spanish newspaper, 'El Pais.' They guessed the sender was Philip's brother, Timothy, and increased the security around the Prime Minister. They advised him to stop holding open constituency surgeries and meet constituents by appointment only and to cease door to door canvassing until they judged it safe to resume. He reluctantly agreed.

Albert and Belinda prepared the papers for the Committal phase of the trial. The two met Charles Harris by appointment to discuss the case, and Albert served all the papers they had prepared for the trial on Charles, as was the procedure. He did not, however, indicate which witnesses he intended to call or how the evidence would be presented. Charles looked at the evidence they had assembled and was shocked. He had guessed at some of it, but the evidence of the diary and the intended elopement to Scotland was a surprise to him.

"I will not contest this evidence at the Committal hearing," he said to Albert. "My client will plead 'not guilty' and I will move for a speedy trial."

"I agree," Albert answered. "I would like a trial as early as September. Let's get it out of the way."

"I agree," Charles said. "Let's make a joint application to the magistrate."

That is what happened. The Committal hearing opened and closed within half an hour as Albert presented the evidence to justify a full trial in paper form to the three magistrates, and Charles made no objection to the evidence as presented. The magistrates withdrew, briefly studied the documents they had received and agreed that there was a case to answer. The two barristers then asked for an early trial, and the Magistrates referred the case to the Central Criminal Court with a request for a court to be found for September or October. Two weeks later both sides were informed that the trial would begin on Monday September 20, 2010, before the Lord Chief Justice, Lord Black. Albert was quietly pleased at the choice of judge. Charles was almost equally dismayed.

In September Belinda and Jonathan received a surprise. They had both been so busy that Belinda had occasionally forgotten to take her contraceptive pills. A week before the trial was due to begin Belinda became worried since she had missed her monthly period. Afraid to tell her mother, she travelled down to 10 Downing Street instead, and spoke to Evelyn, who smiled at her. She had been expecting something like it to happen for some time. She took Belinda to the nearest chemist and brought a testing kit, and, when it showed as positive, took her to the local hospital A and E for confirmation. The hospital asked if she wanted an abortion, and, to Evelyn's pleasure, she said, "No".

When she got home to Blackheath, Jonathan was at home, worried that she was so late and that he had not seen her all day.

"Where have you been, Darling?" he asked. "Albert was asking for you and I didn't know where you'd gone."

"Sit down, Darling," Belinda replied.

He sat next to her, putting his arm around her waist.

Fifty Years After

"I went to see Grandma Evelyn," she said, "and she took me to the hospital. I've just got back from there."

Jonathan was suddenly anxious.

"Are you unwell, Darling? Is there anything I can do?"

Belinda smiled.

"I'm perfectly all right, Darling, but I've been very busy recently, just like you have."

"Do you need to slow down because you're tired? Should we stop doing something – like the book?"

"Stop fussing, Darling, and listen."

Jonathan fell silent.

"Because I was so busy, I forgot to take my pill for several days and, this week, I missed my period."

She held her hand up, as she sensed that Jonathan was about to say something.

"I went to see Grandma and she took me to a chemist and I did a pregnancy test. Later we went to an A & E to get the test confirmed and it was. We're going to have a baby, Darling – and you're going to be a Dad."

Jonathan looked shocked.

"Are you sure? You're not joking?"

"I am sure and I'm not joking. The hospital asked if I wanted an abortion – but I said no. You don't want me to have an abortion do you?"

"Certainly not!" he said, "Come here Darling so I can kiss you."

Once they had emerged from each other's arms, Jonathan spoke again.

"Do you know what this means, Darling?"

"What?"

"We're going to have to tell your parents and mine."

"We'll go this weekend to yours and next weekend to mine, and tell them together."

"My Dad would have told us to go to church at once and get married," Jonathan commented.

"My Dad would like to put a gun behind your back and march you into church!" Belinda said lightly.

"I guess they'll all be glad we booked our Wedding for November 5th," Jonathan said.

"They'll probably think we planned it!" Belinda replied.

27. The Trial opens

September 20 2010
Lord Black opened the trial of Philip Stewart at 3 pm on Monday September 20th, 2010. Fourteen jurors assembled in the well of Court Number One at the Central Criminal Court, more familiarly known as The Old Bailey. Albert noticed that they were a real reflection of London society, young and old, male and female and a variety of ethnic groups. Charles Harris objected to two jurors; a black male and a white female, but they made little difference to the make-up of the jury.

Once everyone was seated, Lord Black addressed the jury.

"Members of the jury, this is going to be a very challenging case. You must forget everything you may have heard about this case and concentrate on the evidence presented before you. You may have heard of the first trial and its result held in June 1961. It will be referred to but you must ignore the outcome of that trial. It has been expunged by the appeal court, which means that legally it never happened. We can't reverse the physical fact that Mark Smith was hanged, but legally that never happened either. What, however, did happen both in fact and in theory was that a successful attempt was made to approach and bribe the jury in that trial to produce the verdict it did. Because of this I have decided to do something exceptional. When I have finished speaking to you I am going to adjourn this case until 10 am tomorrow, when the trial will officially begin and I will talk to you again. I have arranged for you to be driven to your various homes to pack some clothes and other necessities before you are brought back to this building where a coach will be waiting to take you to a hotel of my choice. You must not reveal to anyone where that hotel is and you must report to me anyone who approaches you to ask you about the case or to make you any offer. You will be brought to the court from your hotel and taken back to the hotel by coach every day until the trial is completed. You may be tempted to discuss the case with your colleagues overnight. Please don't do that. Even when I have sent you out to discuss your verdict, it must be done here, in the jury room, not in your hotel.

"Now, I wish you a good night and we will meet again tomorrow morning."

With that, he stood up and left the court, and the jury filled out.

"Well, it's finally started, Albert said to Jonathan and Belinda." Looking at the empty public gallery, he added. "That will be full tomorrow, don't doubt it."

Belinda and Jonathan left the Court together and walked across the road to St Paul's Station to catch the underground to Bank, where they intended to catch the DLR to Lewisham and a bus to Blackheath. They were both excited that the trial had finally begun. For Jonathan it marked the end of a journey of discovery, while for Belinda it was the first step in what she hoped would be a dazzling career. In her dreams she saw herself in the robes and wig that Albert wore, arguing a big case before a senior judge. Both were also still basking in the joy of a first pregnancy and the pleasure that they both had when Jonathan's parents both expressed their happiness at the news. Jonathan particularly was happily surprised because he thought that Martin Greenway would be angry with him. To complete their joy, they had both received letters that morning from the University confirming that they had satisfied the authorities that they had successfully completed the second year course and could proceed to their third year, in residence. Jonathan wrote back on both their behalves accepting the offer, asking for a concession to allow them to live in the city but out of college in view of their soon to be married state and need for continued police protection, to be absent from the university in early November for their wedding, and for Belinda to be

Fifty Years After

excused the final degree exams in May/June 2011 because of her expected confinement and to be permitted to take them in September 2011 with the retakes. He enclosed the medical certificate that the doctor had given to Belinda. They posted the letter on the way to Court and were discussing the likely outcomes. As a result, neither of them noticed the tall, elderly man, who seemed to be going the same way as them until they left the DLR station in Lewisham.

They were unaware of the man's identity, but he soon made himself known.

"Good afternoon, Mr Greenway," he began. "Good afternoon Miss Thompson. My name is Timothy Stewart. You may have heard of me. I have certainly heard of you."

Jonathan and Belinda were startled. Having been unaware of his following them, they had not noticed or heard him come up behind them, and they were not accompanied by their normal police guard, so they felt suddenly very vulnerable.

"Good afternoon, Mr Stewart," Jonathan replied, trying to sound polite, calm and disinterested. "What can we do for you?"

Timothy smiled.

"There's nothing you can do for me or my brother," he said. "You've done as much harm as you can do. You can't do us any more harm."

He smiled again.

"But we can do you a lot of harm. You'd both be dead now, somewhere under the waters of the English Channel, if my brother's plans had worked out. You were lucky then, but you won't always be so lucky."

"Are you trying to frighten us, Mr Stewart?" Belinda asked. "If so, you can forget it. We've lived with the possibility of kidnap and death since January, so it's nothing new."

Fifty Years After

"I saw the film of your Mock Wedding," Timothy said. "I liked the theatrical touch – but, of course, it was meaningless. They're both dead and buried."

"Together, at last," Jonathan added. "We attended Mark's funeral with the police and the relatives of your brother's two victims in July."

"It was a deeply moving service," Belinda added. "Jonathan was asked to read one of the lessons and Luke read a very moving poem. It's a pity you couldn't be there."

Timothy laughed.

"What a load of sentimental rubbish!" he sneered. "You carry out a mock wedding and bury a few bones and you think you're doing something special! I would have given the bones to my dog to chew. That's all they're worth."

"They were the remains of a human being; one who was unjustly killed as a result of a conspiracy organised by your family on behalf of your murderous brother," Jonathan said.

"And in collusion with your family," Timothy added. "The Stewarts remember those who help them and reward them accordingly. They also remember those who frustrate them, and reward those too. Above all, they remember false friends who betray them. Those too they reward."

"Meaning what?" Belinda said, putting her arm around Jonathan's waist and moving close to him for protection.

"Meaning that you've signed your own death warrants, but you've got to wait in the queue. First we will deal with the traitors and then with the open enemies. Sir Marcus comes first. You must take your turn. But, be sure, your turn will come. Philip has decreed the manner of your deaths, and his wishes will be carried out exactly. You'd both better learn to swim!"

Jonathan tried to hide his sudden fear with a show of outward calmness.

"Thank you for the warning Mr Stewart. It was very civil of you. We will walk down the road now and call on

Fifty Years After

Superintendent Donaldson. You may be explaining this conversation to her in an hour or so."

Timothy laughed.

"You are naïf if you think I'm going to hang around for her to come looking for me. Just remember to watch your back and stay away from strange cars and white vans unless you want to go for a sudden unexpected drive and an unplanned one-way boat trip. Don't say you haven't been warned!"

Timothy turned away and walked back to the steps that lead down into the DLR station. Jonathan and Belinda watched him disappear down the steps and, five minutes later, saw a train move out of the station, heading for Greenwich and, ultimately, Bank. They crossed the roundabout and entered Lewisham Police Station, which lies just beyond it on the road into the town centre. Here they found Thomas and reported the conversation to him. He alerted the various ports and airports to look out for Timothy Stewart, but no one stopped Fernando Dos Santos from boarding the evening flight from Gatwick to Malaga.

Next morning Court One was full, as Albert had predicted. Jonathan and Belinda looked around them as they took their seats beside Albert at the front of the court. They saw that all four of their parents, as well as Evelyn and Juliet were present in the court, sitting together. Evelyn and Juliet waved to them. Their four parents just smiled. Belinda walked over to where the visitors were sitting and spoke to her parents.

"Jonathan and I have a surprise for you," she said. "Wait outside the Court when we break for lunch and we'll go over the road to the café there."

Belinda's mother looked across at Jonathan's mother, who smiled at her, and guessed what Belinda's surprise was. Belinda's father looked blank.

"What surprise is that, Darling?" he asked.

Belinda looked at her mother and realised that she knew. She smiled at her father.

"If I tell you now it won't be a surprise, will it?" she said with an impish grin.

There was a stir as a door at the side of the court opened, and the jury filed in and began to take their seats.

"I've got to go now," she said, and she returned to her seat beside Albert.

Jonathan's mother leaned over to Belinda's mother."

"We already know, Catherine," she whispered. "They came to see us last weekend. They were coming to see you on Saturday, but obviously your being here makes it earlier."

Catherine Thompson nodded and turned back and stood up as Lord Black entered the Court.

Lord Black had already broken with tradition, because he had gone down to talk to the Jury who had assembled in a small room near Court One.

"Good morning members of the Jury," he said. "I hope you are comfortable in your hotel and had a good night's sleep."

They all nodded.

"You will have found a printed booklet in your room, giving you the transcript of the original trial in June 1961. I hope everyone of you read it."

Again they all nodded.

"Good. Keep it with you for reference. In itself it's not part of the documents that are exhibits in this trial, but it will be referred to undoubtedly. It's in the public domain, and you need to be aware of it. You will have noticed that you were driven in through the same entrance, that those who have been remanded in custody use and were brought straight here. I have arranged for you to have your lunch brought to you here. You should complete the order form and hand it to the clerk who's looking after you before you go into court each day. We're doing all this because one of the reasons we're all here was that the 1961 jury was

Fifty Years After

bribed to give a particular verdict. We have reason to believe that the group responsible could attempt the same trick again. Remember, don't talk to strangers (or each other) about the case outside of this room until I give you instructions to do so and let me know, through the clerk to the court, if anyone attempts to talk to you."

They all nodded and Lord Black left them. The clerk took their mobile phones and other electronic devices into her care and collected their lunch requests before taking them down to the Court.

Lord Black took his seat and addressed the Court.

"In welcoming you to Court One I wish to remind members of the public that, while you are fully entitled to be here to see and hear what is done in this trial, since in the UK justice is conducted in public unless the security of the nation prevents it, and there are no security issues here, we want to see you but not hear you."

He paused and smiled at them.

"This is obviously an unusual, important, if not to say, historic, trial, and I'm pleased to see so many ladies and gentlemen of the press and other media here. Don't forget that we don't allow recordings, other than the official one, of the proceedings here, and no cameras."

"Now we will open the trial by hearing what the Defendant has to say."

The Clerk to the Court called on Philip to stand.

"Lord Philip Stewart you are charged that on April 26th 1961 you murdered Janet Brown by shooting her to death. Do you plead guilty or not guilty?"

"Not guilty, My Lord."

"You are further charged that on June 21st 1961 you perverted the course of justice and committed perjury while giving your evidence in court. Do you plead guilty or not guilty?"

"Not guilty, My Lord."

The Clerk sat down and the Judge spoke to Philip.

Fifty Years After

"Please sit down Lord Stewart."

Philip sat down and Lord Black turned to the two legal teams.

"This is an unusual trial partly because it is being held under an Act that is no longer in force and which, by law, cannot be enforced. The murder, which is the main subject of this trial, happened in 1961 and, at the Prosecution's request, this trial is being held under the Homicide Act of 1957, which was then the law of the land. That Act stated that if a person was shot to death with a gun, the mandatory sentence was death by hanging. If the Defendant is convicted, that is the sentence that I will be obliged to impose. However, under the circumstances, I shall immediately refer the sentence to the Home Secretary for confirmation, which I know will not be given, so you can expect to return on the following day to hear the actual sentence that the defendant will have to serve if he is found guilty.

"Is that understood by all?"

"Yes, My Lord," Albert answered.

"Mr Harris?"

"Yes, My Lord. It will make a dramatic end to this trial, but, ultimately it will make no difference to the sentence, if you need to give one."

Lord Black smiled and nodded.

"Very well, I'm glad that's settled. Let's get on. Lord Corrigan could you introduce everybody and then begin to present your case?"

Albert stood up.

"Certainly. My Lord."

He turned to face the Jury.

"Members of the Jury, I am Lord Albert Corrigan. I am prosecuting this case. The two young people beside me are my assistants. The first, who you will shortly hear as a witness, is Jonathan Greenway, who will introduce himself. The second is a student at Cambridge University who is reading Law. Her name is Belinda Thompson. She is not a witness but you will hear and see her speak at some point in the trial. On the other side of the Court, representing the Defendant is my colleague, Charles Harris."

Albert looked back at the Judge, who nodded.

"You may proceed; Lord Corrigan."

"Thank you My Lord."

Albert walked over to the Jury box and, standing just two feet from the front row of six, began to speak to them.

"Members of the Jury. This is an unusual case. I understand that you were all given copies of the transcript of the trial of Mark Smith on June 21st and 22nd 1961. That trial dealt with the tragedy that saw a young woman of just 18 years of age callously shot down and killed while she was making love with her fiancé. We will show you that was the relationship between Mark Smith and Janet Brown because they were due to become married within two weeks of the murder. They were planning to elope together the following week. They had bought their tickets and booked a room in the only hotel in Gretna Green. You will hear the present manager, the son of the manager then, confirm that fact to you.

"There were irregularities in that 1961 trial, but you must forget them. The Prosecution are not claiming that the Defendant is in any way responsible for them. The reality is that you face the same dilemma as the jury did in 1961. There was a clear victim – Janet Brown, and two possible suspects – Mark Smith and Philip Stewart. The evidence in 1961 was deliberately skewed by order of the Investigating Officer, D I Alasdair Buchan to point clearly to Mark Smith as the culprit and he was duly found to be guilty and punished according to the law. The work of our first witness ensured that the true background story of that trial was told and the verdict was annulled. You have the same problem. Neither side claimed that a third party may have been present and committed the crime (and then, presumably, disappeared from view). Mark Smith said he

Fifty Years After

did not know who killed Janet Brown. Philip Stewart said he saw Mark Smith do it. You have to judge between them. We intend to prove to you that Mark Smith did not do it. If Mark was innocent, then Philip was not only guilty of the first charge, but also of the second charge."

Albert turned away from the Jury and called Jonathan to the witness box. Jonathan took the oath and stood, facing Albert, who began by asking him his name, address and occupation.

"I am Jonathan Greenway, the grandson of Sir Marcus Greenway. I live at an address given to the Court in the London Borough of Lewisham but which is being kept secret for security reasons and am presently a student reading Information Technology at Cambridge University."

Albert smiled at Jonathan encouragingly.

"I am told that you are to be triply congratulated. You've successfully completed your second year, you and my other assistant, Belinda, are going to be married soon, and you're soon going to be a father, is that right?"

Catherine Thompson grinned triumphantly at Jonathan's mother, who grinned back. Matthew Thompson looked mildly surprised. Jonathan smiled shyly.

"You're right, Lord Corrigan, and thank you for your congratulations. However, I wish you hadn't mentioned the fact that my fiancée is pregnant, since we haven't told her parents yet!"

The Court laughed and Jonathan, who had seemed tense, relaxed.

"Jonathan, would you please tell the Court how you became involved in this case."

"It was basically curiosity, My Lord. I was trying to find out about my Grandfather's career, and learned about the 1961 trial."

"So you looked up the trial on the Internet did you?"

"Yes, My Lord and that's when I discovered that Granddad had helped his Dad prosecute the case. I was surprised because, of course, I knew about the mutual dislike between my Granddad and Lord Stewart,"

"Did you ask your Grandfather about this?"

"I did, and he gave me a book about the trial, which I read with interest."

"What was your reaction to reading the transcript?"

"I was troubled, My Lord. There were aspects about the trial that seemed to be wrong to me."

"What worried you particularly?"

"I read Mr Corrigan's cross examination of Philip Stewart and his summary to the Jury and felt that there was insufficient evidence to say that Mark Smith had been proved to be the murderer beyond reasonable doubt. Under those circumstances, the speed and nature of the Jury's verdict was worrying. I decided that I wanted to know more."

"What did you do?"

"I asked a friend if he could access the original documents."

"Are you prepared to give the Court this friend's name?"

Jonathan smiled and shook his head.

"I don't think that's necessary, My Lord. I don't wish to get him prosecuted."

Lord Black interrupted.

"Mr Greenway, normally I would insist that you name your contact, since he actually broke the law. Your answer would have earned you a stay in the cells below this court for contempt of court, but I do not intend to invoke that power since your technical breach of the law exposed an even greater breach of the law. However, consider yourself rebuked."

"Thank you, My Lord," Albert said with relief. He had been worried lest Charles Harris pursued this issue in cross-examination. He turned back to Jonathan.

"How did the records come to you?"

Fifty Years After

"I received four separate files in a large, tightly sealed package, with a warning to be very careful."

"We are not concerned with three of the files today, Jonathan. Did the four files contain one that was the police case file on the Brown murder?"

"It was a photocopy of the original file, My Lord."

Albert walked over to Belinda who handed him an A4 folder and a manila file.

"Is this the folder what you received?"

"Yes."

"And is this the original of the folder I've just shown you?"

"Yes."

"Let the records indicate that the witness was shown the manila file containing the documents handed to the Court by the Metropolitan Police Records Office following the decision of the Home Secretary to lift the 100 years' closure order."

Albert turned back to Jonathan.

"Thank you, Jonathan. Wait there in case Mr Harris wishes to ask you questions."

Charles Harris approached Jonathan in what he hoped was a menacing manner.

"Mr Greenway, would you agree that you have a somewhat cavalier attitude to the Law?"

Jonathan looked confused.

"I don't understand your question Mr Harris."

Charles smiled.

"Oh you don't do you, Mr Greenway? Surely it's obvious! You deliberately incited someone else to break the Law. I'm sure that your girlfriend didn't exactly approve, since she wants to work in this place one day."

Albert stood up.

"I object, My Lord. Mr Greenway can't speak for Miss Thompson, and she is not a witness in this case."

"I agree, Lord Corrigan," Lord Black responded. "Mr Harris I have already rebuked Mr Greenway gently for his

Fifty Years After

action, but, without his doing what he did, we would have no trial."

"My Lord, I understand what you've just said, but I think the Jury has to understand that Mr Greenway is no plaster saint. He seems happy to drive a coach and four through the Law if it serves his purpose."

"I'm sure the members of the Jury have taken your point, Mr Harris. Do you have any other questions for this witness?"

"No, My Lord."

"Very good. You are excused Mr Greenway. In the words of the Bible – Go away and sin no more," the judge said grinning. "You can resume your seat beside Lord Corrigan – and," grinning broadly, "I suggest you make your peace with Miss Thompson's parents over lunch."

After the Court's laughter had died down and a red-faced Jonathan took his seat beside Belinda, Albert called Julia Donaldson to the witness box. She affirmed that she would tell the truth and introduced herself.

"I am interested in your work on the 1961 Murder file, Superintendent Donaldson, and, most especially the two police reports."

Albert passed a stapled document to Julia.

"Do you recognise this document. Superintendent Donaldson?"

"Yes, My Lord."

"Which document is this?"

"It's the original arrest report signed by P C Adams."

"Would you read it to the Court?"

Julia took the document in her hands and began to read.

"On April 26th last I was walking my beat, which included the roads around the park in Marchfield and the Park itself. I was inside the Park when I passed the site where the body lay about half an hour before the murder occurred. The area was empty and undisturbed. As I turned around to continue my patrol, I saw two young people walking towards me. They appeared to be lovers, because

Fifty Years After

they had their arms around each other's waists and were deep in conversation, which involved both kissing and much laughter on both sides. I passed them and observed them closely because they were a mixed couple – a young black man in his teens and an even younger white woman. I stopped and asked them their names and ages. The man said his name was Mark Smith and he was 18 and the woman said her name was Janet Brown and she was 18. I told them to be careful because lots of people did not like black men going out with white women, and they promised that they would. I looked the boy up and down. He was neatly dressed in a dark suit, white shirt and blue tie. I noticed that his suit pockets were flat and tidy. I saw no sign of the gun he was found with later.

"I left the Park and walked the streets around the perimeter without incident until a white youth, whom I now know to be Philip Stewart, ran out of the Park gates apparently in a panic. He rushed up to me, grabbed my arm and attempted to drag me into the Park. I stopped him, calmed him down, and asked him, 'What's the problem, Son?' He replied, 'A young woman has been murdered in the Park!' Murdered,' I said, 'how?' 'She's been shot,' he replied. I, therefore, accompanied him back into the Park, and followed the path around to the remote area of woodland I had been in earlier. Here I found a naked man kneeling beside a naked woman. I recognised them as the two I had seen earlier. I asked the man what had happened and he said he didn't know. He told me that he and the woman were lovers and had been making love together when the man standing beside me had disturbed them and pulled them apart. He had objected and he alleged Mr Stewart had kicked him in the genital area, causing him to double up in pain. Mr Stewart had then punched him hard on the jaw and he had fallen down and hit his head against one of the trees, knocking himself out. When he recovered consciousness he said he had a gun in his hand and his girlfriend was lying lifeless against the tree where they had been making

Fifty Years After

love. He had gone over to check that she was all right and had just discovered that she had been shot and was plainly dead, when we arrived.

"I asked Mr Stewart what he had seen, as Mr Smith was dressing. He said that he had been taking a walk in the Park when he had come across the two of them. He told me the young woman was struggling with Mr Smith who was plainly pushing himself upon her. He pulled Mr Smith off and both kicked him and punched him, knocking him out briefly, before going to assist the young woman. As he was doing so he heard a footstep behind him and saw Mr Smith coming back with a gun in his hand. He told him that he was going to kill him for what he did and fired the gun twice, missing him but hitting the woman, who was killed. Mr Stewart disarmed Mr Smith and once again rendered him unconscious, using his tie to bind his wrists and Mr Smith's vest to bind his legs.

"I examined the crime scene. Miss Brown was half lying and half sitting, face up and slumped sideways. She had been shot twice. Her clothes lay, neatly folded, in a pile beside the tree. Mr Smith's clothes, equally neatly piled, lay beside them. It looked as though they had been having consensual sex, and that Mr Stewart had misunderstood what he saw.

"I checked that Mr Smith was now properly dressed and told him that I was arresting him on suspicion of murder and that he would have to come with me to the Police Station. I cautioned him, but he said nothing more except the words 'I did not kill her. She was my girlfriend and we were in love. You must have seen that for yourself when you met us earlier.'"

"Do you agree that this report is somewhat different and longer than the report read by the Jury last night and presented to the trial in June 1961?"

"I do, My Lord. There were a number of sentences left out of the final version on the orders of D I Buchan."

"What was the effect of the changes?"

"They strengthened the case against Mark Smith."

"On the basis of this version of the report, what was P C Adams' attitude to this crime?"

"He clearly shows that he had doubts that Mark Smith was the man who fired the gun, My Lord."

"Did D I Buchan submit a report?"

"He did, My Lord."

Albert took a second document from Belinda.

"Is this it, Superintendent?"

"Yes, My Lord."

"Would you read this report for us?"

Julia took the second report and read it, as she had read the first.

"PC Adams, who said he had arrested him on suspicion of the rape and murder of a young white girl, brought Mark Smith into me. I ordered Smith's clothes to be removed and sent for analysis and then interviewed him. He complained that he was cold, as a result of the fact that he was naked. I told him that we had better get on with it quickly. He refused to budge on the story he had given to PC Adams when he was arrested and so I left the interview room, leaving four officers in there with him. When I returned an hour later, his body was bruised in a number of places and he complained that he had been both beaten and sexually assaulted by my men. I asked him if he wanted to make a formal complaint, but he declined. We then continued his interview, but he did not change his story."

Albert interrupted the reading.

"Is there anything about this report that causes you concern, Superintendent?"

Julia nodded.

"There seems to have been an extreme amount of pressure brought on Mark Smith even for that period," she said. "The fact that he was interrogated naked and was

Fifty Years After

beaten up by four police officers should have caused deep concern."

"What did D I Buchan record as Mark's evidence, Superintendent?"

Julia resumed her reading.

"Janet and I were lovers. We first met at a bonfire night party in Marchfield. We were both on our own and we happened to duck to avoid a rocket which some kid had fired into the crowd and bumped each other's head. We both stood up and apologised to each other simultaneously. Then we grinned at each other and I invited her to come for a drink. We left the fireworks party and went to a local pub where we sat and talked over a couple of beers. We decided we liked each other and that we would like to meet again. I walked her home and we fixed a meeting place for next day. We guessed that neither family would approve our continuing to meet. So we used to meet at an agreed spot and I would walk her to the corner of her road and kiss her goodnight there. All four of our parents disapproved, but my brothers and Janet's sister approved.

"We first made love together on St. Valentine's Day, in the Park in Marchfield. Thereafter we often had sex together and would then lie together, naked, in each other's arms, under our favourite tree in the Park, talking. We wanted to get married and Janet wanted to get pregnant with our baby. However, she began to have trouble with Philip Stewart, who began to follow her. I met him once before, on Christmas Eve 1959, when he racially abused me. I punched him on the chin and walked away, but I think he resented me after that and wanted revenge. Janet told me that he had begun to follow her around. We took extra precautions after that to avoid being seen, but I don't know if we were successful.

"April 26th started like every other day. We met up and walked together, with our arms around each other. I noticed that Janet was both excited and nervous and guessed that she had something important to tell me. I suspected that she was pregnant. We had made love often

Fifty Years After

enough for that to happen. I knew she would tell me after our lovemaking. We met PC Adams on the way to our favourite tree. He stopped us and asked our names and ages. I don't think he approved of the fact that we were together, but we weren't breaking any laws, so he could not stop us. He advised us to be careful. We went to our normal tree, took our clothes off and piled them carefully as we always did, and began to make love.

"Suddenly a hand grabbed me by the shoulder and pulled me violently off Janet, hurting her as my erect penis was dragged out of her body, spilling semen all over her. She screamed, and I turned around to face Philip Stewart.

'That's enough of that, you Nigger wanker!' he hissed at me as he first kicked me in the groin and then hit me hard on the chin. I fell backwards and hit my head on something and everything went black. When I woke up I was alone, naked, and holding a gun in my right hand. Janet was lying, not moving, half seated against our tree, and slumped sideways. I threw the gun away and ran over to her, calling her name. She neither moved nor spoke. I reached her and tried to raise her body and give her the kiss of life. That's when I saw the blood on her chest, felt for her pulse, and discovered that she was dead. I was wondering what I should do when PC Adams arrived with Philip Stewart, and I was arrested.

"I do not know what I want to do now. Janet was the only girl I've ever loved and I wanted to share my life with her. As far as I'm concerned my life is over. There's nothing left for me to live for.

"It was signed "Mark Smith" and dated 26th April 1961."

There was silence in the Court and Albert noticed that some of the female jurors were crying. Lord Black noticed too and ordered a ten minutes' adjournment so that the jurors could recover.

On the resumption, Albert asked Julia a further question.

Fifty Years After

"What do you, as a professional and experienced Police Officer, remembering the state that Mark Smith was in following this interrogation – naked and bruised from an apparently severe beating – make of his statement?'

"I believe he was telling the truth, My Lord."

"Does D I Buchan anywhere suggest that Mark changed his story in any significant way?"

"No My Lord."

Albert gave way to Charles.

"Do you think that the Adams document could have been doctored by anyone, Superintendent?"

"I suppose that you are referring to Mr Greenway, Mr Harris. I can confirm that Mr Greenway has never had access to the original documents. They have remained, first in my possession and then in Lord Corrigan's possession. Neither of us altered them in any way. All we have done is ordered that the sections highlighted by D I Buchan should be retained in the copy made for the Court in the same manner as the rest of the document. Anyone can determine the changes by comparing this document with the one presented to the 1961 trial."

"You read D I Buchan's report, Superintendent. Do you agree that Mark's stripping was a standard procedure and that, sadly, some prisoners were roughly handled during interrogations in those days, especially prisoners in murder cases?"

"I wasn't asked to explain what happened, My Lord. I was asked whether I thought Mark Smith was telling the truth. I said I thought he was. That's all."

"You probably agree that you can't judge the conduct of police officers in 1961 by comparing them with the standards that we expect in 2010?"

"Absolutely."

Charles Harris was content with that, and Julia was dismissed, followed by an adjournment for lunch.

There was an embarrassing silence when Belinda and Jonathan met Belinda's parents for lunch.

Fifty Years After

"Well that was an embarrassing morning, you two," Catherine Thompson said.

"I'm sorry, Mum," Belinda replied. "We wanted to talk to you face to face. We saw Jonathan's parents last weekend and we were going to see you on Saturday. I only learnt last week."

"Does Lady Evelyn know?" Malcolm asked.

"I went to her to get her advice. She took me to a chemist to get a testing kit and then to A and E to confirm it."

"Do you ever use the small rectangular devices you both carry around with you for more than playing games?" Malcolm asked them.

"It's my fault, Dad," Jonathan admitted. "I wanted us to tell you personally. I certainly didn't expect Albert to announce it to the world like he did."

"Ah well, it's done now," Malcolm concluded, "and no harm done."

"Are you going to have the baby?" Catherine asked Belinda.

"Of course, Mum," answered Belinda.

"Do you agree?" Catherine asked Jonathan.

"I'm very excited at the prospect and I've written to the University authorities to ask them to postpone Belinda's final exams until September."

"Good," Malcolm commented. "That's very sensible of you. By the way, I thought you did very well in the witness box. I'm proud that you're going to be my son in law. But, next time she gets pregnant, please phone us and tell us, and don't announce it in Number One Court at the Old Bailey with the entire British Press and television corps watching!"

"We won't, Dad," they said together, grinning.

"Good, now let's have lunch," Malcolm said, calling over the waiter.

Fifty Years After

The trial resumed after lunch with the evidence of a Nigerian forensic scientist, Adeloye Adewuni. Albert treated him in the same way as he had treated Julia, getting him to read the original forensic report. He took the report and read it out in a firm voice.

"The deceased was an 18 year old girl. I understand her name was Janet Brown. Death was due to two bullets fired into her body at short range from a handgun. One bullet grazed her heart and the other entered her heart, killing her instantly. The trajectory of the bullets indicated that she was lying on her back when she was killed and suggested that her body had been raised to a half sitting level post mortem. The bullets had entered from her front and exited from her back, suggesting that she was facing her killer. There was evidence of bruising to Janet's face from a blow to her chin and also evidence of blows to her buttocks, possibly from a belt, but these appeared to have been inflicted prior to the day in question. They were at least 24 hours' older. She was also pregnant of over a month's gestation. There was also some evidence to suggest that her hands had been bound a day before her death.

"There was evidence of sexual activity before her death, but no evidence of a struggle or that she had been forced into sex against her will. Semen found within and on her body belonged to Mark Smith. The bullets came from the gun that Mark Smith had thrown away. Mark's fingerprints were on the gun, but I was concerned at the odd angle of those prints. It was almost as though they had been placed there deliberately. The prints were from Mark's right hand from which evidence of gunpowder from recently firing a gun was found. The gunpowder came from the gun that had been used to kill Janet Brown. There was no evidence of bruising from binding on Smith's wrists".

"Mr Adewuni can you tell us how long you have been doing this job?"

Fifty Years After

"I qualified fifteen years ago and have been conducting post mortems since that time. I don't know how many I've conducted."

"With your background, what conclusion do you draw from this report?"

"Always assuming the work was done properly, I draw three conclusions. The first is that Janet Brown was assaulted, probably sexually, the day before her murder. It looks as though her hands were bound tightly and she was hit several times about the head and the body. I cannot say who assaulted her, but I can say that the sexual activity between her and Mark Smith was consensual and that I very much doubt that Mark killed her."

"Why do you say that Mr Adewuni?"

"There were no signs that he had forced an entry into her vagina. I would have expected signs of tearing at the edges. There were none mentioned. Strangely, had she been raped a day or two before, there should have been signs. I do not think that the pathologist did a particularly thorough job. The evidence of the prints on the gun, however, suggests that the pathologist did look at Mark's hands and wrists properly. He said that the finger prints were in an unnatural position, almost as though they were planted on the gun."

"Did you ask for the evidence bag?"

"I did."

"What did you find?"

"I tested the gun. I believe that I proved two things. First there were not two shots fired that afternoon, but four, and second, that the gun had been used in earlier killings associated with the Stewart Gang."

"Why do you conclude that there were four shots?"

"The gun had six bullet chambers. Five bullets had been fired. The Pathologist almost certainly fired one of the bullets. Two bullets were found in Janet's body. Where were the third and fourth bullets?"

"What do you conclude from that?"

"I think that the killer fired two shots at Janet and then tried to frame Mark for the murder by using his hand to fire a third and possibly a fourth shot. The bullet or bullets are probably in the earth near the crime scene."

Albert handed Adeloye over to Charles.

"You've taken a lot on yourself Mr Adewuni. Are you actually simply trying to defend the name of a fellow black man?"

"I find that question to be offensive, Mr Harris. Forensic Science is colour blind."

"If you say so, Mr Adewuni. What do you make of the additions to the original report that was presented to the 1961 trial?"

"I read the original document Mr Harris and I would not call them additions; I would call them deletions. What do I make of them? Their removal strengthened the case against Mr Smith."

"Why do you call them deletions?"

"I read D I Buchan's note written across the bottom of the original document."

"Can you think of any reason why D I Buchan would want to damage Mr Smith's chances of a fair trial?"

Albert got up to object, but Lord Black waved him down.

"The Jury will ignore that question. Mr Harris, shame on you, you should know better than to ask a question like that? Mr Adewuni is a Pathologist, not a mind reader or, perhaps, a Spirit Medium, since the Inspector has been dead for over thirty years."

Charles gave up, and Albert moved on to his next document. He began by calling Luke Smith to the witness box. Luke took the oath and introduced himself.

"Tell me about your brother, Mark." Albert began.

"He was four years older than me and a very quiet and law abiding person. He worked very hard and wanted to make something of himself."

"Did you know about his romance with Janet?"

"Not until the week before the murder."

"Why did he keep it secret?"

"He knew my parents would not approve and would order him to stop seeing Janet. We didn't approve of mixed marriages in those days."

"What did he tell you when he did finally tell you about her?"

"He told me they were going to get married. He said he had bought the tickets and booked a hotel. They were going to elope. He asked me not to tell Mum and Dad, nor my younger brother until after they had gone."

"And did you do as he asked?"

"Yes, My Lord."

Albert took the tickets and the receipt from Belinda.

"Are these the tickets and is this the receipt?"

"Yes?"

"Did you give them to Jonathan Greenway when you met?"

"Yes. I gave him a photograph album as well."

"Why?"

"Mr Greenway convinced me that he was going to try to force a retrial. We had tried to get such a thing for years but had always failed. I tried to help him."

"Did you see your brother after his arrest?"

"Several times, My Lord."

"Did he ever deviate from his statement to D I Buchan?"

"In what way, Lord Corrigan?"

"Did he, for instance, ever admit that he killed Janet?"

"No – he always said he was innocent."

"Did he ever accuse Philip Stewart of the murder or of raping Janet the day before?"

"No – he never knew she had been raped and didn't see who shot her."

"Do you believe that your brother murdered Janet?"

"No, Lord Corrigan. They were going to get married. He was head over heels in love with her, and, according to him, she thought the same thing about him."

"One final point before Mr Harris talks to you, Mr Smith. Do you know if Mark ever owned a gun?"

"He didn't have a gun."

"Did he belong, for instance, to a shooting club?"

"No."

"Thank you Mr Smith."

Albert sat down and Charles replaced him.

"You're a prejudiced witness aren't you, Mr Smith?"

"Prejudiced in what way, Mr Harris?"

"Haven't you been a member of a number of Black Rights Movements?"

"Yes, but I don't think that's relevant to this case."

"The Jury will judge that, Mr Smith," Charles snapped.

"By jailing Lord Stewart, one of the Pillars of the Establishment, you will strike a significant blow against the indigenous majority in this country. That's true isn't it?"

It was the turn of Luke to look confused. Albert began to rise but was again stopped by Lord Black.

"You are asking Mr Smith to make a political judgement that he isn't obviously qualified to make, Mr Harris. I'm striking your question out. The Jury will disregard it and draw no conclusions from Mr Smith's silence."

Charles Harris contrived to look disgustedly at the Jury and sat down.

Hamish Campbell took Luke's place. He introduced himself and went through the file he had given Belinda and Jonathan, explaining how his father had corresponded with first Mark, and then Mark's father, about Mark and Janet's booking.

"Did Jonathan or Belinda come to you to ask for backing for Mark's story?" Albert asked.

"No, Sir," Hamish replied.

"Why were they in your hotel?"

Fifty Years After

"They came up for what I call a Mock Wedding. They had a proxy marriage for Mark and Janet, and stayed with us because that's what that couple planned to do. They talked to me about booking my hotel for their wedding in November and I agreed."

"So who raised the issue of these papers?"

"I did."

"Why?"

"I thought they might be important for this trial to establish the truth about what the young couple intended to do."

"Thank you Mr Campbell."

Albert sat down and Charles rose.

"Why did your father not give this information to the court in 1961?"

"I don't know, Mr Harris, because he never told me."

"Why was that?"

"I was only 6 at the time."

Some of the jury grinned at this. Albert saw this and felt that he was close to victory. This Jury was definitely not hostile to him.

"Who told you about the file?"

"My mother."

Charles gave up and returned to his seat.

Albert called Jennifer to the Witness Box.

"You were Janet's younger sister. Did she confide in you about Mark?" Albert asked.

"Not at first, but she did in February."

"Why did she take so long?"

"She believed that Mum and Dad would not approve and would order her to stop seeing Mark."

"Why?"

"They did not approve of mixed marriages."

"What made her choose to confide in you?"

"It was when she and Mark first made love. She came back in an excited mood and needed to tell someone, so she told me."

"What did you say?"

"I said she was very lucky to find a man who really loved her and did not just want to use her for sex."

"Did she tell you about her diary?"

"No, that was her secret. She wrote it in her bedroom and kept it hidden under her clothes. We discovered it when we went through her possessions after her death."

"Did you write anything in the diary after her death?"

"Certainly not. It wouldn't have been right."

"Did you know anything about the attack on her before her murder."

"Yes, she came home dressed only in her coat and covered with mud. She was crying and I asked her what happened. She told me that Philip Stewart had attacked her and raped her. She gave me a full description."

"What did she tell you? Take your time if you find it distressing."

"She said that Philip had been following her for at least a fortnight. That day he pursued her into the Park and backed her against the wall. He hit her and ordered her to take her shoes and tights off. She did as he told her and he threw her shoes away before he used her tights to tie her hands behind her back. Then he forced her to march, bare foot and with her hands tied, across the park to where there were trees. Once there, he untied her and ordered her to strip. She kicked him and scratched his face and this made him very angry. He hit her so hard that she banged her head against one of the trees and fell down. When she recovered consciousness she was naked, tied up and lying on the ground at Philip Stewart's feet. She tried to get to her feet, but he pushed her down and pulled his belt from his trousers. He rolled her over and used his belt to beat her on her bum, before turning her back over and raping her. The ground was muddy and her hair and body were covered in mud. She had apparently tried to stop him raping her and this made him very angry. He pulled her to her feet and punched her several times, in the body and on her face, which was quite puffy when she came home. Finally, he forced her to lie down on her front, so he could tighten the bonds on her wrists and tie her feet together. He stood with his foot on her back and told her that he was aware of her relationship with Mark. 'If I catch you with that Black wanker again, I will shoot you both dead,' he said. She was terrified of him, but happy because she had just discovered that she was pregnant and was going to tell Mark next day, and they were going to run away together to get married. She told me that Mark had already bought the tickets and booked their hotel. When she untied herself the only clothes she could find was her coat. The rest had gone and her tights were ruined. She guessed that Philip had taken them as a sort of trophy."

"Are you sure she said it was Philip Stewart?"

"Yes, Sir."

"Could Mark have been raping her when Stewart says he found them and pulled them apart by force?"

"No, she was deeply in love with him, and they regularly had sex together in the Park."

"Why did they use the Park?"

"They felt they had no other choice. It wasn't like today when mixed couples have sex and get married or when ordinary couples regularly have sex together. Do you know the meaning of the phrase 'being in trouble' when said by a girl, My Lord?"

"It means being pregnant and unmarried, am I right?" Lord Black asked.

"Yes, My Lord. No one says that today."

"Indeed!" Lord Black agreed.

Albert gave way to Charles, who again adopted a menacing tone.

"Mrs Foster, I put it to you that your evidence is a tissue of lies invented to smear my client in the eyes of this jury. None of this happened and, if it did, it wasn't my client."

"I can only say what Janet told me," Jennifer answered.

"Did anyone else see her come home, barefoot and naked under her coat and covered in mud with a puffy face?"

"No."

"Why did you not tell the police?"

"It wasn't my call to, and Janet did not want me to."

"And after her death?"

"I was only 14. How many 14 year olds would go to the police with a story like that? It's difficult enough for me to tell it now and I'm over 60!"

"I ask the questions, Mrs Foster," Charles responded sharply.

Charles paused, uncertainly, before returning to his seat.

"No more questions," he said.

Albert stood up.

"My Lord, the next witness is more closely related to the content of the diary, which will be the main issue we will be raising tomorrow. It makes sense to link the two together. I suggest we adjourn the trial until tomorrow."

Lord Black looked at his watch, which read 4.15.

"I agree, Lord Corrigan. The trial is adjourned until 10.30 tomorrow as I have a sentencing hearing at 9.30."

He turned to the Jury.

"Members of the Jury, remember the advice I gave you this morning. Don't discuss the case with anyone and do not take anything from the courtroom. Have a good night and we will see you tomorrow."

"That was a good day for us," Albert said to his two assistants. "You did very well Jonathan. I'm sorry to have spilt the beans. I assumed all your parents knew. I hope you weren't told off too severely."

Fifty Years After

"My Dad put each of us across his knees in the café and spanked us," Belinda said, grinning and with her eyes sparkling.

Albert laughed.

"You're a minx, young Belinda," he commented. "You've got a real job on your hands Jonathan when you've married her!"

They laughed as they parted and the police car collected them to take them home, with their armed escort. As they got into the car they saw the coach with the jurors in draw away from the back of the court.

Charles Harris went down to the cells to talk to Philip.

"That was a bad day," he told him. "I didn't manage to shake any of them, and the Jury is against us. I only hope that they mangle their presentation of Janet Brown's diary. You will have to deal with the rape allegation as well as the murder charge. You will have to show something you've not been good at – you've got to show contrition. If you don't you're going down – and for a long time. I doubt whether you will breathe free air again."

"I'm not changing my story Charles. As for the Jury, have you found a way through the defences yet?"

"No. The security around them is impregnable. I haven't yet discovered the hotel they're in. I've got men out looking, but no success so far."

"You've got to get us time, Charles. You didn't do that today."

"It's difficult dealing with witnesses who aren't witnesses, Philip. The Prosecution has been very clever. Tomorrow is going to be very difficult. All I can do is try to do the same thing. I'm going to try to cast doubt on their interpretation of the evidence. You've denied my best defence by what you said last time. If you admit you lied in Court, you will go down for perjury."

"What's your best defence?"

"That neither of you did it. Had you not been so anxious to get Mark Smith hanged we could have used that defence. I hate to say this, but you should have shot him as well and thrown the gun into the Thames."

"I didn't and I had good reason. Except for that damned Greenway kid, it would have worked. I wish my men had seized them and thrown their living bodies into the English Channel."

"For God's sake don't say that on Thursday, Philip, or the jury will take even less time in convicting you than they did in convicting Mark Smith."

"I won't say it – but that's still their destiny, however long it takes. They're going for a swim in the Channel with their wrists handcuffed behind their backs and their legs shackled to weights. I feel about them the same way I felt about the Brown bitch and that wanker Smith in '61 and for the same reason."

Once again, Charles Harris wondered why he was defending Philip Stewart, when he did not share one of his values and attitudes. Almost the only reasons he could think of for defending Philip was that he needed the money Philip was paying him and Philip knew too much about him. He also knew that the Stewart Gang had a very short and violent way of dealing with those they felt had either betrayed them or let them down. He decided it was best to say nothing, said good night, and told Philip he would see him in the morning.

That night the news broadcasts were full of the trial, and the consensus was that it was a good day for the prosecution and a poor one for the defence.

28. Voices from the Past

September 22 2010
Court One was full again on Wednesday, with people outside queuing to get in. As a result, with the exception of family members and connections such as Juliet, the ushers devised an hourly rotation.

Albert called a graphologist to establish that the letters and diary were genuine. He showed him the exercise books that had been collected from Jennifer and Luke and asked him if the writer of the books and the letter and diary were the same. Michael Fairbrother confirmed that the person who wrote the letters was the same as the person who wrote in Mark Smith's book and different from the person who wrote in the diary. He also confirmed that the writer in Janet Brown's book was the writer of the Diary and not of the letters.

Charles challenged this judgement.

"Can you actually say that you have proved that Mark Smith wrote the letters and Janet Brown wrote the Diary?"

"No, I can't honestly say that. There is a finite chance that it could be two other people entirely, but that's extremely unlikely."

"Could Jennifer Foster have written both?"

"I've also looked at one of Jennifer's books and she could not have written either the letters or the diary."

Charles realised that he could not think of another question to ask, and sat down.

Albert rose and addressed the Judge.

"Lord Black, my last witness is a film, made by my two assistants of the diary. The Jury has been shown evidence that the diary is genuine. The exhibits of handwriting from the exercise books and the diary and letters show that. I want the diary to be shown in its entirely and not broken up by lunch so I am asking that we adjourn for an early lunch and return at 1 pm to show the film. I also suggest that, having seen the film myself; it might be better to adjourn for the day after the film has been shown. I cannot see how Mr Harris can ask questions of two people who are dead and the two actors are not qualified to answer for them. Mr Harris can then begin his defence afresh tomorrow morning."

"It's half past 11, Lord Corrigan. I'm prepared to give everyone a long lunch, which will enable me to deal with some routine matters and we will resume at 2 pm for your film."

The Court rose and swiftly emptied, heading for local cafes and the courts' restaurant. Albert turned to his two assistants.

"3-nil to us," he commented and grinned.

Jonathan and Belinda both gave him the thumbs up and the three of them went for lunch with their families and Juliet. Over lunch, the two confided their concerns to Albert.

"I don't want to sit through the film and watch it again," Belinda confessed. "I found it very difficult reading the lines, especially the final entry, and cried my eyes out. I don't want to do that again."

"I agree with Belinda," Jonathan added. "I think that, if we're sitting with Albert, we will distract the Jury from the actual words. They will be listening to the film and watching us instead of the film."

Evelyn nodded.

"They're right, Albert. I've seen the film too, and I know the reaction I had to it. I will take them out and we'll go to Downing Street."

"The problem is, Lady Evelyn, that Charles Harris might want to ask them questions, and they have to be available for that."

"Is Mr Pickering available?" Martin Greenway suddenly asked.

"Yes, Mr Greenway," Albert answered. "Why do you ask?"

"I think it might be a good idea to change your batting order around."

"What do you mean, Mr Greenway?"

"Begin the afternoon with Jonathan and Belinda answering questions about the film and then call on Mr Pickering to give the historical background. That would be relatively uncontroversial and should last less than an hour. Then show the film."

Evelyn agreed.

"You're like a film producer. In a good film, you build to a climax. This film is the climax of your case. To follow it with an explanation would reduce the impact of the film. You want the Jury to go away in tears and with the image of the terrified, raped and battered Janet in their minds. It will stay with them all night; and it will be the main story on the news and in the papers. They'll have it at the back of their minds while listening to the defence experts trying to discredit it. It will destroy their case."

Albert thought about this for a moment before nodding.

"You're right Lady Evelyn, as you usually are. We obviously don't want to distress these two more than they have been already, and, in any case, you never know what effect such distress can have on their unborn child. I'll put the two of them in the box together to answer technical questions from the jury and the defence and follow them with William Pickering. Then you can take these two away and keep them safe. I'll come and tell them what happened in the Court afterwards."

"I think you're very wise," Catherine Thompson commented. "These two have been through a lot. It would be unfair to put them through any more."

Albert stood up.

"I'm going to have to leave you to finish your lunch, since I need to acquaint the Judge, Defence, Jury and Mr Pickering of our intended changes, so there will be no surprises and no objections, but also so that the Jury can think of any questions they want to ask."

Fifty Years After

He left them to return to the Court, and they continued to talk and enjoy their lunch.

They returned to Court One at 2 pm. Albert called Belinda and Jonathan to the witness box, where they found two seats had been provided. The Judge reminded Jonathan that he was still under oath, and watched as Belinda took the oath. Albert stood in front of the Box.

"Would you tell the Court how you made the film?"

"We didn't make the film," Jonathan corrected. "A professional producer made the film and professional cameramen filmed it. We simply acted and read our parts."

"We were given a printed script to learn and a blank diary to appear to write. From time to time the camera focussed on the real diary, but we didn't write anything," Belinda explained.

"What was the purpose?"

"We intended to show the contents of the diary, both the book and the letters," Jonathan answered.

"It's correct, because we checked the script against our photocopy of the original text. Only the last few sentences were added by us," Belinda added.

"Why did you do this?"

Belinda answered.

"We're like Mark and Janet – a mixed race couple. The difference between us is that today no one cares while in 1961 virtually everyone objected. We're going to get married soon with our parents' blessing, whereas their relationship was doomed from the start. What we want from life – love, success, happiness and security – is what they wanted. We know we can have those things – but they had no chance of doing so."

"That's why we feel so close to them," Jonathan added.

Belinda turned away from the Jury to face Philip Stewart.

"I've read what you said in 1961 Mr Stewart and I know you think I'm an animal. As you said, we don't make love with one another; we apparently copulate (your word) in public. Presumably we don't have homes to live in! I want to tell you that I'm not an animal. I'm a human being, and Jonathan and I don't 'copulate' in public. We make love, if we wish to, at home. We also wear clothes as you can see. It is time that you woke up and tasted the coffee."

Charles tried to rise to object, but Lord Black waved him down.

Albert called William Pickering to join them. He squeezed into the witness box between the two lovers.

"Tell me about yourself, Mr Pickering," Albert said to him.

"I'm a lecturer in 20th century British social history at Thames University."

"Have you seen the film we're about to show?"

"Yes."

"Is it realistic?"

"Oh yes. It reflects very accurately the situation in Britain in the early 1960s. I have no doubt that it's genuine."

"How different were things then?"

"Racism was very strong. Mark was right to say that his family would oppose his marriage to Janet. People talk about white parents objecting to mixed marriages, but the fact is that black families were just as hostile. Things are different now, as I'm sure that Luke Smith would tell us."

Albert looked at the Judge, who nodded, and Luke came forward and stood beside the witness box. Led by Albert, he confirmed what William had said.

"Had they gone to Scotland to marry," he said, "They would probably have stayed there. It would have been safer for them after the threats that were made against them. In any case, our families would have disowned them."

Jennifer took advantage of the looser atmosphere in the Court to join Luke and confirm what he had just said. At that point a black member of the Jury also stood up,

Fifty Years After

and, after apologising to the Judge, began to talk about his experience of racism. Charles Harris and Albert Corrigan both realised that the situation had grown a dynamic of its own and was beyond their ability to control and sat down, as several of the Jury began to exchange their experiences of racism with what amounted to a panel of five in and around the witness box. Lord Black decided to let the discussion run on unchecked for a while since it was painting the background to the film in a way that a stylised formal witness session couldn't. Albert felt the same way. Charles felt that the discussion confirmed that there was no way that he could win this case and, even if the Stewarts managed to get through to the Jury, it would have no effect. "This lot can't be bribed into finding Philip not guilty," he thought.

Lord Black eventually looked at his watch, suddenly realising that the discussion had gone on for over an hour. He decided to call time on the discussion. He nodded to the Clerk of the Court who gavelled for silence. The discussion halted immediately.

"This has been a very interesting and illuminating discussion, which illustrates perfectly the dilemma of the two principles. Thank you to all concerned. However, we will now return to the normal practice of a law court and show you a film; Would the five witnesses please return to their seats or leave the Courtroom."

Albert addressed the judge.

"Before we start the film, My Lord, I wish to explain why Jonathan and Belinda are going to leave us for the rest of the afternoon. They both found the making of the film and viewing the final version very distressing. As a result, Lady Greenway has agreed to take them away and look after them while the film is screened. They will rejoin me tomorrow morning."

"I understand, Lord Corrigan. We do not want to impose more distress on them."

The Judge turned to look at them.

Fifty Years After

"I shall give you proper recognition at the end of the trial, but I would like to express this Court's thanks to you both for what you have done in this case so far. Go home and rest and we'll see you both tomorrow morning."

Jonathan thanked Lord Black on behalf of them both and they left, joining Evelyn who met them at the door of the Courtroom before travelling in an official car back to 10 Downing Street. After they left, the lights in the courtroom were dimmed and the television screens were lowered. People moved to ensure that they could see a screen. Philip turned to face the back of the dock where a screen came down for him. A further screen faced the visitors and another came down for the Jury. Albert, Charles, Lord Black and the Clerk of the Court had separate monitors to watch.

The film started with a brief explanation by Albert. He explained that they were presenting the diary that Janet Brown made between November 5th 1960 and April 25th 1961. He spoke directly into the camera.

"Janet Brown and Mark Smith met for the first time by accident on November 5th 1960 at a fireworks party. Janet began to keep a diary from that date and kept it more or less up to date, on a weekly, if not always a daily, basis. She included in her diary photographs that she and Mark took and letters that Mark wrote to her. It tells the story of the developing relationship between the two of them up to the event that severed that relationship on April 26th 1961."

The image of Albert Corrigan faded out to be replaced by a split screen featuring Jonathan writing letters and Belinda writing her diary, with the diary itself imposed across the two. The two wore the identification badges, bearing the images of the people they were representing, that they wore for the proxy wedding. Eventually, the

Fifty Years After

camera focussed on the badge worn by the speaker rather than the speaker's face. That image faded to be replaced by a full screen image of Belinda sitting at a desk with a book open in front of her and a pen in her hand. She spoke and wrote the date: Saturday November 5th 1960 and underlined it with the help of a ruler. Then, after sucking the end of her biro, she apparently began to write.

"Dear Diary,

"This is a new step for me to take because today is the start of a new life for me. I was never good at school. My teachers did not like me and I did not pass any exams. I left school when I was 15, as I was allowed to do, and went out to work. I got a job selling women's clothes at Rosemary's, a shop in Marchfield Green. I'm 17 now, and I still work there. Mrs Taylor, my boss, told me that I'm a good worker and she's going to promote me. I told Mum and she said that so long as she pays me more. It hasn't happened yet, but she told me it would be after Easter, which is on April 18th.

"Today I worked all day and after the shop closed at 5.30 went down to Marchfield Green where they had a big bonfire. My friend Martha and I went down to where they were roasting chestnuts and bought a bag each. We were chewing them when they began to light the fireworks. I've always been a bit afraid of fireworks. I don't like the bangers. I'm afraid of the bangs. They remind me of gunshots and I'm terrified of guns. I don't like war films or crime movies. Unfortunately, a gang of boys were throwing fireworks around as they normally do. Some also fired rockets at us. One came very close to me and I ducked down to avoid it. I banged my head and, looking up to see what I had hit, I found myself looking up into the smiling face of a very handsome boy. My heart missed a beat, literally. He thought I was hurt and asked me if I was all right. I told him I was and asked him his name. He said it was Mark and he was 18. He asked me who I was. I told him I was Janet and I was nearly 18.

"'Let's get away,' he said.

I agreed and we went to a pub, where he bought me a coke and himself a beer. Then we talked. I told him about my job at Rosemary's and Mrs Taylor. He told me that he worked as an Apprentice at Dixon's, a printing company near my shop. We exchanged addresses and we both realised that we live near to each other. I stared at Mark, and he stared at me. But it wasn't like some boys stare at girls. They try to strip us naked with their eyes. He didn't eye me up and down, he stared straight into my face and reached out and held my hand. We were sitting next to each other on a long seat. I thought he would try to put his hand up my skirt, or at least, under my blouse and up my back. Martha told me that her boyfriend did that on their first date and she had to slap his face before he stopped. Mark didn't do that. He didn't even kiss me, but he told me that he liked me and we agreed to go out together next week. Then he escorted me home, acting like a gentleman should.

"Oh, by the way, dear diary, he's black. I don't think that's important, but I hope that other people feel the same way."

The picture of Belinda faded and moved to an image of Jonathan writing a letter.

"Tuesday November 8th 1960."
"Darling Janet,

It was so nice meeting you and I enjoyed it so much that I've been thinking of you ever since. I can't even sleep. My younger brother, Luke, asked me if I was ill. I just told him I'd met a beautiful girl. 'Do you love her?' he asked. I was about to tell him off, when I realised that I do love you. I've never met and talked to a girl before. Our meeting was a lucky accident, otherwise I'd never dreamed of talking to you. My Mum and Dad are always

Fifty Years After

warning me that white girls try to trick black boys into having sex with them. I believed that, and half expected you to put your hands inside my trousers. A friend of mine told me that girls do that. I'm glad you didn't do it to me. I have to admit though, I would probably enjoy it if you did!

"Anyway, I want to meet you again. How would you feel if I collected you from outside your shop and we went for a walk in the Park on Friday after work?
Love you lots
Mark
xxxxxxxxxx"

Belinda as Janet wrote back.
"Wednesday November 9th 1960
Dear Diary

Mark wrote to me and posted it with a 3d stamp – so he must be serious. I've stuck his letter in so you can read it. He told me that he loves me and wants to see me after work on Friday. I told Mrs Taylor that I'd seen a white girl going out with a black boy. She told me that it was a disgusting thing to do – each to her own – she said. I smiled at her and asked her what she'd do if one of her shop girls went out with a black boy. We're all white. She said she would sack her at once. So I wrote to Mark saying that I wanted to meet him and that I loved him too. I confessed that I half expected him to put his hand up my skirt or blouse and was glad he hadn't. However, I told him that I wouldn't mind him putting his hand up my back. I told him that I loved him too – but that he mustn't come and collect me from work. He must wait at the corner and I would join him. What is so disgusting about me falling in love with a handsome, gentle, black boy? People are very strange."

Fifty Years After

"Friday November 11th
Dear Diary

I have been nervous all week, trying to concentrate on my work and, at the same time, willing the time to pass until I could meet Mark again. It's odd how he has become so important to me after just one meeting and one letter – but he has. Like him, I've been dreaming about him all week. I wanted him to kiss me and make me feel special. We met on the corner, as I suggested, and he put his arms around my waist and we walked off together, talking. I told him about what Mrs Taylor said and he agreed it was disgusting. 'Why should it be wrong for you and me to love each other?' he asked. I said we were both human beings after all. We stopped to buy a beef burger at a shop and we were surprised how people looked at us and turned away, as though we were committing a crime. Even the man behind the counter didn't seem keen on serving us. He took our money but made it clear that we were not welcome to eat in his shop. We left his shop and went into the Park nearby. We found a seat in a quiet part of the park and sat down side by side. Mark put his hand under my jumper and felt for my blouse. I suddenly felt excited as his hand pulled gently at the end of my blouse and pulled it out from under my skirt. His hand felt cold against the skin of my back. He moved it up and down slowly. 'Do you like that?' he asked me. I said I did and I didn't want him to stop. 'Why don't you do it to me?' he asked. So I did. His back was muscular and strong. He excited me, especially when he suddenly pulled me to him and kissed me. It was as though my dreams had come true. I kissed him back and we did not talk for a long time. I don't know how it happened, but somehow my jumper and Mark's jacket came off and we were undoing each other's shirt and blouse. I think he undid my blouse before I undid his shirt. We didn't go any further but what we did was to bear hug each other and continue kissing. I put my tongue in his mouth and he did the same to me. All the time he was stroking my back and breasts. I ran my hand over his back and chest and each of us said, 'I love you, Darling,' to the other lots of times.

"No one saw us, but we wouldn't have cared if they did. What's wrong with two teenagers being in love? However, it had been dark for some time and it was getting cold, although our bodies kept us warm. However, the park was certainly closed, so we did up our shirts and put our other clothes on before leaving the park by climbing over the fence. Unfortunately, I tore a hole in my tights. He apologised and offered to pay for a new pair. I told him not to be silly. Then he took me to near my home and kissed me goodnight. I don't think I will sleep tonight".

The camera moved over to Jonathan as Mark.
"Monday November 14th 1960
My Darling

I love you so much it hurts. I dreamed about your lovely body all night on Friday, Saturday and Sunday. I loved holding your body close to mine and I want to kiss it all over, not just your lips. Do you love me as much as I love you? I can't wait until Friday to see you again. But we must find a different café. I know an Indian one where you won't find white racists. Let's try that one.
Love you lots.
M
xxxxxxxx"

Janet wrote back
"Tuesday November 15th, 1960
Dear Diary

Mark has written to me. He loves me so much he wants to kiss me all over my body. I'm not sure I'm ready for him to do that because it means I would have to be naked. I never liked taking my clothes off for PE at school, because I thought the other girls would laugh at my small breasts. They didn't usually do that, but I also think I'm too fat. Some of the girls said that to me. I will let him take my bra off and kiss me all over my body so long as he leaves my skirt and knickers on. I'm not ready for him to take them off yet. I wrote to him to explain that to him, saying I love him as much as he loves me and I want to kiss him all over his body too. I only met him 10 days ago. Why do I love him so much? Mrs Taylor was quite rude today. A black woman came into the shop escorted by a white man. She refused to serve them and told them to leave her shop. 'Cats shouldn't consort with dogs', she said. I think that's just awful! Mark and I are not different types of animal, we're just 2 human beings with different coloured skins that's all."

"Thursday November 17th 1960
My Darling,

So you and I feel the same about each other. Don't worry Darling, I will never take you farther than you want to go. I'm shy too. I hated stripping naked to go into the showers. The other boys always mocked me. They told me because I'm black I should have a big cock. So, why is mine so small? So I'm not ready to be naked either – but you can kiss me all over above my trousers. I'm looking forward to feeling your almost naked body against mine. You're so warm and feeling so soft. Your kisses are like central heating. I can't wait to be with you tomorrow night.
Your ever loving
M
xxxxxxxxxxx"

"Friday November 18 1960
Dear Diary

I allowed Mark to strip me nearly naked. He was very sweet. He kissed me all the time as he took off my jumper and skirt and then my bra. I know he's never been with a girl before because he didn't really know how to unhook my bra. I had to show him. He was much easier to strip than I was. I enjoyed kissing him all over his body but I enjoyed his kissing me even more. He laid me on my back on the grass and lay on top of me, starting with the top of my head and ending with the top of my pants and kissed every bit of me in between. Then he rolled me over and did the same with my back. I felt so excited that things happened inside of me and I wet my knickers. I didn't tell him that! However, when I did the same to him I noticed that a bulge appeared in his trousers at the top in between his legs. He groaned and I became worried in case I was hurting him. I offered to stop, but he begged me to continue. I noticed later that his trousers were wet in front, and grinned when I realised that the same thing happened to him as happened to me.

"I'm afraid, dear Diary, that we still haven't found a café that likes us together. The Indian man treated us just the same as the white man did last week. Mark told me that he's going to be away for three weeks because his Dad's taking him to Jamaica to meet his relatives. We promised to meet up when he returned. Three weeks seems such a long time when you're in love."

"Wednesday November 30 1960
Dear Diary

I've learned to see things through Mark's eyes, and I've noticed things that I'd never noticed before. I've seen newspaper headlines about too many black people coming over to Britain and taking British houses and jobs. I've seen notices in windows saying they wanted tenants but not Blacks or people with dogs or children. I've watched gangs of white boys attacking a black boy and gangs of black boys attacking a white boy. I've seen similar things among schoolgirls. It's horrible. I've also watched a white boy walking out with a black girl being dragged off the girl and beaten up while a gang of white boys raped the girl. It seems as though everybody is against us. I wonder how Mark is getting on in Jamaica. Is he finding what I've found? He should be back next week. I will write to him to tell him I've missed him and still love him, but also what I've seen. We have to be careful. No one wants us to be together but us. It's shameful I can only have the fun my friends have with boys in a park, just because he's black and not white like me. I wish I could paint him white or me black. It's all so unfair."

"Friday December 2nd 1960
Darling,

I'm back and I've bought you a Christmas present. I hope you like it. One day I hope I'll be able to buy you a ring – but it's much too early for that, Darling. I want to hold your body next to mine again and feel your soft and warm breath on my face. Jamaica was good, but I wish I could share it with you. Black and white people get on much better there and we would not stand out so much as we do here. It frightens me sometimes, but I'm determined not to let it get between us. I'll meet you next week, same time and place, and give you your present and kiss you all over. I will even let you take my trousers off – if you will let me remove your skirt. I've always said I would never put my hands up a girl's skirt. That way I won't have to! We'll still be safe so long as we keep our pants on. I love you.
M
xxxxxxxxxxxxxx"

"Monday December 5 1960
Dear Diary

Mark wrote to me when he came back and said Jamaica was good, he's bought a present for me and he still loves me. I think he wants to marry me! I agree with him that it's too early. He also wants to take my skirt off so long as I take his trousers off and leave his pants and my knickers on. I think he's a bit forward, but I like that. I think I'll let him do it – and I've written to him to tell him so. I'll wear my nicest knickers and put some of my favourite scent on. I've got to go out and buy him a Christmas present as well.

Fifty Years After

It's snowed today, so we'll have to look for somewhere inside to meet or else we'll freeze especially if we both wet ourselves like we did last time. I wrote about that as well. I told him that I wet myself because I was so excited and I noticed that he did too. I'm sure he'll be embarrassed because he thought I hadn't noticed! He's a lovely boy, Diary, and I feel so lucky I've found him. I love him so much it hurts."

"Friday December 9 1960
Dear Diary

It was too cold to go to the Park. There was frost on the ground in the morning and it stayed all day. It started to snow in the afternoon. We were very busy in the shop, so Mark had to wait for me to meet him after work because Mrs Taylor kept us back late to clear up. We decided to go to the pictures. The Odeon refused to let Mark in so we had to go to the Embassy – which we all know as the fleapit. When you sit in there, you know why! We sat at the back. The film wasn't very good – but we didn't care. We didn't watch it anyway. We spent our time kissing and cuddling each other. It was good to be back with Mark. I've missed him so much. On our way home he gave me his present, which he has wrapped up for me and told me not to open until Christmas. I have bought him a tie, which I also wrapped up. He told me all about his trip to Jamaica and showed me some photos he took. He gave me three, including one smashing one of him dressed only in swimming trunks, which I've stuck in here with my letters. I gave him a photo of me, which Mum took on the beach at Clacton last summer, wearing only a bikini. It took a long time for him to kiss me goodnight, but I didn't care. He can take as long as he likes."

"Wednesday December 14 1960
Darling Janet,

I'm very sorry but I can't meet you this Friday. Dad's friends are coming over to dinner and I have to be at home to tell them about our Jamaica visit. I won't be able to see you on the following Friday either, because I have to go with the family to Church on Christmas Eve. I will miss you terribly, especially as I didn't see you for three weeks while I was in Jamaica, Darling. Let's spend Boxing Day together. We can meet after lunch and have the afternoon and evening together.

"I've got some good news. I know an old man who has an allotment near Marchfield Green. He has what he calls a potting shed. It's empty, apparently, and no one goes to the allotments in the winter. He has given me the key and told me we can use it to meet there until the spring, when people will go back to the allotments to dig. I told him about you and how people react to us when they see us together. He smiled at me sadly, and said 'That's Britain in 1960 for you.' He told me he had an old paraffin stove in the shed and told me to light it so we could keep warm and then he wished us luck and that we have a merry Christmas. So we will be able to do what we promised each other, even if it snows!

"Have a merry Christmas Darling, and I'll see you on Boxing Day."
Lots and lots of love and kisses,
Mark
xxxxxxxxxxxxxxxxxx(and many more!)"

"Thursday December 15 1960
Dear Diary

I was raped today. Mark wasn't there, of course, when I left work – and I didn't see the white boy who followed me as I walked home because I was thinking about Mark's letter and the fact that he'd found us a place where we could meet in warmth and safety. So it came as a shock to me when a rough hand suddenly bundled me into a side alley and pushed me up against a wall. The boy was older than me and hadn't shaved very well because his face was bristly – unlike Mark's, which is always smooth. He ordered me to take my coat and jumper off, and when I said 'no' he slapped me across the face very hard. I was frightened he would really hurt me so I did as I was told and dropped my coat and jumper onto the pavement. It was dark, because the alley was not lit and no one came by. He made me put my hands on my head as he unbuttoned my blouse and skirt.

"'Take your blouse off and step out of your skirt,' he ordered me. 'Do it quickly, or else.'
I did as he told me, and suddenly felt the cold air on my skin. I knew what he would do next, and I was right as he began to roll down my tights. I suddenly realised, feeling sick, that he must have done this before. I don't know why, but I took my bra off as he removed my tights, lifting my legs to do so. I didn't want him to damage it. He grinned when he saw what I'd done. I think he misunderstood why I did it, because he said 'Good girl.' He reached for my knickers and I tried to push him away. He got angry then, and slapped me a second time before turning me around to face the wall, pulling my arms behind my back, and using my tights to tie my wrists together. Then he turned me back around and took my knickers off. I felt ashamed to stand there naked in front of him, especially when he made me spread my legs out. I watched him take his trousers and pants off – which he did slowly. I've seen my brother's Willie, but never like his was. My brother's always dangles. His was stiff, thick and stood up. He stuck it into my thing without saying anything or doing anything else. He moved it up and down inside me and I could feel it moving and then I felt hot liquid coming into me and he sighed. He took it out and it went floppy, just like my brothers. Then he got dressed again.

'Well, Little girl. I hope you enjoyed that as much as I did. You won't get pregnant because we did it standing up – so don't worry.'

Fifty Years After

I didn't answer him as he untied me and helped me pick up my clothes and get dressed. Afterwards he walked me home, telling me he was protecting me against men who would rape me. I told Mum when I got home, but she didn't blame the boy. She blamed me! 'You must have provoked him!' she said. She ordered me to go and have a bath. I did as she told me and scrubbed myself clean but I don't feel clean. I don't trust any man except Mark. He doesn't take advantage of me and I only feel safe when I'm with him."

"Friday December 16 1960
Dear Diary

I told Mrs Taylor what happened to me yesterday. She was very sympathetic at first.

'It's all these blacks they're allowing to come over here nowadays,' she said. 'No decent girl is safe out alone anymore.'

I told her the boy was white, not black, and her attitude changed.

'Boys will be boys, Janet,' she said sternly. 'I'm sure you must have done something to lead him on, or he wouldn't have done it'

"I was shocked at Mrs Taylor's double standards. Black boys are rapists and white boys are victims of us girls! I didn't tell anyone else, not even Jennifer, my sister, who wouldn't understand any way. She's only 14. I don't know whether to write to Mark to tell him. I wish I could speak to someone about what I feel about Mark, but I can't. I feel so alone. You're the only one I can tell about my feelings, dear Diary, and you can't answer me. It's all so cruel and unfair."

Fifty Years After

"Janet was feeling much happier once Christmas came," Belinda said, "and her next diary entry shows this."

"Christmas Day 1960
Dear Diary

What a lovely day I had today! I woke up and felt the familiar weight of the stocking that Mum always gives us, even though I'm grown up now. I'm 18 next month after all! It was full of sweets and fruit and things I can wear like panties and bras. Then I opened my secret present and Christmas Card. The present was a lovely ring with a big green stone in it. Mark had been very cunning and measured my finger in some way, because he got it right – and I didn't know he'd done it, the Darling. Tomorrow I will put it on when I go out. I dare not wear it indoors, Mum and Dad will notice and demand to know who gave it to me. He sent me a boxed special 'girlfriend' Christmas card. On it he wrote, 'Will you marry me?' as well as wishing me a merry Christmas. I wanted to shout out 'Yes', but I knew he wouldn't hear. I shall have to do it tomorrow. Everything after that was a lovely anti-climax. They all liked my presents and Mum and Dad gave me a lovely red dress. Jennifer bought me a baby doll nightie and Tom bought me a new 1961 diary. Then we had dinner and played games until the evening. I was very tired when I finally got up here, that's why this is so short. Happy Christmas, Diary – don't worry I'm not going to forget you just because I've got a new diary."

"Boxing Day 1960
Dear Diary

Mark was so sweet today. He met me after lunch, as he promised and we walked to the allotments and opened the shed. It was very dusty, so we cleaned it and Mark lit the stove. It smelt a bit, but it kept us warm. We took our top clothes off because we got too warm, especially lying in the sleeping bag that Mark had brought with him, but I would not let him go any further. I told Mark about the

Fifty Years After

boy who raped me and he was very sweet to me. He didn't blame me, but he was upset. 'That's what some boys do, Darling,' he said to me. 'Don't blame yourself. It was not your fault – it was his – but do be careful and avoid dark and lonely places when you're walking home.'

"I promised that I would and told him that I did not feel comfortable with him touching me where he usually did at the moment. He said he understood and instead he cuddled me and rubbed my hair, which I liked, even though he ruined it! We spent the time talking to and kissing each other. I thanked him for his present and showed him I was wearing it, and told him that the answer to his question was a big YES! He thanked me for my present and I had already noticed that he was wearing the tie I bought him. Eventually, the paraffin ran out and the heater stopped working. Mark told me he would buy more paraffin and make sure that we kept some in what we call our house. Then we went home. So now, I'm engaged, diary – although I can only tell you. I hope you like my ring".

Albert's voice came over the image of Jonathan and Belinda.

"There were a few minor entries in January 1961 and early February 1961. You will find them in your copy of the Diary, which we will give you at the end of this screening, members of the Jury. For now, it is sufficient for you to know that Mark and Janet found peace together when they met in what they called their home. The diary shows that Janet slowly recovered from the shock of her rape and Mark gave her the space and time and the loving care which enabled her to do so. We pick up the story on Tuesday February 14th, 1961 – St Valentine's Day. As you would expect, Mark sent her a very special Valentine's Day Card and bought her a very special present. Janet had a special present in mind for him, too."

Fifty Years After

"Valentine's Day, 1961
Dear Diary,

My Darling Mark sent me a lovely Valentine's Day card. He signed it 'with love from your not so secret admirer' and he also sent a large bunch of flowers, which arrived, of course, anonymously. Jennifer knew who sent it, since she knew all about Mark. Mum didn't know and told everyone that I must have a secret boyfriend. I blushed, and denied it, but I could see Mum didn't believe me! That evening Mark met me and we went to our home. I kissed him and thanked him for his lovely card and his present. I told him I had a very special present for him, which I would give him when we got home. He was both confused and excited since I wasn't carrying anything. He tried to tease me into telling him, but I teased him back. He gave up guessing in the end, and told me that he has almost saved enough for our holiday in Margate, which we plan to have at Easter. He's booked our hotel – a bed and breakfast on the seafront – and paid for it. All we have to do is pay our train fares and find spending money. It'll be lovely to get away from all these people who hate seeing us together. I'm really sad that we have to pretend we're not together all the time we're in public. Any way, it's different in our little home! We opened the door and Mark lit the stove, then I told Mark what my present is. 'It's me!' I said. He looked puzzled. 'But we've already given ourselves to each other!' he said. 'Not completely,' I said smiling. His eyes opened wide as he slowly realised what I meant. 'Take my clothes off,' I said to him – 'all of them,' I said, 'but be gentle with me. Remember it's the first time since that boy stripped me naked and raped me.' We took each other's clothes off, and, although Mark's cock grew like the boy's did, it did not seem so threatening to me and he did not use it with the same force. I enjoyed the warmth of his breath, the closeness of his body and the feeling of him inside me. He took his time and he brought me to what I think they told us at school was an orgasm. I shouted out in surprise and he silenced me by kissing me. That's much nicer than putting a hand across my mouth, which is what the other boy did. When we finished we were both sweating and we lay on the sleeping bag together. I have never been happier. Diary, you know all my secrets. I'm sure you know how happy I am. I am much happier even than I was on January 19th when I was 18."

Jonathan's voice spoke over the images.

"Things continued in this way for another six weeks. The two met twice a week and they made love together on most occasions. Mark stopped writing letters, because they were saving for their holiday. The next important day was in the middle of March."

"Friday March 17 1961
Dear Diary

I'm very excited today. After Mark made love to me he told me that he wanted us to get married in May. Because of this, we decided to cancel our planned holiday and concentrate on our wedding. He has a very romantic idea. We will both give up our jobs and elope to Gretna Green. We'll get married there and then go to live in Scotland where we can both find work and where we hope people will be kinder to us. If they're not, he promised he'll take me to Jamaica and we'll live there. I love the sun and the photos he took were lovely. I hate this country because people have been very cruel to us here. I don't know why they're like that. Still, if we get away from here, things can only get better. They can't possibly be worse. We've also lost our home. People are coming back to the allotment to work, including in the evenings. Sadly, most of them are not like Mark's old man. They don't like us here and they've told us so."

Albert spoke again.

"They left the comfort and safety of their little home and began to prepare for their grand adventure in

Fifty Years After

Scotland. Mark found them what he thought was a safe place for them to meet in the park in Marchfield among the trees, and they began to meet there regularly. However, their visits did not go unnoticed. We return to Janet's diary for her account of the final week of her life."

"Wednesday April 19 1961
Dear Diary

I'm very worried. All of last week I thought someone was following me, except for Friday when I was with Mark. Today I'm certain of it. I managed to trick him by slipping into a café on my way home and watching through the window. I will try to describe him. I think he's between 20 and 25, about 5 feet 6 inches tall, with brown hair and well-built muscles. He's white. He's fat. It looks as though he's got plenty of money from the clothes he wears, which look expensive. I don't know who he is or where he comes from, but I think it's creepy the way he's following me about. I wanted to point him out to Mark, but, as I told you, diary, he wasn't there last Friday when Mark and I went to the park and made love."

"Thursday April 20 1961
Dear Diary

He was there again last night. He almost came up to me, but when I turned around, he backed off. I don't know what he's doing – but I don't like it and he frightens me. I've taken to walking home the long way round because there are no back alleys like the one I was raped in before Christmas. I wish Mark was with me. I can't wait for May 5th – that's the day we're travelling to Scotland."

"Friday April 21 1961
Dear Diary

Mark collected me from work today. We don't care about Mrs Taylor's threat to sack me anymore because I've given in my notice anyway. The boy didn't follow me, but I've a horrible feeling that he was around somewhere. I don't know why. Anyway, I felt safe when Mark was with me, and warm when he was making love to me. I've got to tell him that I'm pregnant. I found out last week and I intended to tell Mark he was going to be a Daddy – but the fact the boy was following me made me forget. I don't want to be alone with that boy, so I've asked Mark if he will take me out next Wednesday as well as next Friday. He agreed, and I feel much safer. I wish I was a black girl – then we wouldn't have the problems we have. I don't like white people any more. They've only hurt me."

"Monday April 24 1961
Dear Diary

His name is Philip Stewart and he's 21. He's horrible. He came into the shop and forced me to serve him, although I didn't want to. He said he wanted to buy a bra and panties set and told me it had to be the same size as I wore. I found him a white pair and he bought it. He asked my name and I told him that was for me to know and him to think about and he went off.

He was waiting for me when I left work. He came up to me and told me he was going to escort me home. I told him I didn't need an escort – but he tagged along anyway. It was all right until we got near my home. I ignored him and we walked in silence. However, at the point where Mark usually kisses me goodnight, he suddenly grabbed me and dragged me to him, trying to kiss me. I pushed him away and told him I have a boyfriend already and that I would scream for help if he touched me. He walked off, saying, 'Have it your way girl – but you'll regret it.'"

"Tuesday April 25 1961 (written after midnight on 26 April).
Dear Diary

Philip Stewart raped me today. I have told Jennifer and she has helped me clean myself up – but I was too ashamed to tell her everything. I can only tell you and Mark. I must do that anyway - and I will do it tomorrow (later today that is).

"I was walking home and Philip Stewart followed me as usual. I tried to get away from him, but he would not let me. There's a park on our way home. It's where Mark and I first used to meet. When we got to the gate, he suddenly came up to me and pushed me through it into the park and across the grass to where the outer wall is. I was so surprised I did not resist him. He put his hand in my back. I felt a pin prick in my skin.

'That's a knife,' he hissed in my ear. 'Try anything and I will kill you.'

'Please leave me alone,' I pleaded with him.

'No, chance, Darling,' he said. 'You had an opportunity to be nice to me yesterday and you didn't take it. I warned you that you would regret it. Now walk and look happy!'

He guided me along the side of the park to where some bushes hide the area by the wall. He forced me to stand against the wall and place my hands on my head while he held the knife to my throat.

'Will you do as I tell you or shall I save us both trouble and cut your throat now? he asked me.

'What do you want me to do?' I asked.

'That's better,' he said. 'Put your hands by your sides and stand still.'

I did as I was told and he unbuttoned my coat and pulled it off me. Then he told me to unbutton my blouse and unclip my bra. I did as he said.

'That's much better,' he said. 'I may let you live after all! Now, take them off.'

I made a mistake then. I kicked him in between the legs and scratched his face. That hurt him and made him angry.

'Why, you little bitch!' he said.

Fifty Years After

He hit me several times, punching me on the face and body. He hurt me and I finally fell down, hitting my head against the wall. Everything went black.

"When I came around I was naked and my hands were tied behind my back. A piece of sticking plaster was stuck across my mouth. I was wet and cold. I saw that he had an empty bucket in his hand. I guessed that he had thrown a bucket of cold water over me. I was lying on my back and he was standing over me.

'You bitch,' he said. 'I'm going to punish you for what you did before I fuck you to buggery.'"

"He slowly unbuckled his belt and pulled it out before he turned me onto my face and beat me on the bum and legs with his belt. I don't know how many times he hit me, because I lost count, but I know it hurt and it still hurts. When he'd finished, he rolled me back over onto my back, forced my legs wide apart, took his trousers and pants down, showing me his cock, which was long and stiff like the other boy's and like Mark's is when he makes love to me. Then he raped me. It wasn't like last time, which hurt me, but I don't think it was intentional. Philip deliberately moved upwards and downwards and from side to side in order to hurt me as much as he could. He succeeded and I still hurt down there. When he had finished, he stood up and laughed at me.

'Well, you bitch. Now you know what a real man is like. I'm not one of your Niggers that you love so much. I'm dressed and free. You're naked, tied up and gagged. I'm going to leave you to free yourself and go home – but I'm taking your clothes with me so you have to go home naked. That will teach you a lesson. You'll find that your tights are torn.'

I looked up at him with hatred.

"'Don't look at me like that, bitch!' he ordered. He took his tie off and tied my legs together before he turned me over again, and used his belt on me for a second time. This time he hurt me even more than he did the first time. He left me face down, so I could not look at him. He stood over me, with his foot, with his shoe on, on my back, above my bum, crushing me into the mud. Then he threatened me.

'You belong to me, now bitch. Remember that. If I catch you with that Nigger wanker again, I will kill you both. I will shoot you down like the animals you are!'"

"With that he left me. It took me an hour to free myself and even longer to look for and find my coat. My feet hurt and I was cold and dirty when I got home. I told Jennifer, but not Mum (when she came in from work) and Jennifer helped clean me up and dressed my injuries.

'I'm very frightened diary. I believe Philip Stewart's threat and I think we are both in danger. Tell the Police, if I die tomorrow or next week, and if I'm shot, it was Philip Stewart who killed me and Mark."

Albert came back on the screen.

"Those were Janet's last recorded words. Eight hours later she went out to work. Seventeen hours later she met Mark. Nineteen hours later she was dead, shot dead by a member of the Stewart gang, probably, as she foretold, Philip Stewart. Three months later, Mark was dead too, hanged as a result of the lies and the plotting of Philip Stewart and his family. All that happened nearly fifty years ago. The two were separated all that time; their dreams destroyed with their lives. It took another equally brave young couple to risk their lives in order to find peace for these two doomed young lovers whose only crime was that they wanted to share their lives together. Belinda and Jonathan took their places and married in their name in the place where they intended to marry and we were all present when the mortal remains of the two young lovers were finally brought back together for

Fifty Years After

eternity, enabling them to find, in death, the peace and unity they were unable to find in life."

The film came to an end and the lights went back on in the court. Charles stood up, but Lord Black waved him down.

"Not now Mr Harris. This is not an appropriate time for you to ask questions."

Charles objected and the Judge ordered the court to be cleared except for Albert and Charles. When this was done, he spoke to the defence lawyer.

"Mr Harris, how long have you been practicing law?"

"Thirty years, My Lord."

"Lord Corrigan and I have over 100 years of experience of working with juries between us. We can see that, however worthy your questions would no doubt be, the Jury is not prepared to listen to them or the answers. The women on the Jury went out in tears and the men with a mixture of emotions from tears to raw anger – all directed at your client. It's not my job to direct you, and, if you insist, I will allow your questions – but remember, two of the principals in the film have left the court for the afternoon and the producer and cameraperson were not even here. I will arrange for those two to be here tomorrow and for Lord Corrigan and his two assistants to make themselves available to answer your questions tomorrow morning, if that's what you want. However, my advice, for what it's worth, and I'm sure that Lord Corrigan would agree with me, is that your only chance to save your client is to get on with your defence witnesses and ignore the film."

Albert nodded and Lord Black continued.

"I'll give you one more piece of advice. Your only chance of saving your client from being hanged is to get him to admit what he's done and show contrition both for the rape and the murder. The evidence is compelling and that film's text will be in all the papers tomorrow, since the reporters have been secretly recording the proceedings. I know it and you both know it – but we can't actually stop it with today's technology available to them. It will be read by the prisoners and I assure you that your client will suffer death by hanging before long, although not at the hands of the state, unless he shows some contrition. Remember, too, that there are other charges in the offing against him and others."

Charles nodded.

"Thank you, Lord Black. You have been more than fair with my client and me. I will follow your advice and would be grateful if the five people you mentioned are available tomorrow morning in case I want to ask them questions."

The Court reconvened and was immediately adjourned with the Judge talking to the Jury before they went.

"You have seen some of the most harrowing and disturbing testimony I have ever seen in a court, bearing in mind that they were the last recorded words of a long dead couple. You will each be given a bound copy of the complete diary in its original form with three pages of comparative writing. They're yours to keep. They are a limited edition. One day, no doubt, you will be able to sell them on e bay or at an auction to fund your retirement. Go and try to have a good night's sleep and I will see you all here tomorrow at 10am. Don't forget my warnings. Don't discuss the case among yourselves and don't talk about it with anyone else."

With that, they all stood up as the judge left, and the third day of the trial was over.

29. Philip Stewart

September 23 2010

Charles Harris approached the bench as soon as the case resumed on the fourth morning of the trial.

"My Lord," he said, "I would like to exercise the discretion that your lordship kindly gave me yesterday by recalling one prosecution witness and calling another."

Lord Black smiled at the harassed defender and then at the Jury.

"Members of the Jury, last night Mr Harris wanted to ask some questions about the film we all saw yesterday. I told him that you were in no mood to listen, and advised him to save his fire for this morning."

He turned to face the press box, which was full for the third day and addressed them with mock severity.

"Members of the Press and Media Corps, I recall telling you at the start of this trial that you were not permitted to take photographs or make recordings of these proceedings. I was, therefore, shocked that every major newspaper," he pointed to a stack of newspapers piled in front of him, "carried the text of the film we showed verbatim. Either, every one of you has a much better memory than I have, or you cheated. I am minded to have you all strip searched when you leave the court today."

There was nervous laughter from the journalists, who were not entirely sure that Lord Black was joking. The Judge looked back at the Defence Barrister.

"Very well, Mr Harris. Who do you wish to speak to?"

"First, My Lord, I wish to ask the Producer of the film a couple of questions."

A young man entered the court. The Judge put him as being in his mid-twenties. He had what Lord Black defined as the classic movie look – very trendy in dress and bearing. He introduced himself as Rick Dewhurst, and affirmed rather than swearing the oath.

"Are you the person who devised the film script?" Charles asked.

"I am," Rick replied.

"What were your directions?"

"What do you mean?"

"What were you asked to do?"

"Oh! I was given Janet Brown's diary and asked to make a film presenting it in dramatic form so that the Jury would be able to get a feel of what the writer was feeling when she (and he) wrote what they did."

"Did you write the script yourself?"

"Yes. It was a fairly straightforward task compared to some I've had to do."

"Did you tell the two actors how to interpret the roles and lines you gave them?"

"No. I left that to them. They seemed to understand the characters much better than I did."

Charles thanked Rick Dewhurst and handed him over to Albert who, with a smile, told him that he had no questions and thanked him for coming.

Charles stood up again.

"I would like to request that Belinda Thompson return to the witness box, My Lord."

Belinda stood up and walked forward. She stood uncertainly, wondering what she had to do. Lord Black smiled at her reassuringly.

"Remember, you are still under oath, Miss Thompson."

Belinda nodded and Charles approached her.

"I only have one question for you, Miss Thompson. Who told you how to play the role of Janet Brown?"

"No one did, Mr Harris. Jonathan and I have lived with Mark and Janet for the last nine months. We have experienced some of what they experienced ourselves and both of us have had our lives threatened. On Monday Mr Stewart's brother stopped us on our way home and told us that he planned to kidnap us, strip us, torture us, handcuff

Fifty Years After

us, chain our legs together, and finally throw us, still alive, into the middle of the English Channel, to drown there. I think we know exactly how Janet and Mark felt, especially on that last day."

Charles felt that he really should object to the words about Timothy Stewart, but he no longer cared. He knew he'd lost the case the previous evening, and that Philip Stewart wouldn't do what was necessary to save himself. The Judge also said nothing, partly because he was distracted by a note handed to him by an usher. His face clouded, and he looked at Charles.

"Is that all you wanted to ask this witness, Mr Harris?"

"Yes, My Lord."

"Do you have any questions for Miss Thompson. Lord Corrigan?"

"No, My Lord."

"You can stand down, Miss Thompson."

The judge paused.

"I'm going to call a 15 minutes' adjournment. We will return at 10.30."

Lord Black rose from his seat and returned to his chambers. One of the police officers assigned to protect the Jury was waiting in his room. Lord Black showed him the note.

"Did you write this?" he asked.

"Yes, My Lord."

"You're sure of this?"

"Absolutely, My Lord."

Lord Black read the note aloud.

"A strange man tried to approach one of the Jurors as they walked to the coach this morning. We pushed him away but he continued to hang about and the last we saw of him he was entering the hotel foyer."

"Is that what you wrote and what you saw?"

"Yes, My Lord."

Fifty Years After

"Fine. Go to the driver and travel back with him to the hotel. Ask the staff to pack the jurors' bags and stow them in the coach and then give the coach driver this letter."

Lord Black pulled a sealed letter from his desk drawer.

"Give it to the driver. It's the address of a second hotel, which has kept itself available for us. Tell him to take the bags to the hotel and check the jurors in. Tell him also to say nothing to anyone but to be sure to be the driver on duty this evening."

The Police Officer left. Lord Black sighed with relief that he had been far sighted enough to anticipate what Lord Stewart's unofficial defence would be and to take the steps to scotch it. He had booked sixteen rooms in each of two different hotels, block booked for the week. One was in Central London and the other in Bromley (Kent). "The twelve Jurors will get a pleasant surprise tonight," he thought. He put his wig and gown back on and summoned the court usher to call the court back to order and bring the jury back in. When everyone was in place, he returned.

"Please accept my apologies," he said, "but something came up, which required my immediate attention. Mr Harris, the floor is yours."

Charles Harris rose to his feet. He usually enjoyed this moment. It was what all defence lawyers looked forward to – the privilege of presenting their clients' cases to a judge and jury. Charles knew none of that joy. He knew, just as well as the judge and Lord Corrigan knew, that he had lost the case. He had watched the faces of the twelve jurors as they filed out from the court twice the night before. He could see his defeat in their eyes. Now he felt like Macbeth about to fight the Battle of Dunsinane – a battle he knew he was going to lose. He walked over to the jury box.

"Members of the Jury, you are here to pass judgement on a man who has served his country as an MP, as a minister, and as a peer for most of his life. He stands accused of two heinous crimes – killing a young girl and ensuring the death at the hands of others of a young boy for the terrible crime of falling in love with one another while being of different races. Lord Stewart admits that he has a particular weakness for women and that he does have difficulty in behaving himself properly in female company. He will admit to the separate accusation, for which he is not standing trial, of being too forthright in his pursuit of Janet Brown. However, you have to convince yourself that the Prosecution has proved his guilt of murdering her beyond all reasonable doubt. I am going to show you that there are grounds to have reasonable doubt here."

Charles turned away and called his first witness.

Jill Aymes was fifty years old and had studied handwriting for most of her life. She walked confidently to the witness box and swore the oath.

"Ms Aymes, am I right in thinking that you are a very experienced graphologist?" Charles asked.

"Yes, My Lord."

"Have you studied the book that purports to be the diary of Janet Brown?"

"I have."

"Have you also studied the three school exercise books belonging to Janet Brown, Mark Smith and Jennifer Brown respectively?"

"I have."

"What conclusion have you drawn?"

"I haven't been able to draw a certain conclusion, My Lord. There are points of similarity and points of difference between all three writers and what's in the diary."

"Thank you, Ms Aymes. If you will wait there, Lord Corrigan may want to ask you some questions."

Albert approached the witness box and spoke quietly to the witness.

"You say that you can't give a definite opinion, but, if I pressed you to choose, would you feel the graphical evidence more strongly suggests that the documents are genuine than that they're not?"

"Yes, My Lord."

"Would you also agree that it is highly unlikely that Jennifer Foster forged the documents?"

"I would be stronger than that, My Lord. I would say that it was certain that she didn't."

"Thank you, Ms Aymes."

The second witness was Henry Lewis, a forensic scientist.

"Have you studied the two versions of the forensic report, Mr Lewis?" Charles asked.

"I have," Henry replied.

"What would you say was the original version?"

"The longer one."

Charles looked surprised. This was not what he was told that Henry Lewis would say.

"You seem very certain?"

"I am. I can see a clear reason for the changes and who was responsible for ordering them. There is no evidence that the shorter form was the original. Indeed, except in detective fiction, it is impossible to imagine that anyone could attempt to add to a report without providing a clear reason for the additions."

Charles nodded, walked away, and said "Your witness" to a delighted Albert.

"Let me just underline, Mr Lewis. You agree with Mr Adewuni. Is that right?"

"Yes, Lord Corrigan."

"What about the evidence of the gun?"

"I agree with his conclusions about that as well – two shots were fired at the girl by the killer, killing her; two

Fifty Years After
shots were fired for some reason also by the killer and went wide, and one shot by the police was fired for comparison with the fatal bullets."

"Thank you Mr Lewis."

"My final witness is the defendant, Lord Philip Stewart."

There was a stir and a murmur as the peer left the dock and walked to the witness box to take the oath.

"I swear that the evidence I shall give to this court shall be the truth, the whole truth and nothing but the truth," he intoned in a bored way.

Charles asked the Clerk of the Court to read through the official transcript of Philip's evidence in chief at Mark's trial. At the conclusion of the reading he turned to face Philip. However, before he could speak, Lord Black intervened, to warn Philip about the use of racist language. Then he nodded to Charles who began his questions.

"Do you remember giving that evidence, Lord Stewart?"

"Now it's been read it back to me, yes I do."

"Do you wish to change any of it?"

"No."

"Why not?"

"Because it's the truth?"

"You're certain that Mark Smith shot his girlfriend by accident while trying to shoot you?"

"Certain."

"Can you give me a percentage to show how certain you are?"

"100%"

"So there wasn't another person involved – someone not known to this Court or the court that conducted the 1961 trial?"

"There was no other person involved."

Albert exchanged glances with his two young assistants.

"What's he trying to do?" Belinda whispered. "It's almost as though he's leading the Prosecution."

"I don't know," Albert whispered back.

Charles moved on.

"Yesterday you watched the film made of Janet Brown's Diary. What did you make of it?"

"It was a load of cobblers – sentimental codswallop."

Charles groaned inwardly. This was as bad as he expected.

"Did you first stalk, then harass and finally rape Janet before she was killed?"

"Of course I followed her! She was an attractive bird and I wanted to have her."

"What do you mean by that?"

"The Americans have a phrase for it – it's called getting laid. That's what I intended to do to Janet Brown."

"And did you?"

"Yes. And I enjoyed it?"

"Was Janet's description in her diary correct?"

Charles noticed that the jurors were watching Philip with the same sort of disgusted horror as one does a cobra about to strike at one.

"Not entirely. She didn't know how I stripped her or what I did with her clothes."

"Are you going to complete the story?"

"Sure. After I knocked her down, as she lay unconscious, I ripped off her skirt and then pulled off her tights, tearing them as I did so. I threw her shoes down first, of course. I used her tights to bind her wrists tightly behind her back so she couldn't strike me anymore and then ripped off her flowered pants. Horrible cheap things they were – just like she was. She made herself even cheaper by copulating with a black man. They were no better than animals. Whoever killed them did the world a service."

Charles continued, blank faced.

"I see. What did you do with her clothes?"

"I found a rubbish bin and threw them all in it, making sure they were well down to the bottom. They would have gone to infill next day. I filled a bucket with cold water and came back to where I'd left her. She was still out for the count. I tossed the water over her to bring her round."

"Why did you take her clothes?"

"To maximise her embarrassment. I wanted to humiliate her by forcing her to walk home naked and I also hoped someone would find her naked and, with luck, also have fun with her." He paused before adding ruefully, "Unfortunately, I forgot to destroy her coat."

Charles saw the shock and disgust that these words produced on the faces of the Jurors and wanted to get this over with as soon as possible.

"Did you threaten to shoot her if you caught her with Mark?"

"Yes."

"Did you, in fact, shoot her?"

"No."

"Was the gun yours?"

"No."

Charles turned away with relief.

"Your witness," he said to Albert.

Albert rose from his seat and walked to the witness box.

"So we meet again, Lord Stewart, under somewhat different circumstances to our last meeting in this place!"

He paused dramatically before continuing.

"Have you read the transcript of the trial in 1961 Lord Stewart?"

"Yes."

"Do you wish to change or add to any of your answers to my questions?"

"No, Lord Corrigan."

Albert nodded.

Fifty Years After

"In that trial you posed as the white knight who attempted to rescue a girl who had just been raped. But just now you said to my colleague, Mr Harris, that Janet was cheap and 'made herself even cheaper by copulating with a black man. They were no better than animals. Whoever killed them did the world a service.' Which is the true Philip Stewart?"

"I don't know what you mean, Lord Corrigan."

"Do you not, Lord Stewart?"

Albert pretended to think for a moment, before turning to look at Belinda. He turned back to face Philip.

"What do you think about Belinda Thompson?"

"I think she should go back home. She shouldn't be here taking our jobs and houses."

"And chasing our men?"

"That too, Lord Corrigan."

"I suppose home is what you called Bongobongoland?"

Philip grinned.

"Exactly – all Niggers should go back there."

Lord Black intervened.

"I warned you, Lord Stewart."

"Sorry, My Lord. I should have said 'all black people.'"

"So you think Belinda came from Bongobongoland, do you Lord Stewart?"

"That's where she belongs."

"Would it surprise you to know that she was born in Greenford – as were her parents. I believe that you were born in Greenford as well."

"So what?"

"I believe that, according to you, inhabitants of Bongobongoland run around naked, live in mud huts and copulate in public like animals."

Albert paused.

"That, of course, must include at least five members of the Jury – and, of course, you, Lord Stewart. Do you live in a mud hut, run around naked and copulate in public?"

Philip was silent, and Albert allowed him to remain so, before moving on.

"What do you think of Jonathan Greenway?"

"He's a disgrace to our race. Why can't he find a decent white girl? There were plenty around in Cambridge surely."

"So you think that Jonathan has betrayed you by wanting to marry a black woman, Lord Stewart. Is that the case?"

"Of course it is – cats should not marry dogs as the woman in the diary said – and different races should keep to themselves."

"Would it be true that you consider Jonathan to be even worse than Belinda because of this betrayal?"

"Yes, Lord Corrigan."

Albert walked across to his seat and appeared to look at his papers. After a couple of minutes, he returned to face Philip.

"Is that why you killed Janet Brown, because you saw her as a traitor to your race?"

"I didn't kill Janet Brown, Lord Corrigan. Mark Smith did."

"Let me put it another way – you hated Janet Brown because she was having sex with a black man and not with you and you wanted to humiliate her and punish her."

"Of course."

"On April 26th 1961 you didn't come across the two of them by accident, did you? You were waiting for them. You had been following Janet Brown for some time and you knew where they went. What did you plan to do?"

Philip grinned.

"I was going to teach them both a lesson. I planned to hold them both at gunpoint, and force the boy to strip and the girl to tie him to the tree. Then I was going to burn his clothes before forcing her to strip and throw her clothes into the flames before pegging her out, spread-eagled, on

Fifty Years After

the ground in front of her boyfriend and raping her. Last of all I was going to beat the boy up and then leave them to free themselves and explain to their parents why they had come home naked."

"And, presumably, this was designed to humiliate Janet further and also humiliate Mark?"

"Obviously. It would have taught them not to cross Philip Stewart."

Albert threw a disgusted look at the Jury before continuing.

"So you admit that you lied in your evidence on June 21st 1961? You did not enter the park, see a black boy molesting a white girl, and rush to assist her. Instead you lay in wait for them, equipped with a gun, and, presumably rope and other means of securing them. How did you intend to set fire to their clothes?"

"I intended to use petrol."

"I see," Albert commented. "What caused you to change your mind?"

"I didn't – I wasn't there when they arrived and it was too late when I did get there."

"But you had the gun?"

"I didn't say that."

"Never mind, we'll come back to that later. I recall you were wearing gloves that day. How did you intend tying Janet down with gloved hands?"

"I didn't think of that problem before I left the house."

Albert paused again.

"I see. We'll come back to that again, Lord Stewart."

He paused again.

"Where do you think Mark got the gun from?"

"I don't know. It must have been in his jacket pocket."

"PC Adams makes it clear that there was no gun in Mark's pocket. So where was it?"

"I don't know. Perhaps it was in his trousers pocket."

"Surely you would have heard him rustling among his clothes if that were the case, Lord Stewart? However, you never mentioned that at Mark's trial. You said you heard him step on a twig. Which is the truth?"

"What I said at the trial."

"I see," Albert commented. "So you claim that you told the truth in this court room back in 1961?"

"Of course. I took the words of the oath seriously."

Albert turned away to look meaningfully at the Jury before turning back to resume his cross examination.

"Two new facts have emerged since the last trial when we discovered the original forensic report and the police report. The first fact was that the clothes of Janet Brown and Mark Smith were neatly folded. Does that suggest violent rape to you?"

"Mark may have been a tidy man?

"You didn't leave Janet's clothes neatly folded and piled up the day before did you, Lord Stewart?"

"No," Philip grinned, "I took them away and destroyed them - but I had my reasons."

"What were they?"

"I wanted to humiliate her like she humiliated me and teach her a lesson she would never forget."

"Why did you want to humiliate her?"

"Because she humiliated me when she refused my advances in favour of a Nigger."

"Lord Stewart, remember my warning, I will not say this a third time." Lord Black said sternly.

"I'm sorry, My Lord. I should have said 'a black man.'"

Albert resumed his questions.

"I assume that the humiliation that you're referring to was her refusal to let you force yourself on her the day before."

"Obviously," answered Philip. "She allowed the black man to copulate with her. I could not let her get away with refusing a real man."

Fifty Years After

"If you say so, Lord Philip," commented Albert drily. "I presume the intended lesson was to do whatever you told her and not make any resistance in future."

"That's right."

Albert looked meaningfully at the Jury before moving on.

The second was about the gun. You said that Janet was standing when someone shot her. The evidence says she was on lying on the ground. Which is the truth?"

"What I said."

"The evidence points to four shots being fired. Why were two extra shots fired?"

"Mr Ade-Bongo was wrong – there were only five bullets in the gun."

"What did you say, Lord Stewart?"

"I said there were only five bullets in the gun."

"How do you know?"

"How do I know what?"

"How many bullets were in a gun you claim never to have seen before?"

"There had to be five, that's all," Philip said sullenly.

"I put it to you, Lord Stewart, that you did not attempt to rescue Janet Brown from the unwanted attentions of Mark Smith. Instead you lay in wait for them, intending to assault and humiliate them further. However, when Mark and Janet began to make love together you became angry and attacked Mark before shooting Janet dead as she lay helpless on the ground in front of you. I don't know why you didn't shoot Mark as well as he, too, lay helpless on the ground, but you decided that you would provide the Courts with a victim and a killer and, placing the gun unwittingly in the wrong hand, you made Mark fire a bullet into the grass before going to find P C Archer. I put it to you that the evidence that you gave to the Court in 1961 and here today was and has been today a tissue of lies and that you are guilty of both the offences with which you are charged."

Fifty Years After

Albert stood sternly in front of Philip looking towards the Jury as he awaited Philip's response. Finally, Philip spoke.

"That's complete nonsense."

Albert smiled thinly at Philip.

"Do you really expect the Jury to believe that, Lord Stewart?"

He smiled again.

"It's all right, Lord Stewart, you don't have to answer that, but I would like you to answer this final question. You said you talked with Marcus Greenway before Mark was executed. What did you tell him?"

Evelyn was suddenly afraid, "Be careful, Alfred," she thought.

"I told him the truth."

"And that was?"

Philip hesitated before answering.

"Mark Smith shot Janet Brown twice and killed her."

Evelyn sighed with relief. "You clever, sod, Albert," she thought."

"Thank you, Lord Stewart," said Albert and sat down.

The Judge adjourned the trial for lunch when Charles said that the defence case was concluded. However, one of the jurors felt concerned that the evidence was incomplete, and wrote a note to the Judge, asking three questions and passed it to the Court Usher when she escorted them to the jury room where their lunch was waiting for them. She took the note to Lord Black who summoned Charles and Albert to come to his Chambers. They both arrived within ten minutes and entered Lord Black's room together. He stood up to greet them and asked them to sit down.

"I'm sorry to disturb your lunch, gentlemen and, perhaps more important, your speech writing for this afternoon, but I have received a question from a juror. He feels that the issue of the diary has not been completely dealt with and wants to know three things – First, when and how was the

Fifty Years After

diary found? Second, was it taken to the police and when? Third – if it was – what was the police reaction and if it wasn't – why wasn't it in view of Janet Brown's last comment?"

The two men nodded.

"They're good questions," Albert agreed, "and neither of us raised them."

"What do you want us to do about them, My Lord?" Charles asked.

"I noticed that Jennifer Foster has been here throughout the trial and in court since she gave her evidence. She was here this morning, so it's reasonable that she will be here this afternoon as well," Lord Black replied. "She was your witness, Albert, so I propose to give you the sheet of paper and ask you to recall the witness. You can ask the three questions and you can cross examine on the three questions only if you wish to do so, Charles."

The two men agreed and all three returned to their lunches and preparations for the afternoon. Charles Harris worked alone, but Lord Corrigan deliberately involved Belinda in the preparation of his speech since he felt the experience would be good for her and he found he enjoyed bouncing ideas off her. Jonathan left them to it and had a quiet lunch with his and Belinda's parents, Juliet, and Lady Evelyn. None of them talked much, and all felt nervous as the climax of the trial arrived.

Court One filled up rapidly for the afternoon session and Lord Black arrived promptly at 2 pm. There was a slight murmur when he made his opening announcement.

"Members of the Jury, I told you before you left for lunch that we would use this afternoon for Counsels' summing up. However, we have to delay that slightly since one of you has asked me to raise some important questions with one of the witnesses. That is a right and proper thing to do if you feel that vital evidence has not been dealt with. I have asked Lord Corrigan to recall Mrs Foster to answer the three questions that you asked."

He turned away from the Jury to address Albert.

"Lord Corrigan, would you recall your witness please?"

Jennifer walked from the visitors' area to the witness box, surprised at this turn of events. Lord Black spoke to her.

"Mrs Foster, Lord Corrigan is going to ask you three questions put to us by a member of the Jury. Please remember that you are still under oath."

Jennifer nodded.

"Mrs Foster," Lord Corrigan asked. "You were here yesterday afternoon. Did you watch the film of your late sister's diary?"

"I did, my Lord."

"Did she tell you that she was writing a diary?"

"No, it was her secret diary, and she kept even its existence a secret. You've now read and heard it, so you know why. She felt her diary was her only real and reliable friend. You can see she treated it almost as another human being. There were only two people she trusted absolutely never to betray her – Mark and her diary. She only half trusted me, and she never trusted Tom."

"Could you tell us where Janet put her diary and when and how it was found?"

"She put it in her underwear drawer, under her knickers and bras."

"That was hardly a safe place for a document that contained what to Janet was extremely sensitive information!" Albert commented.

Jennifer laughed and looked at the female members of the Jury, who she noticed were also smiling.

"You're a man, Lord Corrigan, so I can hardly expect you to understand – but I've seen that the women on the Jury do. There is no place safer for a woman to hide something than in her underwear drawer. No other woman would dream of going through it and no man would dare attempt it."

The women in the court shared in the general laughter.

Albert smiled.

"When did you go through her underwear drawer, Jennifer?"

"It was about three years after Janet was killed."

"Why did it take so long?"

"My Dad never recovered from the murder. He refused to let us touch anything in Janet's room. We were not even allowed into it to clean it. Everything was kept exactly as it was at 8am on April 26th, 1961, when Janet left to go to work."

"What caused him to change his mind?"

"He didn't, Lord Corrigan. He died. We all believe he died of a broken heart. Janet was his favourite daughter. When he died Mum asked me to sort Janet's things out. She told me that she could not bring herself to do it. So, I boxed up her possessions, like the school exercise book we gave you for comparison, and collected all her clothes to take to a charity shop. I could not bring myself to wear them. That's when I discovered the diary."

"Did you read it?"

"I did."

"What did you do with it?"

"I sat down and cried my eyes out. Like some people here did yesterday."

"And then?"

"I kept it with me for the time when someone would seriously try to get justice for both her and Mark."

"Did you try to take it to the Police?"

"I did go and talk to Inspector Buchan – but he didn't seem to be interested."

"What did he say?"

"It's too late. I can't bring Mark Smith back to life and it won't change anything. The evidence against him at the

Fifty Years After

trial was overwhelming. There's nothing that the dead girl's diary can tell us that would be relevant."

"So you kept it, as it were, for a rainy day."

"Yes, Lord Corrigan, and Jonathan Greenway was the weatherman. Luke and I can't ever thank him and his fiancée enough for what they've done for Janet and Mark and for both our families."

"Thank you, Mrs Foster. If you wait there, Mr Harris might want to ask you some more questions."

Charles took Albert's place.

"Mrs Foster, thank you for telling us about the history of the Diary. I would like to ask you about your discussion with Inspector Buchan. How well do you remember it?"

"Quite well, My Lord – because I was disappointed at his complete lack of interest."

"Did you tell him anything about the diary's contents?"

"I told him that Philip Stewart had raped her and threatened her life the day before she was killed."

"What did he say?"

"He seemed surprised, but he said that it wasn't evidence that Philip Stewart actually killed Janet. It was a suggestion – but no more significant than if I said that Philip killed her. And – she had not made her rape complaint to the Police before she died. Unfortunately, he said, and he actually smiled when he said it, she's dead – and dead people can't make accusations against the living."

"What did you say?"

"Nothing – I was too shocked and angered by his callous attitude to me and to Janet to say anything. I simply left the Police Station without saying anything. I thought if I said what I thought about Inspector Buchan to him he would have me arrested."

"Did you let him look at the Diary?"

"No. I told him about it and offered to bring it in to show to him. He asked me to describe its contents and I did so. That's when he made his comment."

Fifty Years After

"One final question, if Lord Black will permit it, why did you give the diary to Jonathan Greenway?"

Jennifer looked at the judge, who nodded to her.

"You may answer the question, Mrs Foster."

"Luke met Jonathan and rang me to tell me that I could trust him. So I gave him Janet's diary and he gave me an enlarged and framed photo of Janet and Mark. As I said just now, I can never thank him enough for what he did. He first gave us hope and then gave us all peace. He and his fiancée are a remarkable couple. May God bless them."

The Judge heard several voices from the visitors' area say "Amen."

Charles smiled sadly at Jennifer. He knew already he had lost the case, and also knew what little chance he had depended on the Jury seeing how gracious a loser he could be.

"Thank you Mrs Foster. Can I say that everyone in the courtroom shares the feelings of loss that both you and Luke Smith must both still feel and which can only have been brought back to life during this trial."

"Thank you, Mr Harris. That helps a lot," Jennifer said.

"I can only echo what Mr Harris has just said to you and I'm sure that Lord Corrigan feels the same," Lord Black commented.

Albert nodded.

"Thank you for coming back into the witness box at such short notice. You can stand down now."

Jennifer returned to her seat in the visitor's area and Lord Black turned to look at Charles.

"Very well, Mr Harris. Address the Jury.

Charles rose, laid his papers down, and walked over to the Jury Box.

"This has been a strange case, members of the Jury. In a sense it is a case involving five people. On the Prosecution side you have four very attractive young people. Two of them were just 18 when they died and have emerged from the evidence presented here, especially what we saw yesterday afternoon as very attractive youngsters – remember in 1961 eighteen year olds were seen as children. You became an adult at 21, not 18, as it is today. Of course, the tragic nature of their early deaths and the sufferings they endured in life (because, as Mr Pickering pointed out, racism was a real issue in Britain in 1961) makes their romance gain a halo almost of sainthood. They, in another and perhaps more religious age, would have undoubtedly acquired the halo of martyrs. And then you have the two living youngsters – not much older, at 20, whose actions forced this case back to our attention. They too are an attractive couple – attractive in appearance and in their transparent honesty and the courage with which they have faced and say they still face real dangers to their lives."

Charles paused, to allow the Jury to take in what he had just said. After a minute in which he drank some water and shuffled his papers, he continued.

"On the other hand, you have my client. He is an old man now, and has spent a lifetime in the public service, but he is a flawed man, and does not come across as a particularly pleasant man. The fact that he has a title and is called Lord Stewart or Earl Stewart does not hide the fact that he comes from an ordinary background from the backstreets of North London. His use of, sometimes, inappropriate language for today's more refined taste shows that. He was a family man, but comes across as a racist and a bigot and, according to some, a serial womaniser and, possibly, rapist. He is not a nice man at all. His reaction to Janet's accusation of rape and violent physical assault from beyond the grave shows that. He said, 'after I knocked her down; as she lay unconscious, I ripped off her skirt and then pulled off her tights, tearing them as I did so. I threw her shoes down first, of course. I used her tights to bind her wrists tightly behind her back so she couldn't strike me anymore and then ripped off her flowered pants. Horrible cheap things they were – just like she was. She made herself even cheaper by copulating with a black man. They were no better than animals. Whoever killed them did the world a service.' You might think that such a man isn't worth trying to save, and I would fully understand your point of view if you do think that."

Charles paused again, drank some more water, and returned to the Jury Box.

"However, this case is not about emotion. It's about facts. The Prosecution has tried to prove that Philip is a murderer. He does not challenge the fact that he raped and assaulted Janet Brown on April 25th 1961 – but he's not charged with that. He can't be, because it is out of time. He comes across as a very unpleasant man, I agree, but was he a cold-blooded murderer? It's one thing, in a moment of red passion or rage to say to someone, 'I'll kill you if you do that again!' It's quite another thing, when the anger has gone and the passion has stilled, to carry it out. I'm sure most of you, members of the Jury, have said something similar at some point, but none of you have actually carried out the threat. Of course, you might have ended up in court if the person you threatened coincidentally was killed the next day. That is what happened with Mr Stewart. He is the third victim of this ancient crime."

Charles paused again. He looked along the line of the Jurors, who were listening intently, trying to catch the eye of each one, making them feel that he was talking to each of them individually.

"I warned you not to confuse emotion with facts, and that is what the Prosecution has been trying to do, culminating in the brilliantly produced, directed and acted rendition of what they claim is Janet Brown's diary. I have shown that the identification is not as certain as that, but, even if you believe Janet did write it, it does not prove that Philip Stewart murdered Janet Brown. At best it gives him a motive and opportunity – that's all. Put out of your mind, as well, the brilliant way in which young Belinda and Jonathan portrayed their benighted and unfortunate forebears. You saw Belinda acting and interpreting how Janet felt. You did not see Janet. You have also been told how the evidence at the 1961 trial was rigged against Mark Smith and how the jury at that trial was bribed to convict him. The Prosecution does not claim that Philip Stewart did that. We deplore what happened in June 1961, but it's not proof that Philip Stewart murdered Janet Brown. In short, the Prosecution case is one of innuendo and character assassination, not one of the careful accumulation of facts."

Charles Harris paused again, to allow the Jury to absorb his message, before reaching his conclusion.

"The 1961 Trial was unfair to Mark Smith since it deliberately obscured vital evidence. This trial has corrected that injustice. You have seen all the reports and all the available evidence. What is clear is that you're faced with the same choices as the 1961 Jury was. Either A or B murdered Janet. The Prosecution, facing the same dilemma, has made much of the fact that Mark Smith never changed his story, even though he didn't present it to the Jury in 1961. Perhaps Lord Corrigan, who defended Mark in that trial, will explain why he didn't call him to the witness box as I called Philip Stewart. Philip Stewart has also stuck to his story. What he said in 1961, he confirmed and repeated this morning. The Crown pardoned Mark Smith. You, however, may still decide that, on the basis of the evidence you've been shown that Mark Smith shot his fiancée to death as a result of a tragic accident. Perhaps he should have been spared the rope, but he still killed her. In that case you will find my client not guilty. No one seriously thinks that a third person happened to come around when Philip had gone and found Janet lying by the tree, naked and gazing at her equally naked but unconscious lover, and elected to shoot her dead. So, it comes down to two questions. Who do you believe – the living Philip Stewart or the dead Mark Smith? I don't have to prove that Philip did not kill Janet; the Prosecution has to prove that he did. I am sure you will agree that they have come a long way short of that, and so you must find my client, whether you like him or his attitudes personally or not, not guilty."

Charles sat down with relief, and Albert took his place.

"Ladies and gentlemen of the Jury, I have great sympathy for Mr Harris. Back in 1961, I had Mr Harris's task, trying to argue what I knew was a lost cause, defending a client who was not prepared to help himself. Under the circumstances, I think that Mr Harris has done a good job, but he has not convinced me and I doubt very much that he has convinced you. However, we do agree on a number of points, and I will explain these as I go along. One thing, however, I want you to put out of your mind. Unlike my client in 1961, Philip Stewart does not face the death penalty, even although Lord Black will be forced to pronounce it if you find him guilty, since this trial is held under the 1957 Homicide Act."

Albert walked over to where Jonathan and Belinda were sitting together. He turned back to look at the jury.

"Members of the Jury, the fact that we are here at all is due to the courage and tireless devotion to the pursuit of truth and justice for two long dead young people, of these two exceptional young people sitting here. They have been required to show great personal courage because their own lives have been threatened by agents of Philip Stewart, acting for him but possibly not at his instruction.

Sometimes it requires that sort of courage to right a wrong. I wish I had that sort of courage and I would like to think that I would have acted in the same way that they did – but I'll be honest with you, I very much doubt that, at the age of 20, I would have done so. They did an exceptional job in presenting Mark Smith and Janet Brown to you – but, as Mr Harris pointed out, correctly, they were not and could not be, Mark Smith and Janet Brown. Janet's diary is a very moving book, and they did it justice, but, as Mr Harris says, it is not proof of the fact that Philip Stewart murdered Janet Brown and framed Mark Smith in 1961. However, it does do several important things. It tells you about the relationship between Janet and Mark and what their hopes, dreams and plans were. They were deeply in love and planning to get married. They had faced incredible levels of hostility from everyone, including their parents. However, they still dreamed and hoped for the future – whether in Scotland or Jamaica – and it was a future together. Mark didn't know that Janet was pregnant. She never had a chance to tell him because Philip Stewart killed her before she could tell him. He did know that Philip had assaulted her the day before. Mr Harris asked me to tell you why I didn't call him to give evidence in 1961. The answer is simple. Mark surrendered. He didn't want to live without Janet. He felt he had let her down. She relied on him to protect her. She asked him to take her home and keep her company that night because she was frightened of Philip Stewart and he felt he had failed her. She was dead and he hadn't stopped her killer. He felt responsible and welcomed his death because it enabled him to go back to her and also pay for what he saw as a serious betrayal of her trust. He was Philip Stewart's second victim. Don't forget, too, that there was a third – a tiny spark of life that would have been a 49 year old man or woman now but for Philip Stewart's gunshots."

Albert walked back to his seat, sipped some water, and returned to the Jury.

"So the Diary shows us that Mark would never have deliberately shot at and killed Janet. Did he do so by accident, as Philip Stewart claims? This is where the suppressed parts of the police and forensic reports come in. Philip's story is that he thought that Mark was raping Janet. That was a clever bit of invention for 1961. Remember Janet told us that her employer, Mrs Taylor, automatically assumed that her first rapist was a black boy and commented how black males were always raping white females, until Janet told her that it was a white boy and she found excuses for him. However, gentlemen of the Jury, if you're inclined to believe the stereotype of black males, ask your female colleagues if a rapist or a woman who was having consensual sex with her lover would carefully fold their clothes and put them in a neat pile as they took (or had them taken) off. You all read the transcript of the 1961 trial, which formed part of the background evidence of this trial. There you will see that I pointed out that Mark was left-handed but that the gun was placed in his right hand. There was no evidence that Mark had a gun in his possession when P C Adams saw him, and Luke Smith confirms that Mark never had a gun nor did he belong to a shooting club. I will return to the gun in a moment. There is one final point about Mark Smith. He never gave evidence in court in 1961, but D I Buchan read his evidence out. Despite being put under enormous pressure to confess (he was interviewed naked and was beaten up by four officers) he did not change his story, and he did not accuse Philip Stewart of killing Janet, even though he knew of the threat that Philip had made. He told the truth – he didn't know who killed her because Philip had knocked him out before he shot Janet."

Albert paused again, repeating the same trick that Charles had tried with the Jury.

"Ladies and gentlemen of the Jury, it is clear that Mark Smith did not shoot Janet Brown with the gun produced in

Fifty Years After

court as the murder weapon. He would not have shot her deliberately, even if he had a gun, and could not have shot her accidentally. Philip Stewart alleges that Janet was trying to get up when she was killed, but the forensic evidence states that she was probably laying on her back on the ground. However bad a shot you are, you cannot, at three yards, fire two shots at an upright man, miss him, and hit the prone body of a woman lying on the ground behind him. I have never fired a gun in my life, but I know that even I would not be able to do that!"

There was a murmur of amusement among the jury, and Albert smiled. He knew he had them in the palm of his hand.

"We can't reverse the physical fact that Mark Smith was hanged, but legally it never happened either. I agree that there is no **C** in this case. The killer is either Mark Smith or Philip Stewart. Neither we, nor the defence, pretend otherwise. There is no unknown third person involved. The third person was the tragic figure of Janet Brown. We have shown that it was not Mark Smith, who fired the fatal shots, so it must, by definition, have been Philip Stewart. However, that is not enough for you to convict Philip. I agree with Mr Harris that we have to do more than this – we have to show that he did it. You need three things to establish a murder – means, opportunity and motivation.

"Did Philip Stewart have the **means**? Yes, he did. Forensic testing has shown that the gun was one used in previous crimes by the North London Crime Syndicate known as the Stewart Family Gang. They are, of course, not on trial here, but the fact that the gun was one used by them ties it in with the Stewart family and so with Philip Stewart, the son of the leader of that gang, his father, Jack Stewart. But, of course, Philip Stewart betrayed prior knowledge of the gun when he corrected the pathologist, when he said the gun had not been fully loaded. How did he know that? He could only have known it if he had handled it that day. He refused to take the opportunity of explaining how he had gained this knowledge. I suggest to you that he knew because he took it with him, as he said he intended to do to intimidate Janet and Mark, and, having changed his mind for some reason, fired the three shots: two at Janet, to kill her; and one into the grass, to implicate Mark.

"Did he have **motive**? He certainly had motive. He hated and still hates black people. He denigrated Mark's country of origin, Jamaica, calling it Bongobongoland, and insulted the Nigerian pathologist who gave evidence by calling him Mr Ade-Bongo instead of Mr Adewuni. White racists, however, hate one group of people more than they hate black people – that is white people who consort with or support black people. Janet Brown had a black boyfriend. That was enough for him. Lord Stewart showed his attitude when he condemned Jonathan for falling in love with Belinda rather than a white girl.

"However, Janet had done more – she had spurned him. Janet committed the ultimate sin as far as Philip Stewart was concerned – she had humiliated him twice: once by rejecting him outright and once by choosing a black boy before him. He punished her by beating her and raping her and then, after warning her, shot her dead, like the animal he claimed she was. Why didn't he shoot Mark as well? I don't know, because I've never asked him, but my guess is that he believed that a double shooting would bring 'the third man' into play, which would involve a full police investigation of his involvement. Philip provided a complete case, murder victim and murderer, and let the state carry out his second murder for him. Ironically he and Mark shared a common purpose here. Suicide is a sin in the eyes of Christians and Mark did not want to commit suicide – so he allowed the state to kill him.

Fifty Years After

"Finally, did Philip Stewart have the **opportunity**? Yes, he admitted that he followed the two of them and knew where they were going. As a result, he was able to collect his gun and ambush them. His cover story of the post-prandial walk is almost an insult to our intelligence."

Albert walked away and turned to face the ashen faced Philip Stewart.

"Members of the Jury, two people stand in that dock. One is alive and the other is a ghostly figure. One of them killed Janet Brown. There is no third figure there. Mark Smith did not kill Janet Brown either deliberately or accidentally. Philip Stewart killed Janet Brown deliberately and cold bloodedly, and equally cold bloodedly consigned Mark Smith to the gallows, assisted by the corrupt and criminal police officer in charge of the case, Detective Inspector Alasdair Buchan and the resources of a powerful crime syndicate headed by Philip Stewart's father, Jack Stewart. The blood of three innocent victims cries out for justice. It is your duty and privilege to give it to them."

Albert returned to his seat and sat down. He swallowed the rest of the water in his glass and put his arms approvingly around the shoulders of his two assistants.

Lord Black looked at the clock and at the Jury.
"I'm going to give you an early finish today. Please be back here at 10 am to hear my directions and then I'm going to send you out to consider your verdict. I would suggest that you bring your belongings from the hotel but leave them in the coach. Have a good night and remember that you are not to discuss this case among yourselves or with anyone else. If anyone else does try to speak to you about it call one of your escorting officers and let him or her know immediately."

And so the fourth day of the trial drew to a close.

30. The final day

September 24 2010
The action in Court One was over for the day, but it continued elsewhere. The Jury members were surprised to be taken to a totally different hotel for the night. They had been given no warning but were reassured when their police officer escort assured them the Judge not only knew about the change, but he had organised it and their possessions had been moved to their new rooms by their escort team in the course of the morning.

"If you find anything to be missing, please let one of us know, and we will go and get it for you," the officer told them.

This reassured them, and they settled down for a journey to a small country hotel south of Bromley, in Kent.

Meanwhile, Gethin was a very loud mouthed individual who was in their former hotel, telling anyone who cared to listen that he was the foreman of the Lord Philip Stewart Trial Jury and airing his views about the guilt or otherwise of the Defendant. Susan and Thomas, acting as two Jury members, ostentatiously tried to shut him up, but only made things worse. They all noticed, without apparently doing so, a white male in his fifties, watching them and listening intently from a corner of the room. Once they were convinced they had his full attention, Susan and Thomas noisily left Gethin to finish his drink, saying they were turning in since it was an important day tomorrow. Gethin remained invitingly alone by the bar, drinking his beer, mutely inviting the man who was watching him to come and join him. After watching him for fifteen minutes to check that the other two were not returning, the man wandered over to the bar and sat down beside Gethin. He called the barman and told him to get him a beer and also refill Gethin's glass. Gethin thanked him and asked his name.

"I'm called Bert," the man said. "I'm from North London. Who are you?"

"I'm Gethin," Gethin replied. "I'm normally a public service worker, but I'm tied up with some very hush-hush stuff at the moment. Just between us, I'm the foreman of the Jury trying a murder case at the Old Bailey, trying a real Lord can you believe?"

The man looked impressed.

"Really. Do you mean you're on the Lord Stewart case?"

"The very same," Gethin said triumphantly, puffing up his chest to show his importance.

"Did he do it?" Bert asked.

"Not a chance," said Gethin. "The Blackie did it like they always said he did."

"I agree," Bert said. "These Blacks come over here and think they can get away with anything."

Gethin nodded.

"They won't get away with anything with me – but I'm worried that we've got too many women on the Jury. They're too soft and they've been taken in by that young black girl the Prosecutor's been using."

Gethin finished his glass and put it on the bar, looking pointedly at its empty state. His companion nodded to the barman to refill it, paid, pushed the glass over and got down to business.

"I have friends, Gethin, who would like to help you convince your colleagues."

"Why?" Gethin asked.

"Like you they feel that Black people should stay in Black lands, not come over here taking our homes and jobs and raping our women. They're prepared to put in an investment in ensuring a hard working Lord is not destroyed by these foreign interlopers."

Gethin leaned towards the man in a confidential manner.

Fifty Years After

"Are you suggesting what I think you're suggesting?" he asked.

"It depends on what you think I'm suggesting."

Gethin pretended to consider his answer.

"I'm thinking twelve brown envelopes containing currency notes," he said finally.

"It's a possibility," the man conceded. "How many notes are you thinking?"

"I heard," said Gethin, "that in 1961 the Jury members were given the equivalent of 10 weeks' wages. Something like that would be acceptable."

The man did some quick calculation, and came up with a figure of £5000 each, or £60000 in total.

"I think three big ones," he said.

"That's not enough. We could all go to prison if we're caught. Ten large ones would be better."

"Four?"

"Five, and not a penny less."

"Okay," the man said, "Be down here at 7.30 tomorrow morning. I'll give you 12 envelopes each with ten £500 notes in. Pass them around the jurors at breakfast so they can put them in their bags and avoid the search – and ensure they vote not guilty tomorrow. Don't make the decision too quickly. Spend an hour or two in discussion to give the impression that you considered the case thoroughly."

Gethin nodded, and the man slipped away. Two minutes later he had disappeared. Gethin went into the Hall, found a quiet spot, opened his phone and texted a message to Thomas.

"Got him. £5000 at 7.30am tomorrow – bar. 12 envelopes."

Moments later a reply came back.

"Thanks – see you then."

Charles and Albert went straight back to their homes. Both of them felt tired after their exertions of the week. Lord Black read through his notes and began to draft his words

Fifty Years After

for the next morning. The real Jurors settled into their second hotel of the week and Belinda and Jonathan went home to Blackheath, where they enjoyed a romantic evening together, relaxing for the first time that week. Marcus anxiously asked Evelyn how the trial had gone, and she tried to reassure him that he had been kept out of it all, except for one thing.

"What was that?" Marcus asked.

"Albert managed to get Philip Stewart to say he had told you that Mark killed Janet a day or two before the execution took place."

"That was very clever of Albert," Marcus commented, relieved.

"Yes, that's exactly what I thought," Evelyn confirmed.

In Belmarsh Prison, Philip received a text message from 'Bert' on his illegally acquired mobile phone, confirming that the approach had been made and a suitable deal struck up with the foreman of the Jury. Philip texted the word "thanks" and fell asleep, much relieved in his mind. The job was done. That night he dreamed of the vengeance he would take against Jonathan and Belinda.

Next morning in the empty bar of a Central London hotel a man was arrested by three police officers for attempting to bribe the Jury of the Philip Stewart Trial. They put him in a Police Van and drove him to Lewisham Police Station, where Superintendent Julia Donaldson was very interested to meet him. She was expecting a significant number of other "guests" as well to turn up since she had authorised a series of simultaneous raids at certain addresses across North London. These all took place at 6 am. She and her augmented team settled down for a long day of interviews, interrupted by an expected trip to East Central London to hear the verdict of the Stewart Trial, about which she now had no doubt. In Malaga, Timothy Stewart was scanning the British newspapers and the BBC's 24 Hours news programme to find the outcome of the trial, while also

Fifty Years After

handling the day to day business of the Spanish Franchise, which, that day, included a large bank robbery in Seville.

Lord Black entered Number One Court and surveyed its members for what he hoped was the next to last time. The Court was full again. He was delighted that his foresight had not only prevented jury bribing, but had also brought the intended perpetrator to book. He knew that whatever verdict the Jury came up with, it would be a fair verdict, even if he thought it was the wrong verdict. He sat down and turned towards the Jury.

"Members of the Jury, this has been a unique case, in that we are trying a crime that was committed nearly half a century ago and for which a man was hanged in July 1961. I cannot recall a similar case or one in which the cause of justice was so gravely and brazenly perverted by an officer of the law. We will probably never know why Detective Inspector Buchan did what he did, or what he hoped to achieve by it, but, although its consequences were devastating, not least for Mark Smith, it is not a relevant issue for this trial. You have been shown the transcripts of that earlier trial and you have seen all the reports in their original form and all the evidence that survives appertaining to that terrible event on April 26th 1961, when two young lives were destroyed and a third prevented from coming into existence.

"The question you have to answer, is a familiar one in detective fiction – 'Whodunit'? You have three possibilities for the murderer of Janet Brown – the man originally convicted and hanged in 1961 – her fiancé, Mark Smith; the man accused by the Prosecution and on trial here – Lord Philip Stewart; and the unnamed and unknown outsider – the proverbial tramp of detective fiction. You have to decide in what direction the evidence points.

"You have to consider the original police report from P C Adams, the forensic report from James Arthur and that

Fifty Years After

on the gun from Adeloye Adewuni; the statements of the two men involved; and, of course, the diary of Janet Brown. Be careful with the diary. It tells you a great deal about the tragic story of Janet and Mark, a modern Romeo and Juliet, if ever there was one, but it does not constitute evidence that Philip Stewart murdered Janet. At most Janet Brown is a witness **before** the fact. She is not and cannot be a witness **to** the fact because the fact was that she was murdered and dead people cannot speak for themselves.

"You must sift the evidence and decide what weight to put on each part of it and you must include in that what you have heard in this court from Lord Stewart, as the only person who was present that day who survives. You must decide how likely his story is and also, if you don't think he was telling the truth, what was his reason for not doing so. You may consider the difference in nature between the statements of the two principles. As Lord Corrigan said to you – Mark Smith said he didn't know who killed Janet Brown, but he knew he hadn't; whereas Philip Stewart said, and repeated yesterday, Mark Smith shot his fiancée by accident. Here too you need to consider the reports of P C Adams and James Arthur. Would a rapist have neatly folded and piled up Janet's clothes and his own clothes? Would a left-handed man fire a gun with his right? Was it possible for Mark, however bad a shot he was, to have fired at and missed a standing Philip Stewart at not much more than 3 feet with such disastrous results to a woman lying on the ground behind him?

"I said that there were three possible murderers in this case and you have two charges and two possible verdicts. We're not in Scotland, so you cannot say Not Proven. Philip Stewart is either guilty or not guilty. The second charge (perjury) is a serious one, but I want you to ignore it. Concentrate on the question I asked you – who killed Janet Brown? You have three possibilities.

1. If you think it was Mark Smith, despite his pardon, you find Philip Stewart not guilty of both charges,

because he told the truth and telling the truth is neither perjury nor a perversion of the course of justice.
2. If you think that Philip Stewart killed Janet Brown, you must find him guilty on both counts, because he plainly lied when he accused Mark of killing his fiancée.
3. If however, you think that neither man killed Janet Brown, but she was coincidentally attacked and killed by the proverbial visiting tramp, who was just passing by when presumably Mark was unconscious, Philip was fetching the police and Janet was lying about naked doing nothing in particular in the evening April sun, then you must find Philip Stewart not guilty on the first count (that of murder) and guilty of the second (perjury) because in that case he lied when he said he saw Mark shoot Janet by mistake."

Lord Black paused to sip water from a glass before concluding.

"The Usher will take you out to the Jury Room and you will first elect a foreman from among your number and then consider your verdict. You must reach a verdict that all twelve of you agree upon. Remember that the relevant criterion is that you must be convinced beyond all reasonable doubt, not that you have to be 100% certain."

The Jury spent the next two hours deliberating because three of the members were not convinced of Philip's guilt. The rest waited in different places but all nervously. Only Philip felt certain of the verdict, being convinced that his team had bought the Jury. Lord Black spent lunchtime looking for a black cap and a card with the traditional words of the sentence on.

"If you're going to do something, do it properly," he thought.

Fifty Years After

After the last doubter announced his change of mind the Jury Chairman polled each member individually on the two questions. They were unanimous that he was guilty on both counts. She picked up the phone and called the Usher.

"We have our verdict," she said.

Fifteen minutes later, the Court reconvened.

The Clerk of the Court ordered Philip and the Jury Chairman to stand. He spoke to her.

"Have you reached a verdict upon which all of you are agreed?"

"Yes," she replied.

"On Count One – that he murdered Janet Brown by shooting her, do you find the defendant, Philip Stewart, guilty or not guilty?"

"Guilty."

"And is that the decision of you all?"

"Yes."

"On Count Two – that he committed perjury and perverted the course of justice by claiming that he saw Mark Smith shoot Janet Brown – do you find Philip Stewart guilty or not guilty?'

"Guilty."

"And is that the decision of you all?"

"Yes."

The Clerk told them both to sit down and he handed a sheet of paper with the verdict to Lord Black who began to speak.

"Before pronouncing the sentence, I want to say a word about the two young people sitting beside Lord Corrigan. Both Lord Corrigan and Mr Harris and others have commented on the courage and determination that Jonathan Greenway and Belinda Thompson showed. By their own efforts, supported by Lord Corrigan and Luke Smith and Jennifer Foster they have brought a thoroughly evil individual to justice and reversed a monstrous act of injustice perpetrated in this Court 50 years ago. Lord Stewart, please stand up."

Philip stood.

"As I told your Counsel at the outset of this trial, the crime was committed in 1961 when the law was the Homicide Act of 1957 which laid down death by hanging for murder with a firearm. However, the Abolition Act of 1969 abolished capital punishment for murder, and later, for all remaining capital crimes, while EU law prevents any EU member state from reinstating it. So, I am obliged to pass a sentence while knowing it will not be carried out."

Lord Black put the black cap on his head.

"Philip Stewart you have been found guilty by this court of the capital murder of Janet Brown. This court rules that you shall be taken from hence to the place from whence you came and thence to a place of execution where you shall be hanged by the neck until you be dead and may God have mercy on your soul."

He took the cap off and put the card down, and then spoke less formally to Philip.

"I shall be referring this sentence to the Home Secretary for confirmation, in the certain knowledge that he will commute it. On the second charge I sentence you to fifteen years in prison, to run concurrently with the life sentence that I expect the Home Secretary will commute your death sentence to. I recommend that, in view of your advanced age, a tariff of fifteen years should be set before you become eligible for parole. I understand, however, that more charges are likely to be laid against you, and this may affect the tariff that I have set."

He looked across at Charles Harris.

"Do you understand the situation, Mr Harris?"

"Yes, My Lord."

"Very well. Take the prisoner down," he ordered.

Thirty minutes later Julia, Luke and Jennifer were addressing reporters on the steps of the Court Building, expressing their relief that at last, after 50 years, justice had finally been done and seen to be done in the case of Janet Brown and Mark Smith.

Fifty Years After

Part Four

Death comes as the end (2010 to 2012)

Life is a tale told by an idiot, full of sound and fury, signifying nothing.
(Macbeth Act 5 Scene 5)

Fifty Years After

31. The end of the Stewart Gang.

Autumn and winter 2010 – 2011
That afternoon 'Bert' appeared before a magistrate to answer the charge of attempting to pervert the course of justice by means of bribing a jury. Gethin, Thomas and Susan gave evidence of his arrest and he was remanded in custody on the application of the Prosecution who feared he might abscond.

Jonathan and Belinda spent the afternoon in a mild celebration with their parents, Albert, Juliet, Evelyn and Luke and Jennifer. They were all relieved that the fifty years' long struggle to get justice for Janet and Mark had been successfully completed, but nether Jonathan, nor Belinda, nor Albert nor even Evelyn were so naïf as to assume the battle was over. Albert did not think Charles would appeal, but he did know that the wave of arrests that had happened that morning meant a lot of work and a new trial. He was prepared to finish the job of dismantling the Stewart Family Gang by prosecuting this final trial. He assumed he would again be facing Charles Harris. Jonathan and Belinda knew that their trials were not over either, and would never be so long as Timothy Stewart was free. They knew there was a contract out on them and realised that they could never relax their guard. As Albert told them, "One moment's lapse of concentration could be fatal." He suggested that they should ask the police if they could microchip their bodies, in a similar way to the way some pets were micro chipped.

"If you do that," he said to them, "the police will always be able to find you if you suddenly go missing. It could save your lives."

They thought about this and discussed it together, and with their parents and Jonathan's Grandparents. Eventually they agreed that the potential loss of freedom was worth it for the enhanced security it gave them, and allowed the police to perform the operation.

In the House of Lords, the Speaker accepted a motion to strip Lord Stewart of his membership and to petition the Queen to strip him of his title. The Leader of the House announced the verdict of the trial and the motion was passed unanimously without debate. A week later Lord Stewart's title was rescinded.

Two days after the trial ended Julia rang Jonathan and asked him to come into Lewisham Police Station to see her. He did so next day.

"I've got a job for you – one you like. Despite what I said to you earlier, I want you to do a bit more sleuthing for me."

"What do you want me to find out?"

"My team are up to their necks in work preparing to bring the Stewarts to Court, and Alfred is tied up in the process. For completion, and for your protection incidentally, we want to identify the name that Timothy Stewart is living and travelling under. We know he lives in Malaga and we suspect he has a Spanish passport and possibly a Spanish name."

Julia gave Jonathan a sheet of A4.

"This is a list of flights to Malaga and Madrid on the evening when Timothy accosted you and Belinda. I want you to use your I T skills to get the passenger lists and try to track down the identity he was travelling under."

"May I ask my friend, the Hacker, to help if it proves beyond my skills?" Jonathan asked.

"You haven't heard me say 'yes'," Julia replied, with a twinkle in her eyes. "I can't be seen to condone crime and hacking is a crime."

"Thank you, Superintendent," Jonathan replied. "I will do what I can and bear in mind what you haven't told me not to do."

Fifty Years After

They both laughed as Jonathan turned to go and Julia returned to her files.

Later that afternoon, Jonathan rang Harry Mackintosh and asked for his help. Harry arrived at Jonathan and Belinda's flat two hours later and, after eating a late lunch at Belinda's insistence, settled down with the two of them.

"How can I help you, and is it legal?" he asked, smiling.

"Superintendent Donaldson told me, unofficially, I could call on you if I needed to. She set me the task."

"Which is?"

"To find the name used by the man who has threatened to throw us into the sea and drown us if Philip Stewart went down, as he has."

"Of course I'll help you under those circumstances! What do you have?"

"I have a list of the evening flights to Malaga and Madrid on that day."

"Where does your man live?"

"In Malaga."

"Then forget the Madrid flights. We'll concentrate on Malaga. How many flights were there?"

"Just one – leaving from Gatwick at 2100."

Harry smiled as he unpacked and set up his laptop.

"This should be easy. What are you looking for?"

"The passenger list in the first place."

Harry began to work on his laptop. It took him an hour and a half, but at the end of that time he had a printed list of names and addresses. He and Jonathan studied them intently.

"Most of these were English holiday makers by the look of it – mainly families or couples. Two look as though they were businessmen and probably need to be checked out since they were men travelling alone. There were six Spanish passengers – or people with Spanish names. Four of them are two couples, and so are excluded.

That leaves just two unaccompanied males – Pedro Castanos and Fernando Dos Santos. I suspect your man is one of those."

"Can you narrow it down?"

Harry nodded and returned to his laptop. After another half hour he sighed with satisfaction.

"I was right. The two single Englishmen are bona fide businessmen, resident in UK. One comes from Horsham in Sussex and the other from Crawley, also in Sussex. Now we'll tackle the more difficult part – the Spanish pair. Belinda, could you be a Darling and make me a cup of tea?"

Belinda did as Harry asked and realised afterwards that it was a waste of electricity, time and a tea bag as Harry was so absorbed that he forgot about his tea, and only remembered when it was cold. He drank it anyway, apologetically.

"I think I've found your man. I will do a further check – but I've located Pedro Castanos. He is a student of around your age, so scarcely your sixty year old man."

Belinda made Harry a second cup of tea and this time made him drink it while it was still hot. He did as he was told and briefly talked with Belinda and Jonathan explaining how he had tracked down Pedro Castanos.

"Now I have to do the same for Fernando Dos Santos," he said, resuming his search.

It took another half hour before he gave a satisfied grunt and uttered the words, "Gotcha, you Bastard." He gave the other two a triumphant grin and returned to his search. Finally, he asked for a sheet of paper and wrote down a name and a Malaga address on it.

"There's your man," he said. "He's 67 years old and lives at the address I've given you. He travelled over earlier in the year and returned a week later. He returned to UK a week before he accosted you. He's definitely your man."

Jonathan thanked Harry before ringing Julia to give her the name and address. Jonathan and Belinda took Harry

Fifty Years After

down to the Prince of Wales for a celebration drink, and Julia began the process of securing a European Arrest Warrant for Timothy Stewart, alias Fernando Dos Santos, who received a very unwelcome visit from the Malaga Police a week later. With the Gang leader under arrest and investigation, the Spanish Franchise rapidly disintegrated, as the Spanish police began to arrest members and others tried to save themselves by voluntarily handing themselves in and testifying against their former colleagues.

In England and in Spain the judicial systems began their inexorable and slow grind towards bringing the miscreants to book and ending years of violent and almost unsolvable crime. Two days after the arrest of Timothy Stewart, Julia sent Thomas to Malaga to talk to the Spanish authorities about who had the jurisdiction to try him. The Spanish public prosecutor pointed out that Stewart's crimes in Spain were more serious, long term and varied than his criminal career in UK; at least since he arrived in Malaga in 1980. Thomas thought that this was a fair point, and, subject to the D P P agreeing in UK, concurred. They reached a tentative agreement that the Spanish Court would be informed of the British charges outstanding against Timothy Stewart and hoped that the Court would take account of them in deciding what punishment to impose.

"There's one thing I think I can assure you of, Sergeant Skinner," the Spanish Prosecutor said, "You are unlikely to ever see Mr Stewart answer charges in a British Court. The number and variety of the charges against him here mean that he will get the maximum sentence for each offence. Each offence is separately sentenced and the various sentences run consecutively. Senor Stewart is likely to face a cumulative sentence in excess of one thousand years for all the crimes he has committed or caused to be committed. Would you like us to add an additional ninety for the threats against your Prime Minister and your two twenty year old helpers?"

Thomas laughed.

"You can, I'm sure, but I doubt he will get around to serving the sentences, since they will be tagged on to the end!"

The Prosecutor also laughed, before, putting his arm around Thomas's shoulder, he steered him towards the nearest bar, saying, "Come, my friend, let's go and celebrate our agreement in the traditional British way."

One week later, Julia rang Malaga to confirm that the British Director of Public Prosecutions had confirmed the agreement between Thomas and the Spanish Prosecutor.

Sir Marcus continued to hold on to his office as Prime Minister, despite his own reservations as to the future. The concession that Albert had forcibly wrung from an unwilling Philip Stewart in Court One gave him a breathing space, and Julia's team had yet to focus on his and the other politicians' roles in the cover up of the Stewart Family Gang's crimes. By the time of the Conservative Party Conference in October, he felt positively upbeat. His Conference speech was widely praised and his Government could boast about an improving economic outlook. Even the Tory Euro Sceptics were keeping quiet for once. The only cloud on the horizon was in Afghanistan where British troops were in daily conflict with Islamist terrorists and suffering continual losses, with the result that the British public were increasingly turning against the war and blaming him for getting them involved in it. The Defence Minister warned him that the situation was getting desperate since there was a shortage of suitable equipment and a downturn in recruitment to the Army and Air Force.

"What do you want me to do, Jim?" Marcus asked.

"Give me more money, Marcus. Let me equip our brave men and women properly."

"Talk to Marion," Marcus advised him. "She's the one who will have to find any additional funds."

Meanwhile, in Lahore, two men dressed in white Arab robes were deep in conversation.

"We need to do something dramatic, Saleem," one said.

"What are you thinking of, Asif?" Saleem asked.

"I think we need to think of the assassination of a high level target or targets," Asif replied.

"Do you have any suggestions, Saleem?"

His companion sat silently, cross-legged on the rug he used as a chair. Eventually he spoke.

"I can think of three enemies of Islam; may Allah curse them for ever."

"Who have you in mind?" Asif asked.

"President Kent of the USA, President Le Saux of France and Prime Minister Greenway of Britain. They've all done us great damage and boasted of it. It's time we showed their people that our reach is long."

Asif smiled grimly.

"Such an action would be a strong warning to the West – but it takes careful planning. I will set up three small teams to study the operation, one for each target. When I have their reports, I will come back to you, Saleem."

Back in Blackheath, Belinda and Jonathan were in the final stages of planning their wedding. Study plans were set aside as the wedding dominated all their thinking, even with the help of Evelyn, and their two mothers. Just before they were due to leave for Scotland a Wedding Card arrived in a registered envelope. This surprised the young couple since they thought the precaution taken to ensure the card's safe arrival was a tad excessive. They changed their minds when they opened the envelope. The card was from Luke and Jennifer (to which they had added the names of Janet and Mark) and included two return tickets for a flight to Jamaica following the wedding and a receipted booking for one week in a five-star hotel in Kingston (Jamaica).

Fifty Years After

"They've given us a honeymoon, Darling. That's what they've done," Belinda exclaimed. "I must telephone them to thank them."

She immediately put her words into action. She spoke to Luke.

"Luke," she said. "It's Belinda. Jonathan and I have received your card and your gift. It wasn't necessary and you two shouldn't have done it."

"Don't be silly, Belinda. You and Jonathan risked your lives to get justice for two families you'd never met, but who suffered at the hands of Jonathan's family. Of course you both deserve it! Without you, there would have been no trial and Philip Stewart would still be walking free – free to kill again. It's the least we can do. You both deserve much more. Go and enjoy yourselves in Mark's and my homeland."

A large party gathered for the wedding. Only the immediate family went to the Blacksmith's, but a much larger number of guests, both the invited ones and the villagers, went to the Church Blessing. The Hotel put up a marquee for their Reception and Jonathan, who had chosen Harry to be his Best Man, was delighted that everything worked out as well as they could have wished. He and Belinda went to bed that night, exhausted, but happy. Belinda dreamed that Janet and Mark came to her and hugged her, thanking her and Jonathan for reuniting them and giving them peace at last. Belinda told Jonathan about her dream when they woke up. He was deeply moved and, at breakfast, toasted them.

"To Janet and Mark," he said, raising his glass of fruit juice, "May their spirits rest in peace."

The next day they left Glasgow Airport to fly to Kingston, where they had a memorable holiday. All they had to do was enjoy the sunshine and each other. When they returned Evelyn commented that she couldn't tell the difference between Jonathan's normally pink skin and Belinda's brown skin.

Fifty Years After

The autumn and winter months were dominated by the Stewart trials. The first trial was that of the intended Jury Fixer. He refused to say who had given him his orders and was sentenced to ten years' imprisonment in a very short trial. The main trial, prosecuted by Albert Corrigan and presided over by the Recorder of London, lasted six weeks. Charles Harris represented Philip Stewart as best he could, but the other fifteen defendants had their own lawyers. It was a complicated trial with some harrowing evidence, with the main witness for the Prosecution being Albert Campion. Five of the fifteen defendants pleaded guilty and turned Queen's Evidence against the others in exchange for a reduced sentence. Philip Stewart remained defiant, denying all knowledge of the offences with which he was charged. Tom, the leader of the Cambridge Kidnap gang gave evidence against Philip as well. All fifteen were found guilty and the combined sentences for the fifteen defendants came to over 300 years in total. As foreseen by Lord Black, the Judge increased the tariff on Philip's life sentence to a whole life tariff, in view of the number and severity of his crimes and the total lack of remorse that he showed for his victims' sufferings. At roughly the same time the Spanish Franchise also came to trial and, as foretold by the Prosecutor, most of them received sentences, which meant they would die in prison.

Timothy Stewart was sentenced to 1400 years in jail. Both courts ordered that all the Stewart assets should be seized. Timothy Stewart refused to withdraw the contracts he had placed on Albert Campion, Sir Marcus Greenway and Jonathan and Belinda. However, as he lacked the ability to pay for the services he required, the intended targets considered that it was unlikely that the contracts would be carried out. Albert Campion, however, relocated, with police assistance and a new name, to a village in Northern Yorkshire. Subsequent events proved him to be wise as the children of the Stewart gangsters began to search for him.

32. The Final Curtain

Spring and Summer 2012

2012 turned out to be a very bad year for Philip Stewart as he contemplated the first of what promised to be an endless series of years in one or other maximum-security prison. He quickly learned the truth that no prisoner likes a rapist and no member of a minority ethnic community likes a white racist. In a unique way, Philip Stewart's crimes united the whole prison population, prisoner and prison officer alike, against him. While he was on trial for his crimes, he was relatively safe, although he still had the occasional 'accident' in the shower. However, when the second trial was over, the atmosphere within the prison became increasingly menacing. Especially hostile were prisoners who had been part of the Young Gang. Things came to a head during a hot and sticky day in July 2012. It was a day when the officers in the block where Philip Stewart was held suddenly decided to lay down tools and go to a union meeting in the afternoon. Unaccountably, they forgot to lock the prisoners in their cells before they left. However, they did remember to lock up the block.

Ten minutes after the officers left the block, two burly prisoners, formerly Young Gang members, came for Philip Stewart. He was lying on his bed as they entered his cell.

"Get on your feet, you cunt," the older of the two said, dragging him from the bed.

"You're a disgrace to the prison uniform we all wear," the younger said. "I feel ashamed just seeing you in it. Take it off."

Philip was in no mood to cooperate. He shook his head. The next moment Philip was bent over his bed as one of the men dragged his shoes, socks and trousers off him as the other held his arms behind his back. Philip had barely recovered from this assault on his dignity when he was jerked upright again and the younger man unbuttoned his

Fifty Years After

blue prison shirt. Seconds later, Philip was once again face down, and bent over his bunk, as his shirt was ripped off his back and his wrists were bound tightly behind his back.

"Are you going to rape me?" he asked.

"No, we're going to kill you," replied the older man. "You ordered your gang to kill my old man. I've dreamed of repaying you in kind. Now it's my turn."

They dragged him from his cell, and paraded him before the other prisoners, stripped to his underpants, and with his wrists bound behind his back. The men crowded in behind him as he was forced towards the shower cubicles. Once there, Philip's two captors turned him round to face the others.

"See the rapist and Racist Murderer," the older man said. "He raped and shot an 18 year old pregnant girl to death because she was white skinned and going out with a black boy, who was also 18. Then he fitted up the black boy with his crime and watched him hang for it. The Judge condemned him to death. Does anyone disagree?"

Silence was the only answer. Philip looked around him in terror. He realised what was going to happen to him when he saw the rope in the hands of one of his guards. A prisoner secured the rope around Philip's neck and another two prisoners forced him onto a chair. The rope was thrown around one of the pipes, made taut, and secured. Then they stepped back and watched as a trembling Philip stood on the chair, virtually naked and bound, with the noose around his neck.

"We should tie his legs as well," one of the prisoners commented. "That's the way they always did it."

"You're right, Bill," said the man who had seized Philip. "Someone fetch some more rope and tie it around the bastard's ankles."

Philip helplessly watched one of the prisoners disappear briefly, only to return with a length of skipping rope.

"Will this do, Jack?" he asked.

"It's good enough, Tom," Jack replied, taking the rope and tightly binding Philip's ankles with it.

Jack stood back, and spoke to the helpless Philip.

"Does the condemned man have any last words?" Jack asked. "Say something to make us remember you by or to make us laugh."

Philip wanted to spit his defiance at them. He wanted to keep talking so that the officers would come back and save him, although he realised that no one was coming to save him. He now understood only too well why the officers had suddenly decided to hold a meeting and had neglected to secure the block by locking them in their cells. He shook his head.

"Very well then, have it your own way," Jack said, and suddenly pulled the chair away from Philip's feet. Philip's body dropped slightly as his weight pulled the rope downwards before coming to rest about six inches above the floor, swaying to and fro and making a gurgling noise.

The other prisoners all turned their backs on the dying, choking man, slowly strangling in the rope that attached him to the pipes, and returned to their cells. When the prison officers returned to the block after their meeting, they found Philip hanging and called a doctor, who pronounced him dead. A subsequent investigation of the circumstances failed to find anyone who had seen what happened and who could identify the culprit. As a result, every inmate of that block had five days deducted from their remission as a punishment for their sudden fit of blindness. No action was taken against the prison officers for their oversight in not locking the prisoners in their cells before going to their meeting. Philip's body was taken down and buried in the prison graveyard because no church or municipal graveyard would take him. He was buried in the grave where Mark's body once lay. When Lord Black read about it in his newspaper he remembered

Fifty Years After

his words to Charles Harris during the trial and felt that his warning had been fully justified and his words grimly fulfilled. When Timothy heard of it later in his prison in Madrid, he reissued his contract against Bert, Marcus, Jonathan and Belinda, in the vain hope that someone would carry out the hit. Not even the Stewart Gang children, absorbed in their hunt for Albert Campion, had any interest in the other three.

Life was sweet for Belinda and Jonathan. They returned to the ordered life of the classroom, albeit at a distance from their University. Jonathan took his finals in May and June, obtaining a 2:1, which he felt was brilliant given the circumstances, before being present when Belinda passed her first examination by producing a daughter, whom they named Janet Belinda, and whom Evelyn was convinced resembled Jonathan more than Belinda. Belinda took her final exams at home, under special supervision, and, like her husband, gained a proud 2:1. With Albert Corrigan's help, she was signed on in an inn of court and began to train to be a solicitor. Jonathan worked in a major merchant bank as an I T consultant, where he once again teamed up with Harry Mackintosh. Little Janet grew quickly and was threatening to crawl by the time Christmas came around. After a lot of discussion, they decided that they would baptise their daughter at Easter 2013, and invited Harry, Luke and Jennifer to be her godparents.

Belinda and Jonathan completed the biography of Sir Marcus at the end of August 2012 and presented the draft to Evelyn and Marcus. Evelyn was happy with their work.

"You've done a brilliant job on a difficult subject," she said.

Marcus was not so sure.

"Why have you stopped at the end of the Philip Stewart Trial?" he asked.

"Because we don't want to discuss the links between you and the Stewart family, Granddad," explained Belinda.

"Someone else can do that," added Jonathan.

Marcus's eyes misted over.

"Thank you, Guys," he said eventually, before adding with a distant smile, "'Nihil obstat, Imprimateur', as the Vatican would say. Send it to the publisher."

When Sir Marcus announced his impending resignation, the publisher rushed it into print in time for the Christmas market.

Julia's team knew that their work was only two-thirds completed. They had reversed a monstrous act of injustice and finally given Philip Stewart's two victims justice. Then they had ended the Stewart gang's reign of terror in North London. However, they still had to investigate how the gang had got away with their crimes for so long. How did they apparently become inviolate to the police?

Julia knew that would be their hardest task, but the team, with the expert help of Alfred's skills, were able to pilot their way through the maze of documents and statements to get a fairly clear picture. It was obvious that the Gang had some powerful protectors among politicians at various levels and in all the major Parties. They discovered evidence that Sir Walter Greenway had been on their payroll, as was the Home Secretary in 1961. Other leading politicians were also implicated. Many of them, however, like Sir Walter, were beyond the team's reach because they had died. She pushed these cases aside, and concluded investigations into minor figures among the police and councillors in North London. Many of them appeared in court, and received short prison sentences. Others confessed their crimes and paid back the money they took in bribes and resigned their commissions or their posts.

Fifty Years After

Later Julia dealt with current and former Westminster politicians on both sides of the House, resolving their cases in a similar way to the way she had dealt with the earlier cases, but creating a small number of by-elections. Once this process was completed, Julia disbanded her team and concentrated on the one suspect, the biggest, who remained. It was Sir Marcus Greenway. The files showed that his involvement with the Stewart gang went right back to the trial in 1961 – despite his very public and long maintained public spat with Philip Stewart, which began to appear more and more like a publicity front, to deflect people from the truth. Sir Marcus continued to provide a protective shield for the Gang up until the moment that he authorised Jonathan to see if he could find evidence to exonerate Mark Smith of the murder of Janet Brown. However, Julia knew that Marcus's father had persuaded the Home Secretary to lock the relevant files up for 100 years, so that no fresh enquiry could ever uncover the truth. She also knew that it was Stewart money that bought the Home Secretary's cooperation. However, she did acknowledge that Sir Marcus had approved the fresh enquiry.

Uncertain about what to do, Julia made an appointment to meet the Director of Public Prosecutions. She showed her the evidence against Sir Marcus and asked her advice on what she should do.

"It's quite simple, Superintendent Donaldson. Do your duty. If Sir Marcus Greenway, Prime Minister, were Mr Marcus Greenway, postman, what would you do?"

"I'd call him in and interview him under caution, and then, probably charge him and refer the papers to you."

"Then that's what you have to do. There's no basic difference between them. You know what they say about Bank Managers – strip them naked and they're just the same as the rest of us! Well the Prime Minister is the same. Remember too, the words of Lord Denning when he was Master of the Rolls: 'However high you may be,

Fifty Years After

the law is still above you.' All I would suggest is that you don't bowl up to his office in the House of Commons with one of those lock smashers and blast your way in!"

And so it was in early August 2012 that Julia made an appointment and spoke with Sir Marcus in his office in the House of Commons. She showed the Prime Minister the evidence she had gathered, and asked for his comments.

"There's no point in my trying to hide anything or pretending that I haven't done what you have shown I have done, Superintendent. I've been stupid and failed in my duty as a public servant and a minister of the Crown. I know my father used me to make contact with the Stewart family, but that's no excuse. I knew that Mark Smith was innocent of any crime, and yet I let him hang, and then blocked any investigation into the case no less than five times. I also allowed Inspector Buchan to play fast and loose with the law to protect the Stewarts. I was the local MP and I should have raised his behaviour with the Attorney General and the Home Secretary. I have no defence for my actions and I confess myself guilty as charged to all of them."

Julia noted this response down, and asked Sir Marcus to sign it, which he did, stipulating only that she should not let this leak to the press until after he had resigned. He promised that he would consult with his Party leaders and announce his resignation at the Party Conference in October. Julia promised to hold off until his resignation was effective.

"However, Sir Marcus," she added. "I cannot promise you immunity from prosecution thereafter. It's not in my power to do that. That's a matter for the D P P."

Sir Marcus nodded.

"I understand, Superintendent. I've made my bed over the years, and I have to be prepared to lie on it – wherever it is."

Julia nodded before adding a final question.

"Prime Minister, in view of what you have now confessed to me, why did you let Jonathan investigate this case? You must have seen the danger in it for you."

"I didn't think he would get far and would lose interest at the first check. I was wrong. I misjudged his tenacity, which was very foolish of me. We Greenways are all tenacious."

Sir Marcus smiled sadly.

"Also," he added. "I think I subconsciously wanted to atone for what I have done."

"I see," said Julia getting to her feet and offering her hand to Marcus. "All I can say is, 'Good luck, Sir Marcus.'"

Fifty Years After